A widow with one child—and another on the way.

A career-woman-turned-nanny—with twin five-year-old charges.

An aunt—battling an uncle for custody of her nephew.

All three of these women are about to embark on marriage.

Is it for love...or

About the Author

KATHLEEN EAGLE

is a transplant from New England to Minnesota, where she and her husband, Clyde, make their home with two of their three children. She's considered writing to be her "best talent" since she was about nine years old, and English and history were her "best subjects." After fourteen years of teaching high school students about writing, she saw her own first novel in print in 1984. Since then she's published many more novels with Silhouette Books and Harlequin Historicals that have become favorites for readers worldwide. She also writes mainstream novels and has received awards from the Romance Writers of America, *Romantic Times* and *Affaire de Coeur*.

MARY LYNN BAXTER

sold hundreds of romance novels before she ever wrote one. The D & B Bookstore, right on the main drag in Lufkin, Texas, is her home, as well as the store she owns and manages. She and her husband, Leonard, garden in their spare time. Around five every evening they can be found picking butter beans on their small farm just outside of town.

MARIE FERRARELLA

was born in Europe, raised in New York City and now lives in Southern California. She describes herself as the tired mother of two overenergetic children and the contented wife of one wonderful man. She is thrilled to be following her dream of writing full-time.

For the Baby's Sake

Kathleen Eagle
Mary Lynn Baxter
Marie Ferrarella

FOR THE BABY'S SAKE

Copyright © 1997 by Harlequin Books S.A.

Twenty-Fifth...

The publisher acknowledges the copyright holders of the individual works as follows:

SUMMER...
Copyright...

LOVERS...
Copyright...

BABY...
Copyright © and...

THIRD TIME...
Copyright © by 1991 Marie Rydzynski-Ferrarella

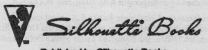

Silhouette Books

Published by Silhouette Books
America's Publisher of Contemporary Romance

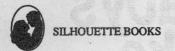 SILHOUETTE BOOKS

by Request

FOR THE BABY'S SAKE

Copyright © 1997 by Harlequin Books S.A.

ISBN 0-373-20132-X

The publisher acknowledges the copyright holders
of the individual works as follows:

BROOMSTICK COWBOY
Copyright © 1993 by Kathleen Eagle

ADDED DELIGHT
Copyright © 1989 by Mary Lynn Baxter

FAMILY MATTERS
Copyright © 1993 by Marie Rydzynski-Ferrarella

Printed in U.S.A.

CONTENTS

A Note from Kathleen Eagle

Dear Reader,

Not long ago a reporter told me that he was surprised to see all the babies on the covers of romance novels of late. "What do babies have to do with romance?" he asked. Since he didn't look much older than my older son, I offered to have a little talk with him off the record. The poor boy lost his cool, turned beet red and sputtered. Like most men, he'll probably never really get it. To this day, I don't think my husband truly understands what a hero he was for me in those hours he spent seeing me through the births of our three babies. A man is especially dear to a woman when he passes the fatherhood test.

Take Tate Harrison, for example. Sexiest cowboy on the rodeo circuit. And he knows it, too. He can see that Amy Becker could use a man around the place, even if she's not ready to admit that Tate is just the man she needs. He can easily ride herd on anything that moves, from her sheep to her little boy. He never dreamed that she'd need him most the night her daughter is born, and he certainly isn't prepared for the way that blessed event makes mush of a cowboy's heart. But, then, neither is Amy. Nor is she prepared to fall hopelessly in love with her late husband's wild and wayward best buddy.

Prepare yourself, dear reader, for the making of a family, Western-style.

All my best,

Kathleen Eagle

BROOMSTICK COWBOY

Kathleen Eagle

For Judy Baer, Sandy Huseby and Pamela Bauer,
on our tenth anniversary.

Vive Prairie Writers' Guild!

Prologue

Tate Harrison cupped his big, calloused hands around his face and peeked through the back door window into the Beckers' kitchen. Except for the two plates standing in the dish drainer along with two forks and a pair of tall tumblers, turned bottoms up, the place was as neat and tidy as the rows in a Kansas cornfield. It was Amy's kitchen, so naturally it would be. The only fingerprints would be those he was making on the glass right now, pressing his face to the window. The floor looked so clean he could almost smell the pine soap, and the stainless-steel sink was flooded with Indian summer sunshine, pouring through the ruffles of a yellow gingham curtain.

He shoved his hands in his jacket pockets and gave the rambler-style farmhouse a cursory inspection on the outside. The yellow trim was in pretty good shape, but the white clapboard siding sure needed a coat of paint. White sheers hung in the side window, but he would bet there were yellow curtains down the hall. Yellow was Amy's color. It looked great with her dark hair and dark eyes. Black-Eyed Susan, he'd called her, but that had been a long time ago.

He rapped on the glass a second time, put his hands back up and peered again. As always, Tate was on the outside looking in. He liked it that way, especially whenever he came home to Overo. The best part of Montana was definitely the outside. Plenty of elbow room. Plenty of scenery. Plenty of opportunity for a cowboy to move on to greener pastures whenever he felt like it. Moving on had become his stock in trade, taking him out of state, even out of the country, but whenever he was in town—and it had been a while—he always looked in on the Beckers.

He'd had mixed feelings this time about paying his more-or-less regular call. Up until a year ago Kenny Becker had been leasing the land Tate had inherited after his stepfather died. He felt a little funny about showing up now to talk business. Kenny was Tate's best friend, and Tate wanted to sell him the land eventually, whenever Kenny could swing the financing. At least, that had always been the plan.

When Kenny had dropped the lease last year, the only explanation had come in a note that said they were "cutting back on the horses." Kenny had assured him that there were plenty of neighbors interested in picking up the lease. But Tate wasn't interested in leasing his land to anyone else. He had called to wish the family a merry Christmas and to tell Kenny to go ahead and use the land, cut the hay on shares. He'd asked only a token percentage for himself, because he knew what Amy would say if she thought he was giving them something for nothing. But he and Kenny were friends, and if times were tough, he wanted to help out. He'd managed to keep his own financial obligations to a minimum.

"You sure you guys are okay?" Tate had asked over the phone. He couldn't imagine Kenny cutting his horse herd. He loved every useless broomtail he kept around the place, and year after year that sentiment had helped him run his operation into the red. But that was Kenny. "You know, if you need to, you can sell my share of the hay and use the cash to—"

"Hey, thanks, buddy, but we're doin' just fine. Amy's got us into this sideline that's...well, it's a long story, but next year things'll start lookin' up. You oughta get married and settle down, Tate. I tell you..."

"I'm doin' fine, too, Ken," Tate had said. "Come fall, we'll take a look at where things stand. If you want to pick up the lease again, fine. If you don't think you're gonna want to buy it like we planned, I'll probably just unload it. My banker tells me the mineral rights are worth more now than the grass."

Lately Tate had been thinking he wouldn't mind selling the land and cutting the last of his ties. He'd left Overo when his stepfather died seven years ago, and hadn't been back in at least the last two, maybe longer. There were a thousand other places where he could be outside without feeling quite so much like an *outsider*. He shouldn't be feeling that way anymore, not when he was standing here on the back step of a house he'd spent as much time in as his own when he was growing up. Kenny Becker was his *best friend*. Always had been.

But Amy was his best friend's wife. And they'd never made a very good threesome.

Damn, he'd knocked three times now, and nothing seemed to be moving except a fat calico cat. She padded across the white linoleum, stopped by the back door and blinked a couple of times, then rounded the corner and ambled down the basement steps. It all made for a pretty

disappointing homecoming. Tate had been looking forward
to surprising them, earning a couple of smiles, maybe even
a couple of hugs and a home-cooked meal. He tried to
remember whether he'd still had his beard the last time he'd
been back. They might not even recognize him since he'd
started shaving regularly again. Well, fairly regularly. No,
Kenny would, he amended. Fifty years from now, when
they were both nearsighted ol' codgers, Ken would still
know him right off.

Amy was another story. She wasn't interested in knowing Tate Harrison. She had no use for his good intentions
or his excuses or his apologies. She tolerated him because
she loved Kenny. He wasn't sure she was really interested
in knowing Kenny, either, not the same Kenny he knew.
But she loved him just as sure as she had no use for his
best friend.

A mystery, that woman. The kind you could stay up all
night reading and never figure out until you hit the very
last page. She was a city girl turned country. One minute
she could be as stiff-necked as an old schoolmarm, the next
she'd be bubbling over like she'd just popped her cork.
Smart and sexy both. Tate figured she'd outsmarted herself
when she'd married Ken, thinking all she had to do to shape
him up was change the company he kept. On her wedding
day, Tate had sincerely wished her luck. From the looks of
things, somebody's luck was stretched a little thin right
about now.

Tate tried the door, but it was locked. That had to mean
they'd gone into town together. Kenny never locked the
door, because he never had a key. If there'd been anybody
out in the barn, they would have peeked out when they
heard the pickup, but just to make sure, Tate walked around
back and gave a holler. The only response came from the
two dogs that had been yappin' to beat hell when he drove

up. A Border collie and a Catahoula Leopard, both trying to see who could jump the highest inside the chain-link kennel. Tate didn't remember the kennel being there, next to the clothesline. The dogs were new, too. He wondered what had happened to the old black Lab he and Kenny used to take with them when they'd go fishing.

On the way to his pickup he turned the corner around the dilapidated yard fence and nearly tripped over a pint-size red-and-white bicycle lying on its side in the gravel. Their little boy couldn't be old enough to ride a bike. Last time Tate had seen the little squirt he'd barely been toddling around, pigeon-toed like his ol' man. His hair was curly like Kenny's, too, only lighter, but he had his mother's big brown eyes. Cute little tyke. Cute enough to make a guy think he might want one of his own someday.

Tate lit a cigarette and leaned his backside against the headlight of his pickup. The crisp October breeze felt good against his face. This was a pretty spot. Plenty of water and grass, and a fine view of the snow-capped mountains. Wouldn't be long before the lowlands would snuggle under a blanket of snow and sleep until springtime. The only time he ever got homesick was when he thought of the Becker place. He'd sold his own house right off the foundation, along with the pole barns, the grain bins, even the damn toolshed. All he'd kept was the land. If you wanted to make a go of it on the land, you had to sacrifice, and you never knew what kind of forfeiture the land might demand. It had taken all it would ever get from Tate. He'd been making a damn good living as a rodeo cowboy, truck driver, construction worker—whatever came along. He'd socked the lease payments away in the bank. He didn't need the land, and it damn sure wasn't claiming his best years.

Didn't look like it was claiming much of the sweat off ol' Kenny's brow, either. He hadn't brought in much hay.

The half section west of the house hadn't been cut. Worse yet, somebody's mangy sheep were grazing on it. Just like Kenny to let a neighbor take advantage of his good nature. But from the looks of things, Kenny couldn't afford to be so damned good-natured. Other than the dogs and the trespassing sheep, Tate didn't see too many signs of life around the place. No horses in the corral out back. Not a cow in sight.

The more he thought about it, the less he liked what he was seeing. Tate dropped his cigarette on the gravel driveway and ground it under his boot heel. Fishing in his jacket for his keys, he jerked the pickup door open. Surely on his way to town he would see a supply of square bales, stacked up in a nice long wall close to the road, where it wouldn't be too hard to reach in the winter. Probably down on his land, near the old homesite, where the access would still be pretty good. Maybe on the alfalfa field, where Kenny should have been able to get a good two cuttings this year. He should have hauled the bales in closer, though, damn his lazy hide.

But, then, that was Kenny.

Chapter One

"**W**hat do you mean, *ever since Kenny Becker kicked the bucket?*"

Tate was ready to pop bartender Ted Staples in the mouth for coming up with such a sick joke. But Ted wasn't smiling. In fact, Ted had stopped pouring drinks. He set the bottle of Jack Daniel's down on the bar as if it were a delicate piece of crystal, and he looked at Tate with about as much surprise as ever registered on the gaunt man's leathery face.

"I mean, ever since Kenny *died*," Ted said more carefully this time. "Is that better? Since Kenny died, the women around here have been drivin' me crazy with phone calls, checkin' up on their men."

"Checking up..." The hinges in Tate's jaw went rusty on him. He could even taste the rust in the back of his mouth. No, the word *died* wasn't any better. For an instant the letters on the neon Pabst sign above the bar swelled up and blurred clean out of focus. Hell, he was only on his first drink, and somehow he'd missed the part where he'd taken a boot in the gut. "What in hell are you talkin' about, Ted?"

"I usually tell 'em the man ain't here or he just left, but you hear that damn he's-been-gone-too-long tone in their voice, kinda scared and trembly, and you know what they're worried about."

"Kenny…"

"Well, you know—" Since they'd hit on a touchy subject, Ted splashed another shot in Tate's glass for good measure. "—it took us a while to find him. Surprised you didn't come back for the funeral, Tate. You two used to be close enough to use the same toothpick. Where you saw one, you saw the other."

"When…" It felt as though somebody had just pulled the walls in a few feet. Tate was suddenly short on air and voice. It took a long pull on his drink to sear the goop out of his pipes. He pressed his lips together and pushed his big black Stetson back so he could get a better look at Ted's face. He needed to make damn sure the old man wasn't putting him on. "When?"

"Why, late last winter." Ted turned to Gene Leslie, who occupied the bar stool on the inside corner. "Was it March?"

"Early March." Gene swept his quilted jacket back with arms akimbo, poking his gut out while he took a moment to puzzle all this out.

Tate was listening, waiting for some sense to be made here. He felt clammy under the back of his shirt, under his hatband. He wanted to shed his jacket, open the door, let some air in the place. But nobody took his jacket off in the Jackalope Bar, because there was no place to put it, and everybody wore a cowboy hat, because you didn't hang out at the Jackalope unless you were a cowboy.

"Take that back," Gene amended contemplatively. "Believe it might've been closer to the middle of the month. Them heifers started calving on the tenth, and I believe..." He squinted, focusing on Tate through a haze of blue smoke. "You didn't know about Kenny?"

Tate shook his head, trying to clear it of the flak and home in on some answers. "Know what? What the hell happened?"

"He was here that day." Ted wiped his hand on the white towel he'd tucked into the front of his belt for an apron, then wagged his finger at the center booth next to the far wall. Two cowboys looked up briefly, then went back to nursing their brews and puffing their smokes as soon as they realized the finger wasn't pointed at them. "Sittin' right over there at that table, horse tradin' with Ticker Thomas 'til late afternoon, early evening. When his wife called, I told her Kenny'd left before suppertime, and I thought sure he was sober."

"Turned out he was, which was too bad," Gene added. "He'd 'a had more alcohol in him, he'd 'a made it through the night. My uncle Amos lived for two days in the middle of November when he went in the ditch that time over by Roundup."

"Your uncle Amos is too ugly to live and too ornery to die," thick-tongued Charlie Dennison said. The story was coming at Tate from all sides now, with Charlie getting into it from his perch near the door.

"You're damn straight. He was tanked up pretty good and glad of it, even when they cut off his frostbit toes." Gene adjusted his hat in a gesture that allowed no two ways about the facts in either story. "Poor ol' Kenny should'a had a few more shots under his belt."

"Kenny only drank beer," Tate said. "I didn't see his old Ford pickup out at his place. Was it a—"

Gene shook his head. "Nah, he didn't wreck his pickup. He got throwed. Ground was still froze hard as rock. Split his head open like a melon."

"Nobody's figured out yet what he was doin' out ridin' that horse that time of night," Ted put in. "Like I said, his ol' lady'd been callin' around to hell and back. Then she went out lookin' for him, so there was nobody home. He must'a drove his pickup out in the pasture, caught a horse and went off ridin' bareback, far as anybody can tell. Damnedest thing."

"Moon was bright as hell that night, and it was cold as a witch's tit," Charlie recalled.

"We used to go out together on nights like that," Tate said. He could picture the moonlight flooding the snow-covered hillsides. Kenny loved those nights, when the big black velvet sky was filled with stars and their voices cracked the cold hush with pithy adolescent wisdom. "Bareback, too, so you'd keep your butt warm. Twice as warm as a woman and half the trouble," he remembered with a melancholy smile.

"Women don't usually buck as hard," Gene said.

"Tell you what, Leslie," Charlie grumbled. "Any woman does any buckin' with *you* has got be three ax handles wide in the hip and horse-faced as hell," Charlie said.

Ted let the perpetual banter go in one ear and out the other, but Tate's difficulty drew rare concern. "They must not've been able to track you down, Tate."

"Maybe they didn't try." Amy, he thought. Maybe Amy hadn't wanted him around when she'd buried her husband.

"That little girl was pretty damn broke up, but I'd be willing to bet she tried to call you or something."

Tate wasn't going to argue. "Who found him?"

"She did."

"Amy?"

"The pickup wasn't back, see, so that kinda threw 'em off for a while. But when they found Kenny's pickup, and then they found the horse still wearin' a hackamore, well, they sent out a helicopter. A bunch of us went out on horseback. But his wife took those dogs of hers, and she went out on foot. She found him."

"He'd slid down into a ravine. Don't know what all he ran into. Head split open like a damn melon." Gene was stuck on the melon image.

It was all a dream. A bad one. The kind that wouldn't go away when he woke up. Tate knew it well; he'd had it before. He cast his gaze at the sooty ceiling and whispered, "Jesus."

Jesus, get me out of here.

Jesus, make it not be true.

Jesus, give him back.

He sighed heavily and dug into his shirt pocket for a cigarette. "Hope she got a decent price for her stock."

"She ain't sold much yet," Ted reported. "She says she's gonna run the place herself, her and the boy."

Tate glanced up from the match he'd struck on his thumbnail. "The kid's only, what? Three or four?"

"Hell, I was feedin' stock when I was four years old," Charlie claimed.

Gene laughed. "The hell you were, Dennison. Even at *forty*-four you wouldn't know which end to feed."

Tate dragged deeply on his cigarette, hoping the smoke would do better than whiskey at calming his innards. One of the cowboys had gotten up from the booth and chucked some change into the jukebox. It rattled its way down the hollow tube and clunked when it hit bottom. If they'd pitched it down Tate's throat, it would have made the same damn sound.

"She hired any help?" he asked. The cowboy punched his numbers, and up came the steel guitars.

"Well, she tried," Ted said. "She run one scarecrow-lookin' guy off with a shotgun after about a week last summer. Said he'd tried to make a pass at her."

"My uncle Amos used to say some widows are just like cask-aged wine, and some are pure vinegar," Gene said.

"Your uncle Amos oughta take another drive out to Roundup," Charlie said. He was listening to Ted's story with increasing interest. "None of her family came to help her out? You woulda thought..."

"Her mother lives in Florida somewhere. She was here for a little while after Kenny died, but she went back." In response to Gene's signal, Ted slid another bottle of Blue Ribbon his way. "Mrs. Becker's got spunk—I'll say that for her. Winter's a bad time to sell, anyway. If she can hold out a few months, I'd say she'll get a good price for the place."

"She's over to the sale barn now," Charlie said. "I was just there. Looks like she's gonna run some horses through."

"Horseflesh is goin' pretty cheap," Gene said as he raised the bottle to his thin lips.

Tate was tempted to stay right where he was and get himself blind drunk, fight absurdity with absurdity. These people were talking about Kenny like it made perfect sense that he was dead. Like it was not possible for Kenny to be the next man to park his old green pickup out front. Like the next guy that flung that creaky front door open and let in a blast of cold air couldn't be Kenny.

It couldn't be true. It was inconceivable that Tate couldn't come home to Overo and buy Kenny a drink, listen to his tall tales and hear that bizarre, high-pitched laugh of his. Kenny was only thirty years old, for God's sake. He couldn't be lying stone cold and silent in a box six feet deep in the ground. That was the meaning of *dead*. His best friend couldn't really be dead.

Blind drunk was one thing, but Tate didn't know if he could pull off a *deaf* drunk, and he didn't think he could handle any more of Hank Williams' "Cold Cold Heart" without getting awkwardly choked up. He tossed the rest of his drink down and stubbed his cigarette in the plastic ashtray. After he slid off the stool he slapped a twenty on the bar.

Ted pushed the cash back across the polished wood. "It's on the house, Tate. I'm real sorry you had to find out this way."

"Good a way as any," Tate answered as he backed away from the bar. "You give these guys another round on me. For Kenny. There were no flowers at his funeral with my name on 'em, so—" his gesture was all-inclusive "—you guys remember Kenny kindly over the next round. He always gave the best he had."

The words tasted a little saccharine in Tate's mouth, but everybody readily agreed with his assessment. Hell, yes, drink up, boys; Kenny Becker was a damn good friend.

"You say she's over at the sale barn?" Out of habit he flipped up the collar of his sheepskin jacket, even though he left it hanging open in front.

"Last I saw."

"Think I'll pay my respects."

Tate didn't feel like pretending to be glad to see people, but it was like old home week the minute he walked into the Overo Livestock Auction. Not too many of his own friends, but several of his stepdad's old cronies recognized him and made a fuss over seeing his picture in *Rodeo Sports News*. It was no big deal, he told them. He'd made a few good rides this summer, but he hadn't made the National Finals yet.

Bill Walker insisted that Tate had "done real good" and his ol' man would be proud of him. To this day Tate couldn't think of Oakie Bain as *his ol' man*, even though he knew his real father only from pictures. But it would have been rude to take exception to the claim aloud. And something in the back of his mind regularly put the skids to downright rudeness.

He stepped around the boxes of baby rabbits and mewling kittens the country kids had for sale near the front door and shook hands with longtime neighbor Myron Olson. Myron wouldn't let go until he'd figured out how long it had been, so Tate had to guess six or seven years before he could slap the old man on the back and head up the steps to the gallery. He didn't look for a seat. Instead he lit a cigarette and leaned against a post near the doorway, where he could observe without being seen.

It didn't take long to spot her. He couldn't see much more than the top of her head, which stood out from all the cowboy hats and straw-hued mops like a fur coat in a dime store. Her hair was the color of a dark bay mare he'd had when he was a kid. You could only see the red tones when she stood out in the sun. Indoors, it was a rich shade of ranch mink. She'd kept it long. Today she had it done up in a braided ponytail. She was sitting way over to the side, down close to the activity, but the crowd was pretty sparse. She was all alone.

She seemed intent on the proceedings in the ring, but maybe she was staring hard because her thoughts were somewhere else. He wondered where. She looked like a high school girl, sitting in class and paying close attention to the teacher. Could have been a foreign language class the way the auctioneer was rattling off numbers a mile a minute. No problem for Amy. He hadn't known her when she was in school, but she was the type who had probably aced every class. Poor Kenny had nearly bombed out, but Tate had loaned him enough of his homework to see Kenny through to graduation.

He wondered if she knew that. She'd pegged Tate for a troublemaker. He'd always been the one getting poor ol' Kenny into hot water. He wondered if she knew he'd also gotten Kenny through school. Didn't matter, Tate told himself. By and large, she had his number.

He watched the numbers flash on the electronic sign. Good saddle horses were going for killer prices. He took a long slow drag on his cigarette as he listened to the auctioneer describe the merits of the next lot. Chief among them, the next four horses had belonged to the late Kenny Becker, who'd raised some of the best quarter horses in the state. According to reliable reports, these were the best of his herd.

Tate figured that auctioneer Cal Swick was likely stretching the truth pretty thin. These were probably the only ones Kenny'd ever managed to break out, despite all his big-scale horse-breeding plans. Kenny was a dreamer, but maybe Cal believed the reliable reports himself.

Saddle horses always sold better if somebody showed them under saddle, so Tate was glad to see that Amy had hired one of the kids who hung around the stock pens to ride her horses through for her. He remembered when he and Kenny used to compete for the same kind of job. They'd bet each other who could get his Saturday chores done first and beat the other one to the sale barn for the chance to earn a few bucks. People usually picked Tate over Kenny if they needed a rider. He'd been born looking the part.

The bidding wasn't going anywhere, so Tate decided to jump in and run the sorrel gelding up a few dollars. He pushed his hat back, gave a subtle nod and a hand signal, skipping over a few increments to make people take a second look. It worked the first time around, but by the time all four horses had gone through, the buyers had dropped the bid on him twice. He was satisfied. Five hundred was a damn good batting average. The only catch would be settling up in the sales office without letting Amy catch him. Then he would go out to the pens and figure out what to do with two horses he didn't need.

He'd bought himself a bald-faced sorrel mare and a buckskin gelding. A five- and a six-year-old, from the looks of their teeth. Well fed, sound legs. He was checking the buckskin's hooves when the woman of the hour caught him red-handed.

"You paid way too much for that one."

Her voice always got to him. Smooth and low for a woman's, it had a seductively smoky quality. He glanced up and connected immediately with earth-mother eyes peering at him between the fence rails. He straightened slowly.

"Hello, Amy."

"It's not like you to wait until after you've paid your money to inspect the goods, Tate Harrison. That was always one of the differences between you and Ken."

"I got here late." He brushed his hands off on his denim-covered thighs, choosing to take the remark the way he took his whiskey. Perfectly straight. "But I can usually spot a good saddle horse in the ring pretty easy."

"So I've heard. Ken swore by your horse sense." She spoke the name so easily that she nearly put him at ease, too. But then she added, "Unfortunately, you took it with you when you left."

He half expected her to take the high ground by climbing the fence and letting him know with another perfectly aimed barb just what the first one was supposed to mean. She didn't. She had all the advantages she needed right now. He was going to have to go to her and find out. "My leavin' didn't disappoint anybody around here too much," he reminded her as he scaled the fence. "People are glad to see me 'bout every two, three years, and for a week or so I'm glad to see them."

He swung one leg over the top rail and paused while she turned her face up to him. He wasn't sure he wanted to get down. Kenny was dead, and, damn, she scared him. He was afraid he would say something stupid, maybe make her cry. The cold autumn air had brought color to her face, but the dark shadows under her eyes canceled out the illusion of rosy-cheeked vitality. It struck him that her black down-filled jacket looked big enough to go around her twice. Then he realized it was Kenny's jacket. Brand-new the last time he'd seen him.

Her eyes held his fast as he lowered his foothold halfway down the fence, then dropped to the ground. His arms hung awkwardly at his sides. He imagined putting them around her, the way he wanted to, but her eyes offered no hint of permission. He flexed his fingers. They were stiff from the cold.

"Why did you buy those horses?" she asked quietly. "You didn't really want them."

"Why didn't you call me, Amy?" She glanced away. "Ed Shaeffer over at the bank always knows how to get hold of me in an emergency. He would have tracked me down if you'd just—"

"There was so much to do. There were so many details,

so many—'' She hugged herself, clutching the voluminous jacket around her. ''There were many things I didn't handle as well as I should have. I was...'' A faintly apologetic smile curved her mouth as she lifted her gaze to meet his again. ''...quite unprepared.''

''I stopped in at the house on my way into town.'' If he told her what he'd been through, maybe she would give him an answer that had something to do with *him*. ''Stopped at the Jackalope. They talked about it like I already knew.''

''I'm sorry.'' He looked away. ''Really, Tate, I'm sorry. I thought about—'' She laid her hand on his sleeve. ''Many times I thought about writing, but I kept putting it off, thinking someone must have told you by now.''

''I would have been back, soon as I heard. You would have seen me the same damn day.'' He stared at her hand. ''That's why you kept puttin' it off, isn't it?''

''Oh, no. Ken would have wanted you to be...'' He looked at her expectantly, waiting for the charge of a dead man. ''To take part in the service.''

''To help carry him to his grave? Damn right he would have. But I haven't been in touch since Christmas, and ol' Kenny, he usually—'' The guilt was his. Always, it was his. ''I should've known something was wrong.''

''Tate.'' She slid her hand down his sleeve and slipped it in his. It felt good—warmer than his, and small but capable. ''You come up with a list of regrets, and mine'll double yours. That's just the way it is. It was all over so quickly. So quickly, it left my head spinning.''

A fleet, flighty gesture parted the front of her jacket. Her pink shirt was too tight. Her belly was too big. He felt as though he'd just walked up to her bedroom window and seen her naked.

''You're...'' He was about to say something totally inane, and there wasn't a damn thing he could do about it. Gates were clattering inside the stock barn, and some guy was calling for lot forty-two. Tate glanced over his shoulder, unconsciously looking for somebody to tell him his eyes weren't lying. "Amy, you're pregnant."

"You're very observant."

"But they were saying over at—" He motioned westward, because suddenly he couldn't get the name of the bar out, or any other word that might offend her. The hand he held in his felt even slighter than it had at first, and he flexed his fingers around it, gently reasserting his hold. "I mean, I heard that you were running the place yourself."

"I'm not letting it go, Tate." And she squeezed back, a secret gesture between two people who shared a loss, letting him know that she was worried about losing still more. "It's my home. Mine and Jody's and..."

"You can't—"

"I'm having a baby, not open-heart surgery."

He allowed himself to get lost in the depths of her eyes, her brave words, her sturdiness. "You got any help?"

"I might be able to hire someone now, maybe parttime—" she smiled and gave a little nod toward the pen "—since I got a good price for those hay-burners."

"How's the little guy doin'? Jody?" She nodded to confirm the name he remembered full well. Kenny had once confided that Tate had been his choice for the boy's godfather, but with him on the rodeo circuit and Amy insisting on having the ceremony "before the little guy went to college," Tate had missed out on the honor.

Amy withdrew her hand, as though the mention of the boy's name had introduced a constraint against handholding. She stepped close to the pen and peeked between the rails again.

Tate followed her lead. "Must be tough for such a little

fella," he said quietly. "Old enough to know the difference, but not to really..." *Understand?* Who *was* old enough to understand?

"He was pretty mad at me today. He used to love to come to the horse sales with his dad. This is the first one I've been to since...since it happened." She leaned her shoulder against the fence and hid her memories beneath lowered lashes. "I wouldn't let Jody come. He wouldn't understand."

Tate stared into the pen. The mare was standing hipshot, neck drooping, eyelids dropping to half-mast. The buckskin's perked ears rotated like radar as he blew thick clouds of mist through flaring nostrils. Whatever was up, the buckskin would be the first to know about it.

"The boy'll know they're gone," Tate said.

"Not right away." Amy sighed. "I didn't want him to watch them go through the ring."

"That must've been hard for you, too."

"Not at all. I'm glad to be rid of them." He glanced at her for an explanation. None was forthcoming. "What will you do with those two?" she wondered.

"Haven't given it much thought," he admitted. Then he smiled. "Just knew I couldn't pass 'em up."

"That's what Ken Becker would've said. Not Tate Harrison." He shrugged. She'd always thought she had them both pegged. "He missed you a lot, Tate," she added gently. "You were the brother he never had."

"He was—" He couldn't say that. He'd had a brother once, a long time ago. Jesse. But he'd grown up with Kenny. That, too, was beginning to seem like a long time ago. "He was the best friend I ever had. Guess I should've missed him more than I did." He turned, leaned his back against the fence and looked up at the distant white clouds. "Guess I'm gonna start now."

"Well..." She wrapped her arms around herself again and they stood there for a long moment of silence, together but apart. One of the stockboys ran by, hollering at someone in the parking lot to wait up.

"How long will you be in town?" she finally asked. "You're welcome to come for supper, if you can find some time. You should see Jody now. He's..."

There it was, he thought. The obligatory invitation. "I'd wanna know more about what happened to Kenny," Tate warned her. "Would you be up to—" She hung her head. "That's okay. I understand. It's just that it's so hard for me to believe he's...gone."

"Dead. There's no way to change that, and that's all there is to know." She looked up, more fire in her eyes than he'd seen so far. "He's dead, Tate. It helps if you just say the word. It happened—" she snapped her fingers "—just like that. You can't believe how fast it happened, and you can't believe it happened until you've said the word. Until you've sold his horses. Until you've given most of his clothes away, and until you've slept..." She sighed, as if the sudden burst of emotion had worn her out. "I have to pick up Jody."

No, he didn't want her to go. He laid a hand on her shoulder. "What can I do?"

"Do?"

"For you and Jody. What—"

"You've already done more than you needed to do." She nodded toward the pen. "You've bought yourself one docile saddle horse and one mean outlaw. You'll have to figure out what you're going to do with *them*."

She kissed his cheek before she walked away. Made him feel like a little boy. Like she'd already come through the fires of hell, and he was too green to notice there was any heat. Even so, he felt favored somehow. Excused. Blessed.

Knighted. Kissed by the princess. It was his cue to rise to the occasion.

He would do it if he knew how.

He decided he would run the mare back through the ring and keep the high-lifed buckskin gelding. The buckskin was obviously the outlaw, which made them two of a kind.

Jody was still mad when Amy picked him up at his aunt Marianne's. Cousin Kitty had slammed his finger in the car door, for one thing, and then Bill, Jr., had jerked the cherry sucker out of his mouth and made him bite his tongue. Marianne assured Amy that she'd checked him over both times and Jody wasn't really hurt. His tongue had hardly bled at all.

Then she'd asked Amy for the two hundredth time about the possibility of having core samples taken on her land, "Just to see if it's worth pursuing."

Amy wasn't interested in Ken's sister's latest scheme. The land Ken's father had left him belonged to her and Jody now. Marianne owned fifty percent of the mineral rights, which the attorney had explained was a technicality that would only become an issue if Amy decided either to sell the land or let people poke holes in it looking for something to mine. Neither proposition interested her, even though she knew one of Overo's poker clubs had a couple of betting pools going—one on her second child's birth date, and the other on the month in which she would file bankruptcy.

But Amy was not giving up. She was tired, and she was nearly broke, but she wouldn't be broken. Nobody was going to poke holes in Becker land or Becker dreams. Even if Ken's plans had frequently been farfetched, he'd been fond of saying that he could depend on Amy to get him turned around. Once he was headed in the right direction, he could make things happen. He could be hell on wheels, he would say. He'd spent much of their marriage spinning his wheels, but she'd known how and when to wedge her small shoulder under his axle and give him a push. He was a good man, a kind-hearted man and he had wonderful intentions. Amy's job was to find a kernel of feasibility in them and build on that.

So at least they had a ranch. It might not have been the kind of ranch Ken had envisioned, but they were raising livestock. They had a home. They had a family. Despite a few impulsive choices, a few setbacks, a few fits and starts, they had come *this* far. Now it was up to her. It hadn't been easy without Ken, but there had been times when it hadn't been easy *with* him, either. Amy would manage, just as she had always managed. She would just have to work harder.

But she did need a little help. Now that she had some money, she needed manpower. A couple of months' worth, she figured. She could have given birth to a new baby, looked after a four-year-old and tended to her business in the summer, no sweat. But winter in Montana could throw a fast-frozen kink into anybody's works.

She wouldn't let herself think about where the money had come from until after she had put Jody to bed and her feet up on two feather pillows and a hassock. It wouldn't have been so hard to sell Ken's saddle horse—especially that outlaw that had been the death of him—if the buyer hadn't turned out to be Tate Harrison. But there was probably some kind of poetic justice in it all. She'd never doubted that she would have to face Tate sooner or later.

In that first rush of confusion, the initial daze and the onslaught of questions and decisions, her first impulse had been to find Tate. It had been a foolish idea, and she'd rebuked whatever infirm hormone it was that had bombarded her brain with such a weak-kneed notion. She'd

breathed the biggest sigh of relief of her life the day Tate
Harrison had left Overo and all but removed his freewheel-
ing influence from her husband's life. She didn't really
know how to get hold of him, not easily, not on such short
notice, and he probably wouldn't have been free to come.
He would come home for a party, but for a funeral? She
doubted it. Or rather, she elected to doubt it. It was simpler
that way.

But, as fate would have it, she'd had to face him with
her excuses right after he'd done his good deed. As if that
weren't bad enough, she'd had to deal with those *stupid*
feelings again. Tate Harrison always made her feel a little
unsteady, slightly unsafe, as though she'd pitched camp on
a geological fault. He made her want to do things she
shouldn't do, just the way he had Ken. There was a look
in his eyes, a challenge to be as bold and as rash as he was.

Even in sorrow, he challenged her. It would have been
easy to let herself go, to break down in his arms. That was
probably exactly what he expected—what everyone expected. It was also exactly the kind of behavior in which
Amy could ill afford to indulge herself. She had responsibilities.

It was late when she heard the pickup drive up. She
turned in her chair just as the headlights played over the
sheers in the front window. Someone was probably stopping to tell her that that damned west gate was open again.
She sighed and hauled herself to her feet. The dogs were
going nuts outside. She would show them; she'd put them
to work. Thank God she had the dogs.

Amy turned the porch light on, then peeked out the window. The face that peered back was disturbingly familiar.
The angles softened earlier by daylight looked harder in the
shadows, the bristly stubble darker, the black eyes less forgiving and the full, firm lips less patient. It was not the

kind of face one welcomed late at night. But she unlocked the door.

Tate felt like the third guy from the left in a police lineup as he stood there waiting. Frost was nipping at his nose while she was looking him over, being none too quick about opening the damn door.

"Oh, Tate." She made his name sound like a protest against any and all surprises. "Come in. We've already eaten, and Jody's—" She shrank back, as though he were muscling his way into her cozy nest.

Feeling awkward and a bit oversize for the small entryway, he stepped over the threshold, tucking his chin as he removed his hat.

"But I can heat something up for you," she added tentatively.

"I didn't come for supper, exactly." He fingered his Stetson's broad black brim. "I'm lookin' for a job."

"A job?" She laughed nervously. Standing there in her dimly-lit kitchen, he looked for all the world like a hulking, humble cowboy. "Did you blow all your money on those horses?" She knew all about that little routine from Kenny. Tate had his foolish habits, but burdening himself with useless horses was not one of them.

"I've got money," he assured her. "What I need is a place to stay for a while."

"Try the motel." She didn't mean to sound sarcastic, but the wounded expression on his face told her that it had come out that way.

"I've had a bellyful of motels." He squared his shoulders and nodded toward the door that led to the basement. "You've got a room downstairs. You need a hired man."

"I don't need—" she took a deep breath while his eyes dared her to effect a complete rejection "—a favor quite that big."

"It won't be a favor. I'm not an easy keeper. I eat a lot and I, uh—" he glanced past her, surveying the homey kitchen "—use a lot of hot water."

"I can't pay you much more than that."

"All I'm askin' for is room and board." He shoved his hands in the front pockets of his jeans and offered a lopsided grin. "And all the shells to the shotgun."

"You heard about that." With few exceptions, she'd always been good at setting people straight. Tate Harrison was one of the few she'd had trouble with. "That happened back in June. I'm a little slower now, but you still won't get any further than he did, so don't—"

"You've got a belly sittin' out there as big as a four-way stop sign." The amusement in his eyes faded. "That's all you need, Amy. A big red stop sign."

Ah, so he remembered. Well, so did she. She'd never told Ken about the time Tate had made his move on her, partly because it had happened before they were married and mostly because she had handled it. There had never been a need to discuss the incident. It would have served no purpose other than to prove that she had been right about Tate. He, of course, had been wrong about her, and he'd admitted it. So maybe it wouldn't hurt to let him help out for a while. Nobody had ever suggested that Tate Harrison wasn't a hard worker when he wanted to be.

And from the spark that flashed in his eyes when she relented with a reluctant nod, he wanted to be.

"You're right. I need a hand," she said. "One I can trust. As long as you have some free time…"

He read the question in her eyes. "I can spare as much as you need."

"I promise you, Tate, I bounce back fast. I did with Jody."

"Every time I laid over with you guys, even for a day

or two, I felt like you were in a rush to kick me out." It was an observation, not a complaint. "I'd try to get you both out of the house, take you out to supper or just honky-tonkin', and you always acted like I was—"

"Ken had responsibilities," she reminded him, although it wasn't something she expected a confirmed bachelor like Tate to understand. She smiled. "If it's any comfort, it was nothing personal. You weren't the only rowdy sidekick I ever bitched out royally."

"Admit it." He gave her a sly wink. "I always got your best shot."

"You earned it."

"I'll get my gear." He stepped back and put his hat back on. "First thing tomorrow morning, it'll give me a world of pleasure to run those flea-bitten bleaters off your land."

"You mean the sheep?"

"Must be a hole in the fence somewhere," he judged. "Either that or—"

"Oh, Tate." There it was again. *Oh, Tate.* This time the coolness was missing. In fact, he'd apparently said something delightfully funny, which was fine with him. He liked the rich sound of her laughter and the way her belly bounced with it.

She touched her hand to her lips, then to his leather sleeve. "Those are *our* sheep, cowboy. You just hired on as a sheepherder."

Chapter Two

Long before Amy had become Ken's wife, Tate Harrison
had been his best friend. She remembered the earlier days
well, but not, she had to admit, without a certain small
niggling of dissatisfaction with herself, a sense that she had
been tested and found wanting. It was not the only time in
her life that her behavior had come up short, of course, and
it would surely not be the last. She was only human.

More irritating, though, was that little voice inside her
head that always had the last say when she thought about
those old bygones. Same voice, same taunting tone, always
suggesting that she had also been *left* wanting. But the idea
was perfectly foolish, absolutely irrational. Amy Becker
was nothing if not prudent. She always had been, even back
then....

From Glendive to Missoula, Tate's reputation as a heart-
breaking hell-raiser had been legend. Amy had never been

interested in men like Tate. She much preferred his friend Ken Becker, whom she'd met when she'd worked at a bank in Billings. When she'd become the head bookkeeper at the small branch in Overo, Ken had come courting. He'd seemed to think his role as bronc rider Tate Harrison's shadow was his best calling card. "We're gonna watch ol' Tate buck one out, and then we'll party," he would say.

It was hard to convince Ken that the best date he could plan with her was a picnic atop one of the beautiful red clay bluffs on his ranch east of the Absaroka foothills. He hadn't been running the place very long, and his goals for his ranching business seemed a bit scattered. But he'd been born to the business, she thought almost enviously. He was the third generation of Becker cattlemen on Becker land. He had the kind of roots Amy craved, and he needed her. She liked that. He was as impressed with her good sense as he was with her good figure. She liked that, too.

Tate Harrison, on the other hand, never seemed to meet a woman who didn't impress him somehow. But it never lasted long. Too often, Amy's dates with Ken would start out as a threesome, and then Tate would pick up a fourth somewhere along the way. Usually it was some empty-headed buckle bunny who couldn't smile prettily and carry on a conversation at the same time, so she would quickly give up on the latter.

The worst of that ilk was Patsy Johnson. Unfortunately, she lasted the longest. She loved to play with the buttons on his shirt and sip on his beer. She never wanted a cigarette of her own, but she was always taking a puff off Tate's. Whenever she did it, she always glanced at Amy, as if to say, *What's his is mine.* As if Amy cared. Amy wasn't interested in Tate's buttons. She didn't like beer. She didn't smoke. Ken had virtually quit, too, except when he was around Tate. In fact, the whole two-stepping, part-

ner-swinging honky-tonk scene seemed to revolve around
Tate, and Amy's little bottom simply wasn't comfortable
on a bar stool.

One night she decided she'd had it with the rowdy cow-
boy-bar scene, where the soft drinks were too expensive,
the music too loud and the women too cute. Ken and his
friends were absolutely right; she did not know how to have
a good time, and she didn't want to interfere with theirs.
She made a trip to the ladies' room, then put in a phone
call to solve her transportation problem. Enough of this
noise, she told herself as she hung up the phone.

"Did you just call for a ride?"

Tate's voice startled her. Her heartbeat skipped into over-
drive, and she had to remind herself that he wasn't catching
her doing anything underhanded, which was almost the way
she felt.

"Yes, I did," she said calmly as she turned to find him
standing too close for comfort in the narrow hallway. The
bare overhead light bulb cast his face in sharp light and
deep shadows, playing up its chiseled angles. The knowing
look in his eyes was unsettling. She was glad she had genuine justification, even if she didn't owe him any. "I have
a headache."

"Does Kenny know?"

"He seems to be having an especially good time." Ken
knew how to enjoy himself, which was part of what made
him so likable, and when he was drinking, he enjoyed himself beyond Amy's ability to keep up. "And we came with
you tonight, so I called—"

"Did he do something?" Amy shook her head quickly,
and Tate laid his hand on his own chest. "Did *I* do something? I said something wrong," he supposed in all sincer-
ity. "If it was that little joke about women in tight pants,

I'm sorry. It didn't apply to you. I've never seen you wear—''

"It has nothing to do with anything you said. I just can't…'' It seemed strange, but she felt as though she could level with him, now that it was just the two of them. He was looking at her intently, as though he were concerned about the fact that she felt so out of place sitting at a table with ashtrays overflowing with cigarette butts and an accumulation of empty beer bottles. "I'm not very good at this kind of thing.'' She gave a helpless gesture, the kind she generally scorned. "The loud music, the smoke… sometimes it gives me a headache, that's all.''

"All you have to do is say something, and we'll—''

"No, just let me—'' She touched her fingertips to her throbbing temple. "I don't want to break up the party. I just want to go home.''

"Come on.'' He put one hand on her shoulder, guiding her toward the side door as he shoved his other hand in his pocket. She shook her head, trying to demur, but he cut her off. "No, I'll take you. It's no trouble.''

"But I've already called—''

"I'll take care of it. Kenny's sister, right?'' She nodded. Reassuring her with a light squeeze of his hand, he signaled the woman who'd been waiting on their table. "Jeri, honey, call Marianne and tell her Amy found another ride. And tell Kenny I'll be back in half an hour, that Amy's okay, but she needs to get home right away.'' He glanced at their empty table as he tucked some money into Jeri's hand. Kenny and Patsy had taken to the dance floor.

Tate put Amy in his pickup and headed across town to the small house she'd rented. It was tiny, but it was the first real house she'd ever lived in. She'd had her own apartment in Billings, and before that she'd lived in apartments and trailer homes with her family. She'd always wanted a real house.

"It's a relief to breathe fresh air," she told Tate. It was also a surprise to her to hear herself confiding, "I feel like a fifth wheel sometimes, especially when Ken has too much to drink." Too quickly she added, "Which he doesn't, usually."

"Well, I'm driving tonight, so Ken doesn't have to worry about having himself a good time."

She didn't understand their definition of having a good time, especially when it was bound to turn into a hangover by morning. "He's beyond the point where it would do any good to ask him to call it a night."

"Did you try?"

"'Just one more,' he said."

"Kenny's crazy about you, you know." He seemed to think he'd offered some great revelation, and he paused to let it sink in before he added, "He's making a lot of big plans. Not that it's any of my business."

"It is your business." Her tone betrayed her resentment. "Whatever his plans are, you'll know all about them before I do."

"We go back a long way, Kenny and me. A guy's gotta talk things out with a close buddy sometimes, especially when he's not too sure what's gonna happen." He dropped his hand and downshifted for a right turn. "He's afraid you'll turn him down." He kept his eyes on the road ahead, shifted again and surprised her by adding, "I'm afraid you won't."

"You think I'd spoil all the fun?" she asked scornfully, but Tate said nothing as he pulled over in front of her house. "There's more to life than rodeos and smoke-filled bars. If that's all you want, then fine, but I think Ken needs—"

"You're probably just what Kenny needs." Tate shut off the ignition, draped his left arm over the steering wheel and turned to her. "But he's not the kind of man you need. Deep down, I think you know that."

"He's a wonderful man," Amy insisted, reflexively bristling in Ken's defense. "He has a good sense of humor and the kindest heart and the gentlest nature of any man I've ever—" she paused and lifted her chin, defying the smile that tugged at the corner of Tate's mouth, for her concluding word came all too quietly "—met."

"You're right about that. Kenny's a nice guy." He laid his right arm along the top of the seat and touched her shoulder lightly. "You'll walk all over him. And he'll let you do it, because when you're done, he'll just pick himself up and do as he pleases. He'll do all that nice-guy stuff he likes to do, the stuff that never amounts to anything and never gets him anywhere. And you'll cover for him, which means he'll be walkin' all over you in his nice-guy way." In the dim light his eyes were completely overshadowed by the brim of his black cowboy hat, but she could feel them studying her. "Is that what you want?" he asked.

She answered tightly. "That's not the way it would be."

"Like I said, Kenny and me..." He shoved his hat back with his thumb and stretched lazily. "We go back a long, long way."

"You said you thought he was crazy about me."

"I *know* he's crazy about you. I know what Kenny thinks long before *he* does." He chuckled. "It won't take you very long to achieve that skill. You're probably halfway there already."

"With friends like you, he certainly doesn't need any enemies."

"I am his friend. I'd back him in the devil's own ambush, and he'd do the same for me." He glanced past the windshield at a pair of oncoming headlights. The car cruised by, and Tate shook his head, smiling wistfully. "But if I was a woman, I sure as hell wouldn't wanna be married to him."

"You wouldn't want to be married to anyone. That's why you go out with women like Patsy Johnson, who'll sit there and rub your thigh while she giggles at every word you say, whether it's supposed to be funny or not. She doesn't expect you to marry her."

"What does she expect?"

"You know what she expects," Amy snapped.

Tate chuckled. "Which part bothers you most? I don't like to be laughed at when I'm not joking, and when I am, you usually laugh, too. So you've got no reason to be jealous there."

"Jealous!"

"But it's hard to resist a woman who's got her hand on your thigh." His amused tone rankled almost as much as his male complacency. "'Specially if you've got no good reason to." He slid closer. "If you wanted to, you could give me a good reason to resist Patsy or any other woman."

"Why would I want to do that?" She knew what a dumb question it was. Dumber still was her willingness to sit still for the answer.

"Because you wanna be the one rubbin' my thigh."

He was smiling, looking just about as irresistible as any man who'd ever donned a Stetson, and she was melting like ice cream in July. She imagined slapping her own cheek to wake herself up, but it was more fascinating to watch him take off his hat and balance it between the dashboard and the steering wheel.

"You know this for a fact?" she asked, fully realizing that this banter was part of the game and she was just taking her silly turn.

"Sure do." He took her shoulders in his hands and turned her to him. "And you want me to be the one takin' you home, because you know damn well you'd never have to ask me twice."

He slowly pulled her close, challenging her to deny the truth in his claim, refusing to let her gaze stray from his. He'd brought her home, hadn't he? The house was only a few yards away, and she was still sitting there. She wanted his kiss, didn't she? When he brushed his palm against the side of her face and slid his fingers into her hair, she knew he was giving her all the time she needed to say otherwise. She couldn't. She parted her lips, but no words would come.

He hooked one arm around her shoulders, lowered his head and kissed her, softly at first, then more insistently, pressing for her response. Her mouth yielded to his as her breath fluttered wildly in her chest. His tongue touched hers like a sportsman testing the direction of the wind. Ah, yes, he seemed to say, that's the way of it, and he turned his head to try another angle.

She liked the sweet whiskey taste of him and the woody scent of his after-shave. His slim waist seemed a good place to put her hand. Her touch was his signal to draw her closer and kiss her harder. He rubbed her back with the heels of his hands, relaxing her, melting her spine, vertebra by vertebra. Then he slipped his hand between their bodies, cupping one breast in his palm while he insinuated his fingertips past her V-neck blouse and stroked the soft swell of its twin. Both nipples tightened in response.

She leaned into his embrace and answered his tongue's probing with the flickerings of hers. She wanted to be closer still. She wanted to feel his hand inside her blouse, skin against warm skin. She wanted to let him guide her, let him show her the way to lose herself in her own senses. Slowly she slid her hand up his long, hard back, up to his shoulder, where she gripped him as though she were teetering and needed support. He groaned, and his kiss became more urgent, more hungry.

"Let's go inside," he whispered.

"Oh, Tate." She wanted to. But making a move required her to open her eyes and realize that she was in the arms of a man who was more than attractive, far beyond adequate and a notch past willing. He was ready to meet her demands, but he would have his own ideas, as well. And he was not Ken.

Ken. The man she was supposed to be with tonight.

"Oh my God. No, Tate, this is all wrong." And it suddenly scared the hell out of her.

Her reluctance didn't seem to surprise him. "It'll be all right once you get it straight in your mind what you really want," he said evenly.

"I want a home. I want a family." Pulling back from him wasn't easy, so she resorted to the kind of ammunition she knew would scare a man like Tate off. "I want love first and then...and *then* sex. Ken—"

It was the name that did it. Tate's shoulders sagged a little as his embrace slackened. Amy closed her eyes and fought the urge to close her hands around his retreating arms before they got away completely. She had to say it again quickly. She had to *hear* it again. "*Ken* and I don't..."

"That's not something we talk over, whether you do or you don't. I'm not interested in hearing any of that," he snapped as he closed his hand around her left wrist and lifted her hand in front of her own face. "You're not wearing his ring. That's all I need to know."

Six months later Tate had known all he'd needed to. He'd carried the small gold band to the altar in his breast pocket, then turned it over to his best friend. He'd witnessed their vows, stood by while they were sealed with a kiss, even put his signature on the official documents. Amy wondered if his participation was Tate's way of backing Ken in "the devil's own ambush." He had kissed the bride properly in his turn and waltzed her once around the Overo Community Hall dance floor. It was the one time Amy could remember that Tate had left the party early—and alone.

On the first morning after he'd talked himself into the lowest-paying job he'd ever had, Tate was lured up the basement stairs by the commingling aromas of bacon and coffee. It had been a long time since he'd been up before the roosters, but he wanted to get started on the right foot with his new boss. He took it as a good sign when she glanced up from the big iron skillet and greeted him with a bright smile, never missing a beat as she turned a row of flapjacks, golden brown side up. It pleased him that she remembered his breakfast preferences.

"Sheep, huh?" He smiled back as he poured himself a cup of strong black coffee.

"Sheep."

"How many head?"

"Three hundred. And they pay the bills." The metal spatula scraped lightly against the skillet as she started dishing out the pancakes. "I can handle sheep, whereas I wasn't much help with the cattle."

"And cattle were the best excuse Kenny could think of for keeping horses around." Tate took a seat at the kitchen table.

"He really just wanted to raise horses, which would have been fine if—"

"If they'd paid the bills."

"Exactly." She wasn't fussy. She intended to keep her home intact. She would raise earthworms if the price were right. "Ken and I made a deal two years ago when he was beginning to realize that my little herd of sheep was more profitable than his whole—"

"You're a better businessperson than Kenny was," Tate said, cutting to the crux of the matter. "Did he ever realize *that* somewhere along the line?"

"Yes, he did. We all have our talents. Anyway, I agreed to the horses, and he agreed to the sheep. We got out of the cattle business."

"Sheep." The traditional bane of the cattleman. Not that Tate was in a position to care all that much, since he didn't own any cattle anymore, just a parcel of land, and it didn't appear that she'd used it to graze sheep. The damn woollies could crop the grass down halfway to China if a stockman didn't use a good rotation plan.

But here he was, offering his personal services, which would mean personal contact. He preferred the smell of cattle over the stink of sheep any day. He thought about it as he sipped his coffee. Finally he shook his head. "Well, you can give my portion of mutton to the dogs and double my ration of hot water."

"I don't serve mutton."

She *did* serve a nice plate of flapjacks and bacon, though, and he took a deep whiff as she set it down in front of him.

"Thank God for small favors. I'm going to have to fix that shower stall before I use it." He tasted the crisp bacon, then elaborated. "It doesn't drain right."

"I usually just mop up the water." The resignation in her voice irritated him. She planted her knuckles against her hip as she turned back to the stove. Her little fist was dwarfed by the basketball of a belly that tested the limits of her pretty pink sweater. "Ken was going to fix that shower, but there were other repairs that were higher on the priority list."

Tate imagined her down on her hands and knees, wiping the floor with a towel. "You give me the list," he ordered as he cut into the stack of flapjacks with his fork. "And a mop, if you don't want me to use your shower upstairs this morning." She wasn't mopping up *his* water.

"You're welcome to use the upstairs bathroom. Just let me check to make sure I've got clean soap and dry—"

"Clean soap?"

"You know, *fresh*. And towels, and Jody's bath toys out of the way."

"Does he have boats? Maybe I'll take a bath instead." He was chuckling happily. She wasn't. He could see her adding another chore to her mental list. "Amy, soap is soap, and I can find the towels. I don't need any special treatment, okay? I'm the hired hand, not a guest from out of town."

"Housekeeping hasn't been tops on my list of priorities lately, but ordinarily—"

"I don't see anything out of place," he assured her. And then, as if on cue, a sleepy-eyed blond moppet appeared in the kitchen doorway. "Hey, who's this big guy?" Tate laughed when his dubious greeting sent the boy scurrying to his mother's side. "Are you the same Jody who used to twist my ear half off when I gave him horseyback rides?"

The little boy looked up at his mother for some hint as to how he was supposed to answer.

"Do you remember Tate, sweetheart? Daddy's good friend?"

Tate, sweetheart. He smiled, enjoying the way it sounded. "You were a little squirt last time I was here, but you sure are getting big."

"I'm almost five," Jody announced bravely as he flashed splayed fingers Tate's way. "If I coulda' been five in August, I'd be in kindergarten."

"Well, next year. You must be big enough to ride a two-wheeler. I almost tripped over one out by the yard fence. Is that yours?"

"It *was* Bill, Jr.'s." Jody ventured a few cautious steps from his mother's side. "I'm gonna give it back to him," he added, clearly for Amy's edification.

"You'll get the hang of it, Jody. Maybe we'll put it away until spring." Amy sighed. "By then it won't be quite so hard for me to get you going."

"You just learning?" Tate asked as Jody joined him at the table.

"I keep falling off when my mom lets go. I'd rather ride a horse."

"I'm with you there, partner. If your mom'll let me use the horse trailer, I'll head into town after I get some chores done around here and bring back your dad's—"

"Breakfast first." Amy cast Tate a warning glance as she plunked a glass of orange juice on the table for Jody.

"My dad's what?"

"Your dad's..."

"Tate is going to help us out for a while, Jody, and he needed a horse, so I sold him—"

"The buckskin," Tate supplied. "That's the one I—" wrong choice, obviously, the way she was rolling her eyes "—kept. He moves out spirited and stylish, and he's got a nice head on him, good chest. The mare was kinda goose-rumped and paunchy." He eyed Amy playfully. "Like mares get sometimes."

"Very funny." Both hands went to her hips as Jody slipped away from the table. "In other words, you weren't about to listen to me."

"I know good horseflesh," Tate pointed out quietly. He hoped Jody wasn't beating feet down the hallway because of something he'd said. He'd just wanted the boy to know that his dad's horse would still be around.

"The buckskin was Ken's favorite, too," Amy said.

"So you were down to the four?"

"No. There are eighteen registered quarter horses out there. The mares aren't bred. The geldings aren't broke. You might say we're horse-poor. I can't afford to keep them, can't afford to give them away." She shook her head sadly. "Not Ken's dream herd."

"Horse-poor, huh," Tate echoed reflectively.

Jody reappeared, carrying a broken stick horse with a missing ear.

"Whatcha got there, partner?" Tate asked. Jody handed over his steed. "Does this guy have a little better handle than that two-wheeler? Looks like he got hogged." Tate ran his hand over the remains of a yarn mane, which had obviously been cut short by an inexperienced groom.

"I buzzed him with the scissors. He's glass-eyed, see?" Jody pointed to the pony's eye, which was indeed made of glass, but a horseman would term him glass-eyed because it was blue. "But whoever heard of a horse with blue-and-white polka dots?"

"You've never seen a blue roan?"

"That's not a roan."

"Looks like a roan to me." Tate turned the stick in his hand as he examined what was clearly a well-loved toy. "I think I can fix him up for you. Do a little fancy blacksmith-in'." He winked at the boy, who listened spellbound at his knee. "And we can probably get that bike of yours at least green-broke while I'm here. When you get throwed, best thing is to climb back into the saddle."

"Ready for pancakes, Jody?"

"Soon as I put Thunder back in his stall."

After the little boy had galloped out of earshot, Amy turned from the stove, plate in hand. "Don't make him any more promises, Tate. Two is enough. He's pretty confused as it is."

"I don't make empty promises." His look challenged her to disagree. When she didn't, he glanced away. "He looks a lot like his dad."

"Yes, he does. And now he reminds me of Peter Pan's shadow, sort of at loose ends." In another part of the house a closet door was opened, then shut. Amy set Jody's plate on the table and spoke softly. "Just be careful. I'm afraid he's looking for a man's boots to attach his little feet to."

"You think I'm gonna drag that little guy along behind me?" He reached for his coffee. "That's not my way, Amy."

"What is your way?"

"With kids?" Tate shrugged. "I don't know. I'm a little short on experience. Just be a friend and stick around while times are tough, I guess. Is that okay?" She nodded, and he smiled. "Good. So far his size doesn't scare me much. Long as I don't have to get on that two-wheeler myself, I'll be all right."

The autumn grass provided the sheep with plenty of roughage, but they needed supplemental feed. Amy laid out her instructions to the letter before turning the chore over to "the guys." Tate shoveled a load of grain into the pickup bed and took Jody along to show him where the feeders were. The sheep trotted across the pasture, bleating to beat hell when they saw the pickup coming.

Tate pulled up to one of the scattered feeders and set about filling the trough with grain. For an almost-five-year-old, Jody seemed pretty grown-up. He often mirrored what

Tate recognized as Amy's instructive manner. "We have to spread it out in the trough so they won't climb all over each other," the boy said soberly as he put his small hands to the task.

"Who's been hauling this out to the sheep since the last man quit?" They'd probably been supplementing for a month or more, Tate figured. He stood back and watched the dingy white merino ewes jostle for position around the trough.

"Me and Mom." Jody squinted one eye against the glare of the morning sun. "We're not as strong as you, so it takes a long time. We put the feed in a lot of small things, like ice-cream buckets, load them up in the pickup and—" with a gesture he drew a beeline in the sky "—buzz on out here. Did you know we're gonna have a baby? That's why my mom has such a big tummy."

"You mean it's not always that big?"

"No, that's a baby inside her. A little baby about—" he held his little round hands inches apart "—I'd say this big. That's why Mom had to stop using the scoop shovel to load the grain. Her big tummy got in the way."

Tate forced a chuckle for Jody's benefit, but it pinched his throat. He thought about Amy wielding that big shovel, and he shook his head. "Brother or sister, do you know?"

"No, that's going to be a surprise. I'm hoping for a brother."

"But a sister would be nice, too. Right?"

"I don't know." Jody scowled, then thrust his hand up for Tate's inspection. "My cousin Kitty slammed the car door on my finger yesterday. See?"

Tate hunkered down behind the open tailgate and studied the purpling fingernail. "Does it still hurt? It looks like it must've hurt like a bit—" *Wrong choice of words.* "*Biddy.*

Like an old biddy with a baseball bat, right? Boy, that can be murder.''

"What's a biddy? Is it a girl, like my dumb ol' cousin Kitty?''

"Yeah. Only older and meaner." He smiled. This curly-haired little fellow was cuter than a spotted colt. "You might get a new fingernail out of this deal. Did your mom tell you that?''

"No." Incredulous, Jody took a closer look at his finger. "You mean my fingernail might fall off?''

"After a while. But it'll be okay, because you'll get a new one. It's happened to me a lot of times.''

"By a biddy hittin' you with a bat?''

"By getting my hand caught in a door or stomped by a horse or banged with a hammer." He ruffled the boy's cotton-candy curls as he stood. "It's not always a girl's fault.''

"I still want a brother," Jody insisted.

"Either way, you'll have a new baby." Tate tossed the shovel into the pickup bed.

"Do you know about babies?" Jody wondered.

"I know they don't play much for the first year or so, and then they start gettin' into things. Have you had pups around, or kittens?" Jody nodded vigorously. "Kinda like that. Brothers get to be more fun when they get a little age on 'em.''

"But he plays around in my mom's tummy right now," Jody disclosed as he followed Tate to the driver's side.

Tate pictured an unborn child "playing around" in a warm, dark, cozy haven. He smiled as he hoisted Jody into the pickup. "What does he play?''

"He kicks." Jody scrambled over on the bench seat to make room for the driver. "Sometimes Mom says it feels like he's playing football. She lets me feel it, too. He kicked my nose once when I was just tryin' to talk to him in there.''

Tate was still smiling as he buckled Jody's seat belt.

"Next time I'll let you feel, too," Jody offered magnanimously.

"Feel what?"

"The baby kicking."

"Oh, well, your mom might, uh..." Let him put his hand on her belly? Yeah, right. But he was *still* smiling. "She might have something to say about that."

"She'll let you. She always lets me."

When they got back to the barn, they found Amy raking out stalls. Her long, chestnut-colored hair was clipped back at the nape, but bits of it had strayed over her face as she worked. She'd tossed Kenny's black parka aside and pushed up the sleeves of her pink sweater. She looked up when she heard them coming, then leaned on the rake handle as she pressed her free hand against the small of her back.

"Whew, I'm working up a sweat here." She wiped her brow with the back of her hand. "Lately it doesn't take much and I'm all in a sweat."

"Go back in the house, Amy. I know where everything is, and I swear to you I've already got the hang of the routine down pat. Jody and me—" She wasn't listening. She'd slid her hand over her ripe, round belly and gotten a funny look on her face. "What's the matter?"

"Is he kickin' again, Mom?"

"*She*—" Amy put her hand under Jody's upturned chin and offered a motherly smile "—is going to be a Rockette. The little rascal is in top form today."

"Where, where, where?" Jody jumped up and down like a pogo-stick rider until Amy took hold of his hand and placed it against the lower left side of her stomach. "Yow!

Mom, that baby kicked me again," Jody chirped. "Let Tate feel."

Bubbling with excitement, Jody was puzzled by the sudden stillness. He looked up at one face, then the other, and he wondered at his power. He'd just created two awkwardly flash-frozen big people, staring dumbly at each other. "Come on, Tate wants to feel, dontcha, Tate?"

"Jody, my hands are pretty—" Tate looked down at hands that might have belonged to someone else, as awkward as they suddenly felt. He flexed his fingers as though he were working out some stiffness in the joints. "They're too dirty and...too cold."

"He won't know that," the boy assured him with exaggerated patience. "He's inside Mom's tummy." He claimed Tate's big, rugged, reluctant hand in his small but sure one. "Where do you feel it now, Mom?"

"Here," Amy said softly. She leaned back against a short stack of square bales as she reached for Tate's hand.

Her skin felt like a firebrick against his. He tipped his hat back with one finger as he sought and found her permission in her soulful, brown, earth-mother eyes. He swallowed convulsively. She directed his hand, pressing it against her as though she were showing him where to find her most personal, most intimate secret. Her belly was harder than he had thought it would be, and wondrously round, like a perfect piece of fruit. He wanted to slip his hand under the sweater—damn pesky wool—and touch taut, smooth skin, but not in an invasive way. More like reverent. It was sure corny, but that was the way he felt. He'd almost forgotten what he was supposed to be feeling *for* until the little critter he couldn't see actually *moved* beneath his hand.

"Ho-ly..." Without thinking, he went down on one knee. As though he were gazing into a crystal ball, he focused his whole attention on this precious part of Amy, the part that held her baby, the part that she permitted *him* to hold in his two hands.

"Hey, Mom, there's Cinnamon Toast." Jody pointed at the feline face peering down at them from the rafters. Neither Amy nor Tate flickered an eyelash. "C'mere, Cinnamon," Jody coaxed as he headed up the ladder to the loft.

"Is that a foot?" Tate asked quietly, afraid he might scare whatever was in there, whatever, *whoever*, seemed to be responding to his touch.

"What does it feel like to you?"

"Like somebody tryin' to fight his way out of a—" He looked into her eyes and gave a teasing half smile. "A balloon?"

"Tactful choice."

"Does he do this all the time?"

"I think she's one of those children who loves to perform for an audience."

"Jeez, she's really—" he moved his hand, following the movement within Amy "—goin' to town here. How long before she's supposed to make her appearance?"

"Three weeks. But you can give or take two. Jody was late. But, then, I know when this one got her start, almost to the hour."

They shared a solemn look. Then an oppressive thought hit Tate like a cannonball. She was speaking of an hour he didn't want to think too much about, not just because it had been one of Kenny's last, but because...because he'd made himself stop thinking about the two of them in that way a long time ago, and he didn't want to start in again. He drew his hands away gradually as he rose from the straw-covered floor.

"Ken never knew," Amy said.

"He knows now."

"Do you believe that?"

"Sure." He sought to put some distance between himself and the bone-melting experience he'd just had by remembering his friend the way he ought to have been remembering him. "I can't see him wearin' a halo or any of that kind of stuff, but I believe he's in a good place, and I think he'll be with you in spirit." Her eyes took on a misty sheen, and her brave smile consecrated his amended efforts. Damn, he could talk nice when he saw a need. "Especially when the baby's born," he added. "I think he'll be there, come hell or high water." He laid a comforting hand on her shoulder. "So to speak."

"So to speak," she echoed softly.

He nodded, and his eyes strayed to her distended belly again. "That's pretty amazing. I mean, you don't realize how amazing until you actually..." He extended his hand impulsively, then arrested the presumptuous move to touch her stomach once more, turning it into an empty-handed gesture. "That's pretty amazing."

"You're blushing, Tate Harrison." He glanced at her, then glanced away, shaking his head. "Yes, you are. You are as pink as—"

Tate chuckled, genuinely embarrassed. *Damn.* Where had this big, dumb cowboy come from? Hadn't he just been doing the silver-tongued knight like a seasoned pro?

"You look like a newborn with a five o'clock shadow." She cupped his bristly cheek in her small hand. "*That* is pretty amazing."

Chapter Three

Tate's plan was to get in a few chores before breakfast, but Amy had already foiled it three days running. The woman didn't know how to sleep in. He could have sworn it was still the middle of the night, but she had him waking up to the smell of coffee. Her time was getting close. Surely she needed more rest. Each time he heard those early-morning footsteps overhead, his first thought was, *Maybe this is it.*

Nah, couldn't be. If anything serious had started, she wouldn't be fooling with the coffeepot at whatever the hell time it was. In order to see the time, he would have to turn the damn light on. He would find out soon enough. He dragged himself out of bed and felt his way to the bathroom door. Once he'd stood in the shower long enough to steam his eyes open, the smell of her coffee drew him up the steps to the kitchen table.

"Oh, did I wake you up?" Amy asked sweetly. "I'm sorry. I really was trying to be quiet."

"You wanna be sneakin' around, you need a different pair of shoes," he told her, his mood lightening gradually. Her hair hung over her shoulder in one thick braid. He liked her light floral, fresh-from-the-shower scent. He also liked the way their fingers touched when she handed him his coffee.

"Ken gave me these." She lifted her foot and glanced down at the plastic heel on her slipper. "They're noisy?"

"Like Mr. Bojangles found a linoleum cloud in heaven."

"I'm hardly that light on my feet," she said with a laugh as she set a plate in front of him. "But see if these scrambled eggs are light and fluffy enough for you. How are you getting along with the dogs?"

"We're on speaking terms." The eggs went down easy. With a wink and a nod, he told her so. "I tell 'em, 'Speak,' and they say, 'Grrr-ruff.' Kinda meanlike, so my guess is we're speaking about territory, and they're tellin' me this is theirs."

"Don't take it personally. They didn't like Ken, either. Do you think you could bring the herd in by yourself?"

"You're talkin' to a professional cowboy here, ma'am." He smiled as she joined him at the table. "Among other things. If I can work cows, I sure as hell don't need any help bringin' in the sheep."

"Good. You'll bring them in, the dogs and I will sort them and we'll take the rest of the lambs to the sale barn tomorrow."

"I can tell the big ones from the little ones, honey. *I'll* do the sorting."

"The dogs do all the work." She studied her coffee for a moment, and he waited for the second shoe to drop. "Tate, I know it's just an expression, but I think it would be better if you'd try not to use it, um…in this particular case.''

''What expression?'' He was truly at a loss. If he'd said a cuss word, it had slipped right out without him even hearing it.

''Honey.''

Honey was bad? ''Just an expression,'' he agreed.

''Jody might hear it and get the wrong impression.''

''Which is—'' he gave her the opening, but she left it to him to fill in the blank ''—that maybe I like you some?''

''*Some?*'' Her indulgent smile rankled *some*. ''Jody wouldn't understand that 'honey' just means 'female' to you.''

''So I should use the word *female?*'' He tried it out. ''I can tell the ewes from the lambs, *female?* Or should I say, I can tell the females from the kids? But kids are goats,'' he amended with a boyish grin. Now that he was rolling, he had her rocking with laughter. ''If I start calling the ewes 'honey,' I want you to get me to a shrink, right away. Sign the commitment papers and tell 'em I'm crazy as a sheepherder.''

''Crazy as a pregnant *female* sheepherder?''

''Uh-uh.'' He shook his head slowly, enjoying the sparkle in her big brown eyes. ''Just 'crazy as a sheepherder.' It's a cowboy expression. You've got a *cowboy* workin' for you, lady. You can boss his hands, but not his mouth.''

''First *ma'am*, then *honey*, and now it's *lady*. I don't know.'' Her laughter dwindled into a sigh. ''They say cowboys are just naturally fickle.''

''Can't live with 'em, can't shoot 'em.''

''Can't resist 'em, either,'' she mumbled, drowning the better part of the comment in her coffee cup.

''What was that?'' Had he heard her right? With a quick

shake of her head, she jumped up from the table, leaving him to guess whether his ears had lied to him.

He shrugged and let it go. "Anyway, what I was trying to say was, I've got a pretty good whistle on me. I can do the sorting. I don't want you out there in those pens until you've calved out."

She returned with the coffeepot and poured him a refill. "Wet your whistle with this, cowboy. You'll need it. It's hard to get the dogs to work for somebody they're not used to. They're my dogs, and they're my pens and I'm not a cripple. I'm just—"

"The mule-headedest woman I ever met. You can supervise, okay? Give orders." His fork clattered on the plate as he took a swipe at his mouth with a paper napkin. "To the dogs, not me. You can tell me what to do, but not how to do it. I might be herdin' your damn sheep, but I've still got some pride left."

"I never doubted that." She smiled complacently as she claimed his empty plate.

He sighed. "So how many head are we sellin'?"

"I sold half the crop as spring lambs back in July, but the price wasn't nearly what I needed to get, so I've been holding off on the balance to put more weight on them." She let her guard down and eyed him solemnly. "I'm running out of time, though."

"They're not spring lambs anymore."

"No, but they're still lambs. Nice ones. They're pretty and plump right now. I was betting on a friendlier fall market, but it hasn't improved much, and my bills need to be paid. I think I'll be able to meet them. I really think I will." She was working hard to convince somebody, but he didn't think it was him.

"Did Ken have any insurance?" Tate asked. Without looking him in the eye, she shook her head. It surprised him a little, but he didn't let it show, because it would have embarrassed her.

"Insurance premiums aren't at the top of the priority list when you've got your whole life ahead of you, and your whole life is tied up in this place."

"Kenny inherited this place."

"And we mortgaged it to stock it and buy equipment. The land and the house. That was Ken's share. The rest was up to him." She slipped the plate into a sink full of soapy water. "When he married me, it was up to *us*."

Tate snagged a toothpick from the little red container that stood next to the pepper shaker. "But he's gone now, and *us* adds up to you and a little—*two* little kids." He slid his chair back from the table.

"It's the life I want for me and my two little kids. So I'm going to fight for it."

"Then I guess I'd better saddle up and move some sheep." He ambled over to the counter, thinking a toothpick was a poor substitute for a cigarette, but a guy had to make do. "Speaking of priority lists, I fixed the shower."

"Already?"

"Didn't take a lot of study, just a little muscle. You tell me what needs doing, and I'll figure out how to do it." He drained the last of his coffee before he handed her the mug. "But if you don't clue me in on the rest of your list, I'll have to come up with one on my own."

"See if you can get the dogs to go with you." She made it sound like a consolation of some kind. "Once you get them out in the pasture, they know what to do. Getting them to work the sheep in the pens takes a little more direction."

See if you can get the dogs to go with you. As if a sheep-dog was going to be particular about keeping company with a cowboy. But when he let the two out of the kennel, they took off hell-bent-for-leather for the tall grass in the shelter belt. An explosive beating of pheasant wings promptly had them yapping their fool heads off as a ring-necked cock sailed majestically out of reach, his coppery feathers stealing a glint of sunrise.

"Nice move, bird," Tate said, turning a squint-eyed grin up to the sky. "To listen to *her* talk, you'd think these two sheepdogs had more brains than a cattleman." He plucked the toothpick from the corner of his mouth and tucked his tongue against his teeth, but then thought better of giving a whistle so close to little Jody's bedroom window. He used the toothpick as a pointer. "Come on, you two, we've got work to do."

All they did was play around. They chased each other around the shed while Tate gathered up his gear. They spooked the buckskin while Tate was trying to get him to take the bit. Damn horse was head-shy as it was. The rowels on Tate's spurs jingled as he gave a hop into the stirrup and swung into the saddle. The dogs ran circles around him as he trotted past the yard-light pole.

"If you two mutts are goin' with me, you can stop actin' like jackrabbits any time now."

"The collie's name is Duke, and the spotted bitch is Daisy," Amy called out. "She's a Catahoula Leopard."

Tate hadn't heard the door open, but there she was, waving to him from the back porch like he was some kind of explorer heading out to sea. "I can see that," he called back.

"She's won two blue ribbons."

"For what? Chasing cars?"

"They know their names." As showy as the pheasant's feathers, Amy's rich chestnut hair trapped a red glint of sunlight. She gave another jaunty wave. "Just call them."

He didn't need her advice on what to call them. "Come on, you fleabags. We're burnin' daylight."

When he topped the rise, he looked back. The dogs had treed some varmint, and their tongues were lolling in apparent expectation that the thing would fall out of the branches and land at their feet. One more chance was all they were going to get.

Tate popped a crisp whistle. "Daisy! Duke! Get your carcasses up here!"

And they came a-running.

The dogs had pushed the sheep along the draws without much coaxing from Tate, but it was a wonder to watch them work the pens for Amy. She whistled like nine different kinds of bird and used hand signals to let the dogs know which animals to drive where. All Tate and Jody had to do was mind the gates.

He still didn't like the idea of letting her get near any livestock so close to her time. Sheep had legs. They could kick. She was already getting kicked pretty good on the inside. When she paused to rub the side of her belly, he whacked the gate shut on the pen where he was working and started to go to her, but then she smiled. Another one of those little kicks. He clenched his fists to stop himself from going to her anyway and putting his hand where hers was. He liked feeling the movement inside her. It was sort of like having a new foal trust him enough to come close and nuzzle his palm, then stand still for a little friendly petting.

"What time are they sending the truck?"

"Five," she told him. "I want to be at the sale barn when they're unloaded so that I can get them settled down and fed."

"You're staying right here." With a quick gesture he cut

off her protest as he strode across the corral, closing in on her. "Look at you. You're all done in. If you wanna go to the sale tomorrow and have your remarkable business-lady wits about you, you'll let me…" He heard footsteps tagging along behind him, at least three steps to his one. Without missing a beat, he scooped Jody up in his arms and patted the back pockets of his pint-size blue-jeans. "You'll let *Jody and me* take care of the grunt work tonight. Right, partner? You think we can handle it?"

Jody nodded vigorously.

"I'm not a business *lady*. I'm a business…"

"Person. Female. Female person. Give me a break, Amy. I got the remarkable part right, didn't I? And I'm just trying to give *you* a break." As part of the effort, he held the gate open for her. "I suggest you take me up on it. It would be downright humiliating if you happened to collapse at the sale barn and I had to carry you out of there. I mean, what if I couldn't lift you?"

She laughed and shook her head as she headed for the house.

"Huh? What if I had to haul you out in a wheelbarrow?" Close on her heels, Tate gave Jody a male-conspiratory wink. "How much does a pregnant lady weigh, anyway? Pregnant *female*, pardon me."

"I *do* think of myself as a lady, but not like, 'Whoa, that's too much for you to handle, *little lady*. Better let a *man* take over for you.'"

"Did I say that? Hey, I've made my reputation as a top hand. You're a *sheep* rancher. You think I'd set my sights on takin' over for a sheep rancher? No, ma'am. Not this cowboy. I'll just be Miz Becker's hired hand, down on his luck and workin' for a dollar a day and board. Only way to hang on to my self-respect."

"A dollar a day?" At the top of the back steps she turned

to him, hands on her hips, and flashed a saucy smile. "When did I give you a raise?"

Amy's lambs did better than most, but prices were depressed. So was Amy. She didn't say a word on the way home from the auction. There wasn't much supper conversation, either, and anything coming from Amy was directed quietly at Jody. Tate felt like an interloper. He helped Jody clear the table. When the boy was told it was his bath time, Tate figured he'd been dismissed from the domestic scene. He went downstairs, flopped back on his bunk and played a few tunes he'd taught himself over the years on the harmonica he'd gotten from his dad. His *real* dad. He thought of him as Carter Harrison, the black-and-white photo phantom. Carter had played the harmonica, too. Sad songs, his mother had told him. Songs to fit his mood, like, "I'm So Lonesome I Could Cry."

"Can you teach me to play that?"

Tate raised his head and smiled. Jody looked small and wide-eyed and shy, standing there in his blue pajamas with the plastic-soled feet. Eagerly awaiting his cue, he gripped the door frame, ready to pop in or vanish, depending on Tate's answer.

"I can try," Tate offered.

Jody fairly leapt across the threshold, skidding to a stop at Tate's knee.

"How much time do we have before you have to be in bed?" The boy managed to shrug his shoulders as high as his ears, but Tate detected a guilty look in his eyes, which probably meant he was supposed to be in bed already. He decided to risk it. "I'd say we've got some time."

The two sat side by side on the narrow bed. Tate tapped the harmonica in his palm a few times, then held it steady for Jody and directed him through a series of notes. "Now the same thing, only a little faster,'' Tate said, and Jody complied intently. ''What song did you play?'' Tate asked at the end.

Jody gave a big-eyed smile, his blond curls shimmering under the overhead light. '''Twinkle, Twinkle Little Star.'''

''That's right. Did you know that's a cowboy's song?'' Jody shook his head. ''Sure is. You're camped out under the stars, you got your saddle for a pillow, your ol' six-shooter handy in case you find a rattler in your bedroll.''

Jody's eyes grew big as saucers as Tate animated his tale with broad gestures.

''You take out your mouth organ, and you serenade the stars. This is their theme song.'' He slid the instrument back and forth across his lips and played the familiar tune again. ''They like that all over, and, man, do they twinkle in that big Montana sky.''

''Let me do it again.''

By the time Jody returned the instrument, Tate was ready to pay him to stop twinkling. They shared a pillow while Tate played every soft, soothing song he knew. Jody finally drifted off to sleep. Tate carried him upstairs and managed to sneak past Amy's room. The desk light was on, and her back was to the door. He figured she was going over the books, dividing the amount of the lamb check among the outstanding bills. She'd been at it awhile. Either she had an extremely long column of numbers, or the check just wasn't big enough.

He decided to take her a comfort offering, and he knew she liked tea. He wanted to let her know that he didn't have to be told what her problems were. He'd been around long enough to take account. He had some ideas, and when she rejected those out of hand, as she was bound to do, he would be prepared with some alternatives. She was a fighter with her back to the wall. She would probably take a swing at him out of frustration, but he was pretty good at ducking. He could also be pretty good at talking sense. And because she was basically a sensible woman, eventually she would hear him out.

But she'd fallen asleep over her books. He stood in the doorway, steaming cup in hand, trying to decide whether he should knock or just walk right in like he owned the place. He wasn't going to leave her slumped over the desk for the night.

She solved his problem by awakening with a start, as though someone had shouted in her ear. She gripped the edge of the little writing desk and turned on him abruptly, her chair swiveling like the lid of a mayonnaise jar. He was sure he hadn't made a sound. Impatiently she swept the mop of errant hair out of her face and, with an indignant look, challenged him to explain himself.

He lifted the cup. "Tea."

She gave him a blank stare.

He was tempted to turn on his heel and leave her to sleep sitting up if it pleased her, but he said, "I thought I could get you to take a break, but I see..."

"For me?"

"Well, yeah. If I'd made it for me, I'd 'a put a kick in it." He sniffed the steam. "Smells like virgin orange."

She smiled. Finally. "What is a *virgin* orange?"

"Pure." He circled the foot of the bed and offered her the cup. "I read the box. It's got some kind of natural sleeping potion in it, but you have to be in bed for it to work."

"It doesn't say you have to be in bed."

"*You* have to be in bed—" he checked his watch as he sat down on the bed "—by midnight, so put the books away. Can I sit here?"

"You've already made your wrinkles in my coverlet."

Flustered, he started to get up again. "Just kidding," she said quickly. "I'm not *that* fussy." She sipped the hot tea, then puzzled over it. "I do have to wonder why you're being so nice to me."

"Why wouldn't I be?" he asked, then added with mock indignation, "What, I don't have it in me to be nice?"

"You have it in you to be...a lot of things, I'm sure."

"Versatility is my stock in trade. I like being a lot of things. Keeps life interesting." He sat spraddle-legged, hands braced on his knees. "But I'm between jobs right now. It's either hire on to push an eighteen-wheeler down the road for a while, or tend sheep. Never had much truck with sheep."

He chuckled at his own wit and caught the weary smile in her eyes, peering at him above the rim of her cup.

"Guess it's something different," he allowed. "Besides, I'll take the view from the back of a horse over a truck cab, any day. Even if it's a view of sheep rumps headin' home."

"I'd like to get rid of the horses. All of them. Especially that outlaw you brought back here."

"One thing I can tell you for sure, Amy. It wasn't ol' Outlaw's fault." He paused for her objection, but she only drank more tea. "I figure he must be the one Kenny was riding that night. He's high-lifed, but he's a good horse. If he got spooked or missed his footing..." She gave him a sharp look, and he added quietly, "Kenny would be the first to tell you not to blame the horse."

"You're saying he shouldn't have been out riding that night."

"I'm saying it happened, and there's no sense to it. It's the kind of thing that could happen to anyone. Kenny drew the wrong cards that night."

"He shouldn't have been playing cards," she said flatly.

"Or drinking. Or riding out there by himself. Or—" Quiet anger rose in her voice, and there was only Tate to be angry with.

"That was Kenny." Her husband, his friend, but they'd both known the same man. "He was a good-hearted, easy-goin' guy who didn't like to think too far ahead."

"Well, I *do* think ahead." She was staring so hard at the papers on her desk that he half expected to see the edges start curling up and smoking. "I plan things. I planned the way I was going to sell the lambs, and I planned on getting more for them. Now I'll have to sell breeding stock so I can buy feed."

"I've been giving that some thought," he said lazily as he folded his hands behind his head and leaned back against her brass headboard. "I know I'm not getting paid to do any thinkin', but, hell, it just happens sometimes. You didn't take any hay off my land this year."

"We hadn't paid the lease." Her eyes darted about the room, finding bits of her explanation in every corner of the room, anywhere except in his eyes. "I didn't have anyone to cut it, anyway. Not that I would have, without your... I know Kenny agreed to cut it on shares, and then... I should have let you know that wasn't happening, so you could have made a deal with someone else, but—" She resigned herself with a long sigh. "I'm sorry. That was irresponsible of me."

"Well, now that you've got that off your chest, you can forget about it, okay? I'm not hurtin' for crop money or lease money or any of that. Come spring, I'll see about selling the land." With a gesture he dismissed the whole issue. He was eager to put forth his plan. "I figure with a little supplement we can put the herd out there and graze them 'til it gets too cold. Meanwhile, I'll shop around for some hay."

"I can't buy hay," she informed him stiffly. "I don't have the money."

"What if I said that I do?" She didn't need to say anything, what with that granite look in her eyes. "Yeah, that's what I thought."

"I should just sell those worthless horses."

"Now, I wouldn't call them worthless. They've got potential." He ignored her delicate sneer. "But if you sold them now, they'd go for killers. Butcher meat and dog food's about the only market for unbroke horses right now."

"They're registered quarter horses."

"And we both know that doesn't matter. Stock prices are low across the board. Nobody's got money for horses right now."

"Ken did." The resentment in her voice did battle with the guilt in her eyes. "He always had money for another great horse bargain."

"That's because he had you, makin' ends meet." Guilt gave way to a flash of gratitude. He understood. He smiled sympathetically. "So now you're done buying horses, and you've sold your lambs, and you're down to your ace-in-the-hole."

"Which is?"

"You've found yourself some cheap labor. You let him do what he can for you."

She looked at him, long and hard, and he could almost hear those gears clicking away inside her head, questioning, always trying to figure the odds and hedge her bets. In her position, he couldn't blame her.

"Why?" she asked finally.

"Because you're a smart woman, Amy. And you've run low on options."

"I mean, why are you willing to do this?"

"It's kinda out of character, isn't it?" He smiled knowingly. "I don't like being too predictable. Every once in a while I like to be nice. I like to be useful to somebody, just for a change."

"I never said you weren't nice...sometimes."

"Boy, that was a squeaker." He laughed and shook his head as he got up to leave. "On that happy note and the strike of the eleventh hour, I'd better drag my tail downstairs."

"I know *I'm* not always nice," she admitted with another sigh. "I didn't even thank you for the tea." She took another drink, just to show him that she wasn't going to let it go to waste. He figured it had to be cold by now. "This is nice, and I thank you."

"My pleasure." He touched her shoulder as he passed. Her surprisingly unguarded look of appreciation made him want to hang around the bedroom a little longer. "I fed the ewes. Tomorrow morning I'll start moving some grain feeders out to my place. I'll be putting the rams out there with them." She raised one brow, but he detected the hint of a smile. "Won't I? I mean, is that your plan, boss lady?"

"We'll have to watch the weather closely if we're going to move them over to your place."

"This is Montana." He chuckled. "What else have we got to do in the winter?"

"Some of the grain feeders might need a little repair," she warned.

"I've already got that covered." He gave her a reassuring wink as he turned to leave.

"Tate?" He glanced over his shoulder, eyebrows raised. "I may not always be nice, either, but I *am* good. I try to be a good person, anyway. I do understand why you're doing all this. I know how you felt about Ken, and I don't want to take advantage of you, especially since I didn't make much of an effort to—"

"If you're seeing some advantage to be taken, I'm makin' progress."

It took him a good part of the morning to make the repairs on the free-standing grain feeders and put them in accessible locations. When he came back he found his lunch waiting for him, but the house was deserted. Jody was playing with a fleet of toy trucks outside the barn, and Amy was inside, sitting in a pile of straw with the shoulders of a one-hundred-and-seventy-pound ewe planted in her lap.

"What the hell do you think you're doing?"

"Poor baby had a nail in her hoof."

Hunkering down next to her, he pulled off one buckskin work glove, pushed her open coat aside and laid his hand protectively over her belly. "*This* is a baby," he corrected, and with a gloved finger he touched the ewe's foot. "This, as you know, is a hoof. This hoof might kick this baby."

"The hoof belongs to a sheep, not a horse or a cow. They have to be trimmed every fall," she explained as she continued to pare the cloven hoof. "And since we're going to move them, I have to get them all done."

"God—*bless*, woman!" The docile, flop-eared ewe sniffed at his jacket, but she was no more intimidated by his exasperated protests than Amy was. Ordinarily he wasn't one to expound much, but he figured a lesson was in order. "A hoof is a hoof." End of chapter one. He sat down on Amy's straw cushion. "Why don't you tell me about these things before you go and—"

"I *always* trim their hooves, twice a year, and I have never gotten hurt doing it. They're gentle animals, Tate."

"Tell that to the two rams I just separated."

"Well, the rams..." She inspected the inner hoof for debris, probing with her parer. "They do butt heads during breeding season. It's a man thing." She spared him a coy glance. "I'll let you take care of the rams."

"I'll tell you something else that's a man thing." He draped his forearms over his knees and removed his other glove. "You see a woman in your condition, you just wanna put her in a pumpkin shell and keep her very well until everything's—" he slapped his palm with the leather glove "—over with. Safe and sound."

"And a woman in my condition happens to have a good deal of energy, especially as the time draws closer. She wants to make sure everything is in order, and nature seems to provide her with the energy to do just that." She looked up at him. "I couldn't breathe in a pumpkin shell. You need your space, Tate. Let me have mine."

"I'll let you show me how to do this," he offered as he scooted the ewe from her lap to his. A hoof was a hoof, he'd said, and he'd trimmed his share. He held his hand out for the knife.

"Actually, I was going to need some help catching them. This one was limping, so she was slower than I was." She relinquished the tool to him. It was useless to argue, and she knew he didn't need much instruction. "I'm used to handling most of it myself, but Jody's helping out, too, now. He can bottle-feed a lamb. He can—"

"Jody's just a little guy." Too young to be given some of the jobs he kept asking for. Tate remembered how it felt to be given the kind of responsibility that made a boy feel like a man. Heady at first, but there was no turning back once you'd taken the step. At least there hadn't been for him.

"I heard you reading that nursery rhyme to him the other night, about the pumpkin shell," he said. It was the kind of kids' stuff he'd sailed right past on his shortcut to manhood. "What's that supposed to mean, 'had a wife but couldn't keep her'? You don't get married unless you've got some way to keep her."

"Keep her what?" Amy teased. "Happy? It's usually the woman's lament, that she had a husband but couldn't keep him."

"Keep him what?" he echoed.

They traded smiles while he switched to the other front hoof. Then he made short work of the back hooves and let the animal go.

"When are you going to settle down?" she wondered. "For longer than a few months, I mean."

"The word *when* supposes I will, sooner or later." The straw rustled beneath him as he shifted, raising his knee for an armrest. "Is that what you suppose? Every man oughta settle down, sooner or later?"

"They don't all want to. I know that. And some try to have it both ways." He looked up, wordlessly asking whether she meant him. "Ken wasn't like that." Missing Tate's message, she went on. "He had built-in roots. I like that. I found a sense of security in it. That's funny, isn't it?"

"Why?" He felt no urge to laugh now that she'd changed the subject to Kenny's attributes.

"Because he found a way to wander off after all, didn't he?" It wasn't the answer he was ready for, nor the one she'd expected to give. She glanced away quickly. "I don't know why I said that. It's a terrible thing to say."

"But it's true. He's gone, and you're still here."

"He didn't mean to," she said sadly as she picked a piece of straw off his thigh. "He never meant to leave us. He didn't even know he was leaving *two* children, and he didn't mean for things to be so—" Here it comes, he thought. He couldn't see her eyes, but her voice was weakening. "—damn hard."

"It's okay." She shook her head as he took her hands in his. "No, come on, Amy, it's okay to tell it like it is."

"It isn't like that. He's not to blame." She glanced at the open barn door, her eyes shining with the threat of tears. "That horse, that crazy horse."

"I'll get rid of the horse," he promised. Her bottom lip trembled, but she said neither aye nor nay. Gently he squeezed her hands. "Will that help?"

"Yes!" She closed her eyes and shook her head again as he moved into position. "No, no, no, it won't do any good."

"Come here, honey." He reached out to her, ready to hold her, anticipating the feel of her weight against him. "It'll do you good to—"

"No," she said firmly, wiping her eyes with one hand and pushing him away with the other. Jody's truck-engine sound effects intruded from a distance. "I can't let Jody see me like this."

"Why not?"

"I'm all he's got." She scrambled to her feet so fast that he missed his chance to offer any gentlemanly assistance. "And I can't come apart now. I don't have time. I have too much to do. I have to—" Her hands were shaking as she struggled for control. "*We* have to get those hooves trimmed."

She'd streaked some dirt across her cheek with the tear she'd banished so quickly. He reached his hand out to her. "Amy, take it easy." He would clean her face if she would let him. He would kiss away her tears.

"Are you going to help me or not?"

Her lips were trembling, and her eyes were wild with an

emotion he couldn't begin to name. He let his hand fall to his side. "I'm gonna do the work," he said gruffly. "You give the damn orders."

Chapter Four

In trade for hay, Tate agreed to break a couple of two-year-olds for Myron Olson. He knew Myron needed green-broke two-year-olds about as much as he needed a swimming pool in his backyard this winter, but Myron happened to have plenty of hay and welcomed the excuse to truck some over to the Becker place. Like some of the other neighbors, he'd offered to help the widow out with whatever she needed, but she always said she was doing just fine.

Just what she needed, Amy grumbled when he unloaded the new stock. More horses around the place. But Tate detected a glint of relief in her eyes when the first load of hay rolled into the yard. He wasn't going to let the horses interfere with his other chores, but he liked to work with them when he was minding Jody, who loved to watch. Tate found himself wishing Amy would come out to observe him in action, too, just to reassure herself that it was perfectly safe to keep horses around.

"Mama, Mama, Mama!"

Jody only called her "Mama" when he was excited or scared. The way his little legs were churning up the gravel, she could tell he was both. She flew out the door and met him at the foot of the back steps.

"Come quick! Tate got kicked!"

"Where!"

"In the head, by one of the—"

She took his hand, and together they trotted across the yard. "Show me where."

"It's nothing," Tate insisted as soon as Amy and Jody burst into the barn. He was sitting on a hay bale, hat in one hand, head in the other, looking like a guy who'd just lost round one. "I'm okay. Just grazed me. No blood spilled." But when he took his hand away from his forehead, he had a glove full of blood. "*Hardly* any blood spilled."

"You're bleeding all over the place!" Amy exclaimed as she knelt beside him, trying to catch her breath. "Can you walk?"

"Legs are fine." He scowled, arching the eyebrow that was catching most of the blood. "You been running?"

"Jody's been running. I've been waddling."

"You shouldn't be running." He took a swipe at the blood with the back of his wrist as he tried to duck away from her scrutiny.

"*You* shouldn't be—" She took his face in her hands and made him look at her. The light was dim, and his eyes were so dark that it was hard to tell anything about his pupils. "Can you walk?"

"You asked me that." He proved he could stand up. "Point me in the right direction."

"You okay, Tate?" Jody asked anxiously.

"If I start to go down, just holler 'Timber!' and get your mom out of the way."

"That's not funny," Amy insisted as she slipped her arm around him. He put his arm around her shoulders, and she gave his flat belly a motherly pat as they headed for the house. "You'll be okay."

"That's what I said. Just feelin' a little booze blind, which is no big deal." But he grabbed for the gatepost as they entered the yard, taking a moment to steady himself without leaning on her. "Except you'd like to start out with some fun before you get the headache."

"You mean you're not having fun yet, cowboy? You and your damned hardheaded horses."

"I'm the hardhead." He closed his eyes briefly, then forced a smile. "The horses are jugheads. There's a difference."

"I'm sure I don't know what that is."

"The difference is, I should have known better. I was sackin' her out, and I should've used a hobble."

"We don't need the hay this bad," she said as Jody scampered up the steps and held the door for them.

"Yes, we do." Neither of them had accented the word *we*, but it resounded in the look they exchanged. "And it's not bad," he assured her quietly. "I'd know if it was bad. I've been kicked before."

"I don't like taking charity."

"It's hardly charity when I'm…" He was looking for a place to sit before he collapsed. She provided a tall kitchen stool close to the sink, and he sank down on it gratefully. "I'm working for the damn hay, and I'm doing it on your time."

"Stop patronizing me. I'm not paying you, and even if

I were, I wouldn't pay you to get kicked in the head by a horse."

"I'll get the doctoring stuff," Jody offered sensibly. He disappeared down the hall.

Amy grumbled as she set to work on Tate's head with a clean towel, soap and water. "I don't want anyone else getting hurt. Horses are dangerous, they're unpredictable, they're..." She worked gently around the cut, brushing his hair back with one hand and blotting the blood with the other. "Tate, this won't stop bleeding. You probably need stitches."

"If you say so." He almost lost himself in the sympathy he saw in her eyes, but Jody's return brought him back to reality. A bottle and two small boxes clattered on the counter. Tate rewarded the boy with a smile. "We'll go get us some stitches. Right, Jody?"

"You mean you can sew his head?"

"I can't," Amy said absently, still trying to staunch the blood. "A doctor can."

"Will it hurt?" Jody backed away slowly. Remembered fear crept into his question. "Is it like an operation? Will he die?"

"Jody, come here." Tate held out his hand. "It's not like an operation, and I'm going to be fine."

"You didn't fall off a horse, did you?" Jody asked anxiously, inching closer.

Tate shook his head as he hooked his hand around the boy's nape and drew him close.

"No," Jody reassured himself. He draped himself over Tate's thigh as though he were hitching a ride. "You got kicked, but you never fell off. That's different."

"I've fallen off lots of horses," Tate admitted, looking to Amy for approval. He was willing to admit to the risks.

"Sometimes you get hurt, but most of the time you just dust off your jeans and climb back on."

"Or you get smart and stay away from them because they're dangerous," she instructed as she peeled adhesive tape from a roll. "Jody knows that."

Tate ruffled Jody's soft curls. "I'm okay, Jody. In a week or so, this will just look like a scratch."

"And don't tell him it doesn't hurt, either, because it does." She sucked air between her teeth, grimacing as she considered the best way to cover the wound. Finally she bit the bullet and applied the bandage. Tate winced. "I'm sorry. Does that hurt?"

"It does hurt a little. You'd probably feel a lot better if I took some aspirin or something."

"We're taking you in for some stitches, and then I want those horses—" She swept them away with a quick gesture.

"Uh-uh." Tate wagged his index finger under her nose. "I took on a job, and I'll get it done. But I'll be more careful."

"You could sue me, and I don't have any liability insurance," she suggested too easily. His steely, dispassionate look set her back on her heels. "I guess you wouldn't sue me."

"I guess I hadn't thought of it."

"I did have insurance, but I didn't pay the premium this fall. That's the next thing on my list, but I haven't had..."

"Jody," Tate began, giving the boy a pat on the back. "Just between us, I don't feel much like driving the pickup. You wanna go look in your mom's sewing box and find me a needle and a piece of thread about—" he thrust his white shirtsleeve in front of Jody's face "—this shade of passin'-out pale?"

Amy threw in the towel. "I'm getting my coat."

A few hours of convalescing went a long way with Tate. And a little TLC was about all Amy had the time for. Otherwise, about the only progress he could say he'd made with her in the time that he'd worked for her was that she didn't seem to hate him. He wasn't sure what more he wanted from her. Not sex, obviously; she wasn't exactly in any shape for a real good roll in the sack. Maybe a little cuddling in the sack, where he could hold her close enough to feel the baby move again.

Hell, what was he thinking? It wasn't even his baby, and she damn sure wasn't his woman. He didn't know why he kept hanging around. She couldn't bring herself to admit she needed his help. If anybody asked, she was honest enough to admit she needed *some* help, but any damn drifter with a strong back would do, long as she kept her shotgun handy in case he had any ideas about...

In case he had the nerve to think about getting her in the sack, where she could put her hands on him the way she had when he'd been hurt. She was the kind of woman who might reject a man's appetite for the roving and rollicking life, but she could still touch him with forgiving, healing, caring hands. Maybe if she would once touch him in the dark, he thought. Maybe if they couldn't see into each other's eyes, they wouldn't be as likely to start the delicious drowning, start the lovely slipping under, then, bam! There was Kenny, floating above their heads like an avenging angel.

And Amy would end up feeling bad about spending any of her affection on Tate. She'd felt bad about it years ago, even before she'd married Kenny, and it would be worse for her now that he was dead. She was too damn hard on herself. She wouldn't think it was a good thing for a good woman to do, and she was good. She had certain standards she tried to live by. She'd made a point of reminding him of that. It wasn't just a matter of being good at what she did. Hell, *he* was good at what he did, not that what he did was any great shakes, but he was good at it. Still, he wasn't *good.*

And just to prove it, he was about to do Saturday night up right.

He started out at the Jackalope, but the atmosphere was too dismal there. Charlie Dennison had gotten his butt in a sling at home. His ol' lady had thrown all his gear into a cardboard box and left it on the back porch. No question that ol' Charlie was completely misunderstood. That put Ticker Thomas in mind of the girl he should have married, damn sure *would* have married if she hadn't run off to Seattle. The music was downhearted, the drinking was solemn and the patrons were all male.

After one drink Tate moved on to the Turkey Track, where the dance floor was hopping. He met up with Kenny's sister, Marianne, who had managed to persuade husband Bill, Sr., Overo's staid, colorless grocer, to shock everybody by taking his wife out on a Saturday night. Marianne professed to be damn glad to see Tate and damn sorry she hadn't tried to get hold of him herself when Kenny died. She'd just assumed—well, everybody knew Tate was footloose.

"You remember Patsy Drexel. Used to be Johnson," Marianne shouted over the strains of "The Devil Went Down to Georgia." She shoved the voluptuous blonde into his arms, and he took a turn around the dance floor with her.

Sure, he remembered Patsy. Patsy was Marianne's friend. Three years ahead of him in school and light-years ahead of him in experience, at least to start out with. Experience had been one hell of a zealous teacher. They'd had some good times together back then, and once or twice in the intervening years, whenever he'd happened to be in town and Patsy had happened to be between husbands.

"Drexel," he said consideringly. That was a new one. "So you got married again, huh?" Before the conversation went the way it usually did with Patsy, he had to get a few things straight. "Where's your ol' man?"

"Which one? The last one ran off to Reno to play guitar in a band. He had the hots for the singer." She looked up and smiled. "It was an even shorter marriage than my first. You think I oughta take back my maiden name now that I'm unattached again?"

"I've still got you down as Johnson in my memory book. Is that your maiden name?" He charmed her with a wink. Here was opportunity tapping a bright red fingernail just above his shoulder blade.

But when he escorted her back to the table, she made the mistake of saying, "Thanks, honey." He wasn't sure where the prickly sensation had come from, but he told himself to ignore it.

"So you're working out to Becker's place for the winter?" Patsy claimed the chair next to Marianne's. "Haven't seen her around town for a while. Bet she's big as a hippo and twice as testy."

"She's all baby," Tate said tightly as he lit a cigarette. "She looks uncomfortable, but I don't hear her complaining."

He eyed Patsy pointedly as he blew a stream of smoke, hoping she'd gotten the message that bad-mouthing Amy wouldn't earn her any points with him, if that was what she was looking for. Patsy was in no position to talk, anyway. From what he could see, all her experience had put more age on her than any UV rays could account for.

"Well, it's real nice of you to help her out," Patsy allowed generously. "But it must be frustrating in a way, considering how you've always kinda carried a torch for her.''

"What are you talking about? Amy's the vine-covered cottage type, and I've never been one to let any grass grow under my feet." There, he thought, that sounded definite. "Besides, she was a one-man woman, and that man was my best friend." For good measure he mentally toasted Kenny before he took a drink.

"You might've been hiding your torch under a bush, Tate, but everyone knew it was there. That's why you left Overo."

He smiled humorlessly as he aligned his glass with the water ring it had left on the table. "I had a lot of reasons for leaving Overo, and Amy Becker wasn't one of them."

"You walked away from your father's land," Marianne said. "That place was rightfully yours, not your stepfather's, from the day your mother died. It was always Harrison land."

"It still is." He glanced at Bill, who was busy people-watching, then at Marianne. Patsy was the woman after his body, but Marianne was a woman after his own heart. Calculating and practical. Cut to the payoff. He just needed to put his basic instincts to work for a change. "Until somebody makes me a good offer."

"Check with some of the oil companies," Marianne advised. "There are about half a dozen speculators looking to take core samples, but some of these old ranchers around here refuse to poke anything but a posthole through the sod. And you know damn well there's money down there somewhere."

Patsy leaned closer. "I can't see you as the sentimental type when it comes to poking holes wherever it suits you, Tate." Her smile was as suggestive as the beat of the music. "Whenever there's a need."

"Leave it to a woman to fancy she can see right through a man's skin," he said smoothly.

"It's in your eyes, sugar. You've got a need."

"Just a simple itch, honey." *Honey.* Damn. He adjusted the brim of his hat, which covered his bandage even while it punished him with a dull headache. He signaled the server for another round of drinks. "Alcohol works wonders."

"Where does it itch? I just had a manicure." Patsy ran her nails up and down his back. "How does that feel? Tell me when I hit on the spot that's bothering you, sugar." Smiling lasciviously, she discovered her favorite thigh. "Am I getting warm?"

"You aren't even close, Patsy." He couldn't believe he was actually moving her hand, patting it apologetically as he settled it in her own lap. Damn his eyes, maybe he *was* getting sentimental in his old age, but he didn't feel much like poking around Patsy or vice versa. "Even if you were, it'd be no use. The itch just keeps on coming back."

"That's because *you* keep coming back."

"So do you." He nodded across the table. "So do *you,* Marianne. Remember when you lit out with that bull rider? Kenny and me had to do some fancy talkin' to keep your dad from headin' into Billings with a shotgun."

"Those were my wilder days." Marianne turned to her husband, who was only half listening. "Can you believe I was ever that wild, honey?"

Bill, Sr., a dubious honey at best, responded with a grunt in the negative.

"We were all born to be wild," Patsy said, cheerfully resigning herself to Tate's rebuff. "That's how I look at it." Then she sang it, pounding on the table for added emphasis. "'Course, if *I* was born to be wild, what about my kids? God, I *dread* having teenagers."

"How many kids do you have?" Tate remembered hearing about one, but Patsy never talked about her children.

"Three. One for each of my two ex's, and one for this guy I used to work for. Thank God Sally's old enough to watch the other two once in a while."

"How old is she?" He was asking for the kind of details he'd always considered none of his business.

"Eleven," Patsy reported without the slightest show of emotion. "Almost twelve. Almost a teenager. Now *her* father was the one I should have kept around if I wanted to be married, but back then the grass looked greener in my boss's bed. Which it was for a while. Then I met the guitar player." She planted her elbow on the table and sank her chin into her hand. "One of these days I'm going to pack up and move to Denver."

"You think you'd like the grass down there better?"

"I don't know. I've just always wanted to live in Denver. Mile-high pie and all that."

"Denver's just like any other place," Tate said as the server appeared with a tray of drinks. "Take my word for it."

"The voice of experience," Patsy quipped sarcastically.

"That's right." Tate wanted to laugh, but he would be laughing *at* her, and he had no right. He was no better. In fact, she was his flip side. She had her experience, he had his.

"I suppose you've spent enough time there to really know."

"As much as I've spent anywhere." There was a dose of sympathy for each of them in his sad smile. "I really *do* know."

"Then you're lucky," Patsy insisted. "Do yourself a favor and don't settle down in any one spot for too long. Before you know it, things'll start to get sticky. You'll have all kinds of baggage and bills, ex-spouses and kids. That stickiness turns out to be glue, Tate. Before you know it—''

"For heaven's sake, Patsy, I try to fix you up with somebody, and you get morbid." Marianne's laughter lightened the mood. "If you can't have a good time with Tate Harrison, then you're over the hill, because, according to my brother, Tate always did know how to have a good time."

"I can vouch for Tate." Patsy gave him a wistful smile. "Even though it's been a long time."

"A long time for what?" Tate figured he could still party, even if he wasn't interested in finding somebody to take him home. "We were dancing just a minute ago."

"You're a great dancer."

"Well, then, let's dance." With a gallant flourish he assisted Patsy with her chair. "Let's just bop 'til we drop, and the hell with all the bills and the baggage."

It didn't do him a damn bit of good to tear up the dance floor with Patsy Johnson Drexel. The way she kept crowding him made slow dancing impossible. He favored a heel-kicking "Cotton-Eyed Joe" or a twirling "Cowboy Two-Step." When his eyes started playing tricks on him and blue-eyed Patsy suddenly went brown-eyed on him, he knew he was beyond dance-dizzy. He decided it was time to quit going through the motions and call it a night.

He was looking forward to falling into bed and spinning himself to sleep, although he realized as he shut off the pickup's engine that there wasn't much night left.

He found Amy standing in the middle of the kitchen, barefoot and dressed only in a pink cotton nightgown. She didn't seem to want to let go of the edge of the sink as she turned to him. Backlit by the light above the kitchen window, the curves of her fecund body made a lovely silhouette beneath the opaque gown. In that instant, Tate knew for certain that God was a woman. A man-God wouldn't have tortured him this way, like making him stand outside a bakery window during Lent.

"Are you just getting up, or just going to bed?" He didn't like the wounded-animal look in her eyes. He wanted to see fiery judgment, so he could say, *Back at you, baby.* But she just stood there while he hung his sheepskin jacket and his hat on the hooks in the back entry. "You weren't waiting up for me, were you?"

"Oh, no," she said quickly. She turned away from him as she tightened her grip on the edge of the sink. "I wouldn't do a foo—fooooolish thinglikethat."

"What's going on?" He crossed the floor in two strides and took her slight shoulders in his hands. "You okay?"

"I could use a top hand." Her shoulders were shaking. She struggled with words and shallow breaths. "You know of one who's not too...too busy? Oh, dear..."

"It's not time yet, is it?" Her whole body went stiff as she nodded vigorously. He pried her hand away from the sink and draped her arm over his shoulder. "We gotta sit you down. You mean, now?"

She pressed her face against his neck and let him lower her into a chair. His mind was spinning, but whiskey wasn't the cause. He'd never sobered up so fast in his life. One thing at a time, he told himself. "You hold on. I'll get you some clothes. I'll get Jody."

"I'm hoping he'll sleep."

"Sleep?" This was no time to argue with her, but it was definitely time to take charge. "Amy, we can't leave him here alone."

"I don't know about you, but I'm not going—" she held on to the seat of the chair as though she were preparing for a bumpy ride "—anywhere. Especially not with you driving."

"I got home all right, didn't I?" Damn right, he was home. *Home,* where he was needed, where it was all up to him now. "I can get you to—"

Her shoulders started to shake again as she dropped her head back. Holy God in heaven, he couldn't take her out on the road like this. The thing was, he had to stay calm. He had to do something quick, and it had to be the right thing. He laid his hand on her shoulder, and the phone on the wall caught his eye.

"You're right, honey. We'll call someone to—Amy!" She groaned softly and pressed the side of her face against his arm. He could feel her hurting. He felt like a powerless lump of male flesh, afraid to step away from her, scared to death not to.

"The first thing to do is get help." He took a step, reached for the phone, pointed a finger at the dial. "Who to call, who to call, who's close, nobody's close..."

"Tate." He hadn't heard her move, but she was leaning against his back now, her hands on his shoulders, just the way he had held her moments ago. "Tate, there's no one else right now. Just you."

"You mean it's coming right *now?* We have to tell them to come." He closed his eyes. His head was devoid of numbers. "Ambulance...police...what's the damn number for—"

"Right *here,* Tate." She laid her cheek against his back. He hung up the phone and turned to take her in his arms. "Having the baby...right here, right—"

"Not on the kitchen floor, honey, let's get you—" He lifted her easily as the answers started to come to him. Make her comfortable first, *then* call. "Okay, let's get you to bed, and I'll call—"

"I've called...the midwife...I've been seeing for pre-natal exams. Left a message."

"Midwife? What is that, some sort of—"

"She'll be here." He laid her on her bed, which she'd apparently prepared in advance with a rubberized sheet. He wasn't sure what to make of all this, or of Amy's soft babbling. "Soon. She'll be here. It came on so f-fassst."

"What if…" A *midwife?* It sounded to him like something out of the Dark Ages. "I'm calling an ambulance."

"No," Amy insisted. She grabbed his arm and with amazing strength pulled him down close to her. "Now, listen to me, Tate, there's no time, and women have been having babies since time began, and they don't…"

He shook his head and tried to pull away, but even as another contraction started, she was having none of his resistance. "I don't have any health insurance, and I don't want any more bills I can't p-p—" She held his arm while he looked on in terror, gripping her shoulders. When it was over, she smiled bravely. "That was a good one."

"It didn't look good."

"Think of it as pulling…as calving out a…no, *easier* than a first-calf heifer, Tate. I'm on my second." Her eyes pleaded with him as she fought to control her breathing. "Tate, I'm afraid you're going to have to do this for me."

"Not me, for God's sake, I'm just as—" Just as what? Scared? Stupid? Weak-kneed as a new foal was the way he felt, but he tried to return that brave smile of hers. He brushed her damp hair back from her forehead. "I don't know anything about this, honey. We need a doctor. Hell, if I make a mistake, you might sue me, like—"

"No, it's not funny. I have to be able to count on you. You have to deliver—"

"No, it's not safe. I might… Let me get you a doctor, honey. When the pain comes, let me just hold your hand until it—"

"Wash yours, damn it!" Then the pain seized her, along

with all the anguish and frustration and anger that came with birthing. "Damn damn damn you, Tate! Look at me!"

"Hey, I wasn't anywhere near—" It didn't matter. The technicality wedged itself in his throat, and it occurred to him that there was no excuse for him. He was a man. Watching Amy suffer made him feel like a worm.

"I'm sorry, honey. I'm sorry." He smoothed her hair back again, kissed her hot temple and whispered, "Kenny's sorry, too."

"You smell like smoke—" She grabbed his hand and squeezed for all she was worth "—and beer, and you...and you...and you..."

"Shhhh, what can I do?"

"I don't wanna shhhh!"

"Yell, then, what can I do?"

"Oooh, oooh—" Pant. Pant. "I think you should wash your hands, and I put all the stuff Mrs....midwife..." She waved her free hand toward the supplies she'd set out on a white towel on the dresser, then groaned. "Scissors and surgical thread...alcohol... Hurry, Tate, hurry—oooooh..."

Crossing the room in a single stride, Tate tore open his cuff and started rolling up his sleeve, but by the time he'd reached the bathroom sink, he'd stripped the shirt off entirely. He washed his hands and his arms up to his T-shirt sleeves. God help him, he was covered with germs and dirt and sin. He grabbed a bottle of rubbing alcohol and doused his hands in it. They seemed relatively steady, even though he felt like he'd swallowed a cement mixer.

"Tate!" Amy called, straining to control her voice. And then, "Taaaate!" She screamed his name as though things were coming apart and he was supposed to be able to put them back together. Like pulling a calf? *Pulling?* Oh, God, why did she have to say *that?* He took a deep breath and a big step.

"Tate!" Eyes wild with terror, Jody stood in the middle of the hallway. "Tate, my mama! Don't let my mama die, Tate!"

Chapter Five

"*My mom can't die of this, can she?*"

That had been Tate's question, too. Even in the best of times his stepfather had been a man of few words, but after his mother had gotten sick, no words had been forthcoming from Oakie Bain. No comfort. No counsel. Tate's questions went unanswered until the day Myron Olson's wife, Joan, had come to take him out of school. "Get your jacket," Joan had said, and he'd stared at the denim thing hanging on a coat hook in the hallway. It hadn't been washed since his mother had gone away to the hospital.

He remembered the sound of Joan's boots clopping down the hallway toward Jesse's classroom. There was his answer, in the sound of a woman's retreating footsteps. Never again would he hear the quiet voice that had willingly given him what answers she'd had. No more would he see the light of approval in his mother's eyes. The terrible reality had fallen over him like a weighted net. He'd felt hot-faced and sick to his stomach, and he'd barely made it to the boys' bathroom.

"Tate?" Jody's brown eyes were as big as basketballs.

Tate took a deep breath. "Your mom's having the baby. It's kinda like lambing. Have you seen a lamb get born?"

"Once," Jody said. "But Mama's screamin' a lot worse than a ewe."

"It hurts her pretty bad right now, but after the baby comes out, it'll stop hurting. It just takes a little while."

He knelt like a supplicant before the boy, holding his arms out awkwardly. "We're going to help her. I'm going to keep the door open, and you're going to sit right outside in the hallway and be ready to run and get me something if I need it, okay?"

Jody nodded hesitantly.

"We can't shake on it, because I have to keep my hands real clean, so put your arms around my neck and give me a hug." The little boy's arms gave him a shot of encouragement. His angel-hair curls clung to the stubble on Tate's jaw. "Thanks, partner."

Amy's breathy pain-ride suddenly sounded less threatening. Clear-eyed confidence took a firm grip on his insides. She needed him, and he was there. The rest would follow in due course.

She was between contractions.

"Do we need to anchor your legs somehow?"

She grimaced and shook her head.

He offered her a sympathetic smile. "Is this it, then? You gonna take this lyin' down, boss lady?"

She nodded again and lifted her chin, returning a tightly drawn, stiff-upper-lipped expression. "There's hardly any letup now." Her voice was stretched thin. "The pains are so bad...won't let me have an-nnnnunhhhh..."

She gripped the brass rails of the headboard as she gathered her forces at her middle. Her stamina amazed him. Unable to touch her, Tate stood watch over her labor.

Anxious eyes peered at him from the dim hallway. Jody was sitting there tight-lipped, clutching his knees, trusting Tate to do whatever needed to be done. Amy rolled her head to the side and saw him there. "Oh, Jody..." Her voice was weak, but her tone took exception to the child's presence.

"Jody's lookin' out for you, too," Tate said softly.

"But I don't want him to see me like thhhhhiii—"

Tate gave a nod. "Jody, I want you to stand guard right by the door, okay? Just like a soldier. And tell me if you hear anyone at the back door."

"Mama, are you gonna die?"

"No!" She turned her head away. "Oh no, oh no, oh no..."

Tate nodded again, and Jody scrambled for his assigned post on the other side of the doorjamb.

"He's scared, honey." He looked down into Amy's eyes, begging her indulgence. He knew she was up to it. He couldn't fathom the extent of her pain, but he could see how strong she was. "We can't shut him out. If you can just tell him you'll be okay..."

"I'm okay, Jody." She was getting hoarse. "I'm okay, I'mokayI'mokay—" She closed her eyes through the next contraction. A gush of water flooded the bed beneath her hips.

"Tate, I think it's time for you to—" Amy pulled her nightgown over her distended belly and spread her knees apart "—check...things...."

This was no time for modesty, and no time for him to back down from a woman's invitation to get personal. Not when a soggy thatch of baby hair was presenting itself at life's door. After the next contraction, Tate quickly swabbed Amy with rubbing alcohol. He'd barely managed to set the bottle aside when she gave a long, deep, terrible groan and pushed. Everything, including his eyes, widened. The tiny head was expelled.

"Good job, Amy!" He felt like a cheerleader in the play-offs—overstimulated and underuseful. "Can you do that again?"

"I can't *not* do it," she barked between gasps. "I can't— ohhhhh..."

"Mama?"

"She's doing fine," Tate said excitedly. His whole being was attuned to the sound of her doglike panting, the smell of life-producing blood and the sight of her body transforming itself in the most miraculous way. "You're doing great, honey. Just one more time."

"Jody, don't..."

"Jody, run get me some more towels," Tate ordered. Jody sprang from his post like a sprinter.

"Ohohohohoh..."

"And peek out the window to see if anyone's coming," Tate called out.

The baby's head turned to the side. Tate cleared its mouth with his big forefinger. Amy whimpered a little as she braced herself for the next onslaught. Tate braced himself against the sound of her pain, which erupted with a fury this time as the baby whooshed into Tate's waiting hands like a tot on a water slide. She bawled the minute he caught her.

"A little girl!"

She was all pink and petite and perfect, and he was actually holding her in his own two hands. A squirming, wrinkled female connected to her mother by a coiled cord, like the receiver on a telephone. Only *Tate* was the receiver. He bore the good news.

"Amy, she's here. Your little girl just made her debut."

"Is she okay?"

"Can't you hear her?" Grinning from ear to ear, he put the slippery prize on Amy's belly. Amy lifted her head, trying to get a peek. Her face was pale and slick with sweat. He took her cool hand in his slippery one and guided it to the baby's head. "She sounds just like you. All pretty and mad."

"Like me?" Chest heaving, Amy dropped her head back. "Not mad," she gasped. "Hardly pretty. But strong. I did it."

"Damn right, you did it. Hold on to her while I do the rest."

He hoped he was doing it right. In some ways it wasn't so different from the nonhuman births he'd attended. His hands were rock steady, and his heart was singing like a meadowlark as he snipped the cord between tiny tourniquets he'd made of surgical thread. "You're on your own now, little girl."

He was wrapping the baby in a white flannel blanket when Amy was seized by another contraction. All she had to do was point to the towels on the nightstand and he understood. They were a team now. He slid one towel in place beneath her, tucked the squalling bundle in the crook of his arm and massaged Amy's belly with the heel of his free hand. "You'll be all done in a New York minute, honey. Just one more good—"

"Awwwwfullll!"

"One more awful pain. God, I could never be a woman. You're amazing, Amy." In both will and body, he thought as she expelled the afterbirth. He rubbed hard. Her belly felt like rubber on the outside and rock underneath. "You made a miracle. I saw it with my own eyes."

The baby squawked angrily as Tate cradled her against his chest. "That's right, little darlin'. Take charge, just like your mama."

But it was Tate who was in charge. He folded the towel around the afterbirth and set it aside. Then he tucked another towel between Amy's legs and covered her with a sheet. She needed a moment to catch her breath.

"Tate?"

He turned, and Jody offered up several towels. "Thanks, partner. Look what we've got." Jody lifted his chin for a peek. Tate chuckled, knowing the crinkled red face hardly met the little boy's expectations.

He sat on the bed and leaned close to Amy. "Soon as I get this little gal acquainted with her mother's face, maybe she won't be quite so..."

The bawling subsided to a whimper when Amy took the baby in her arms. Weary as she was, her pale face lit up like a firefly in a jar.

"That's better," he said. "She wasn't expecting to see my fuzzy face first thing."

"She's glad you were there," Amy said, her eyes smiling up at him. "So am I."

"I never thought I'd..." He shook his head as all words failed him. They looked so pretty together, triumphant mother and tiny daughter. Tate knew damn well he was blushing head to toe. "I'd better clean things up a little."

"Things?"

"You and her." He wasn't sure what to do for Amy now. He knew she might need stitches. The sooner he put in a call for medical help, the better. Then he was going to dispose of the contents of the towel....

"We have to save that," Amy said, reading his intentions. Baffled, he figured the pain had taken its toll on her senses. "It goes in the freezer downstairs, and then into the ground next spring when I plant the baby's tree."

"Oh." He shrugged. "Whatever you say."

"Jody has a tree. Don't you, Jody?" Jody nodded, gratified to hear his name. "Come here and say hello to your new sister. I'm fine now, see? I'm just fine."

The back door opened, and a woman's voice called out, "Anybody home?"

"Mrs. Massey," Amy explained.

The bespectacled woman appeared in the bedroom doorway. Curiously, Tate heard no great flood of relief in Amy's greeting. "You just missed it, Mrs. Massey."

"I can see that." The stocky, middle-aged woman took account, acknowledging Tate with a nod as she removed her red quilted jacket. "My, my, my. Did you steal my job away?"

"I hope I didn't do anything...I mean, I hope I didn't make any mistakes."

"You didn't," Amy said happily. "You were wonderful. I don't know what I would have done if—"

"I should have been here earlier."

"I think that's my line," Mrs. Massey said. "But there are some little details I can attend to. I'm going to scrub up while you put that floor lamp right there next to the bed." She chucked Jody under the chin on her way back out the door. "What do you think, Jody? A brand-new baby. Isn't it fun?"

"Fun?" Hell of a way to spend Saturday night, Tate thought. Then he realized the sun had dawned somewhere along the line and it was actually Sunday morning. He shared a conspiratorial smile with Amy. "How are you feeling? Having fun yet? Can I bring you anything?"

"Mrs. Massey will tie up the loose ends, so to speak."

"I tied one up myself." He was grinning like a kid who'd hit a grand slam.

"Yes, you did. Thank you."

"You sure have a hell of a way of soberin' a guy up, lady." He couldn't understand how he could be steady as a rock and still feeling so high. "Both of you ladies. Look at her. She's sucking on her little hand."

Amy's hand went to the buttons on her nightgown. "Maybe I ought to—"

"Before you do that, let me do my little job," Mrs. Massey instructed as she swooped back into the room.

Tate leaned out of her way, but he was in no hurry to relinquish his post. He wasn't sure he liked the way the midwife took over on the baby, peeling the blanket back to scrutinize her.

"Oh, look at her color. Just what we like to see. Nothing old, nothing new, nothing borrowed, and especially nothing too blue."

Mrs. Massey gave the baby her first test and announced that her score was outstanding. Tate's suspicions fell away as he suppressed the urge to applaud. The woman recognized a perfect kid when she saw one. He was surprised when she bundled the baby back up in the flannel blanket and handed her to him.

"Now, if you and Jody would like to clean the little one up a bit while I tend to Amy..."

"She's so little." And she didn't want a bath. He could tell by the scrunched-up look in her face. "You mean just wash her with ordinary water?"

"Body temperature," Mrs. Massey instructed. "Water will comfort her. You can handle it. You've done fine so far."

He looked down at the tiny prunelike face nestled in the blanket, then glanced at Amy. She looked exhausted, but she nodded, her eyes bright with approval. Even now it amazed him to think she trusted him to take the precious bundle in his big, clumsy hands and leave the room. Instead of pleading incompetence he heard himself promise, "I'll be real careful."

"Jody knows where her clothes are," Amy said. "Jody, remember which drawer has the baby clothes?" Jody bobbed his head. "Will you pick out a little shirt like the one Tate's wearing and a little tiny sleeper like yours?"

"And a baby diaper?"

"Yes, and the pins."

"And get the baby bath stuff?" He was out the door, sliding down the hallway on slick pajama feet. "I know where the baby bath stuff is, Tate. We have a baby towel, too."

Tate followed him to the third bedroom, which had been decorated in white and soft pastels for the long-awaited occupant. Jody opened the third bureau drawer and took out a white sleeper with a row of pink lambs marching across the yoke. "This brand-new one," he decided and held it up for Tate's review.

"Your mother will definitely approve."

"And here's the shirt, and these baby pants to keep her clothes dry and a—"

"What do you think, Jody? I say we turn the heat up a little and treat her just like a newborn calf that maybe took a chill, huh?"

"Uh-huh."

"You're just lucky there was an experienced cowhand in the house tonight, baby girl. And a little broomstick cowboy in training." He might have plopped a calf into the washtub downstairs, but he figured the kitchen sink would work better for this job. He closed the blind against the morning sunlight streaming through the window. Too much shock for a little person fresh out of the womb.

"We're a team, right, Jody?"

"Uh-huh." Jody climbed up on a chair and handed Tate a bottle of liquid baby soap and a soft hooded towel. "This is the stuff we have to use. She sure has messy hair."

"And a lot of it."

Mrs. Massey was right. The water seemed to soothe the infant. Tate ladled it over her with one hand as he cradled her head in his other palm. He didn't want to mess too much with her face, and he figured the white, waxy stuff was probably nature's cold cream, so he left it alone. But he knew a lady didn't like having sticky stuff in her hair. That had to go.

"Your next job is to find the hair dryer, partner."

"I know where it is!" And Jody was off like a shot.

"She's all cleaned up now," Tate announced as he lowered the fussy little one into her mother's arms. "She's just as pretty as a Thoroughbred filly, and she wants her mama right now."

"Oh, yes, come here, sweetie."

"Before I go, I have a few instructions for you menfolk," Mrs. Massey said. "Starting with taking care of Mom. After she rests, we want her to get up and walk a little, but we don't want her to overdo. It's up to you boys to do the cooking and the cleaning up for a few days, you got that? Because if you leave a mess in the kitchen, she's not going to rest until she gets it cleaned up."

"I'm not an invalid, Mrs. Massey."

"She's been using that line on me ever since I started to work for her," Tate said. "I'll snub her to the bedpost if I have to."

"You're the—" the older woman glanced at Amy, then

back to Tate "—hired hand?" He affirmed the title with a humble shrug, and she laughed. "Well, now you can *really* claim to be a jack-of-all-trades. I'll be stopping by daily for a while, but you call me if you need anything." She turned to Amy. "You know what kind of bleeding to expect. Anything heavy, any dizziness or fainting—" The finger was pointed Amy's way, but the final charge was given to Tate. "—she goes to the hospital."

"Got it."

"Don't let that baby keep her from getting her rest. Got a name for her yet?"

"Karen," Amy said—reverently, because it was the first time. "Karen Marie Becker."

It was a nice name, Tate thought. He had an aunt named Karen, but she lived in Texas. And his mother's name had been Mary. He liked it. Karen Marie…Becker.

Of course it was Becker. She was Kenny's daughter. He'd just helped to bring his best friend's daughter into the world, given her her first bath and dressed her for the first time. And now she had a name. Nothing wrong with Karen Marie Becker…except that when Amy had said that last part out loud, it had felt like a pinprick in his euphoric bubble.

Mrs. Massey gave him a colleague's pat on the back before she left, declaring that more duty called her. "The stork's having a field day in Overo. Now that you've got your feet wet, how about—"

"Not a chance," Tate demurred with palms raised in self-defense. "I don't care to press my luck."

"Luck, schmuck. The Lord doesn't always give us what we think we want, but most times He gives us what we need." She punctuated her homily with a nod and a smile. "He gave you stork wings last night, Mister Hired Hand."

Stork wings? Tate flexed the muscles in his back as he

watched Mrs. Massey back her Blazer down the driveway. He did feel a pinch right above the shoulder blades.

He stuck his head in the door of Amy's bedroom. "Can I get you anything? A glass of milk maybe—whoa!" A short-armed tackle pinned him around the knees. He looked down, and Jody looked up, pleading to be noticed.

"Jody..." Amy applied the universal mother's warning tone.

"You got a steer wrestler's grip, there, partner." Tate lifted the boy into his arms. "We got our instructions, and we're at your service, ma'am."

"Karen might take you up on that glass of milk. It's slim pickings until mine comes in."

The baby was asleep in her mother's arms. Tate and Jody looked on like shepherds in a crèche.

"Is there colostrum?" Tate asked absently. He glanced up and caught her eyes laughing at him. Hell, he didn't know. He was just curious.

"Like with cows and sheep? Yes, for the first few days. We mammal mamas are all the same."

"So, you want some kind of oat—" he winked at Jody and teased Amy with a grin "—meal?"

"I want you to sit with us. You and Jody." She nodded toward the wicker rocker next to the bed.

"C'mon, cowboy," Tate said. "Come take a ride on your partner's knee."

"We couldn't have managed this without you two." Amy touched the baby's cheek. "She came a lot quicker than Jody did. She didn't give me much warning at all."

"Women are like that. You never know what to expect." Tate jiggled his knee, and Jody bobbled happily. "You remember that, partner. Every woman's got her own timing, and there's no point in a man tryin' to set his watch by it."

"I can't think of a single comeback, so I guess we'll let

that one stand." She smiled at the sleeping infant. "For now. Right, Karen? When they're good, they're very, very good. And today they were incredible."

"And whenever you're willin' to give in that easy, you have to be very, very tired," Tate observed. "We've already put in a big day, and there's still about sixteen hours to go. You're one of those bosses that doesn't give a guy time to sleep it off."

"I think we'll all be napping today." She couldn't take her eyes off the tiny, tranquil face. "One of us has already started."

"And one more is on her way." Time for the boys to take their leave. "That's you, so if you've got any other surprises, lay them on me before I head out to the barn to get started on the chores. I've got another load of hay coming today."

"No more surprises. Just gratitude."

"Just doin' my job, ma'am."

"You need rest, too," she told him.

"I'll get it eventually." Tate grinned. "Now, if I was a sheepherder, I could lie around on the hillsides all day and do all kinds of cloud-dreamin', but a cowboy's work is never done."

But it didn't matter. Today he had adrenaline to spare.

He'd never imagined himself holding a baby, much less delivering one. Thinking about it made him feel a little weak in the knees. When he told Myron Olson about it, he couldn't help grinning like a sailor on shore leave. Myron was so tickled, he offered to throw in another load of hay. Tate told him he could bring over another horse, too.

He climbed into the driver's seat of Amy's big John Deere 4020. He was beginning to feel the effects of lack of sleep. Once he got Myron's flatbed unloaded and fed all his charges, he figured he would be ready to hit the hay himself.

He didn't know how the dogs had gotten out, but they were making fools of themselves again, chasing a damn tumbleweed. As he started backing the tractor he took a quick check over his shoulder. For a split second he saw Jody's face looking up at him just beyond the rolling ridges of one big black tire. Then it was just the tire.

The whole sky toppled over on him. He heard a piercing scream, and for a moment the world went black. His legs wouldn't work, nor would his arms, and his head wouldn't turn. He was surrounded by shouting, and the scream rose in terror, pitched so high it was beyond the reach of his ears. It was infinite, soundless, nameless and timeless.

When the scream plummeted back to the present, it was lodged in his own throat. He whirled and spat it out as he dropped to the ground. And there stood Jody, looking up at him, wide-eyed, trusting and innocent as always.

Trembling terror overrode reality as Tate towered over the child. He leaned down, his big hands laying claim to slight shoulders, making sure they were real. Sweet Lord, he hadn't been touched, had he? He was still in one—

"I damn near ran over you, boy!"

"I f-found my horse's ear." Shyly, Jody displayed a scrap of leather, as if such an offering might assuage the big man's anger.

"Jody, I just barely saw you. I almost..." Tate sputtered, his heart racing. He pointed a gloved finger and commanded with all the fervor of Moses, "You go in the house now. I'll look at that later. You go inside and stay out of the way."

He saw Jody's lip quiver, saw the tears welling in the little boy's eyes as he turned and ran toward the house. The same tears burned deep in his own brain. Remembered tears. God, it could happen all over again, so easily, in the blink of an eye. He turned and stared the damn tractor down, its bucket-loader lifted skyward as if to say, "Don't blame me. It's Tate Harrison again."

Damn, he hated operating farm equipment. He would rather buck out a horse any day. At least then the only neck he was likely to break was his own.

The house was quiet when he went back inside. He thought about looking for Jody first thing, but he felt so bad about the way he'd barked at him that he decided to make supper instead. He wondered what a person who'd just had a baby would feel like eating. He wondered whether a little person who'd just had his butt chewed out by a big person with a thick head would feel like eating anything at all. Down at the end of the hallway, behind the closed bedroom door, he could hear the baby, bleating like a hungry lamb. The crying ceased abruptly, and Tate wondered whether little Karen was getting real milk yet.

Too soon, he thought, but obviously Amy was able to give the baby what she needed. He wished he had something like that to give Jody right now. Something warm and nourishing, something that would flow easily, without worthless apologies or asinine explanations. Hell, Jody was just a little boy. Tate was the one who had a history of being careless. *Tate* was the one.

He stood awkwardly outside Amy's door, flexed his hand a couple of times before he rapped his knuckles on the wood and quietly announced himself. "Are you girls decent? Can I bring in some food?"

"Come in." Amy braced herself and slid up gingerly, reaching around to adjust her pillows. "Oh, my, we've just been sleeping and nursing, nursing and sleeping. Karen's sleeping again."

"Figured you'd fed her." He handed her a mug of chicken soup, then stuffed an extra pillow behind her. "Figured *I'd* feed *you.*"

"Thank you." She smiled sleepily. "Just for today. You won't have to do this tomorrow."

"I want to." He sat on the edge of the bed. "I'm not real great at it, but I can open a can."

"Have you and Jody eaten?"

"We will in a minute. I wasn't sure where...I mean, I thought he might be in here with you. Guess he must be in his room." He glanced at the bassinet he'd brought in earlier and set next to the bed, within Amy's reach. It hadn't been too long since Jody had slept in that little straw bed. "Did he tell you...that I acted like a jerk a while ago?"

"What do you mean?"

"I didn't know he was outside. I was backing up the tractor. He was standing pretty close." He closed his eyes and gave his head a quick shake. "I...I made him go in the house."

"There's nothing wrong with that, Tate."

"Yeah, but I yelled at him. I haven't been around kids much. All I know is when a calf tries to get himself into a bad place, you put a scare into him, send him packing." He couldn't look at her, but he could feel her looking at him. He could feel her waiting. "I scared Jody. I scared him worse than—" he swallowed hard "—worse than he scared me."

"You yelled at him? Is that all?" she asked quietly, and he heard the fear in her voice.

"I grabbed him by the shoulders. I was so glad he was still standing there, I don't know if I held him too tight, but I shouted right in his face and I...I told him to stay out of the way. Like I was tellin' him it was his fault, when it was mine." He turned to her, his voice as doleful as autumn rain. "I didn't hit him. I wouldn't do that, I swear."

"I didn't think you would, Tate." Wearily he rose to his feet. She caught his hand. "What are you going to do?"

"See if he's awake. Ask him if he's hungry." He squeezed her hand, then let it go as he stepped back from the bed.

"Tell him why you shouted at him."

"What difference does it make why?" Her eyes held his until he knew he needed the answer for himself. "I was scared stupid, that's why."

"Tell him that."

"What if he doesn't want me..." *Around him. Close to him. Breathing his air.* "...want to look at me or anything?"

"Give him the benefit of the doubt, Tate. He's a very mature four-year-old. He knows about safety and responsibility. I've taught him that." She nodded encouragingly. "Just ask him if he's hungry. That'll be a start."

He found Jody sprawled on his stomach, driving his toy cars down the parallel roads in the hardwood floor in his bedroom. He looked up, surprised, but he lowered his chin quickly and went back to his cars.

"Don't mean to interrupt, but I've got some supper ready."

"Not hungry."

"Your mom said you liked those little baby hot dogs in the can. I fixed you some with biscuits and soup." Jody looked up again. "And some chocolate milk," Tate added, encouraged. "You like chocolate milk?"

Jody rolled his toes against the wood and wagged his heels back and forth. But his belly seemed glued to the floor.

Tate noticed the broomstick horse lying on the bed, along

with the detached leather ear. Moving like old molasses, he made himself walk over to the bed. He picked up the broken toy as he seated himself. He felt like a giant in a dollhouse sitting on the youth bed, which hadn't been made that day. The sheets were printed with teddy bear cowboys riding rocking horses and spinning perfect loops above their ten-gallon hats.

"I promised I'd fix this, didn't I?"

"I found the ear in my toy box," Jody reported as he lined two cars up side by side.

"And that was good finding." Tate watched him add a third car to the row, then a fourth. "I'm sorry I yelled at you before." A yellow car came into line, but this one drove up slowly. "I know I sounded like I was mad at you. I wasn't. Not really."

With his thumb on its roof Jody rocked the yellow car back and forth on its diminutive wheels. "I'm not supposed to get around the tractor when it's running," he confided quietly. "The tires are big, and the PTO can grab my hair or my shirt and really get me hurt."

"That's right." As formidable as the huge tires were, the tractor's power takeoff was an appalling threat, and the danger of lost limbs was one of the earliest warnings every ranch kid heard. "Your mom has told you all that, huh?"

"Oh, yeah. And my dad." He sat up, pivoted on his bottom and looked up at Tate. "I just forgot for a minute."

"I know. That can happen." Tate glanced at the yellow car as he laced his fingers together. "You know what happened to me when I looked down and saw you there?"

"No."

"I was scared I was gonna hit you. And I yelled at you because I was mad at myself for not seeing you sooner." His eyes darted back to the anxious little face. "The driver is responsible, Jody. Not you. When you're driving a vehicle, you have to make sure there's nothing behind you, nothing in front of you that you might hit...."

But Tate realized that there was only one thing the boy understood. The big man had been as threatening as the big tractor. "I'm sorry," Tate offered. "I didn't mean to yell at you. It wasn't your fault. It was mine." The boy hung his head. "I scared you, huh?"

Jody nodded. "I was a little bit scared."

"I was a lot scared." Tate lifted his hands and spread them in invitation, and Jody scrambled to his feet and came running. He threw his arms around Tate's neck with grateful abandon, and Tate closed his eyes and hugged him for all he was worth.

"It was a close call, Jody. You know what a close call is?"

"I could have got hit by the tractor?"

"After a close call is all over, it's too late to be scared, but it doesn't matter. It still haunts you for a while, kind of like a bad dream." He leaned back and looked Jody in the eye. "If I'd hurt you, I don't know what I would have done."

"You'd take me to the doctor, wouldn't you?"

"Yes, I would." He lifted the boy onto his lap. "I sure would. We're partners."

"We're partners."

"We birthed a baby together today, didn't we? You and me, we helped your little sister get born." Jody tested the prickliness of Tate's stubble against his palm, and Tate smiled. "'Course, your mom did most of the work. That's why she was making all that noise—because it's hard work pushing the baby out. That's why they call it *labor*. And now she needs rest, so we're gonna do all the work around here, 'cause she's done her share for a while."

"I can fix my own bed, and I can feed Daisy and Duke and Cinnamon Toast."

"And I can feed you," Tate said as he patted Jody's bottom. "You ready to eat?"

Not quite. Jody was still thinking. "It scared me more when *she* yelled," he mused. "I never heard her yell like that before."

"And then I yelled, and you must think all the grown-ups went crazy today. But we're okay now. It's been a crazy, terrible, fantastic day, and we made it through." He squeezed Jody's shoulder. "So let's have ourselves something to eat."

"Are you gonna shave?" Jody asked as they headed toward the kitchen.

"Prob'ly I should."

"Can I watch?"

Amy laid her head back against the pillow and closed her eyes. Tate Harrison was such a difficult man to figure out. One minute he was out boozing with Overo's hell-raisers, and the next he was bringing her daughter into the world with more levelheadedness and every bit as much tender concern as she might have expected from her child's own father. She'd never seen Tate more shaken than he'd been today, or more jubilant.

Vigilant as any brooding hen, she was glad she'd been able to eavesdrop on the conversation he'd had with Jody across the hall. She wasn't sure what to make of the terrible guilt she'd seen in Tate's eyes when he'd told her about the incident with Jody, but she knew he had not harmed her son. She breathed a long, gratified sigh. She was fundamentally independent, but she had trusted Tate with a most intimate and momentous task, and he had come

through for her in spades. Thank God she could continue
to trust him with her son.

She wasn't going to start relying on him, she reminded
herself. The man's feet were made of sand. But he had
more heart than she'd ever given him credit for, and she
was hoping she could lean on that particular muscle and a
few others until she could truly get back on her feet again.
She wouldn't *depend* on his support. But as long as he was
willing to stay, it wouldn't hurt to lean on it, just a little.

Chapter Six

When Amy's milk came in her breasts blew up like twin beach balls. Tate had never seen anything like it. He'd brought her a sandwich and discovered, once again, a changed woman. He tried not to stare, but she caught him at it. She laughed, he thought quite charitably. He stared at the toes of his boots, then tried to zoom back up to her face. But his damned eyes were drawn right back to the same amazing transformation in her otherwise almost-back-to-normal body.

He shook his head and gave up trying to be cool. "Are they gonna stay like that?"

Now she howled. "Lord have mercy, I have finally arrived. Voluptuous at last."

"Well, either way, I mean...I always thought you had a nice—" *Chest on you.* He tore his eyes away as he groped for an alternative. "*Shape.* Really nice. But, you know, this is...nice, too."

"They won't stay this way long." She accepted the proffered plate and gave a quick shrug. "My milk just came in with a vengeance is all."

"Do they hurt?"

"Suck in a real deep breath." He complied. "Now suck in some more. Now a little more. Feel like you're gonna bust yet?" He nodded. She took up the sandwich. "Now hold it for a couple of days and see if it hurts."

He deflated quickly. "I gotta give up those cigarettes. Damn, that pinches."

"Exactly." Amy set her own lunch aside on the signal of soft baby murmurs. "Would you like to hand me my little milk drainer?"

Tate stepped over to the bassinet. Karen had kicked off her pink blanket, tiny legs churning involuntarily. He folded it around her and lifted her in his hands. She was cranking up to cry, but she changed her mind when he cuddled her against his chest. He liked the sweet little sounds she made, even though she was rooting around a dry well.

"Can't help you there, little girl. Your mama's got what you want and then some." He shifted Karen for the transfer as he came to the side of the bed. "You got a preference which side?"

"Ready on the right, ready on the left."

The buttons on Amy's nightgown already lay open between her bulging breasts. Tate swallowed hard. Amy pulled her white gown aside as he laid the baby in the crook of her left arm, positioning the little pink cheek near the source of mother's milk. The miniature mouth fit over the distended nipple like a trailer coupling. Tate felt a surge of excitement that had nothing to do with hunger and little to do with sex. Pride, maybe. He wasn't ogling, but he was having a hell of a time tearing his eyes away.

"Would you hand me a bath towel off the dresser?" Amy asked.

He snatched it up and returned to her, glanced in her eyes for permission, then admired the tranquil activity at her breast again. A wet spot was quickly growing over her right breast, and he understood the need for the towel. Impulsively he knelt beside the bed. She lifted her right elbow. He tucked the towel under her side and arranged it over her breast.

"I keep getting everything wet."

"I'll change the bed when you're done." The baby's contented little noises made him smile. "Seems like a waste of good produce."

"There's such an abundance to start with. If I were a ewe, I'd probably have twins. Two mouths to suckle."

Now it *did* have something to do with sex, something to do with a man's urge to kiss a woman at the damnedest times. His head was falling fast. He was drowning in her eyes, sinking like a stone, going under for the third time. When the authorities dredged up his corpse, it would be obvious where he carried the lead weight that had pulled him under. He hoped she would be able to explain it away in the eulogy.

Amy saw it coming, and she met it head-on with a warm, wet, open-mouthed kiss.

Just one kiss, but it was a real breath-stealer. When it was over, he couldn't quite draw away. Forehead to forehead they rested, their mouths sharing hot breath, their nostrils filled with the scent of sweet milk.

"I couldn't help myself," he whispered.

"It's all right." She drew a long, slow breath. "A woman needs a man's kiss when she's..." He lifted his head and looked expectantly into her eyes. She glanced away. "I heard you talking to Jody. I get scared, too, sometimes. When I realized I was in labor, and I knew I was alone, I really got scared.''

She wasn't alone now. He wanted her to know that. He cupped his hand around her cheek and kissed her again, more gently this time. He couldn't remember when he'd ever gotten down on his knees to kiss a woman. He told himself that he just wanted to assure her that he was there, but her lips were remarkably responsive, and she tasted so damn good.

She took his hand, put it on her belly, then covered it with hers and pressed it tight. He felt a bulge in her stomach, but it was hard, like muscle.

"It hurts when the baby nurses," she explained quietly. "It's nature's way of making my uterus contract back down to size, but it…" Her fingers dug into the back of his hand. He took the hint and began kneading the knot in her belly. "I've had enough of pain," she said.

"Yes, you have." If he could take it away, he would thank her for the privilege. "It doesn't seem fair. It was hard to watch you suffer with it. It's no wonder you were scared."

"I was afraid for my baby. I was afraid I wasn't strong enough." She tipped her head back against the pillow, eyes closed as she remembered. "I was going to call someone else, the sheriff or someone, but I was afraid it was too late for anyone to…" She gave him her soft earth-mother smile. "Thank you for coming back in time, Tate."

"I shouldn't have left."

He never should have left Overo in the first place, not without her. He should have stayed and fought for her instead of letting Kenny…

Oh, hell, he'd been through all this before, beating himself up inside in a way that no other judge or critic could manage. It was pointless. Kenny was the family man, not Tate.

"I shouldn't have left at all *that night*," he clarified, still kneading her gently. "I knew your time was close. I shouldn't have left you alone."

"But you're not my husband, so you didn't owe me that kind of commitment."

"No." He knew she meant to absolve him. He wasn't sure why it felt like a rejection. "I'm not your husband. But I'm your husband's best friend. I'm, uh…" Reluctantly he drew his hand back and pushed himself to his feet. "Committed to him. His memory. To taking good care of his wife and his—"

"Tate, don't—"

"And his kids. Anything for Kenny's family. You need anything—food, sheets, towels…" He tossed her a cocky wink. "You need a man's kiss, honey, you just call on me anytime."

He brooded on that scene for the rest of the day. He would have gone into town and gotten himself good and drunk if it weren't for the fact that there was so damn much work to do around the place. That night he fixed Jody's broomstick horse. He gave it a new horsehair mane. He'd culled the black hair from a trimming he'd given the gelding he'd stopped thinking of as Kenny's horse and started calling Outlaw. He fixed the ears and the frayed rein, and he gave it a whole new broomstick.

Jody's response to the refurbished toy couldn't have been more rewarding for Tate if he'd bought the boy something grand and new and presented it all tied up with a big red bow. Jody announced that his horse's new name was Outlaw, Jr., and that he was going to ride him "up and down and all around the town." He was Amy's mounted escort when she went out to the barn "just to say hello" to a ewe that Tate had brought back from the pasture and treated for foot rot. And Tate was the baby-sitter.

"How's my little girl?" he whispered as he knelt beside the bassinet. Since nobody but Karen could hear him, he figured he could indulge himself in the possessive claim. The baby knew what he meant. She grabbed his forefinger, and they shook on it.

He liked the soft little baby sounds she made as she waved her fist and turned her head from side to side, trying to focus on his face. "What are you telling me, huh? What do you see? It's not your mama's face. Kinda bristly. Needs a shave, same as it did the first time you saw it. Remember how you bawled? Was I that scary?"

He picked her up, taking a yellow flannel blanket with her, and he held her high against his shoulder. "Not anymore, huh? Wanna go for a little walk and see some more stuff?" *Just you and me, kid. Nobody else hears me babbling like this.* "You know what? You're not scary anymore, either. I've gotten used to you being such a little tyke."

He rubbed her flannel-covered back as he carried her into the living room, just for a change of scene. "'Course, this is as little as you'll ever be. Next time I come to visit..." She rewarded his back rubbing with what seemed like a very big burp for one so small. Having unwittingly done her a service, he smiled as he went on talking. "Well, you'll be a lot bigger next time. You'll be walking tall and talking big, just like your brother, Jody." His smile faded as he stared out the window at the distant mountain peaks. "And you won't remember me."

Amy came through the back door with a mighty, "Whew! Feels like I just ran the marathon." Tate could hear "Outlaw, Jr." clopping at her side across the kitchen floor. Amy looked surprised when she saw him in the living room with the baby. "Is she already hungry again?"

"No, but she was awake, and she's wantin' to tell the world hello, too, just like her mama."

"I have to get active and get my strength back." Her cheeks were rosy. From where Tate stood she was looking pretty bright-eyed, bushy-tailed and back in charge as she took the baby from him. "I'll make supper," she said.

"Tired of my canned soup and cold meat sandwiches?"

"I know you guys are ready for a change. Chicken and dumplings?" A pint-size lasso loop landed over the back of a chair. "Jody, I asked you not to do that in the house. Maybe Tate could give you a bike-riding lesson while I make supper?"

"We could play with the baby while you cook," Tate suggested.

"She doesn't know how to play." She rocked the baby in the crook of her arm. "And anyway, she's almost asleep."

"C'mon, partner." Disgusted, Tate reached for his jacket. "We're gettin' kicked out of the kitchen."

"It'll be worth your while, I promise."

Yeah, right. Tate left the house feeling as peevish as a wet cat. Jody followed at his heels in the same mood. He kicked a tire on his bicycle as he passed it in the yard. Tate turned, one eyebrow cocked solicitously.

"I don't wanna ride that ol' bike." Jody pouted. "I like to ride horses. When I get big, I'm gonna have a real horse, but I won't fall off, and I won't get killed. I'm gonna be a cowboy, like you."

"What should we do with this?" Tate's nod indicated the bike.

"Put it in the shed."

"Good idea." He lifted the offending toy by its handlebars, and they headed for the shed together. "Out of your mother's sight, out of her mind, huh?"

"She just came out here and petted that ewe that's limping around, and then she went back to that baby."

"Uh-oh." Tate remembered what it was like to be upstaged by an attention-grabbing new baby. "How do you like the new baby, Jody?"

"She doesn't *do* nuthin'. She just cries and smells funny." Jody kicked at the gravel in his path. "I told you a brother would be better than a sister. I wanted a baby brother."

"And I told you, they're both the same at first. They don't do much. Karen couldn't go out to the corral with me and help me feed Outlaw."

"I could!"

"And since she can't even sit up yet, I couldn't put her up on Outlaw's back and lead her around."

"You could do that with me. I can sit up." His feet suddenly stopped dragging.

By the time they'd reached the shed, Tate wondered whether Jody had springs on the bottoms of his tennis shoes. "That's just what I was thinkin'. The thing is, we might not wanna mention it to your mom." He spared the boy a warning glance as he turned the handle on the door. "I mean, unless she asks. Then we'd have to 'fess up."

"What does *'fess up* mean?"

"Means a cowboy tells the truth when his mom puts a question to him. It's part of the code."

"What's a code?"

He didn't mind Jody's questions. He took a shot at answering every one. Too many of his own questions had been ignored when he was a kid, and he'd been looking for answers ever since. He'd found a few, but he was still looking for the big ones. Fortunately, either Jody hadn't thought up the big questions, or he'd decided to break Tate in easy. Baby girls were easily explained. Women were something else.

At bedtime Amy read Jody two extra stories, sticking with it until he fell asleep. When she returned to her room, she was surprised to find Tate sitting on the bed with Karen. Wonder of wonders, he was pinning on a clean diaper. Amy tried to remember the last time she'd seen a man voluntarily tend to that particular chore.

"I was eavesdropping on the stories again," he admitted. "Jody says he wants to be a cowboy, and when he follows me out to the pickup, he tries to take steps as big as mine." Intent on his job, he didn't look up until he'd finished carefully fastening the second pin. "But he's not quite done being your first baby."

"I'm afraid he's going to grow up faster than either of us really wants him to."

"Either of *us*?"

"Either him or me." She couldn't help smiling. "I never thought I'd see Tate Harrison change a baby's diaper."

"Nothin' to it. Right, Karen?" He slid both hands under the baby and lifted her to his shoulder. "Only one thing ol' Tate can't do for you, and that's feed you. That's up to Mom, whose—" his eyes danced mischievously as he glanced at Amy "—jugs appear to be getting smaller, so I'd say you'd better get while the gettin's still good."

"Jugs?" She postured, hands on hips. "You'd better watch it, cowboy."

"Hey, just because you domesticate me a little, it doesn't mean I'm show-ring material."

She glanced down at her chest. "There's no less milk, just a little less pouf. I'm not show-ring material, either."

"You did a lot today." He piled the pillows against the

headboard to make a backrest for her as she joined him on the bed. "I read somewhere that having a baby's like having major surgery. Takes a while to get your strength back."

"Where did you read that?"

"One of the magazines in that pile downstairs." Reluctantly Tate handed the baby over to her mother.

"Wouldn't be Ken's old *Quarter Horse Journal*s. Must be one of my old *Parents* magazines."

"Yeah, well, I've already read all the horse stuff." He planted his hands on his knees. "I'll go check on—"

"Stay, Tate." She worked the buttons on her nightgown with one hand. "We haven't talked much since—" the soft look in her eyes personalized her invitation "—since the last time you watched me do this."

"You don't mind if I watch you take your—" That's not it, he told himself, and he gripped his knees a little tighter as the last button slid though its hole. "Watch you feed the baby?"

"You've seen all there is to see. More than my husband saw, in fact." The blue-flowered flannel slid away, baring her round, scarlet nipple. "I went to the hospital when I had Jody. Kenny wasn't there."

"Really?" Tate didn't want to know why. He didn't want to talk about Kenny at all right now. Not with Amy's breast bared for the baby and blessings bestowed on his voyeurism. He wondered whether her nipples were sore. "Do you need a towel?"

"I have one." She patted the bed, offering him the spot right next to her. "I promise not to squirt you."

"You could squirt me?" Mesmerized, he moved closer.

"On a good day I have a six-foot range."

"Does it taste like regular milk?" He glanced up and caught her smiling indulgently, the way he might look at

Jody. Hell, he had his questions, too. He told himself to watch the baby suckle, think warm milk, and he would have the general idea. "I guess I've had it, but I don't..."

She uncovered her free breast.

He lifted his gaze to hers. "...remember."

She couldn't make the offer in words, but her eyes were willing, mainly because he'd always been so easy on them. He was a beautiful man. His dark eyes held her gaze as he dipped his head slightly. Then he glanced down at the blue-white liquid dribbling down the underside of her breast. His full, sensuous lips parted as he looked into her eyes one more time to make sure. She nodded almost imperceptibly. He touched her nipple with the tip of his tongue.

She held her breath as he passed his tongue back and forth. The flow increased, and he took the bud of her nipple gently between his lips and let the milk leak into his mouth. He was cautious, like a humble petitioner, asking only to glean the overflow, while the tiny mouth on the left side was all business, working her like a milkmaid.

"Is it awful?" Amy asked timidly.

He made a low, contented sound, brushing his nose against her, scarcely moving his head in demurral. She forgot about her soreness. She forgot about feeling a little shy around him because she had been extraordinarily vulnerable and exposed, and she'd had time to reflect on what he might have seen and thought and felt. But for the moment misgivings and discomfort took a back seat in the presence of pure and natural tenderness.

He put his hand over her belly and felt for the distended muscle he'd learned so much about in recent days. He found it and massaged slowly, testing her receptiveness. "Does it still hurt here?" His lips hovered close to their post.

"Not as much, but..." *Yes, do that. Oh, yes, Tate, help me heal.*

"Will it hurt if I...suck a little?"

"Not if you're gentle."

He was gentle. The man who was wildness personified now suckled her with exquisite gentleness. She could not think how wanton she must be to permit such a thing. She could only feel. Deeply touched by the potential of his power bridled by his own tight control, she relinquished her doubts and permitted herself a separation from anxiety, however brief.

"It's warm and sweet," he murmured appreciatively. "Am I taking candy from the..." A tear slipped silently from the corner of Amy's eye and slid down her cheek. His heart fell with it.

"She's fallen asleep," Amy said quickly. He drew back, and she covered herself with her open nightgown as she got up to put Karen to bed. "Does it taste like candy?"

Propped on one elbow, feeling foolish and deserted, he watched her bend over the bassinet, absently clutching her nightgown together in front. What kind of stupid, juvenile thing had he done, and what in hell was he going to do with the ache it had left him with?

She straightened slowly and laid her hand over her eyes. His problem was minor. She turned, her face full of desolate tears and confusion, and he knew that, no matter who she was looking for on her bed, Tate Harrison was all she had. She sat down next to him. His problem was major again.

"Would you hold me for a while?" she asked.

"Sure." He reached for her, and she buried her face against his neck. He knew better than to expect an outpouring of emotion. This was Amy. She was stingy with her tears, and she sure as hell didn't shed them over spilled milk. "You were thinking about…somebody besides me."

"No." She put her arms around his middle and sighed. "Ken would never have done what you just did."

"I was just curious," he claimed.

She looked up at him, smiling through unshed tears.

"Okay, so maybe *curious* isn't the right word. Maybe I was just flyin' by the seat of my pants." Maybe that was exactly what he'd been doing since he'd first heard about Kenny's death, telling himself he had nothing but good intentions. "I'm sorry if I embarrassed you or made you feel…guilty or something."

She closed her eyes and buried her face again. This time he could feel her trembling. "Don't cry, honey."

"I can't help it," she sobbed. "I have to cry. Isn't that stupid?"

"No stupider than what I did. I didn't mean to do anything bad, I just—"

"It wasn't bad," she insisted, sniffling. "You were trying to make me feel…to help me…" She hated it when she got like this. "There's no reason for this ridiculous crying, so I'm stopping right now. See?" She used her hand until he plucked a tissue from the box on the night table and handed it to her.

She glanced ruefully at his shirt as she wiped her nose. "I'm getting you wet."

"Don't worry about it. It's a release, like we all need from time to time." *If she only knew.* "It's a natural thing, honey. Perfectly natural."

"Yes, I suppose. I try to convince myself I'm above those things, but obviously…" She gestured in frustration, the pink tissue balled up in her hand. "I do know the only thing I have to be embarrassed about is the way I've always——'' She glanced up, red-eyed and apologetic. "I've always sold you short."

"You mean I ain't as cheap as what you thought?" he drawled with half a smile.

"It didn't surprise me that you bid the horses up. It was the kind of grand gesture I would have expected, and, after all, it was *only* money." Still shaky, she took a deep, steadying breath. "But the Tate Harrison I *thought* I knew would have walked away after that, satisfied he'd done his duty to his old *compadre*."

He had come close to doing just that. "Honey, if I'd known you'd taken up sheepherdin'..."

"One favor," she entreated. "Try to remember not to call me 'honey.'"

"Is that what Kenny called you?"

"No." She smiled. "He called me 'Aims.' I don't want you to call me that, either." With a quick motion she erased the very idea. "I've heard you call at least a dozen other women 'honey.' It rolls off your tongue too easily, and it doesn't fit me."

"How about Bossy?"

She pressed her hand to her lactating breast and groaned.

"How about 'Black-Eyed Susan'?" he offered quietly, and the bittersweet reminder of "the road not taken" gave them both sober pause. He glanced away. "I'll come up with something better. Just give me a little time."

Her real question was, how much time would he give her?

His real question was, how much would she accept?

"Would you like me to fill the tub for you?" he asked.

"I guess you've noticed it's one of my favorite places to be lately."

"I can't imagine why." His smile faded as he searched her eyes. "Does everything...seem to be healing up the way it's supposed to? I asked Mrs. Massey if everything was okay when she checked you over the other day, and she said, 'Just fine, and how are you?' Like I was askin' after *her* health.'' He gave a quick shrug. ''Which I could have been, for all the conversation I had with her. She probably thought that was all the hired hand needed to know.''

''She's a woman of few words, and that was all the news. But I have one more important thing to say.'' She took his hand in hers, and he lost himself in her eyes. ''Thanks for asking.''

He nodded. ''Nice and warm, but not too hot, right?''

She nodded, too.

Half an hour later Amy emerged from the bathroom in her long white terry-cloth robe. Tate was watching TV in the living room when she came in to say good-night.

''Can I get you anything else?'' he offered as he rose from the chair. He'd made himself some coffee. ''Maybe some milk or some tea?''

''If you don't stop being so nice, I'm going to start crying again.''

But she offered no objections when he took her in his arms again. Her hair was damp, and she smelled of strawberry soap. Hugging her felt right. Kissing her would feel even better. ''Ask me to hold you through the night, Amy.''

''Tate, I can't have—''

''I know that. It's just good to hold you. It made me feel good when you asked me to.''

''I think maybe we're both kind of turned inside out right now, Tate. I know I am, and I know it would be a mistake for us to spend the night in the same bed.'' She leaned back and gripped his arms as she looked up at him. ''A big, big mistake.''

''Turned inside out'' was a good way of putting it. He

told himself to keep that in mind while he straightened up the kitchen and thumbed through a magazine. His damn ear had turned itself inside out. He wasn't sure when he'd started keeping it cocked for the baby's cry or for the sound of little pajama-covered feet shuffling down the hallway.

He heard the telltale squeak of Jody's bedroom door open. No footsteps. Amy was looking in on him. Maybe she was thinking about changing her mind about Tate. Maybe if Jody was sound asleep, and maybe if Amy was having second thoughts about her own empty bed, then *maybe* Tate wouldn't be spending another night tossing and turning on that wretched cot.

But the family slept upstairs. Their hired hand slept in the basement. Damn it all, it wasn't *his* family. She wasn't his wife and they weren't his kids. He was doing it all for the *late* Kenny Becker, his best friend. He heard her footsteps and the softer chirp Tate had learned to recognize as the hinges on her bedroom door. There was a pause.

"Good night, Tate."

"Good night."

By Thanksgiving there was snow, and it was time to bring the sheep closer to home. Tate wanted to leave Daisy and Duke at home, but Amy insisted that the dogs would save him time. They might have saved *Amy* time, but they were playing games with Tate this time out. When he dismounted and opened a gate, the dogs turned the herd and ran them down the fence line. Tate waved his arms and whistled and cussed to no avail. The sheep were scattered to hell and back, and all the dogs wanted to do was frolic in the wet snow.

By the time Tate had bunched the herd up again, the dogs were nowhere in sight, which was just fine by him. It was nightfall, and he was cold and hungry. He and Outlaw could push the herd without the help of any fancy dogs, just as soon as he figured out where the hell he was. The snow had thawed some during the day, but dropping temperatures had formed a crust that glistened by moonlight. The rolling hills all looked the same. But for the crunch of hooves breaking the snow crust and the creak of leather, the night was calm and quiet. It was the kind of night that used to bring Kenny over to his place for a moonlight ride.

This was no time to let himself start thinking about Kenny. Tate's butt was getting numb. His face was stiff with the cold. If Amy was his friend, she would have a hot bath and a shot of whiskey waiting for him.

But Kenny was his friend, or had been, and Tate had an eerie feeling that he was surveying the same moonscape Kenny had been looking at that last night. He sensed that he was hearing the last sounds Kenny had heard. "Did you lose your bearings that night, buddy?" he asked the night breeze. "Did you get turned around the way we used to sometimes?"

Kenny had been out joyriding that night. Tate was doing a job. He was trying to bring Amy's herd in. Not that he was drawing any comparisons or thinking any critical thoughts concerning the dead.

"I never interfered with you, man, except that once. But she was your woman, 'til death do you part. And she misses you. Hell, *I* miss you. So I'm tryin' to do the right thing, here, helpin' her out." He tipped his hat in unconscious deference to the myriad stars. "She's one hell of a woman. She always was, even though it seemed like she was afraid to loosen up and just have fun."

Okay, so maybe his wits had left camp temporarily, but he figured he could count on the witnesses to keep his secret.

"I have a feeling you can hear me tonight, Kenny. Either that, or I'm talkin' to myself. Or a bunch of dumb sheep."

Amazing how close the big ewe's bleating resembled laughter.

"What's that, you big pile of wool? You're sayin' I'm the one who's lost? Hell, I know where I am. I'm back in Montana. Big Sky Country." He lifted his eyes to the diamond-studded, black velvet sky. "I hope. It damn sure ain't heaven if Tate Harrison's allowed in, right, buddy?"

Tate read his answer in the distant glow of Amy's yard light. He managed a stiff-lipped grin. "But it's likely as close as I'll ever come."

Chapter Seven

"**M**om, where's Tate?"

Amy turned from the window. "He's bringing the sheep in, Jody." But the pens were still empty, the west gate was still closed and there was nothing stirring on the snow-covered hill above it. "He's out in the pasture, rounding up the sheep."

Jody was satisfied with Amy's answer for all of ten minutes, which was the time it took her to cut up vegetables for the stew she was planning for supper.

"Mom, when's Tate coming back?"

"Soon, Jody. He'll be back soon now." She glanced out the window again, this time noting the rosy streaks in the western sky. Sundown had a way of sneaking up on a person this time of year.

Not five minutes later Jody's broomstick horse was dragging its tail on the kitchen floor again. "Mom, what's taking Tate so—"

"I don't know!"

The moment the words were out, Amy regretted her tone. Jody's big eyes displayed the same kind of worry she'd been trying so hard to disown. He came to her and put his little arms around her hips, not looking for a hug, but offering one. She dropped to his eye level and took him in her arms.

"Tate rides really good," Jody assured her. "He hardly ever gets bucked off when he rides saddle bronc."

"Did he tell you that?"

"He showed me one of his buckles. They're like prizes you get for winning in rodeos. Tate rides *real* good."

So did your father. Horses were his life.

"You don't have to worry, Mom."

"You don't, either." She raked her fingers through the polka-dot horse's new mane. "Daisy and Duke aren't used to Tate, so he probably can't get them to work for him as fast as they do for me." The explanation sounded good. It even made sense.

It even made Amy herself actually smile. "Tate may be good with horses, but your mom is the dog expert around here." She gave Jody another good squeeze. "Of course, if he had the common sense of a good sheepherder, he'd take them the long way, which would take him safely along the highway. We could drive out a little ways and take a look."

Taking a look was better than sitting around worrying, Amy decided. She bundled up the children and drove her pickup several miles down the two-lane road, but there was no sign of sheep, dogs or horseman. Still nothing to worry about, she told Jody. If Tate was trying to get back before dark, he had to cut across the pasture. In that case, they wouldn't have been able to see him from the highway. But it was getting dark. When the dogs came back on their own, Amy called the sheriff.

"Miz Becker, it ain't all that cold out yet, and it ain't all that late," Sheriff Jim Katz told her over the phone.

Amy snorted disgustedly. When it got to be thirty below in the dead of winter, she would have to remember to ask the sheriff if it was cold enough for him yet.

"Man's got a job to do, y'gotta give him time to do it, Miz Becker."

"How long is that, Sheriff?" One glance at Jody's anxious face reminded her to curb the bitterness that burned the tip of her tongue. For the moment, anyway.

"I'd say ol' Tate oughta have them sheep penned up by eight and be warmin' up his innards at the Jackalope not long after. Once you start callin' the bars, if you can't track him down by midnight, you give me another call."

"Midnight. I'll make a note of that, Sheriff. Thank you."

"I understand you bein' touchy, Miz Becker. You've had more'n your share. But you gotta understand, I can't send out a search party every time a man rides out in his pasture."

"It's mostly my pasture, and it's dark and Tate's not familiar with—"

"Tate Harrison knows his way around, Miz Becker." Katz chuckled. "Give him a little more time. Then give a holler over to the Jackalope."

Amy wasn't tracking *anybody* down at the Jackalope. Men never took anything seriously until the situation was long past serious. She went about her business, and feeding her children came first. Twice during supper she jumped up from the table to check on the noise she thought she'd heard outside.

After she cleaned up the dishes she congratulated herself for getting the laundry done during the off-peak hours when electricity rates were cheaper. She left the baskets of folded clothes downstairs, thinking she would ask Tate to carry them up. Not that she couldn't lift them herself, she mused as she glanced out the window for the fifteenth time, but knowing Tate, she would be in for a reprimand if he caught her at it. He would tell her it was too soon for her to be hauling heavy loads up the stairs.

She was the perfect image of calm, repeatedly reassuring Jody as she bathed both children. After she'd put them to bed, she showered and dressed for bed herself, even though she fully intended to keep vigil. She turned the lights out so she could see through the window, but nothing stirred in the bright circle cast by the yard light. Nothing—absolutely nothing. She folded her arms on the back of the sofa, rested her head in the nest they made and kept watch out the side window.

The yard light was a homing beacon, but Tate was disappointed to see that the house was dark. Not even a light left on in the kitchen. The vehicles were all lined up in a row, present and accounted for. No one was looking for him. That was a relief, of course. It didn't make any sense to take the kids out on a cold night and drive around looking when she wouldn't have had a prayer of finding him, anyway. Not on the trail he'd taken. He had half a mind to backtrack tomorrow and see just where in hell he'd been.

He got the sheep bedded down and his horse rubbed down. Outlaw deserved that and then some for getting him home—getting him *back,* back to the house. When he'd first seen that yard light, he'd really felt as though he'd found his way home. He'd had to remind himself that it was the Becker place. Just a house. Just a dark house, where everybody was tucked up in bed, nice and cozy the way they ought to be.

Amy sat bolt upright when the back door opened. Somehow she had let herself doze off, lost track of time, neglected her fretting. She sprang to her feet, but she managed to affect some measure of composure by the time she reached the kitchen.

"Tate?"

There he stood in the shadows just inside the door. He was safe. He was home at last. He was unscathed, breathing normally, filling her kitchen doorway with his broad shoulders and the fresh scent of a winter's night.

He glanced up from pulling his gloves off. "You still up?"

"I've been waiting, but I guess I dozed off." She crossed the cold floor on bare feet, stopping short of arm's reach. "Did you have trouble?"

"Damn dogs wouldn't listen to me," he complained. She could tell his lips were stiff. "Other than that...I kinda got lost. Whole countryside's crusted over with snow. Looks like a huge white lake. You try to set your course, and just when you think you've got yourself lined out, you cross your own tracks. Pretty soon you start talkin' to yourself, tryin' to keep your brain from wanderin' away from camp."

Now that he was inside, his teeth had started chattering. "I brought 'em all back, though." He fumbled with the buttons on his sheepskin coat. "Every last bleatin' one of 'em. I counted."

"Let me help you." Her heart pounded out a jubilant rhythm as she took over the job of undoing his buttons. "Are your fingers...?"

"A little stiff, is all."

She pushed his jacket off his shoulders, then reached up to take his hat, then the scarf he'd tied under it. "How about your ears?"

He groaned when she put her hands over them. She knew the shock of her warmth must hurt, but he stood still for her inspection. There was even an indulgent smile in his voice. "They're still there."

"Oh, but so cold, and your cheeks..." Vulnerable places, all. She cupped her palms over his cheeks. If she turned on the light, would she find a healthy flame in his skin, or dark discoloration? She could feel his body shaking. Hers joined in, whether from relief or panic, she didn't know.

He put his hands over hers, sandwiching her warmth and pressing it to his face. She ached sympathetically with the stiffness in his hands.

"I don't know if I can get my boots off without a crowbar. My feet have turned to ice."

"I'll take them off. Sit here." She dragged a chair back from the table. The offer seemed to surprise him, but he complied, raising one leg so she could get a grip on his boot heel. "Can you wiggle your foot just a little?"

"Sorry, ma'am. 'Fraid I'm plumb out of wiggle."

"Okay, then, just hold still while I—" She turned her back, straddled his leg and tugged. His foot was forced to bend as the boot came loose, and he sucked his breath quickly between his teeth with the pain.

"If it hurts, you're starting to thaw," she said as she stepped over one leg and on to the next.

"I'm thawing, then. Hungry, too. Anything left from supper?"

"I'm going to fix you something, and it's also my turn to fill the tub for you, and I want to make sure..."

When the second boot came off, she found herself sitting on his knee. He settled his hands over her hips, and she looked at him over her shoulder. It was her turn to be surprised.

He grinned. "Why are we sittin' in the dark?"

Smiling shyly, she felt like a child sitting on Santa's knee. Partly uneasy, but mostly delighted. "Because I was watching out the window."

"I thought you'd gone to bed." He toyed with the white sash of her robe, tugging, turning her toward him. "The house was dark, so I thought…"

"I didn't know what to do. I took the kids and drove up the road. I called the sheriff, but he said to give you…to wait a while, to…" She closed her eyes as he touched her cheek. "Oh, Tate, your hands are still so cold."

"Your face is warm."

"I wasn't sure—"

His arms encircled her, and his kiss put an end to uncertainty. He was there, in the flesh. She touched his face, his ears, his neck, hoping to transfer her warmth to his chilled skin. But his lips were warm. His embrace tightened as he tilted his head for a new angle, for better access to her lips and the recesses of her mouth. She welcomed his tongue's gentle onslaught. She was more than glad to have him home.

She tucked her hands into the open neck of his flannel work shirt and smoothed them over cool combed cotton. He had the neck and shoulder muscles of a breeding stud. The feel of him thrilled her, and when he broke the kiss, she knew he could read that weakness in her eyes. He could hear it in every fluttery breath she took.

She traced his collarbones with her thumbs. "Just a plain T-shirt instead of long johns, Tate? What were you thinking?"

"It started out to be a nice.…" He closed his eyes, and his mighty shoulders quivered beneath her hands. "Oh, God, Amy, if you wanna undress me all the way…my fingers are still pretty stiff."

It would hardly be a difficult task, she thought. She could easily warm his body with hers. She could readily banish the chill from his bones and ease whatever stiffness plagued him. It was so good to have him safe in her arms that it was hard to remember any doubts she'd ever had about holding him close.

About trying to hold him at all.

"Let me start the water." She got up quickly and pulled him out of the chair. "We need to get you into some warm water right away."

"I think I'm gonna like this part."

"It's all part of thawing out. How do you like it so far?" It was impossible to interpret his low groan, so she tackled another subject. "Jody was awfully worried. He couldn't help thinking about what happened to Ken, you know? And he kept asking and asking, 'Where's Tate?'"

She turned the hall light on. He blinked and squinted like a man who'd just awakened.

"I'll go in and tell him I'm back. Would it be okay to wake him up?"

"I think it would be a good idea. I made him go to bed, but if he's asleep, he's probably not *sound* asleep, because there's that—" She touched his sleeve, pressed her lips together briefly and nodded. "That worry."

Tate nodded stiffly. She wanted to say what he wanted to hear, what she had not quite managed to claim—that it was her worry, too. He turned on his sock-clad heel and made his way down the hall. She listened for the low creaking sound she identified with Jody's door. Even with the bathwater running, she was able to tune in to their voices—one small and high, the other deep and comforting. Tears stung her eyes. She wiped them away quickly and made herself busy. Busyness kept sentimentality at bay.

"You were right," Tate said when he returned from his

mission. "He was awake. I think I lost a few points with him when I told him I got lost. He says if Santa Claus brings him a real horse this year, he's goin' with me next time, because he knows the way home." He smiled as he tackled his shirt buttons. "I think that's a hint."

"I've heard it before. That broomstick is the only kind of horse Santa Claus is ever dropping down *this* chimney." She hand-tested the temperature of the water. "I'm surprised he didn't pounce on you the minute you walked in."

"He heard us whispering, and he couldn't make out who it was. He was afraid to come out and see." He pulled his shirttail free of his jeans. "Sometimes a little kid gets scared when he hears adults whispering. He's afraid something bad has happened." He shrugged as he unbuttoned his cuffs. "Or he *knows* something bad has happened, and he's afraid of what might come next."

"You're still talking about Jody?" she asked carefully. She remembered Ken telling her that Tate had lost his mother when he was a boy, but she knew nothing about the circumstances.

"Sure, Jody. Or any little guy." He shed the plaid flannel shirt and whisked his T-shirt over his head. "He thought maybe the sheriff was here."

"He remembers the last time I called the sheriff," she said absently. She was staring. Tate's chest seemed so much bigger now that it was bare.

"So now he knows it doesn't always end up like that." He unbuckled his belt and gave her a crooked smile. "You wanna stick around and wash my back?"

"I'm sorry. I didn't mean to keep..." It wasn't easy to tear her eyes away. "I want to get some hot food in you, and this is one time I wish I had some liquor in the house."

She supposed she had that sinister-sounding chuckle coming.

He supposed turnabout chest-ogling was fair play.

"I think there's a bottle downstairs with a genie named Jack inside who could grant you that wish." His favorite brand. He hadn't brought it in, but she didn't need to know that. He figured Kenny had left it right where Tate would find it, in a drawer in the gun cabinet, alongside the liniment and the Ace bandages.

"Then we'll break the seal and let the genie out." She waltzed out the door, adding cheerfully, "For medicinal purposes, of course."

"Of course."

The water burned like hell at first, even though he knew it wasn't that hot. But he closed his eyes and rubbed it over him, letting it do its work. He didn't see any sign of frostbite, which was good, but restoring his circulation was a painful process.

"Tate?" It was Amy's voice, calling out just above a whisper. "I brought you something to put on. Ken's things. Is that okay?"

"Sure. The door's unlocked." He slid the shower door closed. "There. I'm behind glass. Just set it inside."

But she came into the room. "I found your genie, too."

"The one in the gun cabinet?"

"You and Ken must think alike. I mean, the two of you must *have thought*…"

"Like two pups in a basket, in some ways." Through the opaque glass he could see her, an obscure shape in a white robe, hanging some sort of reddish stuff on a hook on the back of the door. "Maybe we're still on the same wavelength. I knew right where to look."

"So did I." She gave a small laugh as she left the room, closing the door softly behind her.

After he toweled off, he debated with himself about putting his own clothes back on. It bothered him that the maroon terry-cloth robe smelled like somebody else's shaving lotion. And plaid flannel pajamas. He never wore pajamas. He figured for the sake of decency he ought to put on the pants, but the hell with that shirt. He couldn't believe Kenny had worn such a thing to bed. The sheepskin slippers were pretty dudish, too, but they were warm.

Tate tied the belt on the robe and checked himself out in the mirror. He needed a shave, but his razor was downstairs, and he didn't want to use the shaving cream in the medicine cabinet. He didn't like the smell of that, either. It wasn't his brand.

He shuffled into the kitchen and enjoyed having Amy wait on him at such a late hour. Beef stew and homemade bread warmed his shivering insides. Her robe was similar to his—or Kenny's—but hers was long and white. He wanted her to sit down with him without having to ask her to, but she kept bouncing in and out of the room.

Then he heard a crackling sound in the living room, and he turned to find her standing in the doorway and looking strangely hesitant. "Would you like to sit by the fire for a while?"

"Not alone."

"No." She watched him wash his soup bowl. "I'll have to feed the baby soon anyway."

He glanced at the clock.

"A couple of hours," she amended.

"A shot of whiskey and a warm fire would do me just fine, then."

He pushed the sofa closer to the fire. She poured him a shot of whiskey. She even warmed it over a flame before she handed it to him. "Dr. Jack," he said as he raised his glass to the fire.

"Was there water in the stock tank?" she wondered as she joined him on the sofa.

"I ran the pump."

"And how about the barn? And did you open the door to the shed in the far pen, in case—"

"I opened the door."

"I should have put fresh straw—"

"I put down fresh straw." He glanced askance at her. She was back to testing him. "I took care of it, Amy."

"I wasn't sure you'd think of—"

"I damn near froze my tail off getting your sheep back to the fold, lady. You think I'm gonna leave the job half done?"

"No."

She turned quietly to watch the fire, and he watched the firelight burnish her face while the flames danced in her eyes. He sipped his drink and toyed with the thought of going to bed with her. Not seducing her. Just getting up off the sofa when the time came and going to bed with her, as if he were her man.

"You think nobody else can do it quite as good as Amy can," he observed flatly.

"I couldn't have..." The words got stuck in her throat.

"Go on." He waited, then coaxed with a gesture. "You couldn't have what?"

"Well, I probably couldn't have—"

"Uh-uh, it was better the other way." He smiled, enjoying her struggle. "Come on, now, I worked hard for this."

"I couldn't have done any better myself."

"Damn right you couldn't have. I froze my—"

"I know, and I do appreciate that special sacrifice."

"I fed them and watered them and tucked them in for the night. I was gonna sing to them, but they said not to bother. They'd heard enough of that on the way home. On the way *back*." He drained his glass, and she poured him a refill in what he figured to be her bottom-line show of appreciation. "Hell, I don't even like sheep, and here I am, treatin' 'em like—"

"Children?"

"Cattle." He had half a mind to push his luck and light up a cigarette. "I'm a cowboy, remember?"

"I remember." She set the bottle on the hearth and studied it for a moment. "And I remember how I used to treat you after I married Ken."

"You always invited me to stay for supper. I always knew I could bunk in here for a night or two as long as I wasn't raisin' any hell." He smiled, remembering. "If Kenny and me went out and tied one on, I knew better than to set foot in your kitchen. I didn't blame you for that."

"You always saw that he got home."

"This was where he belonged. He had somebody waitin' for him."

"In most ways he was a very good husband. He didn't spend much time in the bars, except..."

"Except when I was around. Right?" She didn't have to answer. She was still staring at the bottle. "You know why married women are always tryin' to fix the single guys up and get 'em married off?" She shook her head. "They think their husbands envy our freedom. And maybe they do sometimes."

"They probably do."

"But it works both ways. We envy them, too, sometimes. Like when it's time to go home." He laid his arm along the back of the sofa and leaned closer, changing his mind about the cigarette. He liked the fresh scent of her hair. "How come you never tried to fix me up with somebody, Amy? Why weren't you introducing me to your sister? 'Fraid I'd ruin her?"

"My sister is older," she said evasively. "She was already married."

"A friend, then. Somebody just like you."

"It wouldn't be fair. You only want a home *sometimes*, Tate. Like when you're cold and tired."

He wasn't listening. "You don't have any friends just like you." He touched the softly curling ends of her hair. "There aren't any more like you, Amy. I've looked."

She looked at him skeptically. "Where?"

"Church socials. PTA meetings. Choir concerts."

"Don't you mean truck stops, rodeos and bars?"

He grinned lazily. "Don't tell me I'm lookin' for love in the wrong places."

"Don't tell me you're looking for love."

"Just lookin' for comfort tonight," he said lightly. "A warm fire and a hot meal." He sipped his whiskey, thinking maybe there was some kind of love to be found somewhere in the whole combination.

The baby's soft cry from the back room made him smile again. "Sounds like I'm not the only one." He caught Amy's hand as she started away. "You comin' back?"

"I'll bring her in here."

He poured himself another drink, resettled himself on the sofa and watched the sparks sail up the flue while he waited.

"I had to change her completely," Amy explained when she came back with the baby. "She was soaked through."

"Thought maybe you'd gone shy on me and decided to stay in the bedroom."

Baring her breast, she held his gaze with eyes that said she kept her promises. She'd promised to sit next to him while he warmed himself with fire and whiskey. And now she warmed him with a special intimacy.

"I like to watch you feed her. I haven't spent much time around babies. Or mothers feeding babies this way." He set his glass down and leaned over Amy's shoulder to watch the busy little mouth. "Not human mothers, anyway."

A feeling of possessiveness surged through him, and he wanted to physically become a shelter around this little family so that he could keep it safe from the cold night. He cupped his big weather-roughened hand over the baby's tiny head. Her downy hair felt precious and delicate against his palm. He remembered his first glimpse of it, what a wet, sticky, welcome and glorious sight the top of this little head had been, and it occurred to him that he'd put the cart before the horse. He had never made love to Amy, but in a sense he'd given her this child. He hadn't planted the seed, but he'd delivered the baby into her arms.

Little Karen drank herself to sleep, which was what Tate thought he would do, right there in front of the fire, after Amy took the baby back to bed. But Amy came back and sat beside him, as though it were her place. He tried not to think about the fact that he was wearing Kenny's robe, which smelled like Kenny's after-shave.

"You have a wonderful way with Jody," she told him. "I don't know whether I've mentioned that."

"No, you haven't."

"You seem to know all the right things to say. He's had to grow up a lot these past few months. He's been my strong little man."

"He still needs time to be your little boy. I'm not sayin' you don't do right by him, because you do. And you've had a lot on your mind. It's just that—" He shook his head. He knew he had to be half-shot if he was coming up with advice about raising kids. But she was looking at him as though she thought *he* thought she'd done something wrong, so he had to explain. "Sometimes when you get a new baby in the house, the older kid gets to feelin' like a milk bucket sittin' under a he-goat."

"While the mean old nanny——"

"Now, I didn't say that at all." He drew a deep breath and sighed. "And I don't wanna be buttin' into your business. I especially don't wanna be buttin' heads with you right now. I might crack."

"So enough about goats?"

"Enough about goats," he agreed. He dropped his hand on his thigh and rubbed his palm against the terry cloth. "I've got no right to talk, anyway, after the way I got after the little fella the day I was unloading hay."

Amy touched the back of his hand. "How old were you when your mother died, Tate?"

"Ten." He wasn't sure where that question had come from, but her touch would be his undoing. He could tell that right now. "She had some kind of routine surgery—gall bladder, I think—and there were complications. But I was almost grown. It wasn't like Jody, losing his dad before he even had a chance to——"

"Ten is hardly almost grown."

"When you live on a ranch, it is. The gospel according to Oakie Bain says that twelve is old enough to do a man's work." He turned his palm to hers, and their fingers seemed to lace together of their own accord. "All I'm saying is, just don't rush it. It'll happen soon enough. Once you give him a man's responsibilities, he won't be a boy anymore. And there's no such thing as a *little* man."

"You had a younger brother, didn't you?" He turned his face to the fire. "Ken told me."

"He told you what happened?"

"He said that your brother was killed in a farm accident when he was quite young. That's what you're thinking about, isn't it?"

"I'm talking about Jody." He tried to shrug it off. "Just

making a simple observation. Take a look at it, or leave it alone.''

"I'll take a hard look at it, Tate. It's a lot more than a simple observation." She paused, but it was too late to step back. "What was his name?"

"Jesse." His voice became distant, alien, drifting in desolation. "My brother's name was Jesse. Half brother. Oakie was his father, not mine." That was enough, he told himself. She'd only asked for his name. But his mouth wouldn't be still. "Jesse was only nine years old. By anybody's standards, that's still a boy."

"What happened?"

"I backed over him with the tractor." Damn the whiskey and damn his thick tongue. "Ran a 4020 just like yours right over his...right over him." He heard the catch in her breath. She didn't need any more details. "I figured Kenny must've told you the whole story."

"No." She squeezed his hand, and he could feel the pressure in the pit of his stomach. "Can *you* tell me?"

"I just did. I killed him. That's all she wrote."

"But it was an accident," she assured him softly.

"It was a crazed tractor," he countered. "One like you read about in a horror novel." With a look, she questioned his judgment. He studied the contents of his glass as he recalled some of his best recriminations. "Or else it could have been a booby trap that some prowler set to trip Jesse up. Or an earthquake sort of threw us both off balance. Anything but an accident. Accidents happen when people get careless."

"How old were you?"

"Twelve." He gave a long, hollow sigh. "I remember it like it was last night's dream. Real vivid, you know, but just beyond your grasp. Just past the point where you can turn it around and shake it up and make some sense out of it. All you can do is let it play itself out. You open your mouth to scream, and nothing comes out. You watch yourself slam on the brake, and you see the look on Oakie's face, and he's waving his arms. Is he saying go forward? Go back? And you get that awful, sick feeling all over again when you realize your brother's under the tire.''

He saw it all again in slow motion, for the umpteen-hundredth time. His hands were shaking, foiling his attempts to make the throttle work, to find the gear that would change the course of more than the tractor. He didn't see Oakie coming, and suddenly he was trying to turn a fall into a jump, then scrabbling out of the way. That was when he glimpsed Jesse's brown hair, and the outstretched hand, and the blood, just before he buried his own face in the alfalfa stubble and tasted dirt and bile and tears.

He felt untouchable, the way he always felt when he remembered, the way he had felt that day. He remembered thinking they would put him in jail, which was where he belonged. But instead, the sheriff had asked Oakie all the questions, sparing Tate a glance once in a while as Oakie had given the awful answers. ''Is that right, son?'' the sheriff kept saying. Tate didn't know; he'd just stared at his useless hands and nodded. His whole worthless body had gone numb. And no one had tried to touch him then.

But Amy touched him now. He wasn't sure what had happened to his drink, or what he'd said last. Suddenly Amy was holding both of his hands. He hated the way they were shaking. ''One minute he was playing with a spotted pup Oakie had given him,'' Tate said distantly. ''The next he was underneath the damn tire.''

She bowed her head and pressed the back of his hand to her cheek. ''You saw him, didn't you?'' she whispered. ''You found him broken and bleeding, the same way…''

The same way Kenny had been when she'd found him. Another shared intimacy. They knew the same nightmares.

"It wasn't your fault, Tate."

"How do you know?"

"You were only twelve years old," she reminded him. "Still a child yourself. You didn't kill your brother. It was a terrible—"

"Accident," he recited. "Tragic accident, horrible accident. I hate the word. It grates on my ears like somebody grinding his teeth." He watched the fire. "The sheriff said it was an accident. The neighbors, when they brought over their hot dishes and offered to help with the chores, they called it an accident. Oakie didn't say much of anything, not for a long time. Kids from school said, 'Sorry about what happened, Tate' and that was that. Nobody talked about it much after we buried Jesse. Or if they did, they talked around it."

"It's always in the back of your mind when you farm," Amy said quietly as she rubbed her thumbs over the backs of his hands. "You like to think it's a good way to raise kids. And it is. You want them to take part in the work because it builds character, and they learn so much."

She closed her eyes, and a lone tear slipped down her cheek. She shifted a little, hoping he hadn't seen it. "But there are the accidents. They happen, Tate. They happen more often than most people want to realize. They happen with adults at the controls. You were only—"

"A boy?" He shook his head. "I was doing a man's job. I was expected to act like a man. Stand up like a man. Own up to my mistakes like a man, meaning you don't make excuses and you keep your blubbering to yourself." He was quoting now, almost verbatim.

"You weren't allowed to—"

"Cry? No way. Not unless I wanted Oakie to, uh—" He

recalled his stepfather's favorite warning. "Give me something to cry about. The only person I ever talked to about it was Kenny, and that was only after I'd had a few drinks, like now." Still staring into the fire, he gave a humorless smile. "Ol' Kenny and me, we learned to act like men. Drank and smoked like men. Cussed and scrapped it out like men. Chased us some girls and had us some women, just like real men."

With a groan she tried to be subtle about drying her cheek on her own shoulder. "Now you're beginning to sound like the other Tate."

"What other Tate?" He took her chin in his hand and made her look at him. "There is only one Tate Harrison."

"Maybe so." She took a deep, steadying breath. "But he has an outside and an inside."

"Just like everybody else." He found the dampness on her cheek with his finger.

"You've worked hard at toughening up the outside. You've done a better job than anyone I know. But when the chips are down, you always come through. You'd go out drinking, and Kenny was always the one who got plastered. You were the one who brought him home. You were always watching out for him."

His mouth quirked slightly as the knowing smile flashed in his eyes. "Hornin' in on your territory?"

"He was my husband."

"Kenny had his head in the clouds most of the time, but he didn't worry much since he had us both watchin' out for him." He raised one brow. "Trouble is, he got away from us one night. And you've been thinkin' you should've gotten to him sooner, while I've been thinkin' I should've been here."

"Crazy, isn't it?"

"It'll drive you crazy. Believe me, I know."

"I want Jody to be...different. I don't want him to *act* like a man. I want him to *be* a man. Independent. Responsible."

"Like his mom?" She was all set to take exception, but he laid a finger against her lips. "Relax a little. Let him be a boy first. I told you about Jesse because..." The name came hard, as always, but this time he had Amy's hand in his, and her acceptance. "Because of Jody."

Which wasn't the whole of it, and she knew that as well as he did, but it was easier to advocate for the boy. "He watches you with the baby," he said, remembering, looking down at their clasped hands, now lying in her lap. "I told him how the baby wasn't going to be much fun for a while, and he's trying hard to understand all that, but he needs—" She looked up, and he looked into her eyes and said almost inaudibly, "He needs you to hold him."

"I can do that," she said gently. He leaned closer, and she put her arms around him and laid her cheek against his chest.

A man's need to touch a woman was a given, but the need to be touched by her was something else. He felt the need so strongly, he was almost afraid to return the gesture, afraid he would give himself away.

They wouldn't touch him. He'd done an awful thing, and nobody wanted to touch him.

"This isn't what I learned about acting like a man," he said as he slid his arms around her. He closed his eyes and nestled his face in her hair. "Hangin' on to you for dear life like this."

"Is that what you're doing?"

He didn't think he could hold her close enough, but she found a way to surround him with more warmth than the fire in the hearth radiated. He breathed deeply of the sweet strawberry-and-smoke scent of her. "I feel like the kid who got lost in the woods. It sure was dark out there."

"Could you use a kiss, too?"

"Not the kind you'd give to a kid."

She slid her fingers into his thick hair and pulled his face down to hers, kissing him as hungrily, as greedily, as fervently, as he'd ever been kissed. He'd never wanted anything more desperately than he craved her touch right now, but not if he had to ask. And he didn't. Suddenly her hands were all over him under the robe, caressing his hair-spattered chest, his shoulders, his flat nipples. He sucked in a deep breath and offered her access to his belly. He was on his way to heaven when she touched him there.

He untied the sash and drew the robe back, trying to shrug out of it without changing her course. "This thing smells like somebody else, Amy." Her fingertips curled into his waist, and she went still. He dropped his head back against the sofa. "Is that what you want?" he demanded quietly. "You want me to be somebody else?"

"No." She pressed her forehead against his chest and breathed soft words on his skin. "God help me, no."

"I want you so bad. You know that, don't you?" She nodded against him. "But I'm not Kenny. I don't own a robe and slippers. I don't wear pajamas. I'm not—" He couldn't be, not even if he had the heart to try, and she had to accept that. "I don't ever want you to call me by the wrong name."

She sighed. "Tate, I know who you are." She lifted her head and met his gaze. "I'm beginning to, anyway. You're the man who delivered my baby, the man who fixed my son's broomstick horse, the man who—"

He touched his finger to her lips. He didn't want her gratitude. "I want to make love to you."

"It's too soon."

"Because of the baby?" He searched the depths of her eyes for her answer. "Or because of Kenny?"

"Both," she admitted. She closed her eyes against the disappointment she saw in his. "Both."

He nodded and withdrew.

"That doesn't mean we can't give each other—" She extended her hand to him quickly, then closed it on a second thought. "I started to say 'what *we've* been giving.' But you've been giving, and I've been taking."

"It hasn't been easy, has it?" She looked at him, perplexed. "Taking help from Tate Harrison."

"Oh, Tate," she said as she took him back in her arms.

It had been *too* easy. Too quickly she had come to rely on him. Too readily she had let him lay claim to a too-large piece of her heart. She'd made it all too obvious. She hugged him, but she gave him no more of an answer. At least she could try not to show him *how* readily and *how* easily and *how* much.

He kissed the top of her hair and held her close. "It hasn't been easy givin' it, either."

Chapter Eight

Thanksgiving seemed to creep up overnight, but it did not pass without a traditional dinner. Tate was invited to carve the turkey and sit at the head of the table. He obliged. Even though he hardly considered himself a jack of the turkey-carving trade, he figured it out without asking for any pointers. Sitting in Kenny's chair at feast time felt a lot like wearing Kenny's robe and slippers, which Tate had quietly returned to the bedroom closet and never worn again. The prospect of an opportunity to play Santa Claus would have held considerable appeal except for the idea of filling someone else's boots again. Tate had his own boots. They were broken in nicely and fitted him just fine.

Amy hadn't been into town since the horse sale. The roads were icy, and she was glad when Tate volunteered to drive her in for the requisite six-week checkup. She had to take Jody along for a throat culture, and he and the baby were both fussy. The waiting room at the rural clinic was packed with whining children and cranky mothers. Tate excused himself to do some errands and promised to meet Amy and the kids at the Big Cup Café, two doors down the street.

It bothered her to find him sitting at a booth with her sister-in-law and Patsy Drexel. Marianne was working her way through a club sandwich, and Tate and Patsy were sharing a laugh and a cigarette. She was just passing it back to him, and he was about to take a drag when he saw Amy. One quick puff and, to his credit, he put it out before she brought the children to the table.

Patsy eyed the ashtray regretfully, as though she hadn't gotten her fill. Too bad, Amy thought.

"You guys ready for lunch?" Tate tipped his hat back and smiled. "I've been waitin' to order."

Amy shook her head. "We can wait 'til we get home. I have plenty of—"

"Mom, can I have a hamburger?" Jody pleaded.

"You can sit right up here with me and have anything you want, partner." Tate reached over the backrest and nabbed a booster seat from the empty booth on the other side. "We're too hungry to wait, aren't we? How's your throat?"

"They stuck a stick down it." Jody demonstrated with his forefinger. "Yech!"

"What you need is a big, fat hamburger and maybe some hot—" Tate glanced at Amy "—soup? Some orange juice?"

A little late to be asking my opinion, Amy thought. Jody had already scrambled into the booster seat, which Tate had pulled close to his side. She sighed and nodded, eyeing the remaining space on the horn of the half-moon booth. "Whatever he orders will be hard for him to swallow, and it's coming out of your wages, Harrison."

"That's all right," he said, chuckling as he signaled waitress Madge Jensen. "I've been meaning to suggest a pay cut, anyway. The seconds are killing my boyish figure."

Marianne offered to hold the baby, and Patsy spared the bundle a cursory glance as Amy wearily took a seat. She felt as though she'd just been to the doctor for anemia and he'd prescribed leeches. The bill—like all bills these days—had been higher than she'd expected. It worried her that she hadn't been able to pay it in full. She needed the cup of tea Tate suggested. She *wanted* the lunch he offered that she wouldn't have to prepare herself.

"We need anything from the store?" Tate asked.

The question surprised her. Tate had been picking up milk and eggs when he went to town, and he knew how well stocked her freezer and pantry were with her own produce. Now that she was doing the cooking again, she made everything from scratch. No more canned soup.

"Thought maybe I could take you grocery shopping." He sipped his coffee, then offered a teasing grin. "Wouldn't that be fun?"

Compared to what? Amy wondered. Delivering babies? All the fun things he could do with Patsy?

"I don't have my coupons with me." She glared at him. *How do you like that for mundane?*

"Amy and her coupons." Marianne chortled. "Bill, Sr., never had to bother with coupons and weekly specials until Amy moved in and started talking it up. But since our store is a franchise..." She smiled sweetly. "Well, we went along with it, so everything's up-to-date in Overo now. I just don't see where you find the time to mess with all that stuff, Amy. Clipping coupons and watching for bargains."

"I'm organized," Amy said dryly. A quick glance at

Tate forced her to add, "Usually. And I don't buy what I don't need."

"What do you need for lunch?" Tate's nod turned her attention to the waitress, who was standing near Amy's shoulder, pencil and pad ready.

"Just a glass of water, please, Madge."

"You are the stubbornest woman I've ever known," Tate grumbled under his breath after he and Jody had put in their orders.

"I'll have to agree with that," Marianne put in. "Have you given any more thought to having a geological survey done? Tobart Mining is still interested."

Tate tucked his cigarettes into his jacket pocket. "They've approached me, too."

"What are *you* going to do?" Marianne asked.

"I don't know." He picked up his coffee cup. "I've been thinking about selling out altogether. If I do, I guess I'll hang on to the mineral rights."

"So in a year or two I'm likely to be looking at a strip mine right down the road," Amy surmised with blatant disgust.

"Just because you let them take core samples doesn't mean you're asking for strip mining."

"Really?" The look she gave him was cold enough to freeze beer. "What do you think they'll find in our basin, Tate? Gold nuggets?"

"Well, there could be oil, natural gas. There could be a lot of things." He dismissed the possibilities with a disinterested shrug. "They reclaim the land."

"We're ranchers." Amy turned to her husband's sister. "That was all Ken ever wanted. A working ranch."

"I think you mean a working *wife*," Marianne said. She shifted the baby to her shoulder. "Ranches don't work. *People* work. And you work too hard, Amy."

That was her choice. "Your father left Ken his land and you his money." *Mine gave me a strong back.*

"I also own half the mineral rights."

"Which are useless to you unless I agree to exploration. The land is Ken's legacy to his children," Amy said firmly. "It won't be mined. Now, can we talk about something else, please?" She offered a tight smile as Madge appeared with coffee refills. "I believe I will have a cup of tea and a BLT, Madge. Are you ready for Christmas, Marianne? How about you, Patsy? Have you done all your shopping?"

"I've done some," Patsy drawled. She glanced Tate's way and sighed. "Seems like I'm always shopping around."

Amy had turned the heat down before she left, and the house was cold. Almost as chilly as the attitude she had given him since they'd left the café, Tate thought. It couldn't have been over the comment about stopping at the store. Hadn't she been the one wishing aloud for some fresh fruit just the other day? Besides apples, she'd said. She had apples in the pantry.

He wasn't just sure what he'd done, but he figured it had to do with Patsy Drexel. If that were the case, he could afford to feel a little smug, considering his innocence. He went about his business, feeding the livestock, mending a hasp on one of the gates and sneaking his morning's purchases down to his room when everyone was napping. He was feeling pretty damned organized, too, now that he'd done some Christmas shopping. He'd never wrapped a Christmas present in his life, and he'd thought about leaving the stuff with Marianne or Patsy, along with a hint that he hadn't used a pair of scissors since he was in grade school. But he'd missed his chance.

The gun cabinet had obviously been one of Kenny's

places for secreting things. Since Amy hadn't disturbed Kenny's whiskey stash or checked the guns, Tate took the cabinet to be property left untended, now that its owner was gone. It wouldn't hold everything he'd bought, but there was plenty of room for the things he didn't want Amy to find. He heard her footsteps on the stairs just in time to shut the door and lock it.

"Another drink to warm up?"

He didn't know why the question stung him. He'd thought about it himself, actually, but he'd changed his mind. He didn't like the way she was standing in the shadows at the foot of the stairs and looking at him like he was some kid who ought to know better. Maybe he'd just change his mind back again.

She wagged her head and sighed disgustedly. "Ken always thought he was so clever. If you insist on having it in the house, you might as well keep it in the kitchen and use a glass."

"What's left from Ken's stock *is* in the kitchen. I just needed a place to stash a few things under lock and key." Working hard to keep his cool, he bounced the key in his hand for her benefit. "The lock doesn't do much good with the key sittin' right in it."

Slowly she walked over to the gun cabinet, stared at the glass door for a moment, then ran her hand over the carved molding. "It's been a slow process, dealing with Ken's things—his drawers, his side of the closet, his boxes and boxes of keepsakes. He never threw anything away." Her hand dropped to her side. "I haven't gotten to this yet, but the guns aren't loaded."

"The .22 pistol had two rounds in the clip."

"Oh, Ken." She drew a deep breath and cast her glance heavenward. "Why were you always so...?" With a quick shake of her head, she took the blame herself. "I should have thought to check. I should have been more careful."

"Everything's unloaded now. If you don't have any use for them, you could probably get a good price for some of them. Maybe keep one around for—"

"They're Jody's." She folded her arms and turned away from the cabinet. "They will be when he's old enough. Some of them belonged to Ken's father. One was his grandfather's." She stepped closer to Tate, distancing herself from the Becker family heirlooms. "Otherwise, I wouldn't have them around."

He wondered whether she'd ever told Kenny any of this. He remembered that the cabinet itself had been in Kenny's family forever, as had the love of guns. Tate owned a couple of hunting rifles, too. He figured most guys did.

"Out here alone, you've got predators to worry about, maybe prowlers." No surprise to her, he thought. If Kenny had been good for nothing else, he'd been capable of protecting what was his. "If you don't know how to use a gun, I can sure teach you."

"You're going to sell your land, aren't you, Tate?" The question came out of left field. He missed the catch, so she pitched her charge again. "You're just going to sell out to the highest bidder."

Was she kidding? For years the bidding had been closed to anyone but Kenny. "I've only kept it this long because Kenny wanted it. When you guys dropped the lease, I kinda figured—"

"It's been in your family. It belonged to your father."

"Yeah, well, he died young because he worked too damn hard. He had a bad heart. This is no life for a man with a weak heart." He thought better of adding, *Or a woman with two little kids.* "That's about all I know about him, too. He died when I was even younger than Jody."

Damn, he was at it again, spilling personal history like a leaky washtub.

"Jody won't remember much about his father, either, but he'll have the home his father left him."

"Forever and ever, amen?"

"A home is important." She jabbed his shirt button with her forefinger. "Roots, Tate. Roots are important. They give you a strong sense of who you are."

"You have a strong sense of who *you* are." He closed his hand around hers. "You've only lived here since you married Kenny. Where are your roots?"

"They're here. They grew fast, once they had fertile ground."

"Like the tree you fed from your own womb?" He didn't realize he was going to take her shoulders in his hands until he felt their slightness. "Aren't you afraid this land might suck the life right out of you, maybe through those roots you put down?"

"No," she said, standing her ground without pushing him away, as he might have expected. "I've brought new life here. I've made a home. A permanent home. You sold your family's house, and now you're going to sell the land it sat on."

"I don't have any use for it."

"They'll rape it, Tate. The speculators, the investors, the miners. They'll strip it down and violate it."

A caustic comeback sprang to the tip of his tongue, but he couldn't quite spit it out. He couldn't accuse her of being melodramatic, not with that look on her face and the image that the word *rape* brought to his mind. It was more than a risk to the land. It was a threat to Amy, to her power to make life flourish, to the essence of her femininity. In her eyes he revisited her pain and her triumph in the moment she'd given birth.

"You want it?" he demanded flippantly. The life force burned so strongly in her eyes that he was forced to turn away. "Take it," he said, his bravado deflating. "Christmas present, free and clear. I'll sign over the title."

"Don't be ridiculous," she tossed back.

He turned like a cornered gunfighter, the words piercing him as sharply as any bullet could have. "You've said that to me before, Amy. Remember?" *Remember the night I drove you home? You made your choice that night.* "'Don't be ridiculous, Tate.'"

She stared, frowning slightly, trying to dredge up some recollection of the details in her mind. Clearly it wasn't an easy task for her. Maybe it wasn't much of a memory for anybody but Tate.

"There was no way I was gonna hang around this town after you married Kenny and set up your *permanent* housekeeping with him. *That* would have been ridiculous."

"So you chose to live like a gypsy."

"A cowboy," he corrected with a cocky grin. "Don't gypsies raise *sheep?*"

"I don't know. All I know is that they wander from place to place, and their children just—" she gestured expansively "—wander with them."

"I don't have any children, so what difference does it make how I choose to live my life?" His eyes challenged her. He folded his arms and braced his shoulder against the gun cabinet. "What difference does it make to *you*, Amy. Why should you give a damn?"

"You were my husband's friend."

"It has nothing to do with Kenny, and you know it. It has to do with you and me, and it always has."

"There was no 'you and me.' You weren't really—"

His hand shot out and grabbed her shoulder again. "The only thing I wasn't really was the kind of man you were looking for. You chose your husband carefully, didn't you?"

She stiffened. "Yes, and you were his friend, which made you *our* friend."

"Give me a break." With a groan he released her and turned away, patting his empty shirt pocket. His cigarettes must have been in his jacket. It was about time for a smoke and the drink she'd first accused him of sneaking.

But at his back, she persisted with her crusade. "You know, you could have built something on that land instead of tearing down what was left and going off—"

Great suggestion. "You would have enjoyed that, would you?" He confronted her again, trying hard not to sneer. "You married to Kenny, and me living just down the road?"

"It wouldn't have bothered me."

"Yeah, right. Well, it would have bothered the livin' hell out of me."

"I just meant that..." They stood face-to-face, but they were talking past each other. Intentionally. He knew what she meant, and he could tell by the look in her eyes that she knew damn well what *he* meant.

She shook her head and softened her tone. "You don't understand about the land because you've never been one to settle down. It's just not in you."

"I understand something about the land, Amy. I grew up here." He glanced away. He didn't like that soulful look she was giving him. "I guess I don't understand about the roots. Mine must have eroded. What was left after Jesse died was me and Oakie. Two people who tolerated each other. Barely."

"Why do you keep coming back, then?"

"To see Kenny." *What, was she blind?*

"Kenny's not here anymore."

"I'm stickin' around to help his wife and kids get through the winter."

"I'm his *widow*."

"Which means what? Besides the fact that you need a man?"

"I *don't* need a man!" Fingers rigidly splayed, she swept the idea away with an abrupt gesture, then calmly echoed, "I'm not talking about that. I'm saying you've come back to—"

"No, let's stop talking *around* it, Amy. I'm living under your roof, and Kenny's dead." He braced his arms on the gun cabinet, trapping her between them to keep her from turning away. "Several years ago you said it was wrong. Several cold nights ago you told me it was too soon. What are you tellin' me now?"

They stared at one another, and finally it was he who had to turn away. If he got hold of her again, he would begin trying to shake some sense into her. Or he would be kissing her senseless—one of the two. He sighed. "What do you want from me, Amy?"

"I haven't asked for anything."

"Doesn't it mean anything to you that you haven't *had* to?"

Her lips parted. He arched an eyebrow, waiting, but she pressed those lips together again. He gave a dry chuckle, as short on patience as she was on answers.

"I'm goin' out for a smoke," he told her as he headed for the stairs. "Call me when supper's ready. Whatever supper you think you can spare your hired *gypsy*."

Tate thought a lot about "roots" when he and Jody rode into the hills—*his* hills, on his land—and selected a Christmas tree. He'd taken it as a somewhat positive sign when Amy hadn't refused to let Jody go along after Jody assured her that his throat wasn't "one bit sore anymore." The horseback part of the journey would be short, Tate had promised. They had trailered Outlaw as close in as they could. Then he'd put Jody in the saddle and mounted up behind him.

Maybe he did have some roots in the foothills, he thought. The huge, pale winter sky rose high overhead and slid down in the distance behind the snow-capped western peaks. The morning freshness was filled with sage and pine. It felt good to fill his chest with something besides smoke, to get himself light-headed on pure air.

"What we're gonna end up with is a juniper or a ponderosa pine. You think that's okay?" Tate wondered as he surveyed the snow-spattered red cuts and the flat-topped slopes.

Jody nodded vigorously, the bill on his little flap-eared plaid cap bobbing up and down like a barfly's eyelashes.

"They don't make the best Christmas trees, but we'll find a good one. We can't use a limber pine. See that one up there?" The boy nodded again. "The wind's turned it into a pretzel."

"Mom and me bought our tree last year," Jody reported. "Did your dad used to go cut your Christmas tree himself?"

"My stepdad did, yeah."

"Did he take you with him?"

"He did. This is where we'd always come lookin', too."

He remembered the year a bobcat had spooked the horses. Jesse had been just about Jody's age, and Tate and Jesse had been riding double. Their sixteen-hand palomino had laid his ears back, and they'd gone streaking across the flat, with Jesse hanging on to the saddle horn and Tate, mounted behind him, gripping the swells. He could still see that jackleg fence up ahead. Just when he'd thought they were goners, the big horse had sailed over the rails like a trained jumper and kept right on galloping until he wore himself out. Oakie's face had been whiter than the December snow cover, but he'd said he'd never seen any cowboy stick a horse better, and he'd been looking Tate straight in the eye when he'd said it.

"We always found a good one out here," Tate said, surprising himself as he echoed Oakie's annual pronouncement. "You can't get 'em any fresher."

They chose a small juniper. Even though it didn't have the pointed crown they were looking for, it had a straight trunk, and it was already decorated with cones that looked more like pale blue berries. Entrusted with Outlaw's reins, Jody was content to stand back and watch Tate cut the tree down. But the notion of roots bedeviled Tate as he swung the ax. He would take the tree away, but the roots would remain. If he came back to this spot years later, he knew he'd find juniper saplings. For every one that he pulled down, Amy would probably plant two more, with or without a placenta to nourish its roots. That was the way she was. A nester, like his mother, whose life had been hard and brief. His mother hadn't lived long enough to see the get of her womb reach manhood.

The tree went down, and Jody cheered. Tate straightened his shoulders and flashed a smile the boy's way. It was good for a boy to have a man to look out for him, too, Tate thought. And it was good for a man to remember that times weren't *all* bad when he was a boy.

Amy had been keeping to herself a lot lately, spending hours behind closed doors in the bedroom with the sewing machine whirring. The tree pleased her. She emerged long enough to give it her special homespun touch, adding brightly colored calico bows, along with small hanging pillows shaped like rag dolls and toy soldiers and teddy tears. She gave the top berth to a lacy angel, then stepped back and announced that she'd never seen a prettier tree.

After letting it be known that offers to entertain the baby would be more than welcome, Amy went back to her sewing machine. Tate and Jody discovered that Karen had an ear for harmonica music. Now that she could hold her head up, she liked to bob along with their songs.

After several hours of late-night work, Tate managed to get his packages wrapped. The paper was cut funny in places, and he'd had to use a lot of tape, but he felt good when he arranged the gifts under the tree. He'd saved all the receipts. Half the stuff probably wouldn't fit. The other half was probably purely frivolous, but he didn't care. He'd picked out things he wanted his...he wanted *them* to have.

Amy didn't say much when she saw all the packages, but Jody was bursting with excitement when he asked, rather cautiously, whether any of the packages might be for him. Tate pointed to his name on one of the tags and challenged him to find the others.

Jody found one small box to be especially fascinating. He kept checking it over, shaking it, staring as though he were trying to develop X-ray vision, and muttering his guesses as though the package might respond if he hit on the right word. By Christmas Eve he had almost become a fixture beneath the tree.

After a supper of what Amy called her Christmas Eve chowder, she disappeared into the bedroom one more time and emerged with an armload of packages and a broad smile. "I have some things to add to the booty," she told Tate as they met in the hallway.

"Can you use some help?" Karen had fallen asleep in his arms, and he'd just put her down in the crib in her nursery. "Looks like you've been busy."

"You guys probably thought I was avoiding you these last couple of weeks. I wasn't." She let him take the top half of her pile of packages. "Mine are all homemade."

"Makes them more special."

"Jody's too young to see it that way. I know he's excited about your gifts, and I'm trying not to be an old Scrooge about it."

With a quick frown he questioned her choice of words.

"What I mean to say is, I'm sure you bought him the kinds of things a little boy wants for Christmas."

"I was a little boy again when I did my shopping. You don't begrudge me that, do you?"

"No." They stood across from each other in the narrow hallway, his armload of boxes touching hers. A big red bow grazed her chin. "I appreciate it. It's the first Christmas without Ken, and I dreaded it. But you're here, and I'm glad, and—" She shrugged. "I guess I feel a little guilty about being glad."

He groaned. "You are so full of—" With a soft chuckle he tipped his head back against the wall. "The word that comes to mind...well, you'd take it wrong."

"Baloney?"

"That's not right, either. I know how you feel. I miss Kenny, too. Maybe not the same way you do, but I miss him." He ducked a little closer to her ear, as though he was sharing a secret. "I think it's okay to be glad about some things at Christmas, and still be sad about others. And I'm glad I'm here."

"Where would you be if you weren't here?"

"No place special." Probably hanging around Reno or Denver, or maybe working the holidays for some trucking outfit, but she was looking at him as though she thought he was sitting on the keys to some pleasure palace. "That's the truth, Amy. No place anywhere near this special."

Jody had fallen asleep under the tree. Quietly Tate set his armload of packages aside and knelt beside the boy. The colored lights from the tree cast a rainbow of soft hues over his soft blond curls and his sleeping-in-heavenly-peace face. The warm glow seemed to seep into Tate's skin, like the gleam of approval he'd been seeing in the child's eyes lately.

That was a gift, he realized. The best gift anyone had ever given him. Nobody had ever accepted him unconditionally, the way Jody did. He imagined himself claiming his gift from under the tree as he lifted Jody into his arms, carried him to bed and tucked him in.

Amy had a steaming cup of apple cider waiting for him when he came back to join her on the sofa. "Homemade," she said as she watched him take a sip. "But it doesn't have much kick to it."

"I like it the way it is." He pressed his lips together, savoring the cinnamon flavor. "Homemade."

She nodded toward the packages under the tree. "It's that small box that fascinates him, but I don't think it's sugarplums he has dancing in his head. What's in it?"

"A gift for him and a surprise for you."

"The day you don't surprise me will be a surprise, Tate Harrison. I hope you didn't go overboard."

"I didn't." Not as far as he was concerned. "Anyway, what's done is done, and you're long overdue for a few pleasant surprises. And I'm just the man who can provide them, because you don't expect much." He gave her a mischievous wink. "I can look pretty damn good just by taking some time off from being bad."

"I wouldn't say that."

"You wouldn't say I look good?"

"You look—" she gave him a pointed once-over "—the way you've always looked." The observation made him squirm a little, which made her laugh. "Truthfully, I've always thought you looked good even when you were being your baddest."

"Baddest man in Overo?"

"Sometimes. You know darn well you turn a lot of heads, cowboy. You always have."

"But not yours."

"You know better than that," she admitted. "But I've always managed to be fairly practical."

"*Very* practical."

"I'm certainly not going to be unrealistic about a cowboy whose pickup odometer turns over every year." She glanced away from him, her attention drawn to the lights on the tree. "I do hate to see you sell your land, though. Someday you might wish you had a familiar place to park that pickup."

"I'm familiar with a lot of parking places."

"So was my father." She sighed deeply, and the lights twinkled in her eyes like distant memories. "My family moved all the time when I was growing up. When people ask me where I'm from originally, I still get all flustered with the need to explain. I used to launch into a complete history, but I've learned to simply pick a place." Her wistful smile seemed almost apologetic. "Or just to say that I'm from here now, because I *am*. I really am."

"Permanently planted, I'd say." Slipping his arm around her shoulders seemed a natural gesture. "Was your father in the military?"

"He should have been, but that was probably one of the few things he didn't try. He never held a job very long. He got bored." His hand curved comfortingly around her shoulder as her voice drifted and became almost childlike. "And I was never in one school for more than a year. He left us one winter when my mother decided that the trailer court we were living in was going to be home." A deep breath and a quick toss of her head grounded her in the present again. "She's still there, in Florida."

"Smart woman. I wouldn't wanna leave Florida in the winter, either. Where was the ol' man headed?"

"Who knows? I haven't seen him since."

He started to drink his cider, but a word from a previous conversation nagged at him. "Would you call him a gypsy?"

"Among other things." She offered a knowing smile. "He was a rover. He was a jack-of-all-trades. He was a lovable man in his way."

"Would you say he was a dreamer?"

"Oh, yes, he was that."

He looked her in the eye. "You know, you married a dreamer, too."

"Ken was not at all like my father. He may not have been much of a businessman, but he gave his family a home." She shrugged. "I'm surprised my father didn't try cowboying. It would have suited him well, I think."

"It would suit me well, too." Suit him just fine, he thought, as he drew his arm back and cradled the warm mug in both hands. "Except that I've been stuck with a damn flock of sheep lately."

"You're not stuck with them." She bit her lower lip, and he knew damn well she was thinking up a good one. Without looking up, she said quietly, "You're free to leave anytime."

"I was just..." *Damn*, she was a tough nut to crack. "I've made up my mind to see you and the kids through the winter, and that's what I'm doin'. I'm not sellin' any land before spring, and I'm not in any hurry to hit the road." He slid her a hard glance. "Unless you want me to."

"I just don't want you to feel obligated."

"I don't. I've got nothin' better to do. Simple as that."

Simple, hell. They stared at the Christmas lights until he couldn't stand the silence anymore. It was loaded with complications.

"Can't think of any place I'd rather spend the winter than Montana, freezin' my damn—" He glanced at her, and he thought he detected the hint of a smile in her eyes. "I don't know anyone in Florida who'd put me up for the winter, do you?"

"Not a soul."

"Besides, it's Christmas." He reached for her hand. "I'm not goin' anywhere at Christmas."

"Peace to you, then, cowboy." She gave him a peck on the cheek and whispered, "And merry Christmas."

Chapter Nine

Jody didn't see Tate sitting at the kitchen table when he rode his broomstick horse into the living room on Christmas morning. Tate had already made coffee, and he was quietly biding his time as he sipped the first cup of the morning. Just waiting. He smiled to himself when he heard Jody's, "Whoa." There was a pause, and then, "Whoa! Mom! Tate! Hurry, come look!"

Tate hitched up his beltless jeans and poured coffee into a second cup, which he passed across the counter to Amy as she came around the corner carrying the baby against her shoulder. "Santa even made coffee this year?" she marveled with a sleepy smile. "What a guy."

"Special Christmas service for people who do two-o'clock feedings," Tate returned as he walked around her and touched the baby's cheek with one finger. "Happy first Christmas, little darlin'."

Eyes as big as saucers seemed to be asking him what all

the fuss was about. "This is Christmas," he explained, sliding his finger under her soft baby chin. "Are you ready for all the excitement?" She bounced her head up and down over her mother's shoulder and rewarded him with a smile.

Her brother galloped onto the kitchen scene, waving both arms wildly. "Come on, you guys! Hurry!"

Amy gave a throaty, morning laugh that sent shivers down Tate's back. "There's nothing in there that's about to run away, Jody." On second thought she cast Tate a warning glance as they headed for the living room. "Better not be anything on the hoof."

"There might be a few little tracks on the roof, but no new livestock this time around."

"Look at me, Mom!" Jody bounced astride the small saddle Santa had left under the tree. A small gasp escaped his mother's throat. "Just my size. Maybe there's a little horse for me outside!"

"Santa always takes these things one step at a time," Tate said. "I know for a fact that he never brings live animals without Mom's permission." Amy's soft sigh of relief made him grin. "But Santa knows every cowboy needs a good saddle, just in case."

A soft-body baby doll that was bigger than Karen earned a discreet test squeeze from her mother. The fancy stroller that could be converted for half a dozen uses obviously pleased Amy, too. "Santa heard that the stroller Jody used was ready for retirement," Tate said.

"Santa's insight was remarkable this year." Amy lifted the padded seat out of the stroller frame. On the floor it became a handy infant seat with handles that also served as rockers. Karen settled into it comfortably and quietly watched her first Christmas morning unfold.

No one tore through the gift wrap faster than Jody. He announced what each gift was, barely able to contain himself as he pulled it out of the box. "Cowboy hat—thanks, Tate! Cowboy pajamas—thanks, Mom! Record player—thanks, Tate! Monkey with a button nose—thanks, Mom!"

Amy opened a box and lifted out the ruffled dress he'd picked for Karen. He blushed when she held up the frilly bloomers. "I liked the bows on it." He shrugged and sipped his coffee. "The one you made for her is prettier, though."

"This one is fancier." Amy's eyes glistened. "I love it, Tate. It's just darling."

"Well, see what you think of this," he said, urging her to open another box. He'd decided that a woman who'd just put aside her maternity clothes probably needed some pretty new things in her normal size, and he'd chosen a sweater, slacks, blouse and a down-filled jacket with fur trim on the hood.

"I saved the receipts in case there's something you don't like." He reached behind the sofa and pulled out a huge fruit basket, wrapped in red cellophane and tied with a green bow. "Except this. We're eatin' this."

"That's enough for an army!" It made him feel warm inside to hear Amy laugh so readily. "I like everything, but we'll see what you guys think about the clothes when I try them on. I can't even guess what size I am now."

"I don't know if the styles are right." Tate eyed her appreciatively and gave a slow smile. "But I'll bet you two oranges and a banana that I didn't mess up on your size."

"You sound awfully confident." Her smile was coy. "Did you seek expert advice?"

"Didn't need any," he drawled. "Got a damn good eye."

She ducked under the far side of the tree and delivered a gaily wrapped box into his hands. "There aren't any receipts for yours. About all I can alter is the fit."

He couldn't believe she'd made the Western shirt herself, with its piped yoke, pearlized snaps and crisply tailored collar and cuffs. And the plush royal blue robe she'd made was monogrammed with his initials and a tiny horseshoe. Tate smiled a little self-consciously as he tried the robe on over his T-shirt and jeans. He'd never been big on clothes to wear around the house, but he could see how it might come in handy for a guy who had a house to hang around in. He thought about breaking it in with his own brand of after-shave.

"Do you like the color?"

"It's a great color." It didn't look anything like Kenny's. "We knew you were busy back there, but we had no idea *how* busy. Did we, Jody? Ma'am, you sure outdid yourself on that sewing machine."

"I'll take that as the stamp of approval." Admiring the way it looked on him, she assessed the sleeve length and adjusted the fluffy lapels, smoothing her hands over them to make sure they lay just right over his robust frame. "Does it feel comfortable in the shoulders?"

"It fits great."

"I thought you'd like a pocket," she said.

With two fingers he traced the large *H* in the middle of the monogram. "How did you know my middle name?"

"I sneaked a peek at your driver's license."

"Picked my pocket, huh?"

"You're an easy mark," she said lightly. "You left your pants in the bathroom. But your license only says 'Tate C. Harrison,' so I'm still wondering what the *C* stands for."

"Carter," he said. "After my father."

Their eyes met briefly, exchanging myriad feelings neither dared name. He wanted to kiss her, long and hard. She wanted to put her arms around him and hug him in the new robe she'd made for him.

But she smiled and patted its single pocket. "This isn't made to hold cigarettes."

"What's it for?"

"I don't know." She gave him a saucy smile. "Maybe your billfold."

"I do like to keep that handy."

Amy sat on the floor next to the baby and tested out the rocker as she surveyed the colorful torn-paper chaos. "What was in that small box, Jody? Did I miss that?"

"Didn't open it yet," Jody said as he withdrew the last box from underneath the tree. "I was saving it."

"Well, let's see what it is." Tate's eagerness shone in his eyes as he watched Jody unwrap the gift.

"The harmonica." With wide eyes and a voice full of wonder, Jody took the instrument from the box. "The silver-and-black one."

"Is that yours, Tate?" Amy asked quietly.

"I have a couple of them," he said absently. He was busy cherishing the look in the little boy's eyes. "This is Jody's favorite. Right, partner?"

"Tate's gramma gave him this," Jody reported. "It was his grampa's."

"Oh, Tate—"

"Jody has a surprise for you." He gave an encouraging nod. "Go ahead, son."

The word *son* was out before Tate knew it was coming. Jody didn't seem to notice, and neither did Amy. She was too intent on listening to Jody play "Jingle Bells" and "Frosty the Snowman." Tate figured he'd only used the word because right now it suited the way he felt. He wasn't trying to take anybody's place. But he was just as proud of the boy's accomplishment as any father could possibly be.

By afternoon the snow was falling thick and piling up fast. By nightfall the wind had picked up. When Tate went out to the barn to put the sheep to bed, he found that the snowdrifts were getting bigger. He hadn't thought it possible, but the sheep were getting stupider. The shed was three-sided, and the solid wood doors on the barn had to be left open whenever the building was used for a sheep shelter. There were no deadlier conditions for sheep than moist air in close and closed quarters. He'd been meaning to build slatted doors for the barn, but he hadn't gotten around to it yet. Now the dumb beasts were huddled in every corner of the pens outside, and the drifts were mounting around them.

Daisy and Duke seemed to realize right off the bat that this was no time to play games with the cowboy, even if his signals were a little off the mark. They took the cue to drive every last woolly creature under a roof. Tate couldn't help marveling at the dogs' work. He vowed that the pair would feast on T-bones or soup bones, whatever he could rustle up from Amy's freezer. After supper they would be bunking in his room for the night. When the chips were down, the cowboy and the sheepdogs made a remarkable team.

Amy didn't object when the dogs stumbled in the back door with him, blown in on a big wind. He could tell she'd been waiting anxiously, just as she had the night he'd trailed the sheep back from his pasture. Not that he wanted her to worry, but there was something pretty nice about being met at the door.

"Visibility must be down to zero out there," he announced as he shooed the dogs down the basement steps to keep them from shaking snow all over the kitchen. "Ol' Daisy and Duke sure did earn their—"

"Where's Jody?"

The question slammed the brakes on Tate's heart. He stared dumbly.

"He's not in the house, Tate. I was ready to brain you for taking him outside in this, but..." She kept looking behind him, as though she expected the boy to appear at his heels. "He's not anywhere in the house."

"Get me the biggest flashlight you've got." Tate jerked the back door open and whistled for the dogs.

"I'll get dressed."

"You stay with the baby. We'll find him."

It was the kind of windy whiteout that spawned Western disaster tales, and the worst kind was about the child who slipped outside unnoticed and froze to death only yards away from the house. Galvanized by fear, Tate called out as he followed the fence line toward the pens, but the dogs bounded through the drifts in a different direction. They seemed to be headed for the machine shed.

With every inch in every direction turned completely to snow, there were no directions. There was no order, no sense to anything. A mere man was almost useless. The snow stung Tate's face as he followed the two canine tails, which were about all he could see. The flashlight probably wasn't penetrating more than a few feet, and the wind had his lung power beat all to hell. He had to trust the dogs' keener senses.

But when he ran smack into the chain-link fence surrounding their kennel, he cursed the dogs roundly. "I said find *Jody* you dumb sons of—"

"Here I am!"

Daisy and Duke were already digging the snow away from the doghouse door. Jody emerged like a snowball, tumbling into Tate's arms. He'd had the good sense to dress warmly, and he'd found a snug place to take shelter. Throat clotted with a burning flood of relief, Tate hugged him close. A whistle for the dogs was the only sound he could manage.

"He's okay," Tate announced as he came through the door again, his legs considerably less steady this time. "He was in the doghouse."

"In the doghouse?" Laughing and crying at once, Amy reached out like a desperate beggar and took the boy in her arms. She sat him on the kitchen counter and peeled his ice-coated scarf away from his face. She laughed again, relieved to uncover a cherry-red nose and quivering lips. "How was it in there?"

"Cold as ice," Jody blurted out.

"I guess one trip to the doghouse is enough for tonight." She took off his hat and combed her fingers through his matted curls. "Oh, Jody, I was so scared."

"M-me, too. I was worried about Tate. Th-thought I c-could help him get done with his chores f-faster." His teeth chattered. "I couldn't f-find the b-barn."

"You didn't know how bad it was out there, did you, partner?" Tate offered as he glanced anxiously at Amy.

The looks they exchanged over Jody's head acknowledged the internal mélange of emotion that defied words. Terror was slow to give way to complete, bountiful relief. Amy didn't know whether to scold her son or simply hug him to pieces, then do the same for his rescuer. Tate didn't quite know what to do with himself, either, other than to try to shake off most of the snow in the vicinity of the scatter rug by the back door. Amy handed him Jody's jacket, and he hung it on a hook next to his.

From the back room came Karen's call for her supper. One look in Amy's eyes and Tate knew that the woman had finally reached her limit, emotionally and otherwise. She couldn't stand the idea of coming apart in front of anyone. She needed a few moments to herself.

"I'll give Jody a bath while you feed the baby."

"Are you—" She pressed her lips together tightly and cupped Jody's cheeks in her hands. "Toes hurt?" she croaked.

Jody shook his head. "I just went out...'bout three or seven minutes ag-go."

"I don't think he was out too long," Tate said. "We'll go in the bathroom and get ourselves thawed out."

Amy nodded and fled to answer the baby's call.

Jody pulled one of his boots off and dropped it on the floor. "She's real mad, ain't she?" he asked quietly.

"*Isn't* she." The correction rolled off Tate's tongue as though teaching the boy proper English was something he did every day. Where had *that* come from? he wondered as he hunkered down to pick up the boot. Jody handed him the second one. "She's not really mad. She was afraid you were lost in the snow, and I was, too. It was a mistake to go outside, Jody."

"A bad mistake," the boy agreed.

"But it's not like you were being a bad boy. The rule is that you don't go outside without asking. Right?"

"She wouldn't have let me go."

"And now you know why." He set the boots by the back door, then turned with his big hands outstretched. "Come on up here, partner." They traded bear-and-cub hugs. "Oh, that feels good. A bath will warm you up just fine. I know that from experience. First you, then me."

But it was a couple of hours before Tate got his shower, and by then it wasn't quite as much of a treat. He'd said good-night to Jody and left him to make peace with his mom, who offered to read him three stories instead of the usual one long one or two short ones. Tate had used the little shower downstairs, trying not to use up too much hot water, in case Amy still wanted some, and he'd wrapped himself up in his brand-new bathrobe. Then he'd plunked himself down on the bed with a magazine and sat there listening to the wind whistling above the window wells.

Since he'd taken up residence with Amy and the kids, he'd made a point to limit his smoking to the great outdoors, but this was one night when he figured he'd earned a shot of whiskey and a cigarette. Trouble was, even though the whiskey felt good going down and the smoke steadied him some, it made him feel lonely.

It was Christmas, and here he was sitting on a single bed in the basement of the first place that had felt like home to him in one hell of a lot of years. It was *Christmas*, and he was indulging himself in two of his favorite vices. Big thrill. Daisy and Duke were curled up as close together as cloves on a Christmas ham, and Tate felt like a man who'd been relegated to the doghouse.

His blue mood didn't make much sense. This was the spare bedroom, after all. Hired hand or guest, this was where the Beckers had always put him up. It was comfortable enough, and he had his privacy. It didn't make sense that the four white walls made him feel so damn lonesome, not with Amy and the kids right upstairs.

But he'd spent this Christmas on an emotional roller coaster. His head was spinning with a hundred joys and fears, and there was no such thing as sense. If truth be told, he would have to say he'd started losing touch with his faculties the day he'd knocked on Amy's door and offered her a hand.

Offered to *be* her hand, and for next to nothing. In lieu of flowers, just the way he'd planned, just as the obituaries always said. Hell, he'd turned himself into a living memorial. Now he was turning himself inside out, like the kid looking for one last piece of candy in his Christmas stocking.

Pathetic. He damn sure didn't need steel guitars whining in the background to put him in a melancholy mood. But, then, he was a cowboy, and all a cowboy had to do was pour himself a drink and *think* lonesome. He finished his cigarette, tossed back the last of his drink, turned the light out, took his clothes off and crawled into bed.

Damn, those sheets were cold.

Three quiet taps on his door brought him up on one elbow.

"Tate?"

Just like a woman. She could smell smoke in the middle of a blizzard, and she'd come to give him hell about it. Man, she'd sure tiptoed down the steps quieter than a feather duster.

"I'm...here."

The door opened slowly, and there she stood in her nightgown, backlit by the light in the stairwell. "The kids are in bed, and it's so quiet upstairs," she said in a small, shy voice. "I...well, I thought...the lights look pretty on the tree, and...it *is* nice and quiet." She paused, obviously waiting for him to jump at the chance to go up and sit with her. "I guess you're tired."

"Yeah," he said finally. "I'm tired." Seeing the way her shoulders sagged slightly brought him a small surge of satisfaction. Minute, actually, compared to the surge of hot current that was suddenly running strong and lusty through his body and heading straight for his lightning rod.

Amy stepped back as though she'd felt the shock. She was about to retreat just as quietly as she'd come.

He turned over on one hip. "Amy?" She paused. He could almost hear her misgivings, but he could see they weren't strong enough to take her away. She was caught in the balance.

"Amy, you gotta know that I'm down here bunkin' in

the same room with two wet dogs who are huggin' each other up somethin' fierce, and my nerves are wound tighter than a spring, and I'm thinkin' if I could just get close to you right now…''

She went to him. Drifted across the floor like an apparition and knelt beside his bed. He swung his legs over the side of the bed and sat up, pulling the sheet over his lap. ''Honey, I don't wear…any kind of pajamas.''

''I noticed you were uncomfortable in them before.''

''Amy, what I'm trying to tell you is I can't—'' With her back to the dim light, he couldn't see her face. He could smell that strawberry soap she always used, and he forgot all about wet dogs. He took her face in his hands, touching the soft contours of her cheeks with his thumbs. ''I want you so bad, I can hardly…''

''Hardly what?'' She slid her hands over his upper arms, caressing hard muscle. ''What would you be doing if you could get close to me tonight?''

''I'd be lovin' you up so good, you'd stop—'' He drew her into his arms, lifting her into his lap. ''You'd stop thinkin', stop worryin', stop—''

''I should warn you, Tate, I'm not very good at this.''

''Good at what?'' He knew damn well what, but he was going to make her say it. Here she was, cuddled against him like a kitten, and she was taking that instructive tone with him again, the one she used to protect herself. He'd always been a threat to her somehow, and, as always, she was trying to keep one foot on the floor, just in case she decided to run. Well, he wasn't about to *let* her run. Not tonight.

''I'm not the best lover.'' She drew a shaky breath. Tate wondered when and how she'd arrived at that conclusion. ''I want to be good at it, but I know I'm not.''

She just knew, and that was that. The rest he would have to figure out for himself.

"I am." He lifted her hair and traced the delicate arch of her ear with the tip of his tongue. "You want me to show you how?"

"I don't know." She shivered when he blazed a damp trail down her neck. "You probably think this is a funny conversation to be having with a woman who's somehow managed to produce two children."

"You hear me laughin'?"

"No. I appreciate that." She slipped her arms around him, shifting in his lap. "Is there room for me here? With you?"

"If we stick close together." He slid his hands up and down her back, teasing himself with the feel of soft flannel and the knowledge that there was nothing beneath it but Amy. "Is it still too soon? I know how to make love to you, Amy, but there are some things about a woman's body that are still a mystery to me."

"You've seen me at my...well, my least appealing."

She couldn't stand the idea of coming apart in front of anyone.

Oh, Amy. Her struggle with words and images touched him almost as deeply as her struggle with pain. "Why do you think of it that way? Because I was there?"

"No. I guess I shouldn't think of it at all." She pressed her face against his neck and kissed him there. "I guess I'm afraid it might bother you, and I'm afraid I'm not pretty enough or sexy enough or——"

"You trusted me then because you had to." He slid back, cradling her, entreating her as he took her into bed with him. "Trust me now because you want to. Let me decide how beautiful you are."

He peppered her face with kisses while he unbuttoned

her nightgown. "I want to kiss your breasts," he whispered, sliding down into position. "I'll be gentle."

He laved each one carefully, nuzzling, kissing, making them tighten. He could feel the passion rising in her, but he knew from the tension he felt in her body that she struggled still. Her instinct was to hold back. "I taste milk," he said.

"I'm sorry. I can't—"

"Don't keep it from me." He swirled his tongue over her peak, relishing it like an ice-cream cone. "Amy's milk. It's the only kind I like."

"Oh, Tate, you'll make me…"

"Does it feel good?"

"It makes me want…"

"Good." He kissed the valley between her breasts. She buried her fingers in his hair and held him while she gulped deep breaths, struggling to regain control.

He wasn't going to give it to her. He knew damn well it was the last thing she needed right now. She needed to *lose* control, and by damn, he was just the man. He was *just* the man. He whisked her nightgown over her head and slid down more, licking a stray drop of milk as he kissed the underside of one breast. "Do they hurt?" he asked. "Are they too full?"

"No, I just fed…but all you have to do is…"

"Shh, don't worry about that." He kissed her, sharing the sticky sweetness that clung to his lips. "Just tell me if anything hurts you. I'd cut off my arm before I'd hurt you, sweetheart, so just tell me."

"Your arm?"

Okay, so the protrusion straining against her thigh wasn't an arm, but he wasn't going to hurt her with it, either. Damn, she was teasing him. She touched her lips to his forehead, and in the dark he could feel the curve of her smile. "You don't get to laugh, either, woman." He slid his hand over her belly and kneaded gently, the way he had weeks ago. "Is it back to its normal size?" he wondered.

"I think it's—" She caught her breath as he caressed her, his hand nearly bridging the span of her pelvic cradle. "I'm flabby there," she said, but her soft groan told him that she was also aroused there. And lower. He sensed that the tension inside her was drifting lower, and he chased it with a slow hand. He didn't have to hurry. He knew where it was going, and he knew he would catch up.

He kissed her tenderly and hungrily, supplicating and demanding, and gaining wondrous kisses in return. He was gaining on her. "Relax for me, sweetheart."

Ah, her thighs were strong and stubborn, but her need was growing stronger. His tongue stroked hers, while down below he explored her springing hair, her damp folds, her soft, warm secrets. Deep in his loins he throbbed like a swollen thumb, but he knew what Amy's body had endured, and self-restraint was within his power. "Tell me when we have to stop."

With a delicate touch he stroked her until she responded urgently, pressing herself against his hand, inviting a deeper touch. "Don't stop," she pleaded. "Oh, Tate, don't stop."

He hovered over her, brushed her hair back from her face and kissed her. He was fully prepared to make the magic just for her, but he wasn't prepared for her quick gasp when he tried to slide his finger deeper. "Oh, sweetheart, I'm hurting you." He withdrew, stroking her thighs in the hope of comforting her.

"No, it's okay. I'm okay, Tate. My checkup...I'm—"

"Shh, you're not ready." He wasn't sure where it had come from, but he kissed away the dampness on her cheeks.

She groaned, running her hands up his back, digging her

blunt nails in when she reached his shoulders. "That's for me to decide," she said huskily. "It might have to hurt a little."

"I can go as slow as you want."

"How about as fast as I want?"

"That, too. But if I hurt you inside, you tell me, okay?" As he spoke, he reached into the drawer in the nightstand and withdrew a foil packet. "You don't have to be strong for me, Amy. If I can't give you pleasure now, I won't—"

"I can't get pregnant now, Tate. At least, I *probably*—"

He smiled, palming the packet as he smoothed his thumb over her forehead, hoping to banish all probably-nots. "This doesn't sound like my cautious little Black-Eyed Susan."

"I told you I wasn't very good at this." She slid one tentative hand over his hard buttock. "But I want to be. I want to be…memorable for you."

He would never forget her shy, gentle hand on his hip. "Keep touching me, and I'll remember."

She did, and he returned the favor. He caressed her until she lost the last vestige of tight control and quivered in his hand, entrusting him with a rare moment of complete vulnerability. She was eager for him now, open to him with no reservations, no limitations, save the one he willingly placed on himself for her protection. She greeted his penetration with a soft, welcoming sound.

He groaned with the pleasure of immersing himself fully in her warm passage. "Put your hands on my chest," he implored. "Feel my heart beating and touch my…" His own nipples were sensitive, as she discovered with her fingertips. "Mmm, that's good. You can talk to me, Amy."

"I don't want to sound—ooooh, Tate."

"I want you to sound 'oh, Tate.' I'll remember every soft, sweet word."

"I'm afraid to talk," she whispered as she rolled her hips to meet the thrust of his. "This feels too good."

"Ain't that the..." The truth, which was ecstasy, which was bearing down upon him faster and without regard for... "Come with me, Amy."

She drew a quick breath, coming apart, shattering deliciously in his arms. "Stay with me, Tate."

"Like this, yes," he crooned close to her ear as he drew her knees up to his waist. "Let me take you with me."

She clamped her legs around him as she arched and lifted, unfurled and set sail.

Neither could move at first, and when they stirred, it was like a dance in slow motion. They nestled together, eyes closed, hands languidly touching damp skin, ears hearing the soft whistle of cold winds and hearts content in the shelter of a loving embrace.

"You okay?" he asked finally.

She nodded, and then in a small voice asked, "You?"

"Oh, yeah."

Over in the corner, one of the dogs yawned.

"Who asked you?" Tate's chuckle rumbled deep in his chest. "I'd have to say this is the best I've been in I don't know how long."

"That's for me to say, isn't it?"

"Pardon me." He traced his finger along the top of her shoulder before he kissed it. "Was I okay?"

"Best I've ever—" she pressed her face against his neck and whispered "—*had,* and I know I shouldn't say that."

"Give it a rest, honey." He caught himself and groaned. "I didn't mean 'honey.' I meant—" he kissed her again "—for both of us to give it a rest. This whole routine between us. Just give it a rest and let ourselves be together the way we've both been dreamin' about lately." He brushed his lips across her forehead. "Haven't we? I know I have."

"And now you know I have. And I shouldn't." He groaned, and she stretched her arm around him, hugging him close. "I'm not regretting anything, except... Well, just look what happened tonight. Jody got out of the house without my knowledge. Where was my head?"

"Were you thinking about me? Were you thinkin' that the weather was bad, and I'd been outside for quite a while, freezin' my—"

"—tail off, I know. It's a nice one, too." She reached down and patted one rock-hard cheek. "Yes, I was thinking about you, hoping you were all right, wondering any one of the many things I've been wondering about you."

"Satisfy any of that curiosity tonight?"

"Satisfied...something. Not the questions, but—"

"The woman." Thank God. He'd been a little worried at first. "That's good. You're more woman than anyone I've ever known, my pretty Black-Eyed Susan, and you're a challenge and a half."

"Really," she said lightly. "I don't know who you're comparing me to, but when I said 'the best I've had—'" She huddled against him, as if she wanted him to hide her from something. "I didn't mean it the way it sounded."

"It didn't sound any *way*. I knew what you meant." He turned her in his arms, belly to belly, knees to knees. "You need a man, Amy. There's no shame in that."

"Then why does it sound so...shameful?"

"Maybe because—" he kissed the soft swell of her breast, and she sighed "—you know I'm the man you need."

She groped for a denial, but none would come when he

touched her breast as reverently as he did. Silence, followed by soft, mingled breaths and appreciative sighs, spoke of sweet accord. He claimed his point with a kiss.

Chapter Ten

As quickly as it had come, the Montana blizzard blew across the Dakota plains to become a Minnesota blizzard, leaving drifts of snow glistening in the morning sun. Jody had already forgotten the terror of blowing snow sweeping him across the yard on Christmas night. Snow pillows were friendlier, and he was ready to play in them. Amy bundled him up in his snowsuit and sent the dogs outside with him. "Stay right in the yard," she warned.

"I'm going to make a snow castle."

"I want to be able to see it from the window, okay?"

She later took her coffee into the living room, tapped on the window and waved. Jody waved back and pointed his mittened hand at the snow angel he'd just made. Then he waved again, and Amy turned to find Tate standing just behind her, waving back.

"You certainly move quietly," she said.

"Not as quietly as you do." The smile in his eyes said

they shared some new secrets. "Did you find the quarters a little cramped last night?"

She glanced back out the window. New secrets posed new problems for her this morning.

"I didn't expect you to stay," he said quietly. "Just wanted you to know I missed you."

"I don't want Jody to think..." She kept her eyes on what was going on outside the window. Her child was playing with his plastic snow-block maker, thinking only that his mother and his new cowboy idol were inside watching him. "Obviously, he knows that moms and dads sleep in the same bed. I don't want to confuse him with other...ideas."

"You're still a good mother, Amy. A good woman." Tate stepped up close behind her and laid his hands on her shoulders. "What happened last night didn't change that."

She closed her eyes, allowing the light, woodsy scent of his after-shave to fill her head with erotic images of the night before, but only briefly. It was as risky an indulgence as enjoying the feel of his strong hands. She opened her eyes wide and trained them on her busy little boy as she gripped the warm stoneware mug in both hands. "You mean, what happened last night with Jody?" she asked tightly.

"You know what I mean." He leaned close to her ear, his chin brushing the thick braid that lay over one shoulder. "I mean, what happened with me."

"I went looking for it, didn't I?" Her voice went a little hoarse. She cleared her throat, determined to be nothing more than matter-of-fact. "I asked for it."

"*It?*"

"You." She set her coffee on the lamp table and turned to look him in the eye. "I went looking for you, Tate. I wanted *you*."

It galled her that the confession clearly pleased him. He tried to take her in his arms, and she saw the confusion she caused him when she stepped out of his reach. She bolstered her resolve by telling herself that he was taking certain things for granted after just one night. He didn't understand her situation at all. Just like a man.

"I've decided to sell out, come spring."

He stared, confounded by the news. "When did you make that decision?"

"To sell out?" She shrugged, turning to the window again. "It's always been one of the options under consideration. Lately I've had to think about it more seriously. I have two small children. It's foolish for me to think I can give them the attention they need while I'm trying to run a business that demands..." She spared him a glance. "Well, you know what it demands."

"A lot of work. You need help." *You need me, Amy.*

"Hired help isn't always reliable." *But I do need you, Tate.* "If I can get through lambing, I'll make some money. My herd will be worth more with the lambs on the ground. But I need to know—" Watching Jody arrange a row of snow blocks gave her time to swallow some pride. *I need you, but how long can I count on you?* "How long can you stay, Tate?"

Now he was watching Jody, too, and his answer came without emotion. "I told you I'd get you through the winter."

"Last night complicated things, didn't it?"

"How so?" He gave a mirthless chuckle. "You think I'm gonna require more than room and board?"

"You didn't require anything." She faced him. "I was the one."

"Amy—"

"I want to pay you, Tate." She *had* to pay him. She

knew it wouldn't keep him there any longer than this whim of his lasted, but it was the only way she could make peace with the way she felt about their tenuous arrangement. He was doing her too damn many favors.

"For what?" he demanded.

"For all that you've done."

"I've done what you needed me to do."

"Yes." She folded her arms, hugging herself tightly. "More than you bargained for. More than you hired yourself out to—"

"Stop it!" he growled. "Why can't you just ask me?" He closed his hands over her shoulders and recited the words carefully, as though she might be hard of hearing. "'I need you, Tate.' Is that so hard to say?"

She lifted her chin and turned her face away. One, two deep breaths helped her fight back the tears that threatened to betray her. She'd admitted to the mistake of wanting him, but *wanting* was different. With the exception of an occasional human indulgence, she routinely did without many of the things she wanted. Wanting could be kept under control, but needs had to be met. The children's needs, her own needs—it was up to Amy to provide for those. It always had been.

"Ken left some good horses," she told Tate in her most controlled, informative tone. "All registered stock, but they're not saddle-broke. I know horse prices aren't great right now, but I want you to take your pick. For every month that you've been here, every month that you stay, I want you to have one of those horses."

"What kind of services are you trying to pay me for, Amy?"

She pressed her lips together firmly. She wouldn't let his anger scare her. She could feel the power in the hands that gripped her shoulders, but she could also feel his restraint.

He couldn't intimidate her. No man could. He could leave today if he wanted to, and she would get along fine without him.

"I'll stay. I told you that." He released her, his arms dropping heavily to his sides. "I'll stay and do what needs doing. Herd your sheep, deliver your baby, have a talk with your son—whatever."

She stared, startled by the knowledge that deep down she believed in his promise.

"Oh, yeah, and I can also take you to bed and give you the best damn lovin' you've ever had." He quirked a cocky smile. "Jack-of-all-trades, that's me. All that for a few broom tails?"

She affected a careless shrug. "It's all I can come up with right now."

"Well, I ain't that cheap, lady. I'm gonna cost you dearly."

"The wages of sin, I suppose."

"What sin? You mean what I got last night? Was that supposed to be my wages and your sin?" He took advantage of the momentary paralysis of her tongue. "Or was it the other way around? Damn, you've got me confused."

"I don't want to take advantage of you," she said tightly.

"Likewise," he assured her with a smug grin. "So I'm not about to take my wages out in trade. You'll have to come up with something better."

"I wasn't *offering* to pay for your..." She was tempted to put a bag over that grin. "I need your help, Tate," she said, forcing an even tone, "and I'm not suggesting any- thing—" *Stop that aggravating nodding.* "—unseemly. I'm only trying to—"

"That's a start. 'I need your *help*, Tate.'" He was on his way out of the room, wagging his finger and being a damn smart aleck as he went. "I like the sound of that. That's gettin' there."

"Where are you going?"

"The baby's cryin'." He paused. At first it was quiet, but then came the muffled squall. Tate's tone mimicked her at her most indulgently instructive. "I'm going to pick her up. And if I had the equipment," he said, hands on his T-shirt-clad chest, "I'd feed her, too. But even a jack-of-all-trades has his limits."

He knew she didn't want to need him. Needing his *help* was difficult enough for Amy, but needing *him*—needing Tate Harrison—was like having the flu. She figured she would get over it. And maybe she would. If she did, hell, he'd never really pictured himself being tied down, especially not to a bunch of sheep and a piece of ground just outside Overo, Montana, and halfway to nowhere.

The Christmas blizzard gave way to a January thaw, and Tate used the respite to his advantage. He built the slatted barn door he'd mentally devised before Amy had declared her intention to sell out. His design allowed for a choice of doors. Amy was impressed. She also liked his wall-mounted hayracks and grain feeders, which he modestly claimed were "real easy to knock together." She was less excited when he rigged up a corral, using portable steel fence panels, and began breaking horses.

He figured he could have at least four or five green-broke by spring thaw. He didn't have time to make good saddle horses out of them, but some of them had potential. He enjoyed lecturing Jody on the subject, pointing out each animal's strengths and weaknesses, from conformation to temperament. He predicted which ones would really be worth something when Amy decided to sell them and lamented the fact that they would be worth even more if he had more time to work with them. The summer, maybe.

Given the chance, Jody would make a good horseman someday, if Amy would ever ease up on the rules. He had to stay off the fence, stay in the pickup, stay away from the horses when Tate wasn't around, stay away from the hooves, stay away from the teeth, and on and on. To her credit, Amy never said, "Your dad was killed by a horse," but her distress was apparent every time she came out to the corral when Tate was working the horses. And it annoyed the hell out of him every time she called Jody into the house because he'd been "bothering Tate long enough."

"Nobody in this house bothers me except you," he told her privately when she came out to the corral one day. "And you bother me plenty."

"Nobody's got you tied to the hitching post, cowboy. You can mosey on anytime."

"Cute." He watched the boy and his trusty stick-horse disappear into the toolshed, where he'd been sent to fetch a leather punch. "Are you trying to keep Jody away from me?"

"Of course not. He loves you like a brother."

"Brother?" He felt slighted, and feeling slighted made him feel mean. He gave her a mean-spirited smile. "What's the matter with *uncle?* You don't like that word?"

"Big brothers eventually move on, and they never realize how much little brothers miss them."

"Yeah, well, Kenny was like a brother to me, so the analogy doesn't quite work."

Jody appeared in the doorway of the toolshed. He waved the leather punch in the air, and Tate nodded his approval.

"You're right about one thing, though," Tate confided absently. He was pleased to see that Jody wasn't forgetting to close the door, and that he was carrying the tool back at a sedate walk, exactly as instructed. "The boy loves me. Unconditionally, no questions asked. And I love him right back the same way." He adjusted his hat as he looked Amy in the eye. "Believe it or not, I am capable of that. I don't care whose kid he is, I love him like my own."

She believed him. Now that she knew he was capable of giving more of himself than she'd ever thought possible, her heart ached all the more with the need to ask for another little piece of him for herself. But she was too proud. He'd been spending more of his evenings in town lately, which she regarded as a warm-up activity for a man with itchy feet. She tried not to lie awake and listen for the sound of his pickup. When she heard it, she tried not to notice what numbers were illuminated on her bedside clock. And when she didn't hear it, she tried not to imagine what or who might be keeping him out so late.

The month of February was torn off the Overo Farm and Ranch Co-Op calendar, and March came in with a lamb.

"We've got a baby comin'," Tate announced from the back door as he pulled off his work gloves.

"Already?" Amy pulled the plug on the dishwater and reached for a hen-and-chick print towel. "You're sure?"

"I suspect the signs are about the same for a ewe as they are for a cow or a mare." Tate tipped his hat back and grinned. "Human females like to keep you guessin', but you take their clothes off, the signs are probably pretty much the same."

"That's true. That's absolutely true." From the look in his eye, she could have sworn he was just as excited about the prospect of lambing as she was. Maybe he was the wolf at her door. "Your lunch is ready."

Tate's news seemed to wake up the house. Jody turned

off the Saturday-morning cartoons, and Karen called from her crib. But Amy had to hurry out to the barn and see for herself what was going on. She'd counted the days and figured on almost another week before lambing would start. Now she would have to count on Tate, who was helping himself to a cup of coffee, and Jody, who was slurping up a bowl of cereal. They would have to spell her from a few duties while she did the job she felt called to do.

"You'll change your mind about sheep when you see the lambs, Tate. They're just as cute as—" She put Karen in his arms and smiled when the baby grabbed his chin. "Well, not as cute as *human* babies, but cuter than calves. I forgot to tell you about the lambing pens."

"I found them," he said. "I've already got a couple set up, and as soon as I have a cup of coffee..." He smiled down at Karen, who was trying to examine his teeth. "A cup of coffee and a couple of little baby fingers..."

"Lambing is my job."

With a glance he questioned her good sense.

"Your hands are too big, Tate." To emphasize the contrast, she put her hand over the back of his just as Karen laid claim to his thumb.

"Hey, that looks like Papa Bear, Mama Bear and Baby Bear," Jody managed to announce despite a mouth full of milk.

The look in Tate's eyes softened as one dilemma crowded out another. Amy nodded, smiling wistfully. "Mine are just the right size, you see. I have to help my mamas get their babies born. That much I owe them."

Tate had been party to many a calving, but delivering Karen had changed his outlook on the miracle of birth. Amy was right about the lambs. Those little wobbly-legged woollies were irresistible. Her skill and patience as a midwife were remarkable. Tate was content to observe the process while he tended the children. Some of the ewes required Amy's help in delivery, which often meant slipping a deft hand into the birth canal to assist a lamb in making its debut.

Most of the ewes produced twins, and one even had healthy triplets. Amy determined that the runt of the three would have to be bottle-fed. The death of three young ewes left orphans, two of which were successfully "grafted" on to ewes that had lost their lambs. Amy wrapped the pelts of the dead lambs around the orphans so that the adoptive mothers would accept them as their own. She graciously accepted Tate's offer to do the skinning.

That left two lambs to become "bottle babies," which pleased Jody immensely. Amy confided that raising orphans on the bottle was never profitable, and most sheep men didn't bother. "Sheep *women*," she said, "are different. When we sell the herd, we'll be keeping those bottle babies."

They were different, all right, Tate thought. She tried to talk offhandedly about selling her sheep, and she probably could have fooled almost anybody else. But Tate saw the pain in her eyes. Once lambing was over, she would use up what feed she had, and then she would put the herd on the market. Before the fields were lush with grass, she would sell out. She wouldn't have to worry about predators this year, she declared with artificial cheer. And shearing would be someone else's problem.

Leaving Amy and the kids would be Tate's problem. The more she mused about making her own preparations, the less he had to say about anything at all. The ground had thawed, and the first pale blooms of camas and sego lilies were beginning to dot the hillsides among the first green spikes of new grass. If he were planning to graze the livestock, he would take note of the poisonous camas and keep the animals away from them. He would be looking for coyotes, and he would be thinking about replacing a couple of sections of fence with the lamb creeps he'd been building. He'd modeled them after a picture he'd found in one of Amy's sheep-raising books. Not that he'd *read* it; he'd just sort of flipped through the pages. And not that he was thinking seriously about *any* of this stuff. A grazing plan had just sort of crossed his mind.

When he ran into Marianne and Patsy at the bar one night, he quietly took exception to a comment Marianne made about his "cozy little arrangement with Amy." But he wasn't about to tell the women that Amy was talking about selling out. Marianne would have been on the phone with her lawyer in a New York minute, trying to find out how soon she could get her damn core samples taken. Not that he cared about a few holes punched in the pasture, but Marianne's claim that there was money lurking below ground didn't impress him much, either. If they found anything, it was likely to be coal. And he had to agree with Amy about strip mining. It wasn't a pretty sight.

Faced with Amy's quandary, he'd forgotten all about his own plans to sell his land. When Marianne brought that issue up, he paid for his drink and called it a night. He wasn't sure why he was grinding his back teeth as he left the bar. Probably had something to do with the smell of Patsy's perfume.

It was almost midnight, but the kitchen light was still on, and Amy was still up. She was sitting at the table paging through a magazine, a steaming cup of tea close at hand. If he didn't know any better, he would think she wasn't planning to be up at her usual predawn hour.

"Waiting up for me?" He was trying for a touch of

sarcasm, but it just wasn't there. He liked the idea too damn much to make light of it.

"The baby's been fussy."

"Seems pretty quiet to me." Little Karen had been sleeping through the night for weeks now.

"Would you like some coffee?"

"No, thanks. I'm sober enough." He tossed his denim jacket over a hook, thinking that if he couldn't work up any sarcasm, maybe he could bait her just a little. "You've got no business waiting up for me, Amy. What I do is my business."

"I wasn't waiting up for you. But you're early."

"Compared to what?" He pulled out the chair across from her, spun it around and straddled it, folding his arms over the back. "Compared to last week? Last month?" She glanced up from her magazine. "Compared to when Kenny used to come home?"

"Kenny always came home." She gave him a pointed look—though what her point was, he wasn't sure—then turned a page and found something that seemed to interest her more than he did. She tore into a corner of the page as she rattled on. "Ken had his faults and his weaknesses, but he gave us a home, and he was part of it. Always."

"Good for him." She glanced up, and he nodded. "I mean that. He inherited this place. Big deal. The truth is, *you* were good for *him*. How good was *he,* Amy?" Her eyes betrayed nothing as she carefully laid the coupon aside. "How good was he for *you?*" Tate demanded quietly.

"I don't see how his best friend could ask a question like that." She turned another page. "He gave me two children."

"*I* was here the night Karen was born," Tate reminded her. Her hand went still, the page stalled at an angle. "I

was with you that night. She came—'' Amy looked into
his eyes as he gestured poignantly ''—from your body into
my hands. I've never felt so...''

''So...what?'' she asked, as mesmerized by the memory
as he was.

''Yeah, so what.'' He stood abruptly and jammed his
hands into his front pockets, bursting the bubble with a
shrug. ''I shouldn't have said 'big deal.' I didn't mean to
knock Kenny or anything the two of you...had. Okay?''

''I think you misunderstood, Tate. I meant...'' But he
was done. He was getting his jacket back off the hook.
''Where are you going?'' she asked.

Back to the Jackalope, he should have said, but her question had sounded sufficiently meek to warrant an honest
response. ''Out to the barn.'' Downstairs first, for something to keep him warm. Maybe blankets would be enough.
''I need to take care of some things before I turn in.''

She should just leave him alone, she told herself as she
headed across the yard. He hadn't been out there very long,
and he was probably having a cigarette. It was a clear, crisp
night. Nice night to be outside. She visited Daisy and Duke
in their kennel, then told herself to go back into the house.
But herself wasn't listening very well. The light was still
on in the barn. She pushed the side door open.

''Tate?''

''Up here.'' She saw his black cowboy hat first, then his
face, then his denim collar turned up to his jawline. He
peered down from the loft. ''What's up? Kids okay?''

''They're fine. They're sound asleep.'' As she closed the
door behind her, she noticed a pair of green feline eyes
peeking down from the loft, too. ''What are you doing?''

''I had a crazy yen to sleep out here tonight.''

''In the barn?''

"Ol' Cinnamon Toast has been up here cleaning out the mice, and I just mucked out the pens today. Put down fresh straw." He flipped open a green wool blanket. "It's aboveground, which is a real plus. I feel like campin' out tonight." The hat disappeared, and there was some rustling of hay. "Could you hit the light on your way out?"

When the light went out, it was pitch-dark for a moment, but then her eyes adjusted to the dimmer light emitted through the clerestory windows directly across from the loft. The moonlight would be nice, she thought. It would flood across his makeshift bed like stardust. She climbed the steps quietly, although she knew he heard her coming.

"Tate? You'll get cold out here."

"If I do, I know where the house is."

She climbed over the top of the ladder and stood at the foot of the pallet he'd made. He'd pulled the blanket up to his chest, pillowed his neck in his hands and covered his face with his cowboy hat. His boots stuck out at the end of the blanket. He looked incredibly long. And he was ignoring her.

Amy cleared her throat. "As long as you've declared a truce, maybe we could..."

"Have ourselves a roll in the hay?"

"Have a talk about...the best way to go about selling the livestock." She knelt on the corner of the pallet. "I'll need your help, but I don't want you to think you have to—"

"I don't think I *have* to. Go back to the house, Amy. Give me some peace."

"It's too cold out here," she insisted. "I won't have you sleeping in the barn."

"What're you gonna do about it?"

"Well..." Good question. "I'm just going to sit here." He shoved his hat back as he braced himself on his elbows and gave her a cool stare. "You can't control me the way you did Kenny. That's what scares you about me, isn't it?"

"Control? I couldn't control Ken. He puttered around with his horses and talked about all the things he was going to do around here, but I couldn't get him to make a *real* decision about anything important to—" her hands flopped against her knees in frustration "—to save his life."

"Kenny was my friend. He was a good-hearted guy, and we had some good times together. But he never took charge of anything." He sat up, leaned across his own knees and reached for her hand. "A woman wants a man to take charge once in a while, doesn't she?"

"Yes, but not—"

"Not to push her around." He tugged on her hand, cautiously reeling her into his bed. "Not to take her security away, but just to say, 'Lean on me for a while.'"

"That would be nice."

"Damn right." He lifted the edge of the top blanket and drew her underneath it. "So I'm gonna show you just how a man takes charge."

There was no more talk of selling anything. There was very little talk at all, and when they spoke, it was only of what was happening between them at the moment. They didn't undress completely. Instead they delighted in undoing buttons, one at a time, and finding places that needed kissing. Each piece of clothing became an envelope to be expertly unsealed, the contents to be secretly investigated without being removed. They were like first lovers, exploring one another, sharing secrets in a secret place. They teased one another about wanting to get into each other's pants, tortured each other by dragging zippers down and touching warm skin with cool hands. Inevitably the torture became exquisitely sensuous as hands and lips sought the deeper secrets nestled in the wedge-shaped envelopes of open zippers.

He had not hoped to love her this way again. Reckless as he was, he had never been the right man, but he would do for now. And for now, he would do well.

She had not expected to be held and touched this way again. Sensible as she was, she always sought moderation, but not tonight. Tonight she abandoned caution and demanded no compromise. Tonight his way was better.

Tonight she whispered love words while she suckled him. Tonight she made him moan as relentlessly as he did her. They kissed and touched with feverish abandon. He called her *honey,* because, he said, she tasted like honey. "And I've never said that to anyone before."

He was, she told him, a man for all seasons and all times of the day, but especially beautiful in the moonlight. Her hands cherished his every contour. "Like polished marble all over, all over, all over."

"We're going to shoot the moon," he promised as he eased himself inside her. It took some ardent stroking, some rhythmic pumping and some zealous writhing, but they did. They not only shot the moon, they made a whole new crater.

"Don't go yet," he said when she'd recovered strength enough to move. "Stay with me a little longer."

"We should go inside. We could..." She wanted to take him to her bed, but Jody might find him there. His room was right across the hall. Amy's good judgment put her wanting in its place.

And Tate didn't need any diagrams. "We'd have to get dressed," he lamented as he cradled her against his chest. "I'd have to fasten this." He couldn't locate a bra cup without brushing the back of his hand across her nipple.

"And then I couldn't do this anymore." He smiled when he'd coaxed her nipple into a bead.

"You're a tricky one, Tate Harrison," she whispered contentedly.

He tongued her nipple gently, just one more time. Just for good measure. "How long will you nurse Karen?"

She answered with a soft groan.

He tightened his arms around her hips, holding her to him as he pressed his face between her breasts. "Who gets weaned first, her or me?"

Like his lovemaking, his teasing hurt sometimes, but she could hide the hurt as long as he couldn't see her face. She tunneled her fingers into his hair and held him, his ear a scant inch from her thrumming heart. "Whoever grows up first, I guess."

Chapter Eleven

He woke up shivering in his blankets, and Amy was gone. Responsible Amy. She had children to look after—thank God she was responsible. He would have kept her up in that loft, rolling in his arms, halfway into summer. A loft was much better than a pumpkin shell, not that he owned either one. But he had a pickup, a passbook savings account and a piece of Montana ground. He was worth *something*, anyway. If the woman couldn't see that, it was time to point it out to her. The sun would be up soon. He decided that sunrise would be a damn good time.

He showered and shaved, and while he was getting himself dressed in the shirt she'd made for him, he could hear activity overhead. Karen was making those cute little baby noises. She was just naturally an early bird, but it was unusual for Jody to be clomping around the kitchen in his prized cowboy boots at this hour.

They were all outside by the time he got upstairs. He

could see them through the front window, Karen all bundled up in her stroller and Jody standing out there hipshot like a cool cowhand, leaning on his broomstick horse as if it were the gatepost on the approach to a ten-thousand-acre spread. Amy was dragging something out of the back of her pickup, which she'd backed up to the edge of the yard. Early-morning light brightened the sky all around them. The lavender hills sloped in silhouette against the pale yellow dawn.

Tate grabbed his hat and headed out the back, slamming the storm door shut behind him. Amy looked up and smiled. ''We were just about to go looking for you. We're planting Karen's tree.''

''You're gonna plant a tree just before you move out?''

''Whether we're moving or not, these things have to be done in their season, and it's the season for tree planting.'' She hooked a stray lock of hair behind her ear and pointed across the yard. ''Jody's tree is that paper birch. See how nice and tall it's growing?''

Jody trotted across the yard to reacquaint himself with his birch tree. ''It's budding, too,'' he boasted.

''We thought Karen's should be a Christmas tree.'' Tate took over the job of unloading the young nursery-raised blue spruce from the back of the pickup. ''I don't want to block the view from the window, though,'' Amy mused as she surveyed the yard.

She wore an old yellow sweatshirt and faded blue jeans, and she looked as fresh and naturally pretty as the morning sky. She caught him staring at her, though, so he had to tear his eyes away and give some serious consideration to the problem at hand.

''I've been thinkin' we needed a windbreak over there by your garden.'' He quirked her a questioning brow, and she nodded. He carried the tree and pushed the stroller.

Jody and Outlaw, Jr., galloped along behind, while Amy donned her gardening gloves and brought up the rear. She carried the shovel.

Jody cut a wide circle around his sister's stroller. "Remember when we went out and got the Christmas tree, Tate?"

"I remember." Along with Christmas trees past, he thought. Trees had a way of making nice memories. He set the tree down close to where he wanted to see it take root, then he turned, eyeing the shovel. "You gonna let me do the digging on this project?"

"If you want to."

He took the shovel from Amy's hands and stabbed the ground with its point. He could feel her watching him with those earth-mother eyes of hers. When she was satisfied that he could handle the job, she dashed into the house and came back with a bucket of water and a plastic sack.

"Does that look big enough?" He knew it was plenty big, but he wanted to make sure she was satisfied with his work. This was one morning he wasn't giving her anything to complain about.

"It looks perfect." She knelt beside the tree and started tapping the pot to loosen the roots.

"Here, let me help." Tate hunkered down beside her and took the plastic pot in his big hands, breaking it down the side. Then he took out his jackknife. "The tool-of-all-trades for the jack-of-all-trades." He was really going to impress her now. He'd had a seasonal job with the Forest Service years ago. He knew that a competent planter of trees always scored the root ball.

The sun appeared in a crotch in the foothills, spilling fruit-basket colors across the sky as Tate lifted Karen from the stroller. They all gathered around Tate's hole in the earth and watched Amy empty the contents of the plastic zipper bag. There was nothing unbeautiful about the blood from Amy's body, the tissue that had nourished her unborn baby. Tate held the tree steady with one hand. With the other he raked black loam into the hole. Other fingers plunged to his aid—Amy's slender ones, Jody's short ones and Karen's chubby ones. They pounded the first layer down, added water, and dug in again.

"Who's going to tend it?" Tate asked after the job was done.

"God takes care of the trees," Jody reported confidently. "Doesn't He, Mom?"

"The trees and the sparrows." Amy squinted against the sun's glare as she looked up at Tate. "Who's tending yours?" He looked at her questioningly. "The ones along the driveway that used to lead to your old house. There's a huge clump of daylilies that blooms there every summer. Did your mother plant those?"

"Probably." He remembered his mother's daylilies and her hollyhocks. He'd had to weed them every damn spring when she was alive. "They're still there?"

"Like Jody said, God takes care of them." She shifted Karen from one hip to the other and started toward the house. "Besides, you can't even get rid of daylilies with an eight-bottom plow."

Jody fed his orphan lambs with a huge plastic baby bottle. Amy and Tate sat side by side on the back step and watched them romp around the yard together. From their backyard kennel, Daisy and Duke let it be known that they were ready to romp, too. The lambs ignored the barking. They listened only to Jody, the voice of the milk supply.

"When Jody goes to school, he'll have two lambs on his tail," Tate said with a bemused smile. "Think that'll make the children laugh and play?"

Amy laughed as she bounced Karen on her knees.

"You've been eavesdropping on the bedtime reading again."

"Karen and me both, right, sweetie?" He chucked the baby under her chin. "One night last week I walked the floor with her a little bit, and Jody's door was open just a crack. We didn't wanna interrupt, but we heard something about little lambs, and we were just curious."

"Tate, about last night..."

"You let me say something about last night, okay?" He detected an unusual timidity in the look she slid him. "Short and sweet."

"Yes," she said quietly. "Short, but very, very sweet."

He whispered in her ear, "I kept it up as long as I could, boss lady," and she closed her eyes and smiled. "I meant that my say will be short and sweet. *Maybe*." She glanced up, and he chuckled. "Why is it we're always explaining what we meant after we say what we say?"

"To each other?" He nodded. She shrugged. "Maybe we don't speak the same language."

"We did last night," he recalled. The blush in her cheeks was so pretty, it stung his eyes. He had to look at something else while he said his piece. He chose Jody, tumbling in the new grass with a leggy lamb.

"I've been doin' a lot of thinking lately," Tate began cautiously. "You know, you can keep horses and sheep together real easy. They complement each other well, the way they graze. Sheep will eat plants that horses don't like, and sheep dung is good fertilizer for horse pasture. They seem like opposites, but each improves the pasture for the other."

"You have to separate them at lambing time," Amy pointed out quietly.

"So you make a few allowances." He turned to her. "You really plannin' to sell this place?"

"You really planning to sell yours?" He was ready to tell her that he wasn't sure, but she had a piece she had to say, too. "If you'd stop running long enough, you'd realize how useless all this running is. You were born to this land, Tate, this life, and it still shows, no matter how far you've tried to put it behind you."

"You wanted something different from the life you grew up with," he reminded her. "So do I. I want—"

"What?"

He smiled. "Listen to me, now. I'm trying to draw you this harmony-between-sheep-and-horses comparison."

"And I want you to tell me straight-out," she insisted. "What are you looking for, Tate?"

"I want a home and family. I want to feel like I belong, like I'm wanted and needed." He looked across the yard at Jody again. "Like somebody believes in me, trusts me. I screwed up bad once, but—"

"You were just a boy."

"I didn't know that. I thought I was supposed to be a man." He paused for a moment, thinking about that ghost and a few others. Here was an opening for him to try to put their ghosts to rest. "Kenny thought it was still okay for him to be a boy, even after he was married. He let you carry most of the load." He turned to her. "I wouldn't do that, Amy. I'm just as strong-willed as you are. We'd put it all together—what's mine with what's yours. But you'd have to be willing to share decisions with me, fifty-fifty."

She was doing her damnedest to bank up the coals on a warm smile. "Would you be wanting a few cows, too, cowboy?"

"I might. But if I can live with sheep—"

"I think I could live with cows if I had a real cowboy around," she said, too quickly, too eagerly. It was as though she'd caught herself on the verge of being happy, and it scared her, made her feel guilty. The implicit contrast was like a bucket of cold water dumped between them.

Dredging up a somber note, she glanced away. "I did love Ken."

"I know." Tate slipped his arm around her. "He was my best friend. Always." *Even when I wanted his girl for my own. Even when I wanted his wife. Even when I wanted to punch him in the face because he didn't know any better than to take the woman I wanted for granted.* "I loved him, too, Amy, but that doesn't have to come between us. He loved us. And we both did right by him."

"What you said about why we haven't always gotten along... Why I might have been...afraid of you in a way." She looked up at him again. "You might have a point."

"I might have a point." He claimed the baby, who shrieked with delight as he lifted her toward the sky in a joyful toast. "Ha-ha, I might have a *point!*"

"There's a chance we could become great compromisers," Amy said tentatively.

"We'd probably butt heads once in a while, but we'd take care of each other, too. You'd lean on me, and I'd lean on you, sort of like a jackleg fence." He was riding high now, with a pretty girl tucked under each arm. "And the kids, they'd be like the cross pieces, you know? There's a lot I could teach Jody."

"You've been like a father to him these last few months."

"I thought it was *brother.*"

"Father," she amended belatedly. "And there aren't too many fathers who can say they've actually delivered their daughters into the world."

He bounced Karen in his arm. "You remember that night, little darlin'? You popped your head into the world, and this was the first face to greet you." She patted his smooth-shaven cheek with a chubby hand. "It was a little bristly that night, as I recall."

"She was glad you were there." Amy put her arm around his waist and smiled up at him. "So was her mom."

"I know you needed me that night," he said. "How about now? Not just my help, Amy. *Me*." He needed to hear her say it. "It's not a weakness to need someone," he professed, as much for his own benefit as for hers. And suddenly, for better or for worse, he didn't mind saying, "I need you."

"For what?"

"For a companion," he offered. She wasn't buying yet. "For my partner, how's that?" Better, he could tell. "For my lover," he growled in her ear. "How's that?"

"It would be a lovely thought." She challenged him with a look. "If you loved me."

"I don't remember when I didn't love you."

Now she smiled, and the light in her silk chocolate eyes was like sunrise at sea.

"And I always will, Amy. How's *that*?"

"Is it...really true?"

"You know it's true."

She did. She'd known it for some time. And she'd known there would be heartache if he left her and risks if he stayed.

"I think my father loved my mother, too, in his own way. And we loved him, but..." Oh, God, could she keep a man like Tate happy? If she gave him a place in her heart and her home, would he find it too confining for his long, tall cowboy form and being?

She sighed. "I can be good in all the roles you named, but I'm not a good gypsy. You'd have to—"

"Settle down, I know. I'm feelin' pretty settled. I've

been a pretty good hired hand, haven't I?'' She nodded slowly. ''Fire me.''

''What?''

''I want to be your husband. I want to be a father to your children.'' He searched the depths of her eyes. ''If you think you could love me.''

''I've been afraid to love you, but I've been loving you anyway. It couldn't be helped.'' She lowered her head and rubbed her cheek against his shoulder. His heart swelled when she finally confessed, ''I need you, Tate. If you ever left me now...''

''I would die inside.'' She lifted her chin, then lifted her eyes to his. He smiled. ''I've been runnin' in circles, endin' up back home every time.''

He dipped his head, and their lips met for a long slow kiss. Karen smacked his cheek once, but it didn't faze him. Not when he heard the catch in Amy's breath over his fancy tongue stroking.

''Oh, mush,'' said a voice at his knee.

Tate groaned. He opened his eyes and reluctantly broke the kiss. Amy giggled as he turned a sheepish glance Jody's way. ''Mush?''

''You guys gotta get married if you're gonna be kissin' like that.''

''You think we'd better?'' Tate asked expectantly. Jody wrinkled his nose. ''Do I have your permission to marry your mom, partner?'' Tate's nod summoned Jody for an exchange between cohorts. The boy leaned in closer. ''Say yes, and I'll see what I can do about a horse to go with that saddle.''

Jody's pogo-stick legs sprang into action. ''Yes! Whoa, can you marry her today?''

''Jody!'' Amy complained buoyantly. ''You probably

could have bid him up. I'm certainly worth more than one horse.''

"I only want one." He grabbed Tate's knee, anchoring himself for one quick, anxious inquiry. "Will you be my dad then?''

"I will if your mom stops playing hard to get and says yes.''

"Can we still be partners?''

"We can always be partners." He looked into the face of the only woman he'd ever petitioned for such an agreement. "You wanna be partners, Amy?''

"Kiss her again, Tate! She'll say yes if you kiss her again.''

So he did kiss her. And she did say, "Yes.''

* * * * *

A Note from Mary Lynn Baxter

Dear Reader,

This was a fun book to write because it's another of my books that is set in my beloved Texas. In fact, *Added Delight* takes place only twenty miles from the town where I was born and raised.

In addition to the setting, I enjoyed venturing into the world of children, choosing to take on five-year-old twins who are not only precocious and mischievous, but who are determined to play matchmaker to two hardheaded adults not interested in ties that bind.

Widower Joshua Malone doesn't have time for another woman in his life, not with his work and his children. Melissa Banning doesn't have time for a cynical man set in his ways.

But when Melissa goes to work for Joshua, she takes over not only his home, but his heart as well, but only after a few sparks fly, to say the least.

Mary Lynn Baxter

One

"You didn't!"

"I did."

"Naw, I don't believe you. There's no way you just waltzed into the director of nurses' office and said you were through."

While sitting cross-legged in the middle of Laurie's bed, Melissa Banning eyed her friend with a troubled expression on her face. "Well, I didn't say I was through, not in the true sense of the word. What I said was that I'd had it, that I needed a break or..."

"Or what?" Laurie asked, looking as if she still couldn't believe what she was hearing.

Melissa didn't mince any words. "Burn out completely."

"I'm still having trouble believing that your job has gotten to you that much, my friend." With bold gray eyes, Laurie actively searched Melissa's face. "Why, you're a born nurse if there ever was one. Nursing is all you've thought about, talked about for as long as I can remember.'' When Melissa didn't respond, she went on, ''And this past year, in light of the tragedy, I shudder to think what you would've done without it. It's been your salvation.''

What Laurie said was true. A year and a half ago Melissa's parents and younger brother had been killed in a boating accident. For months Melissa had been inconsolable. But then she had regrouped, channeling her grief into something positive. Her work as a registered nurse had taken on new meaning. Nursing suddenly had become her reason for living and had remained so until recently.

Under Laurie's close scrutiny, Melissa bowed her head and shut her eyelids, squeezing back the tears that were threatening. ''You're exactly right,'' she said struggling to get a grip on her emotions.

''So why chuck it all now?'' Laurie stood to her full five feet nine inches and wandered to the window, her movements jerky.

For a moment Melissa forgot her troubles, mesmerized by the way the sunlight pooled through the miniblinds and settled on Laurie's mane of straight black hair. It was dazzling in its effect. But then everything about Laurie was dazzling, especially her personality. Though not beautiful, not even pretty, she more than made up for that when she smiled—and she smiled a lot. At this point in her life Melissa didn't know what she would have done without her friendship and support.

Though it had been a month since she had walked out of the hospital, Melissa had only this morning called Laurie at her public-relations firm in Nacogdoches and asked if she could visit her for a few days. Without requiring any explanations, Laurie had encouraged her to come right away.

Now, as Melissa watched her stuff her hands into the side pockets of her slacks, she saw the concern mirrored on her friend's face. "You think I'm crazy, don't you?" It was more a statement than a question.

Laurie shook her head. "No, not crazy. Confused is probably a better word. It's just not like you to do anything rash. You're the most organized, rational person I know."

Melissa shifted her position on the bed, leaning heavily against the pillow at her back. "Not anymore. The pressure finally got to me."

"Trust me, I'm not criticizing," Laurie said hastily. "There's no way I could be a nurse. And even if I could, the intensive care unit would be too much to handle." Laurie paused with an outward shiver. "I'm a people person all right, but I'd as soon not be around them when they're ill. Just the thought of sticking anyone with a needle makes me sick to my stomach."

Melissa smiled at that, but the smile didn't reach her eyes. "You always were a chicken."

"Yeah, and proud of it, too," Laurie said, grinning back.

"You're hopeless." This time Melissa's smile was genuine. But then it disappeared as quickly as it appeared. "Speaking of hopeless, I guess that about sums me up. But I just couldn't take it anymore, Laurie. At twenty-eight, I'm suddenly finding myself in a full-fledged mid-life crisis."

Laurie rolled her eyes. "You were facing a crisis all right, but hardly a mid-life one."

"You know what I mean."

"What was it that really got to you?" Laurie's eyes were sympathetic.

Melissa raised an unsteady hand to her forehead. "It wasn't any one thing. I guess it's the combination of the fallout from my family's death, the horrendous working hours and the stress."

"Once you were in charge of the unit, they tended to dump everything on you, right?"

"Let's just say I was the one who bore the brunt of the work, especially in light of the nursing shortage."

Laurie pushed away from the wall where she had been leaning. "I'm not surprised. The newspapers are full of ads for both R.N.s and L.V.N.s." She paused, then moved toward the bedroom door. "I don't know about you," she added, changing the subject, "but I'm dying of thirst. You want a Coke or glass of iced tea?"

Melissa's face relaxed into a smile. "Tea sounds good."

"Sounds good to me, too. Nowhere but east Texas can you drink iced tea all year long and enjoy it." She frowned suddenly. "I guess you think I'm a poor hostess for not offering you anything sooner."

Melissa waved her hand. "I thought nothing of the sort. Anyway, you've been too busy letting me cry on your shoulder to think of anything else."

"You'd do the same for me," Laurie quipped before walking across the threshold.

Minutes later she returned with two glasses filled to the brim with tea, a lemon wedge in each.

They sipped for a moment in silence. Then Laurie asked, "How much did they give you?"

Melissa pushed a wisp of dark hair off her cheek and frowned. "How much what?"

"Time," Laurie clarified. "How much time?"

Melissa blinked. "Oh. How long is my leave, you mean?"

"Right."

"I told the director I wanted six months to a year."

Laurie whistled. "That long. You are serious."

"I'm serious," Melissa said flatly. "I've never been more serious about anything in my life."

"Do you think they'll give you that long?"

"I doubt it, but I asked for it anyway."

They were both sitting cross-legged now in the middle of Laurie's king-size bed. The sun, having just settled on the horizon, left a slight chill in the air. Due to the seriousness of the conversation, however, both were oblivious to the change in the climate as well as the chime of the miniature grandfather clock sitting on top of the television set.

"What are you going to do?" Laurie asked at last, her forehead wrinkled.

Melissa concentrated on rearranging the napkin, now soggy, around her glass. "Would you believe I haven't thought that far ahead, though I know I'll have to get some type of job, part-time maybe. I have a little money saved, but I certainly don't want to have to live on it. Anyway, the monthly payment on my condo is awful."

Laurie was quiet for a minute, then she said, "How long have you known about this? I guess what I'm trying to say is, why haven't you confided in me before now?"

Melissa's face clouded. "Because I haven't been fit company for anyone, that's why. I've been sleeping long hours, doing aerobics, walking. In essence I've been trying to heal my exhausted body and soul."

"That bad, huh?"

"That bad. I don't think I've ever been more frustrated or dissatisfied with myself or my work."

"But you do intend to go back to the hospital eventually, don't you?"

Melissa didn't hesitate. "Of course. I have every reason to believe that after I'm away from the rat race for a while, I'll return a new woman, ready to tackle my job again with the same enthusiasm that I've always had."

"I don't think your lack of enthusiasm is all job related," Laurie asserted bluntly.

"What makes you say that?" Melissa's tone was guarded; she had a feeling she knew what Laurie was getting at.

"Don't take that tone with me, Melissa Banning. You know since you and Martin called it quits, you haven't been the same."

"Please," Melissa said, a strident note in her voice. "Let's not rehash that again. Martin English is back home where he belongs with his wife and child."

"Only it's not that simple, is it, Melissa?"

"No...yes!" Melissa's voice wavered.

"I know something happened, something you've never told me. There's an underlying sadness about you that I can't quite put my finger on."

Melissa refused to meet her gaze. "Please..."

"All right," Laurie said with a sigh. "I won't push it. But one of these days you're going to have to open up."

Melissa sighed. "Maybe, but not today, okay?"

"Okay, I'll let you off the hook, but only because I'm afraid you won't stay with me if I don't. That spare bedroom down the hall has your name on it, you know."

Melissa set her glass on the bedside table, then, reaching over, she gave her friend a quick hug. "I don't know what I'd do without you, Laurie Deaton." She blinked furiously to keep the tears back.

"Hey, hey, let's not get maudlin, okay?" Although Laurie's tone was serious, there was a wide grin on her face. "What we need to do instead is find you a job." Her grin broadened. "I simply can't stand the thought of you being idle while I'm busting my buns."

Melissa grimaced. "Come on, show a little mercy, will you? I'm not ready to hunt for a job. See—" she paused and pointed to her eyes ''—if these circles get any darker or deeper, I'll never be able to take off my sunglasses.''

"And you're too thin, too."

"I like to think of myself as slender," Melissa said airily. Suddenly a frown creased her brow. Granted, she had been scrimping on meals lately in order to meet her demanding schedule. However, she hoped to remedy that soon.

"Whatever you say."

Melissa laughed and changed the subject. "Speaking of jobs, have you come across anything lately that sounds interesting? I know you're forever perusing the want ads."

"Now that you mention it, I have." Laurie bolted off the bed, a mischievous twinkle in her eyes. Then with glass in hand, she darted across the room to the small desk sitting in one corner. She grabbed the classified section and came back to the bed.

Melissa stared at her wide-eyed. "Surely *you're* not thinking of changing jobs?"

"Not really, but it's fun to see what's available. Here, take a look." Laurie sat down and thrust the paper at Melissa.

The room was quiet while Melissa read the portion circled in red ink. When she looked up, her eyes twinkled. "You've got a point. It does sound intriguing."

"For me, but not for you."

"Mmm, I don't know so much about that."

Laurie's mouth went slack. "Please tell me you're not thinking what I think you're thinking?"

"Oh, but I am." Melissa flashed her a wide grin. "Sounds exactly like what I'm looking for."

"You can't be serious?"

"Oh, but I am."

"But...but," Laurie spluttered, "the ad is for a live-in

housekeeper and baby-sitter for a widower with two children.''

"So." Melissa's expression was as bland as her tone.

"So!"

"Don't you see?" Melissa said, scrambling to a sitting position on the bed, her eyes brimming with excitement. "That's exactly the type of job I need. Compared to what I've been doing, it'll be a piece of cake."

"Melissa!"

Ignoring Laurie, she went on, "You know I've always loved children and keeping house—well, how difficult can that be?"

Laurie rolled her eyes and gave an unladylike snort.

"Go ahead, make fun. I don't care. But I see this as an opportunity to get away from having to make life-saving decisions day after day and still do something worthwhile."

"You're really not kidding, are you?"

"No, in fact I'm going to call the number listed right now."

"For God's sake, Melissa Banning, you can't even cook."

Melissa smiled innocently. "So what? I'm not too old to learn."

"This is nuts. *You're* nuts," Laurie muttered, shaking her head.

She was still shaking her head minutes later when Melissa placed the receiver back on the hook and said, "Well, aren't you the least bit curious?"

"No," Laurie said glumly. "I'm not going to be a party to this madness."

"Ah, come on, be a sport. If this works out, we'll get to see each other more often than once every couple of months." Melissa's tone was coaxing.

Laurie gave in. "Okay. What did you find out?"

"I spoke to the man's sister, a Dee Johnson. She told me she had recently married. You know her?"

"Nope."

"Well anyway, her brother's name is Joshua Malone. Does that name ring a bell?"

"No, I don't think…" Laurie suddenly snapped her fingers. "There's a Malone that owns a construction company. Is he the one?"

"He's the one. His wife's been dead for three years. He has five-year-old twins."

"Twins. God, this gets more ridiculous by the minute."

"Where's your sense of adventure? Come on, be a sport. Anyway, she's certainly aroused my curiosity," Melissa added, "especially after she told me I was the only one who had applied."

"That ought to tell you something."

Melissa feigned innocence. "And what might that be?"

"Run like hell."

Melissa laughed. "Not me. I'm supposed to go to Joshua Malone's place north of town in the morning."

"There's nothing I can do to talk you out of it?"

"I may be a nut, but I'm going to see it through."

By the time Melissa found the turnoff that led up a winding, narrow road on the outskirts of Nacogdoches, she began to think Laurie's concerns were valid.

Throughout the previous evening, while munching on pizza and watching a movie on the VCR, Laurie had thrown her several strange looks. But she had refrained from asking any more questions, much to Melissa's relief. She was certain part of the reason was that Laurie didn't think she would go through with it, that when she, Melissa, awakened the following morning, she would have changed her mind.

She hadn't. She was determined at least to check the job out, first and foremost because it truly appealed to her and second because it would get her away from Houston, away from pain and disillusionment.

But now, the farther she drove along the poorly maintained road, she began to have her doubts. When Dee Johnson had given her directions, she hadn't said that Melissa would have to travel a road that would put her kidneys in jeopardy.

"Damn," Melissa muttered, squeezing her legs tighter together, fearing she would have an accident if this went on much longer.

Then, miraculously, the house came into view. Still, she felt no sense of jubilation. The instant she switched off the engine and stepped down onto the uneven ground, she pinpointed the reason.

Neglect. The entire place reeked of it.

While the house seemed nice enough, a sprawling red brick ranch, it had an unkempt appearance. The grass in the large yard, while not yet knee high, certainly needed mowing. The flower beds bordering the front sidewalk were crammed with weeds. The swing on the porch, which ran the length of the house, was broken, one end sagging from the attached chain. It reminded Melissa of a broken arm on a doll she'd had as a child.

On closer observation, the place looked deserted. Surely that was not the case. She brightened somewhat when she spotted a pickup truck in the garage.

With her dark hair swept back casually from her fine-boned face, Melissa walked toward the house, looking tall and self-assured. Inside, however, her nerves were jumping. Sighing deeply, she shifted her purse to the other shoulder and shoved one hand down into her skirt pocket before continuing her cautious trek up the walkway.

Hoping for the best but fearing the worst, Melissa stepped onto the porch and pushed the doorbell. It was only after she'd removed her sunglasses and ground her finger into the button a second time that her ears picked up the sound of footsteps.

In anticipation of meeting her would-be employer, Melissa plastered a smile across her face. But the minute the door opened and a large man wearing a cowboy hat filled the doorway, Melissa's smile vanished as quickly as sand in a wind storm.

He was staring at her through narrowed, hostile eyes.

"Look, lady, I don't know what you're selling, but whatever the hell it is, I'm not buying."

While her mouth was agape, the door slammed shut with a definite bang.

Two

For an instant, Melissa was too stunned to move. Then sucking in a deep, sharp breath, she unconsciously stepped back and felt the blood slowly drain from her face.

"Of all the nerve," she muttered under her breath.

What on earth had happened? It was obvious she wasn't expected. Had Dee Johnson failed to tell her brother about the appointment? Melissa didn't know the answers, but one thing she did know, she was going to get the hell out of this place.

She had just turned and placed a foot on the top step when she heard the door open behind her. Something made her swing around. Maybe it was curiosity, maybe it was pride.

The same man was standing in the doorway. His hat now rested back on his head, allowing her to see his face. Instantly, dark brown eyes met and clashed with Paul Newman-blue ones.

Before Melissa could respond to his brazen stare, he asked in an East Texas drawl, "You wouldn't by any chance be the lady inquiring about the job?"

Arrogant bastard, she thought, wanting desperately to tell him what he could do with his job. Instead she curbed her quick tongue and murmured with false sweetness, "As a matter of fact I am."

His eyes continued to move over her, this time more slowly and thoroughly. She stood helplessly as they paused on her breasts, which the thin silk blouse did little to camouflage. She could feel her nipples harden and push against the soft fabric of her bra, and she tried in vain to convince herself that the response resulted from the crisp air and not this man's stare.

Nevertheless, Melissa squirmed inwardly, feeling like a bug under a microscope.

"Sorry if I offended you," he said at last, the smooth deep voice not sounding sorry in the least.

Melissa wanted to say something, anything, that would not only put this man in his place but force him to look away. To her dismay, she couldn't utter a word. Her throat was clogged.

For the first time in years, she was totally unnerved by a man's stare. To make matters worse, he was smiling, a blatant, sexy smile as if he knew the effect he was having on her.

Gritting her teeth, Melissa stiffened her spine. "You didn't offend me," she said, her voice biting. "Trust me, it takes more than a rude...cowboy like yourself to accomplish that."

His eyes shone with devilment. "What do you say we begin this conversation over? On the right foot this time."

"Under the circumstances, I don't think that's possible," Melissa said primly, then blushed in shocked surprise. She was behaving as rudely as he had, which for her was completely out of character.

"Then you are here about the job?"

"Yes, I *was*." She stressed the *was* making sure he didn't miss the past tense.

They locked gazes, both of them suddenly flushed with anger.

"Look, this conversation is pointless." Melissa, trying to dispel the tension, strove to make her voice light. "It's obvious I'm wasting your time, and you're certainly wasting mine."

His eyebrows rose a fraction. "As long as you're here, you might as well stay."

"I don't think..." The rest of her sentence faded into thin air as he grinned and stuck out his hand.

"I'm Joshua Malone."

Why she didn't tell him to go to hell, she would never know. The fact that she ignored his outstretched hand was of little consolation, especially when she looked up at him and said a trifle breathlessly, "And I'm Melissa Banning."

"Ah, you are the one my sister called and told me about."

"If you were expecting me, Mr. Malone, then why the rude reception?"

The twinkle faded from his eyes, and another scowl darkened his features. "Because, dammit, you weren't what I was expecting."

"And what exactly was that?" Again Melissa spoke with that strain of false sweetness in her tone.

"For starters, someone a whole helluva lot older and uglier than you."

At first his bluntness robbed her of a suitable comeback, but then she rebounded. "Look, Mr. Malone, as I've already pointed out, this conversation is a waste of time."

He caught her arm as she turned to leave. "Don't go."

"Give me one good reason why I shouldn't."

"You need a job."

"Not good enough."

"Okay, so I need a housekeeper."

"Still not good enough."

"Want me to beg?"

He was laughing at her. And instead of loosening her up, it made her madder. "This is all too ridiculous for words. Now please let go of my arm."

She hardly felt his touch, but he was much too close. Her nostrils filled with the aroma of his cologne and the clean, pungent scent of his skin, and she could see the brilliant centers of his blue eyes.

"What if I told you I was desperate?" he asked, letting go of her arm.

"Are you?" she asked, curious in spite of herself.

"Yes," he admitted tersely. "I'm desperate."

She raised her eyebrows. "Go on."

"Since my sister left three months ago, I've had three housekeepers. Need I say more?"

She gripped her purse tighter. Sympathy could be her ruin. "What makes you think I'll be any different?"

"I don't." He shrugged. "But I can always hope."

When Melissa didn't say anything, he went on in a persuasive tone, "What'd you say? You're here. What have you got to lose?"

"Oh, all right." Her voice lowered but lost none of its brittleness. "The least I can do is listen to your sales pitch."

"Thanks." His thin lips were set in a taut line.

Melissa knew that begging did not come easily to a man like Joshua Malone, even though he had joked about it only moments before. No, she knew he was a man who liked to be in control of any and all situations and was unhappy when he wasn't. At the moment he was not in control.

Feeling her curiosity reach an advanced level, she looked on in silence as he stepped aside and beckoned for her to enter.

"Welcome to our friendly abode," he said, his tone mocking.

Ignoring him, Melissa walked into the dimly lighted entry hall, where she paused, then blinked, trying to adjust her eyes.

"Having second thoughts?"

She turned to find him close behind her, so close this time that she could feel his warm breath on the back of her neck. She shivered. The husky note in his voice was the least of her worries; she could handle that. But his close proximity she could not.

Squaring her shoulders, she took a hurried step forward, ignoring her increased heart beat, only to suddenly freeze in her tracks.

"Oh, my God," she whispered, more to herself than to Joshua, who had now moved to her side.

He gave an apologetic shrug. "Terrible, isn't it?"

"Terrible" was such a gross understatement, the word seemed ludicrous. The room was a wreck. Papers, clothes and dishes were strewn everywhere. It could have passed for a battleground or worse, Melissa thought with a sinking feeling in the pit of her stomach.

Beside her, Joshua shrugged again. "Like I said, my sister's been gone three months."

Melissa faced him, wide-eyed. "How...I mean..." Her voice faded while she groped for the words to say what was on her mind.

"I should have warned you, I guess."

"I don't think you could have," Melissa said flatly, sarcastically.

"No, probably not," he responded, seeming to take no offense at her caustic tone. He then tossed his hat onto the table against the wall. Just as it landed, all hell broke loose.

The door burst open, and two children raced into the room with two dogs in tow, both barking at the tops of their lungs.

"That's enough!" Joshua shouted, striding farther into the room. Immediately he curtailed the yelping animals by grasping their collars and giving them an easy jerk.

Instantly, the room fell silent.

Melissa could not have moved or spoken if she'd wanted to. Ever since she'd faced Joshua Malone, she had been at a loss for words more times than she'd ever been in her life. All she could do was stare in stunned amazement at the two disheveled, pint-size individuals now flanking Joshua. The twins.

He couldn't deny them, Melissa thought irrationally. They were like clones. Both had blond hair, the same surfer's blonde as Joshua's, the same-shaped nose and mouth. The only noticeable difference was the color of the twins' eyes—theirs were green instead of blue. At the moment those vivid green eyes were staring up at her with a mixture of curiosity and hostility.

Joshua's deep voice broke the heavy silence. "Melissa Banning, meet Sam and Sara, who are five going on twenty-five."

Melissa cleared her throat and forced a smile. "Hello," she said gently, quelling the urge to sweep them into her arms, rush into the bathroom and scrub their grubby hands and faces.

"They've been playing outside all morning," Joshua said, as if that excused their appearance.

Melissa paled. It was uncanny how this man could read her mind. Unconsciously she took a step backward, panic making her cold on the inside. The quicker she got away from the Malones, the better off she would be.

Both Sam and Sara were anxiously looking up at Joshua, but it was Sam who asked in a petulant tone, "Who's that lady?"

Joshua tousled his blond curls. "Ms. Banning to you, young man. If we're lucky, she'll be our new housekeeper and baby-sitter."

"Aw shucks, Dad, we don't need anyone to take care of us."

"That's right, Daddy," Sara chimed in her squeaky little voice. "We can take care of ourselves. And we can take care of you, too," she added in a proud voice.

Joshua hugged them both close to his legs, while a sigh erupted from the depths of his big chest. "I wish that were true, sweetheart, but I'm afraid it's not. Anyway, Daddy needs someone not only to look after you but the house, as well, so I can work."

For the time being, his explanation seemed to pacify the twins. They disentangled themselves and plopped down on the floor beside the dogs.

Switching his gaze to Melissa, Joshua pointed to the chair in front of her. "Please, sit down."

Melissa wasn't sure why she sank onto the cushion littered with papers, because there was nothing about the situation she liked, especially the way the children were staring at her as though she were from another planet and wishing she would return to it.

"Uh, how 'bout something to drink?" Joshua's rough-edged voice cut into her thoughts.

"No. No, thank you," she said, licking her lips. "I'm fine."

He didn't look convinced, but he didn't say anything. Instead he crossed the room to a long window, where he fiddled with the miniblinds until the room was flooded with light.

Sighing inwardly, Melissa permitted herself a sidelong glance in his direction. To her relief, he seemed unaware of her scrutiny, and she was able to observe him without his knowledge, watching as his muscled arms emerged from the worn, cotton T-shirt, his shoulder blades moving against the cloth.

She tried to force her gaze away, but she couldn't. He was in his thirties—thirty-five, maybe—and he was beautiful. Flawless, in fact. More than six feet of rock-hard body, chiseled face with cheekbones any woman would kill for and the trim look of a marathon runner. So what if he looked as though he could use a shower and change of clothes? In his case it merely honed his looks to greater perfection.

Even though she would admit she found him attractive, that was as far as she would go. She had no use for men. That part of her life was finished. Besides, he was the type she made it a point to steer clear of, the type who wanted everything but was unwilling to give in return, the type who could break a woman's heart.

"Hey, kids, why don't you take Sugar and Spice outside while I talk to Ms. Banning?"

Again Joshua's compelling voice was the tonic needed to jerk her back to the moment at hand. She remained silent while the children begrudgingly got up and pulled on the dogs' thick manes and headed toward the door. It was after they had reached the threshold that they spun around. Melissa was their target.

"Go away," they cried in unison. "We don't want you here."

Melissa caught her breath.

Letting loose a string of curses, Joshua moved swiftly across the room, not stopping until he loomed over them. "Sam, Sara, apologize to Ms. Banning right now."

If he'd spoken to her in that tone, Melissa wouldn't have argued. They didn't, either. Hanging their heads, they pawed the floor with the toes of their tennis shoes, then raised their eyes toward Melissa.

"I'm sorry," Sam mumbled.

"Me, too," Sara said, raising her head, her tiny, lower lip quivering.

Again it was all Melissa could do not to go to them and jerk them into her arms. An unfamiliar ache rose again in her throat. She wanted to hug them until they hurt.

"That's more like it," Joshua said. "Now, go on outside and play."

Once she and Joshua were alone, a heavy silence fell over the room. Melissa had long ago deserted the chair and was now standing beside it. Joshua, near, was leaning against the mantel.

"Sorry about that," he said, a brooding expression on his face. "They know better."

"I'm sure they do," Melissa said softly, then eased herself toward the couch. His scrutiny was making it impossible for her to think rationally.

"I'm curious as to why a woman like yourself would apply for this job?" he asked once she was seated.

Melissa responded with a question. "Did your sister tell you anything about me?"

"Only that you're a registered nurse living and working in Houston."

"Well, that just about sums it up."

His gaze was intent. "I find that hard to believe."

"It's true. Nursing has been the prime interest in my life for a long time now."

"So why aren't you nursing?"

"I needed a change of scenery," Melissa said honestly.

"Burnout, huh?"

She was taken aback. "How did you know?"

"Just guessed. The news is always belaboring the nursing shortage and how overworked the good nurses are."

"In this case the news is not exaggerating."

"I take it, then, you've had no experience in this type of work?"

"None."

He sighed. "Well, as you can see, we're no prize package, either. So it seems neither of us can be choosey, especially me. It's obvious our lives are in an upheaval." He paused and rubbed the back of his neck. "With my work, it's just not possible to function without a housekeeper."

"You're a building contractor."

"And a widower." His tone was as blunt as his words. "My wife died three years ago. But I suppose Dee told you that."

"Yes, she did, and I'm sorry," Melissa said for lack of anything better to say.

"Yeah, me too."

Melissa looked away, certain that what she saw lurking in his eyes was pain.

"My job requires long hours," he said after another long moment. "Sometimes daylight till dark. But these last months I've had to depend on my foreman to carry the heavy load, which won't work much longer because we just landed the bid on a high-rise office building."

"Congratulations."

"Thanks."

A short silence fell between them.

"So what's it going to be, Ms. Banning?" He fixed her with an ice-blue gaze so intense that Melissa felt a shiver along the back of her neck. "Are you willing to take us on?"

"It probably won't work out," Melissa said desperately.

"We won't know till we try."

"The twins already don't like me."

A smile reshaped his lips. "I'm not worried. They'll come around."

"You haven't checked my references."

"Dee did, said there were no skeletons in your closet."

His attempt at humor failed to draw a smile from Melissa. "Do you always have an answer for everything, Mr. Malone?"

"Most everything, Ms. Banning," he said easily.

Melissa's head was reeling. If there ever was a family that needed help, it was this one. But heaven help her, she wasn't at all sure she was the one to give it. The situation was not what she had expected, nor was Joshua Malone.

Yet she knew what her answer would be and was amazed at how calm she was.

"Well, Ms. Banning?" His voice interrupted her racing thoughts.

Her gaze swept up to his face. "I'll take the job."

Three

Melissa idly tapped a red-lacquered nail against the side of her coffee cup.

"Nervous?" Laurie asked with a mischievous smile.

"You're enjoying the hell out of this, aren't you?" Melissa snapped, though the small smile on her lips went a long way toward toning down the sting of her words.

Laurie laughed outright this time. "You bet I am. And before this is all over, I will have said 'I told you so' a thousand times."

They were sitting in the warm comfort of Laurie's glassed-in breakfast room, which jutted off her kitchen, drinking coffee. The temperature outside wasn't nearly as charitable. Not only was the Sunday morning cloudy, but chilly, as well.

It had been two days since Melissa had accepted Joshua Malone's offer. And she wasn't sure she had done the right thing, not by a long shot. In fact she wondered if she hadn't taken leave of her senses.

After having returned to Houston to pack her things, she had gone so far as to pick up the phone, determined to tell Joshua she had changed her mind. But then the memory of the twins' beautiful little faces had returned to her, and she'd dropped the receiver as though it were a hot potato.

And Joshua—well, she'd decided that she wasn't going to think about him. As long as she kept in mind that he was her employer, she would be fine.

Melissa forced a smile. "You're wrong. I won't regret this, and I'll prove it."

"We'll see," Laurie said, reaching for a pack of cigarettes and lighter. Without taking her eyes off Melissa, she lit one.

Melissa made a face. "When did you start puffing on those foul things again? You told me you had quit."

"I have and I haven't," Laurie moaned, slipping her saucer from beneath her cup and grinding the head of the cigarette into it. "I'm trying damned hard, but so far I haven't been able to shake them."

"I know it's hard, but if you've come this far, don't backslide now."

"Yes, Mama."

Melissa grinned. "I'm the one who's nervous, remember?"

"Ah, so you're finally going to admit to it?"

Melissa drew her eyebrows together. "I shouldn't have to admit it. The fact that I landed unannounced on your doorstep at seven o'clock this morning is a dead give-away."

"Oh, it is," Laurie replied with a sparkle in her gray eyes, "but I didn't mind."

"It's a good thing. I woke up at four this morning, got

dressed, threw my suitcases in the car and locked up the condo, all in that order. By five I found myself heading north." Melissa smiled wanly. "And here I am."

"What time are Mr. Joshua Malone and children expecting you?"

"I told him I'd be there around noon or before."

"Ah, just in time to make lunch."

Melissa's mouth fell open. "Do you think…" She broke off, suddenly seeing the grin on Laurie's face. "I'll get you for that."

"I just couldn't pass that one up."

"Well, if they're hungry, there's always Kentucky Fried Chicken."

"You don't have to go through with this if you don't want to, you know. Nothing's written in stone."

Melissa sighed. "I know, but if you could have seen those kids…" She let her voice trail off.

"Pitiful, huh?"

"Worse than that."

"And Joshua Malone?"

"There's not much to say," Melissa responded evasively. "I told you what he looked like."

"A hunk, right?" Laurie grinned.

Melissa gave her an exasperated look. "Well, some women might think so."

"But not you." Mirth danced in Laurie's eyes.

"Of course not." Melissa's response was curt.

Laurie took no offense. She merely shook her head and smiled. "What I'd like to know is what would be so terrible if you *were* attracted to this man?"

Melissa flushed. "Can it, Laurie. You know better than that."

"Sorry," Laurie said. "It seems that every time I mention men, I strike a nerve."

"You're right. A man in my life is the last thing I need or want." Especially one like Joshua Malone, she added silently. "Lord knows I've got enough complications without adding another one. Right now all I want is to learn how to relax, how to laugh again."

"And you still think this job is the right tonic?"

Melissa didn't hesitate. "Yes, I honestly do. It's obvious the family needs some stability in their lives." She smiled. "Anyway, I think it'll be both interesting and a challenge."

"So what's going to happen when you leave?" Laurie asked bluntly. "We both know the hospital is not going to let you off the hook for long. Don't you feel like you're cheating them?"

Melissa drew her eyebrows together in a frown. "Do you think that's what I'd be doing, cheating them?"

Laurie looked contrite. "Sorry again. That was a low blow, and I shouldn't have said it. It's just that I don't want you to get in too deep over your head, especially with those motherless children."

"Don't worry. I'm approaching this job with my head instead of my heart. And if I stay only one or two months, it'll be better than what they have now, which is nothing or no one. I can guarantee you that."

"So what are you going to find the most challenging?" Laurie asked, lifting her cup to her lips and draining the last of her coffee. She eyed Melissa carefully over the rim.

Ignoring her question, Melissa stood, a grin spreading across her face.

"Are you leaving?" Laurie asked, getting to her feet.

"Got to. It's getting late."

"You haven't answered my question."

"What if I don't know the answer?"

"Oh, you know, all right. Don't forget who you're talking to. Besides, I saw that grin on your face, like a cat who's just been given a bowl of rich cream.''

Melissa threw back her head and laughed. ''All right, you win. I'm going to enjoy putting the man of the house in his place more than anything I've done in a long time.''

Joshua had just locked the temporary building that served as an office on the site of his next job. While he shifted the set of plans from under one arm to the other, his gaze drifted to the newly printed sign posted close to the street.

In spite of himself, Joshua felt his chest swell with pride. He was reacting like a kid, he knew, the same way Sam or Sara reacted when he complimented them on something they had done well. But he couldn't help it. When he'd bid on this new office complex, he'd pulled off a coup that had surprised even him. It was the chance he'd been waiting for, and now that he'd gotten it, nothing was going to get in his way. Malone Construction was on its way to becoming a viable company.

However, he was no fool. Completing the project on time and keeping the costs within the budget would definitely be a challenge. But then, he'd never been one to back down from a challenge.

He'd always thought of himself as a ''good ole boy'' from the wrong side of the tracks who was left to make his own way early in life. As a result, he'd had to work doubly hard, not only to beat insurmountable odds in turning his small construction company into a success, but just to survive. Survive he had. With the completion of this project, he hoped to have it made.

Now removing his gaze from the sign, he slipped the keys into his jeans pocket and began making his way toward the truck. He was halfway there when a maroon two-door Buick pulled up and stopped beside him, blocking his way.

A blonde was behind the wheel. She rolled the window down and smiled up at him.

"You're a hard person to catch," she said peevishly.

"I try," Joshua responded evenly.

"Oh, you're impossible, you know that?"

Joshua grinned mockingly. "So I've been told."

"Aren't you ever serious?"

His lips curled. "Just get to the point, Gladys. Why were you looking for me?"

"I thought you might like to come to lunch."

Gladys Powers was the ex-wife of one of the local bankers. Since her divorce had become final several weeks ago, she had chased after Joshua.

Normally he would have been more responsive. She was great on the eyes and had a body that had caused his control to slip on more than one occasion. Taking her to bed would be a conquest in its own right. But not this morning. Catering to her would be more trouble than it was worth. Anyway, Melissa Banning was due to arrive by noon.

Gladys's husky laugh brought him out of his thoughts.

"Are you thinking what I'm thinking?" she asked seductively.

"Depends on what you're thinking."

She grinned slyly. "Why don't I tell you that when you come to lunch?"

"Thanks for the invite, but I can't make it, not today."

"Can't or won't?" she whined.

Joshua's eyes narrowed slightly. "It's Sunday, Gladys. I have to spend it with the kids."

"You sure that's the only reason?"

He took in the pouting slant of her red mouth and her

accusing eyes for a moment, then said, "You must realize I don't owe you an explanation."

"You're a bastard, Joshua Malone."

"I know."

She tightened her lips and jammed the car into gear. "Well, some other time, then?"

Joshua touched the brim of his Stetson with a finger and grinned humorlessly. "Some other time."

Immediately after she drove off, leaving a trail of dust behind her, he jumped into the truck and headed for his closest neighbors, the Sinclairs, where he'd left the twins.

But thirty minutes later when he walked into the office at the house, he was alone. Alice Sinclair had persuaded him to let the twins stay for lunch, then accompany her girls to a birthday party shortly thereafter. The Sinclairs' two girls were nine and ten, and they loved looking after Sam and Sara.

The only reason he'd consented was because it might be easier if the twins were not there when Melissa Banning arrived, which should be at any moment now, he reminded himself with a deep sigh. They needed to discuss so much, and as the twins had not yet accepted the idea of another housekeeper, he'd just as soon tackle the orientation alone.

He laid the building plans on the desk, but instead of sitting down and working on them as he should, he walked to the window and peered outside. His office faced the front of the house, with a clear view of the drive, which meant he would see Melissa when she arrived.

While he waited and watched, he moved his shoulders up and down, trying to work the kinks out of them. He both dreaded and looked forward to the new housekeeper's arrival. Yet he had thought of little else since he'd met her, which in itself was ridiculous and extremely disconcerting. Nevertheless, Melissa Banning intrigued him, and regardless of how hard he tried, he couldn't imagine her in the role of his housekeeper, or anyone else's for that matter.

She simply had too much class and too much breeding. And was far too beautiful. But then he guessed she had her reasons for leaving her chosen profession and seeking other work. As long as she did her job, why should he care?

He did, though, and that was what galled him. He wanted to see Melissa as just another housekeeper in a long line of many, but he could not. Maybe it was that hint of raw sexuality about her that he found disturbing, that kept him thinking about her, about the way her dark, dark hair surrounded her face, the way her breasts had thrust proudly against the material of her blouse when she'd been agitated.

But it wasn't just her beauty that attracted him; something more, something deeper stirred him. Maybe it was her voice, a voice that was soft and bright-sounding, as though filled with sunshine. Or better still, maybe it was her temper. A grin slowly crossed his lips. When riled she was as prickly as a porcupine. And damned electrifying.

Leaving a string of muttered expletives behind him, Joshua left the window and sat down at his desk. Still he did not unroll the plans. He stared at them with a scowl on his face.

The last thing he needed or wanted was to get involved with a woman, any woman. He had had ample opportunity to remarry during the three years he'd been a widower, having been chased by half the women who knew him. But he was not interested in remarrying and prided himself on remaining uncommitted.

Still it had seemed he had forgotten the simple art of breathing until Melissa left the room. And when a puzzled frown had marred her forehead, he'd wondered what it would be like to put his lips on that spot.

"This is crazy, Malone!" he shouted to the empty room. "You're crazy!"

But even as he leaped out of his chair at the same time a car door slammed, he knew that crazy or not, his new housekeeper was the reason Gladys's offer had been easy to turn down.

Four

The second Melissa shifted her car into park and turned the key to off, she leaned across the seat and grabbed her purse, a canvas bag and briefcase.

It wasn't until she reached the Malones' front door that she realized she had tried to carry too much, especially with her windbreaker determined to slip off her shoulders. Pausing to regroup, she took a whiff of the crisp morning air. Earlier the sky had been dreary and overcast; now it was clear. Close by she heard a bird chirrup.

These were good omens, she reflected with a smile, a sign she had definitely made the right decision in taking this job.

Because her arms were loaded, she used her elbow to knock on the door. She was concentrating on holding on to her luggage when the door opened from the inside, causing her to lose her balance.

"Damn," she cried, clawing at the air, knowing at any moment she was going to fall flat on her face.

Muscled arms prevented that, although her briefcase and windbreaker went flying in her struggle to maintain her equilibrium. But the only thing she was aware of was that her shock-racked body was plastered against a hard frame. Strong, masculine fingers dug into the flesh of one bare arm, while another hand cupped the underside of her derriere.

She clung to him, blood pounding in her head. Her nipples sprang erect at the embarrassingly intimate contact, and she felt the stirrings of warmth in her lower stomach and between her thighs.

"Take it easy," Joshua murmured in her ear. "I've got you."

She was so close to him that she could see every perfect pore in his face, count individual eyelashes, see the tiny weblike lines in the irises of eyes that watched her intently.

"You okay?"

"I'm...fine," she whispered, struggling to draw her gaze from his.

"Sure?"

"I'm sure." But she wasn't sure; she wasn't sure at all.

"Did you know that your eyes shine like blackberries in the sun?" His voice was low and husky.

Her heartbeat roared in her ears as she watched the amusing glint in his eyes darken and begin to simmer.

Melissa barely managed to eke out a "No."

"Well, they do."

She opened her mouth, then snapped it shut. He smiled. She smiled back.

Then suddenly their smiles faded, leaving them staring at each other in stunned surprise. Their eyes locked with a different sensation, but one just as potent as surprise.

Together they realized they were still fitted like pieces of a puzzle, stomach against stomach, thighs against thighs. Her nipples also remained buried in his chest. She heard his sharp intake of breath, felt the tautness of his arms.

With superhuman effort, Melissa gathered her scattered wits and gazed up at him with wide eyes, while he tenderly pushed her to arm's length. Heat scalded her cheeks.

"Nothing like making an entrance," he said lightly, though his ragged breathing made a mockery of his outer calm.

"No, I guess not," she replied with an embarrassed smile. Suddenly realizing that his hands were still on her arms, she took another step back. His hands fell automatically to his sides.

Then after looking at her a moment longer, he asked, "How 'bout a cup of coffee?"

"Sounds wonderful." She couldn't keep the slight tremor from her voice.

"Good. Does to me, too. Come on, we'll get the rest of your things out of the car later."

His voice now was even and controlled, as if the encounter had never happened. Melissa couldn't help but envy him, as every nerve in her body still felt exposed.

Once they entered the kitchen, Melissa eased her purse and tote bag off her shoulder and onto the nearest chair, which was already littered with newspapers.

Joshua had crossed to the cabinet and was leaning his back against it. "I was going to straighten things before you came," he said with an apologetic shrug, "but somehow the morning got away from me, and the twins—"

"Speaking of the twins," Melissa interrupted, latching on to a safe subject, "where are they?"

"They're with the neighbors at a family birthday party.

It's a good thing, too. With those two little motor mouths around, we wouldn't be able to discuss anything.''

Melissa ran her tongue over her lower lip. "They still aren't thrilled about my coming, are they?" In spite of herself, her voice held hope.

"No, but like I told you, you'll win them over," he said, twisting around and opening the cabinet behind him. "It's just a matter of time." Lifting his arms, he reached for the can of coffee.

Melissa couldn't help but notice the way his T-shirt clung to the corded muscles of his back, the way his hair, sadly in need of a trim, grazed his neck.

"Here, let me make it," she said suddenly, feeling the need to occupy her hands as well as her mind.

He faced her and grinned, a grin that merely added to his sexual charisma. Melissa groaned inwardly.

"Believe I will." He moved out of the way. "I never learned to make the stuff worth a damn, anyway. Gwen used to say my coffee tasted like stump water."

That analogy brought a smile to Melissa's lips. "Was that your wife's name?" she asked shyly.

"Yeah."

"How did she—" Melissa began, only to abruptly swallow the rest of the sentence. Her face flooded with color. What right did she have to be so inquisitive?

"Die," he finished for her. "It's all right. You can say the word."

She felt the color deepen in her cheeks.

"She had uterine cancer," he said, gazing at her directly.

Melissa took a deep breath and let it out slowly. "God, how awful."

"The doctors did everything to save her, but it just wasn't meant to be."

She didn't say anything because there wasn't anything

to say. Instead she watched as he crossed to the table, sat down and stretched his legs in front of him.

"How 'bout you?" he asked, pinning her with his blue eyes.

"What do you want to know?"

"Everything you didn't tell the other day."

"I told you—"

"I know what you told me, and I told you I didn't believe you. And I still don't."

She gave him a hard stare; the last thing she wanted was a repeat of their earlier conversation.

"You ever been married?"

Holding on to her patience by a mere thread, she said, "No." Then, turning, she busied herself by placing five level teaspoons of coffee into the filter.

"Ever been close?" he pressed.

"No," she said again, not liking in the least the direction the conversation was taking. Hoping to forestall any further questions, she turned on the water at the sink with more force than necessary and watched as the container filled to the brim.

"For some reason I don't believe that, either," he drawled.

She whirled around. "For some reason I don't care what you think."

The glimmer in his eyes brightened. "How come?"

"How come what?" Not only was her patience wearing thin, but so were her nerves.

"How come you've never married? A beautiful woman like you."

She stiffened. "That's none of your business."

"I'll concede that, but I'm still curious."

Why she satisfied that curiosity, she would never know. "Let's just say I was too busy getting my career on track."

The corners of his mouth lifted. "A career that you've now abandoned for another."

His remark stung. "I've already explained that."

"So you did."

"What about you, Mr. Malone?"

"What about me?" His tone was alarmingly smooth.

"Have you ever come close to remarrying?" she asked brazenly, her eyes flashing, bent on giving back as good as she'd gotten.

He grinned as though he saw through her ploy. "Nope, not interested."

"Oh?"

He looked squarely at her, amusement lurking in his eyes. "But that doesn't mean I'm not interested in women."

"Somehow I don't find that surprising," she said, her voice laced with sarcasm.

"I hope not, Ms. Banning," he drawled, that devilish glint in his eyes again.

Damn him. He was laughing at her, enjoying her discomfort to the hilt.

Finally Melissa lifted her chin a bit higher. "Look, while I concede you have a right to know my background, there are limits. My sex life just happens to be off-limits. It's none of your concern, nor is yours mine. So if it's all the same to you, let's stick to the basics, shall we?"

The only sound in the room at the moment was the coffee pleasantly gurgling in the pot, filling the air with its rich aroma.

"Whatever you say." His mouth twisted in a half smile. "So, tell me about your family."

Melissa tensed. "Both my parents and my brother were killed in a boating accident just last year." Even to herself, her voice sounded high and light.

She heard him draw in his breath in a horrified gasp.

Not wanting to discuss it further, she quickly asked a question of her own. "What about you, Mr. Malone? Any other family beside your sister?"

"Drop the mister, okay? Joshua will do just fine."

Caught off guard, she could only nod, knowing his given name would not come easily to her lips.

"In answer to your question, no, I don't have any other family. Not close, anyway. My mother died when we were young, and Dad a few years later from cirrhosis of the liver. He drank himself to death." His expression turned bitter, as if old memories rose to haunt him. "Now that Dee's married, it's just the twins and myself."

"Well, that's a wonderful family in itself." Melissa smiled, relieved that the tension hovering over the room had dispelled somewhat.

"Kinda thought so myself."

"Since you mentioned the twins, when do they go to kindergarten, morning or afternoon?" Her tone was brisk, businesslike. While waiting for him to answer, she removed two cups from the cabinet and filled them with coffee. It was only after he'd sampled it that he answered her.

"They go to the morning session. Alice Sinclair takes them, and the bus brings them home."

"Should I take them?"

"Not unless you want to. The bus could do both, but Alice likes to chauffeur them along with her girls."

"What about extracurricular activities?"

"Like what?"

"Oh, you know, gymnastics, soccer, dance." She raised her cup to her lips and took a slow sip.

He frowned. "You sound just like Alice. She's always nagging at me about stuff like that."

"In other words the answer's no."

Not intimidated by her reproving tone, he leaned across the table and studied her, a mocking smile on his face.

For another long moment the silence was heavy as his gaze locked on her mouth, then moved to the slender column of her neck before settling on the unsteady rise and fall of her chest.

Melissa squirmed, that bold look recreating that hot sensation she'd felt when she'd melted against him. What had possessed her? She had never reacted to Martin like that, and she had thought she loved him, for God's sake.

Joshua was the first to break the silence. "Do whatever you think best. While I don't pretend to be the father of the year, my kids don't want for anything that counts."

"I wasn't criticizing," she began.

"Yes, you were," he cut in. A hard note had crept into his voice. "And just so you'll stop looking down your nose, I'm crazy about my kids and will do anything for them."

Melissa bristled. However, before she could make a suitable comeback, several car doors slammed simultaneously. Joshua pushed himself up from the chair and sauntered to the window.

"It's the twins," he said, his back to Melissa. "Something must've happened or their plans changed." When he turned, his face was creased into a deep frown. "It's way too early for them to be home."

Sharing his concern, Melissa stood and peered beyond his shoulder and watched as the woman standing on the edge of the sidewalk waved.

Seconds later the front door opened, then banged shut, all in one smooth motion.

"Daddy, Daddy."

"In here, son," Joshua responded, striding toward the door.

Their little bodies heaving, Sam and Sara dashed into the room.

"Daddy, Daddy," Sam said again, rushing up to Joshua, his eyes filled with excitement. "Guess what? Sara's tooth came out, and blood was everywhere. It was awesome!"

Five

Sara had come to an abrupt halt behind Sam, her lower lip protruding and tears trickling down her cheeks.

"You meany!" she cried, hitting her brother in the middle of the back with a tiny fist. "I wanted to tell Daddy."

Melissa tried to keep a straight face, but it wasn't easy, especially when she saw Joshua's lips twitch at the same time as he dropped to one knee and pulled Sara around Sam and into his arms.

"Here, here, sweetheart, don't cry," he said in a deep, tender voice, all the while smoothing errant curls away from her face. "Is that why you didn't go to the party?"

"Yes, sir." Her breath caught on a sob.

"Let Daddy have a look."

Without having to be asked a second time, Sara opened her mouth and stuck the tip of her tongue through the empty space.

Melissa watched the interplay between father and child,

a bemused expression on her face. Sara looked adorable dressed in a pair of pleated baggy jeans with a Mickey Mouse sweatshirt and absurd-looking high-top tennis shoes with red laces.

Joshua laughed and hugged her to him. Then gazing beyond the child's shoulder, his eyes connected with Melissa's. He winked, then smiled, and her heart turned over. Damn that sexy smile.

"Ugh, I hope that don't happen to me," Sam chimed in, determined to get his share of the attention.

He, too, looked adorable in a boyish way in his jeans, T-shirt and blue jean jacket.

"Doesn't happen to you," Joshua corrected mildly, rising to his feet.

"Okay, but you should've seen the blood, Dad. It ran down her lip."

"Did not!" Sara exclaimed.

"Did, too!" Sam countered.

"Hush, both of you. This is no way to act in front of Ms. Banning." He paused and beckoned to Melissa, who still hadn't said anything. Her thoughts were in chaos. There was so much she had to learn about children. She couldn't help wondering if she was up to the challenge after all.

"Sara, where did you put your tooth?" Melissa asked finally, her voice soft.

Instead of answering, Sara hid her face against Joshua's thigh.

"Ah, now, don't be shy," Joshua coaxed. "Come on, show Ms. Banning your tooth. I'd like to see it, too."

"Me, too," Sam added. "Aunt Alice wrapped it in a napkin and put it in Sara's pocket."

Slowly and carefully, as if she were uncovering the rarest

of jewels, Sara eased the tissue out of her jeans pocket and held out her hand.

"Go ahead, open it," Melissa prodded. "I can't wait to see." She smiled, hoping to put the child at ease.

"Yeah, hurry up, Sis. I wanna see if it still has some blood on it."

"Sam," Joshua said shaking his head, "when did you get to be so bloodthirsty?" Then to Sara, "We're waiting, sweetheart, open it."

The instant Sara uncovered her prize, cheers and claps rent the air. She giggled, once again hiding her face against Joshua's leg.

Joshua rested a large hand against Sara's cheek, and Melissa was forced to admit, albeit grudgingly, that he did have nice hands. Though his knuckles were rough and even scarred, his fingers were long and tan with sun-washed hairs detailed in the light.

"Do you know about the tooth fairy?" Melissa asked, bending over so that she was on eye level with the child.

Sara looked puzzled. "No."

"No, ma'am." Joshua's tone was gentle, but it brooked no argument.

"No, ma'am," Sara muttered, still gazing at Melissa with suspicion.

"Me, neither," Sam put in, moving next to his sister. Yet he, too, looked at Melissa with mistrust.

At least they weren't being flagrantly hostile, Melissa thought, her smile widening into a grin. "Every time you lose a tooth, you're supposed to put it under your pillow, and when you wake up the next morning, there'll be money under it."

"Who puts it there?" Sara asked cautiously.

Although Melissa rose to her feet, she didn't take her eyes off the child. "The tooth fairy, like I said."

Sara cut her gaze to Joshua. "How much money does it leave, Daddy?"

Joshua rolled his eyes. "Can you beat that, Ms. Banning? I have one child who's bloodthirsty and another who's mercenary."

"Sounds like a winning combination to me," Melissa responded, her lips twitching.

Reverting his attention to his daughter, he said, "All I can tell you, sweetheart, is to do like Ms. Banning said and put the tooth under your pillow. We'll see what happens then. But for now, I want you and your brother to hightail it to your rooms and get busy cleaning." Ignoring their groans, he continued, his glance resting on Melissa. "Ms. Banning will supervise."

"We don't want her to," Sam said, his tone having turned hostile once again.

"What if I help you," Melissa responded quickly, wanting to strangle Joshua for making her the bugger bear in this. "When we're finished, I'll read you both a story."

In spite of its inauspicious beginning, the rest of the afternoon was not half as bad as Melissa had anticipated. She had to admit, though, that most of its success was due to Joshua's willingness to pitch in and help. His purely impersonal attitude toward her also contributed to its success.

It was as if she had never plummeted into his arms or felt the bold imprint of his body against hers or felt his hot gaze on her. If she hadn't known differently, the entire episode could have been a figment of her imagination.

By the time she made her way into the kitchen and finished preparing dinner, she was exhausted. She had never worked so hard and had so little to show for it. Even though the three-bedroom-two-bath house was in better condition than when she'd arrived, it was by no means clean. But at least she and Joshua had cleared a path through the den and kitchen before he had shut himself up in his office.

Now, as she eyed the glass dish filled with steaming hot meat loaf and the bowl of salad next to it, she couldn't help but feel a sense of pride. Her very first meal. If it tasted half as good as it looked, the dinner would be an unqualified success. But it had been no easy feat. She'd had to get a recipe book out of the drawer and follow it step by step, while trying to remember how her mother had operated in the kitchen. With that uppermost in her mind, she'd added a few spices that weren't in the recipe.

"Eat your heart out, Julia Child," she murmured, placing the dishes on the table.

"As long as you don't answer yourself, you'll be all right."

Joshua's deep baritone vibrated with amusement. Melissa whipped around, her heart skipping a beat. He was lounging negligently against the door frame. His hair was damp, as if he'd just gotten out of the shower. From where she stood, she could smell the fresh scent of his cologne.

"I'll try to remember those words of wisdom," she finally said, blushing. To cover her nervousness, she leaned forward and checked the French bread wrapped in foil.

Joshua pushed away from the door and ambled toward her, a slow smile lighting his eyes, causing them to crimp at the corners. Even at that he looked tired, or was *frustrated* a better word? She assumed his job was to blame. She knew he was under pressure to get the high-rise office complex started and finished on time.

"Mmm, something smells good."

His tone sounded faintly mocking, but she couldn't be sure. No way could he know this was the first family meal she had ever prepared.

Striving to make her voice light, she said, "If you'll call the children, we can eat."

Minutes later they were all seated around the table, their plates covered with food. An uneasy silence fell over the room before Sam whined, "Daddy, do I have to eat? I'm not hungry."

"Yes, son, you have to eat," Joshua replied patiently, then proceeded to take a healthy bite of the meat loaf.

Melissa's breath hung suspended, waiting for the compliment she knew was sure to come. To her disappointment, he didn't say a word, and if she weren't mistaken, he made it a point to steer clear of her eyes as he took a second forkful.

Swinging to Sam, Melissa's gaze rested on him, watching as he chewed his first bite.

Before he had so much as swallowed it, his fork clanked to the plate. "Yuk, that tastes awful."

"Sam, that's enough." Joshua's tone was firm and cold. Sam hung his head.

"I don't like it, either, Daddy," Sara whined, pushing her plate away.

Scowling, Joshua slammed his napkin on the table and stood. "Both of you go to your rooms, on the double. I'll deal with you later."

"Yes, sir," they mumbled, sliding out of their chairs.

Once the children had gone, the silence in the room swelled to a thundering pitch. Melissa, shaking from head to toe, rose quickly and began carting the plates to the cabinet.

She felt rather than saw Joshua's gaze track her every move.

"Look," he said, "I'm sorry. The meat loaf...it wasn't that bad."

She swung around, furious. "How dare you patronize

me? I saw that look on your face. You didn't like it, either. So why don't you just come out and say I'm a lousy cook?'' She was practically shouting, yet she couldn't seem to stop, humiliated as she was that her meal was a failure.

An angry flush spread beneath the tanned skin. "All right, so you're a lousy cook. Do you feel better now?"

"No," she snapped, the lump in her throat increasing in size.

Joshua's mouth tightened in an exasperated line. "Wouldn't you know that I'd get a housekeeper that can't cook. Damn!"

"How do you know I can't cook?"

"Well, can you?"

They glared at each other.

She dug her fists into her hips. "No, as a matter of fact I can't."

"Lord, help me," he said again, lifting his eyes to the ceiling.

"So, what are you going to do about it, fire me?"

His brow drew together in a heavy frown that lightened only slightly when he spoke. "I just might do that."

"Good," she countered, focusing her attention on the stack of dirty dishes and silverware now piled in the sink. But it was hard to see them because tears hampered her vision.

"Melissa, for God's—"

Her sudden gasp of pain stopped his words.

"Melissa!" He was beside her in record time. "What the hell...?"

She was staring at her index finger as if in a trance. It was covered with blood.

His dark gaze lingered on her hand, then returned to her face. "How the hell did you do that?" A muscle jerked in his jaw.

"There's...there's a knife on top of the plate..." Her voice trailed off.

"You're not going to faint on me, are you?"

"No," she muttered weakly. "At least I don't think so."

"Here," he said huskily, "give me your hand."

"Joshua..." It was a plea for something, she didn't know what.

Tenderly, as if he were handling the rarest of porcelain, he gently maneuvered her hand under the faucet. When the blood had washed away under the running water, he bent his head and examined it closely. With rough fingers he gently probed the torn, tender flesh.

Trying to downplay the effect his touch was once again having on her, she made light of the situation. "I've... never been so accident prone in my life." Her voice wavered slightly. "Two in one day is quite a record."

His hand stilled, and he looked up into her eyes. "Well, nurse, I hardly think this one will require major surgery."

"Are you sure?" she asked, her breath coming in short spurts.

"Just to make sure, we'd better take another look."

Before Melissa realized his intentions, he brought the tip of her finger to his mouth and kissed it.

For the second time in a few hours, she was speechless.

By the time he lowered her finger, his breathing was shallow. "When I kiss Sara's sore bleedies, it always makes them better."

His gaze never flickered, holding her transfixed, breathless.

She felt herself drowning. "I...I should clean up this mess," she whispered, hardly recognizing her own voice.

"You're exhausted," he said softly. "Why don't you call it a night. I'll load the dishwasher and put the kids to bed."

She shook her head. "No...I can't let you do that."

He was looking at her again with that strange light in his eyes. "I think you'd best go."

She went.

Six

Three days had passed since Melissa cut her finger, and during that time her and Joshua's paths crossed very little. Awakening at her usual time, she'd gone into the kitchen where there had been no sign of him, except for an empty cup in the sink.

The morning following her accident, there had been a note on the table, in Joshua's manly scrawl, telling her that he was opening a household checking account so that she could buy groceries and pay for other necessary items, such as gymnastics.

When she'd sat at the table, a smile had crossed her face. Losing no time, she'd made a list of things that needed to be done.

From then on she hadn't stopped. It had been a hectic three days, but with no major upsets. Though the twins had still not accepted her, they hadn't been openly antagonistic, either.

The one thing in her favor, when it came to Sara, had been the appearance of the tooth fairy. Sara had been ecstatic with the results. She had dashed into Melissa's room, waving the five-dollar bill that Joshua had slipped under her pillow while she was taking a bath.

"Lookey what the fairy left me, Ms. Banning."

"Why don't you call me Melissa. Ms. Banning is a mouthful."

"Okay, Lissa," she said, her silky curls bouncing.

Melissa couldn't help but smile at the shortened version of her name. Somehow it fit.

"So, tell me what you're going to do with all that money," Melissa said at last.

"Hide it from my brother."

Melissa laughed and hugged the child, then helped her and Sam get ready for school.

Even that hadn't turned out to be the trauma Melissa had expected. It was while she'd checked their drawers and closet for suitable clothing that she noticed how skimpy their wardrobes were. She'd vowed to correct that.

However, she had spent the majority of time cleaning, determined to take one room at a time, beginning with the kitchen. But she'd been hampered by interruptions.

Laurie had called, and they had chatted for at least thirty minutes. Then two of her nursing friends had called her, bringing her up-to-date on hospital gossip. Melissa had thought she would experience pangs of regret when the nurses had given her a blow-by-blow account of what was happening at the hospital. But she hadn't. Instead, she had felt a sense of relief that she was not there.

Despite those interruptions, she had accomplished more than she'd thought possible in such a short time. Not only had she turned the kitchen into a sparkling room of beauty, but she had shopped for groceries and filled the pantry to capacity. She'd also signed Sam up for soccer and Sara for gymnastics and dance.

Most important of all, she had made an effort to spend time with the twins, though it hadn't been easy. Joshua had punished them for their behavior at the dinner table, and they had blamed her. Still she'd had an after-school activity planned each day. So far she had been pleased with the result.

Joshua, however, was a different matter. She had told herself she must stop thinking about him. When she'd been forced to communicate with him, which had been only for a short time in the evenings before he shut himself up in his office, she had kept it brief and businesslike, as had he.

Despite her efforts, he had crept into her thoughts. He was like a force of nature, appearing at the most unexpected moments. Like now, when she was in the utility room loading the washer with clothes.

She sighed as she jammed the last of Joshua's jeans into the cold water and slammed the lid down on the machine.

"What's the matter with you?" she muttered aloud, thoroughly vexed with herself.

Then, as if by keeping her hands busy she could run from her thoughts, Melissa began straightening the items on the shelf in front of her.

No such luck. Joshua's face flashed before her eyes, and her sigh deepened. The chemical reaction between them made no sense, she argued furiously. She couldn't begin to come to grips with it. Yet denying it made no sense, either. Every time she looked at him, she felt it.

He turned her on. That was it in a nutshell. On both occasions when he'd touched her, he had started a fire inside her body. He'd made her feel feminine again, a feeling she hadn't experienced in years, a feeling she thought she'd never experience again. And that was where the danger lay.

Since Martin's betrayal and her family's deaths, she had thought her emotions were dead and buried, never to be resurrected. Was she ever wrong. Joshua Malone, with his blue eyes, cocky smile and gorgeous body, had the power to turn her bones to water the instant he came near her. Even if he never touched her again—and she would make sure he didn't—she knew that it wouldn't just go away.

"Are you at a stopping place?"

She jerked around, her heart in her throat. "Lord, but you scared me half to death."

Joshua's eyebrows drew together. "Sorry, thought you heard me when I came through the door. Obviously not, huh?"

"No," she said, sounding winded, his face and body filling her vision.

"Sorry, didn't mean to scare you."

Melissa removed her hand from her heart, though it was still racing like a runaway freight train. He was staring at her, one eyebrow arched high, his mouth twisted in a near smile. Oh, God, had he read her thoughts? Nervously, she ran her tongue over her dry lips.

"You're...home earlier than usual."

"Yep."

She frowned. "Is anything wrong?"

"Does something have to be wrong for me to knock off early?"

"No, of course not," Melissa said stiffly. "It's just that—"

"I don't make a habit of doing that. Was that what you were going to say?"

"Yes," she responded, shifting her shoulders, suddenly recognizing how tightly she had been holding them.

"Well, I was about to tell you why when you jumped

like you'd been shot. You always that jittery? Or is it just when I'm around?''

Melissa shot him a scorching look. ''Maybe a little of both.''

To her amazement, he threw back his head and laughed.

Flushing in annoyance, she averted her gaze, determined not to let him know how that deep laugh had affected her or how she couldn't stop noticing the way his worn jeans molded his muscled thighs to perfection or how his blue chambray shirt, open halfway down the front, exposed the hairs on his chest.

''By the way, where are the twins?'' he asked, bridging the ongoing silence. ''It's much too quiet for them to be around.''

Thankful for the reprieve from her disturbing thoughts, Melissa answered quickly, ''Alice's girls took them for a ride on their bicycles.''

''Ah, so you've met the Sinclairs?''

''Alice introduced herself first thing Monday morning when she came after the twins.''

''She's a character, isn't she?''

Melissa smiled. ''That's for sure. But I liked her on the spot.''

''I'm glad. She's a good friend to have.''

''The twins are certainly crazy about her.''

As if he heard the dejected note in her voice, he said, ''Your time's coming.''

''I wish I shared your confidence, although I will admit things are better, especially with Sara.''

His eyes softened slightly. ''It's because you care about them, whether they admit it or not.''

''I'm trying, that's for sure.''

''At least they're eating your food,'' he said, a smile

tugging at the corners of his lips. "And not complaining," he added.

The corners of her own lips twitched. "Maybe it's because I've been following the recipe book to a T and not improvising." It felt wonderful to be able to laugh at herself again.

Joshua chuckled. "You said that, I didn't. But since we're on the subject of food, how's your finger?"

She could feel the color rise in her face. "Fine. Just fine."

He hooked a thumb through a belt loop, a smug grin curling his lips. "Then my home remedy worked?"

Her voice betrayed no emotion except an uncommon huskiness. "Yes, it worked."

He stared at her steadily for another moment, then shoved his Stetson back and swiped at his forehead with the back of his hand. "Damn, but it's hot. I'm wondering what happened to those cool Septembers we used to have. Here I am sweating like a judge at a close election."

That brought another smile to Melissa's lips. "You're not alone. I called time and temperature a little while ago, and it was 85 degrees." She tipped her head sideways. "Is that the reason you're home early?"

"Hardly," he said, his blue eyes searching her face. "You don't remember my original question, do you?"

She thought for a moment. "No, I guess I don't."

"I asked if you were at a stopping place. The washing is what I was referring to."

"Why, do you need me to do something?"

"Yeah. Go to the softball game. You and the twins." She blinked. "Me?"

"Yes, you," he mimicked.

"Now?"

He glanced down at his watch. "Oh, say in about thirty minutes."

"But...I don't understand. I mean..."

He shrugged. "Just thought you might like to go, that's all."

"Are you going to play?"

"Sure am."

"What position?"

He looked surprised, and when he spoke, his tone was faintly mocking. "Shortstop."

She turned away with the pretense of checking the machine, all the while trying to sort through her confused thoughts.

"Well, you wanna come or not?"

She faced him again. "I'll go, but I'll have to change clothes."

"Why?"

"Because I can't go looking like this, that's why."

Her red mane was drawn in a severe topknot, with only a few wayward strands escaping around her temples and her creamy nape. She had on cutoff jeans and a green T-shirt that had the words Methodist Hospital splattered across both breasts. On top of that, she was barefooted.

"You look fine to me." His voice had dropped an octave.

She swallowed. "I...wouldn't feel right."

He drew in a breath. "Suit yourself."

Then before she could reply, he turned his back and ambled down the hall toward his bedroom. Melissa sagged against the machine and watched him, her body too weak to move.

Seven

"I see you got conned into this, too."

Melissa swung around, then smiled. "Oh, hi, Alice," she said, her smile widening. "Since you weren't with the girls, I didn't think you were coming."

"No such luck," Alice replied. "Travis would have a fit if I didn't come watch him play."

With the exception of the Sinclairs, Joshua had gotten her and the twins to the softball park practically before anybody else. Melissa had been sitting by herself while the twins sat several bleachers below with the Sinclair girls, Mitzi and Jane, having a good time. But she hadn't been bored; when she wasn't keeping an eye on the twins, she was watching Joshua and Travis warm up.

Every so often Joshua would look her way and wink, and her pulse rate would escalate wildly.

"Want some company?"

"Sure." Melissa scooted over. "Have a seat."

With a soft grunt, Alice lowered her short, overweight body onto the hard wooden seat. She had light brown hair sprinkled with gray and lovely brown eyes that even the glasses she wore couldn't hide.

At the moment there was a twinkle in those eyes. "Well, what do you think?"

"If the way your husband is pitching that ball is anything to judge by, the Wallbangers are going to win."

Alice's gaze followed Melissa's. "Yeah, even if I do say so myself, Travis is the best pitcher in the league." She grinned. "But that wasn't what I meant."

"What did you mean, then?" Melissa plucked at the white string that was clinging to one leg of her jeans.

"I was referring to your job. Actually, I was referring to Joshua and the twins."

Melissa sighed. "To tell the truth, I don't know. I...don't see a lot of Joshua, and the twins—well, they tolerate me and that's about all."

Alice leaned over and patted her on the knee. "Please don't give up. Those kids need you. Ever since Gwen died, their lives have been topsy-turvy. Joshua's tried—oh, Lord, how he's tried. But with his job and all, it's been hell."

"What was she like, Gwen I mean?" Even as the words left her mouth, Melissa wished she could call them back. She grimaced guiltily. For some crazy reason, she felt as though she were prying.

The sunlight was dwindling. Twilight was near. The darkening leaves rustled in the trees in the distance, and night was falling.

"There's nothing wrong with your curiosity," Alice said gently. "In fact, it's only natural."

"While I feel I'm making strides with Sara, Sam's a different story." Melissa shook her head. "He seems to remember his mother more than Sara."

"Well, she doted on them both, that's for sure. Her babies were her life." Alice shoved her glasses higher up the bridge of her nose. "Gwen was quiet and rather shy, really. But she loved to cook and kept an immaculate house."

"Sounds like she was, *is*, a tough act to follow." Melissa tried her best to keep the despondency out of her voice.

Apparently she failed, for the look Alice gave her was sympathetic. "I agree, only..."

"Only what?" Melissa prodded when the other woman hesitated.

Alice sighed. "I shouldn't say this, but sometimes I think Gwen neglected Joshua." She paused, gesturing with her hand. "Forget I said that, will you? My tongue has a way of running away with me sometimes."

Melissa would have liked to have heard more, though she didn't voice that thought. Instead she asked, "What about his sister?"

"Oh, she did a great job until she up and married. As you know, from then on it's been one housekeeper after another. For whatever reason, they don't stay. It's the twins, though around me and the girls, they're angels."

Melissa lifted her chin. "Well, I don't intend to let them run me off."

"Atta girl."

They fell silent for a moment and listened as the starting lineups were announced over the loudspeaker. It was only after the enthusiastic applause with loud whistles ripping through the air that Melissa realized the stands had filled to near capacity.

Joshua and Travis's team, the Wallbangers, were the first to take the field. The whistles grew louder.

Alice, getting to her feet, cupped her hands on either side of her mouth and yelled, "Come on, Trav honey, you can do it. Pitch 'em over the plate."

Melissa stood beside her and began clapping. "Are the Wallbangers picked to win?"

Alice threw her an outrageous glance. "Don't you dare let Joshua hear you ask that. Those men, especially your boss, think that every time they put on their uniform, they're going to win."

"But do they?"

Alice laughed again. "Of course, they'll win, if Joshua's bat is as hot as it usually is."

Melissa didn't say anything as her eyes locked on Joshua, who was at the shortstop position, flexing his muscles as he limbered up. He filled out his knit uniform nicely, she thought, better than any man she'd seen on the covers of magazines lately.

A frown creased her brow, and at the same time Alice punched her on the arm. "Sam's trying to get your attention. I think there's trouble brewing."

"Oh, brother," Melissa murmured, lowering her head and meeting Sam's upturned gaze. "What's wrong, honey?" Her tone was pleasant in spite of the peevish expression on Sam's face.

"Sara keeps hitting me, Ms. Banning," he whined. "Make her stop."

Alice smiled and raised her eyes heavenward. "I'm surprised it hasn't happened sooner. Have fun."

"Thanks," Melissa replied dryly with a watered-down grin. She then made her way carefully down the bleachers until she was sitting behind the children.

"Sara, honey, are you being a pain in the neck?"

Sara turned rounded eyes up at Melissa. "He hit me first."

"She's lying," Sam said quickly, defiantly.

"Sam, you mustn't call your sister a liar," Melissa scolded. "That's not a nice word."

"But—" he began.

"Let me finish. Did you hit her first?"

He hung his head. "Yes, ma'am."

"Now, him's the pain in the neck." Sara flashed her an endearing grin.

Mitzi and Jane snickered.

Sheer willpower kept Melissa from following suit. "Sam, I think you should tell your sister you're sorry, don't you?"

Sam cut his eyes to her and was quiet for a minute. "Do I havta?"

"You havta," Melissa stressed softly, reaching out and straightening the collar on his jogging suit. For once, he didn't pull away, but it was with reluctance that he complied with her order.

"I'm sorry," he muttered.

"Thank you." Melissa patted him on the back. Then turning to Sara, she said, "Young lady, I think it'd be best if you sat on the other side of Mitzi."

"Can we have some popcorn?" Sam asked once Sara had scrambled off the seat to do as she was told.

"I don't see why not," Melissa said.

Minutes later Melissa kept the Sinclair girls and the twins in sight until they had rounded the corner at the far end of the bleachers. Shaking her head, she climbed up and once again sat beside Alice.

Alice grinned. "You handled that like a pro."

"Oh, I don't know," Melissa groaned. "Sometimes the enormity of this job hits me like a ton of bricks. And then sometimes I feel so sorry for them because they don't have a mother, and I just want to hug them, assure them everything is going to be all right. Does that make sense?"

"Yes, because I feel the same way. There are times when

I'd like to hug Joshua, tell him the same thing. That man's been through hell.''

"I'm surprised he never remarried. I know there are women who—" Melissa broke off.

Alice made a clucking sound with her tongue. "That's an understatement. While Dee was living with them, he saw a different one practically every night, but now he doesn't seem to go out as much, though I'm sure he's not celibate."

Melissa tried her best to ignore the tiny wound to her heart. "I'm sure."

Alice gave her a strange look, though she didn't say anything, and after that they talked very little, turning their full attention to the game. Each time Joshua came to bat or caught a ball, Melissa found herself standing, hollering and cheering along with the rest of the spectators.

"I can't believe he's so good," Melissa exclaimed, turning a flushed face toward Alice after Joshua had hit a line drive into left field, driving in a run.

Sam and Sara were jumping up and down. "Daddy, Daddy, Daddy."

Alice stomped on the bleachers. "Yeah, isn't he something."

"Yeah, he sure is," Melissa whispered to herself.

She was still thinking that when the ball game finally ended and she, Alice and the kids wandered to the dugout. They had been there only a minute when Joshua headed toward them.

Sam and Sara ran to meet him.

"Daddy, you were awesome!" Sam cried, reaching him first. "You made the winning run."

"Yeah, Daddy, you were awesome," Sara echoed, her soft curls swirling around her heart-shaped face.

"Proud of your old man, huh?" Joshua grinned, placing

his arms around each of their shoulders. But his eyes sought Melissa. "Well?"

"Well what?" Melissa asked innocently.

"You know..."

At that moment Travis Sinclair came up behind Joshua and clapped him on the back. He was a big, brawny man with dark hair and a mustache.

He winked at Melissa. "He wants you to tell him how great he did, that's what."

Alice made a face. "You men and your macho egos. Talk about women."

"You did play a great game," Melissa said, her gaze connecting with Joshua's again. For a heartbeat, it seemed as if they were alone.

"I hope you had a good time," he said finally, his voice warm.

"I had a wonderful time."

Sam's sudden, "Daddy, can we have some more popcorn?" shattered the moment.

As if giving his ragged breath time to even out, Joshua slowly and methodically removed his cap and wiped his brow before he answered. "No, son, it's late. It's time to go home."

Melissa couldn't help but notice the way he looked at her when he said the word "home."

She felt warm and cold at the same time.

The giggles coming from the bathroom could be heard throughout the house.

Melissa had drawn the twins' bathwater and filled the tub with bubble bath. Each had a washcloth, though not much progress had been made toward washing their bodies. They were too busy playing. The boat that she had bought at the grocery store that morning was a big hit.

"You two need to hurry," Melissa said, leaning over the tub and pushing Sara's curls off her forehead. "It's getting late. Remember school's tomorrow."

Sam lifted inquiring eyes to her from the soapy depths of the bubbles, two red spots on his cheeks. "Where's Daddy? I thought he was coming to bathe us."

"Lissa's bathing us, silly," Sara pointed out before slapping at the water with her tiny palm.

"He'll be here in a minute, I'm sure," Melissa said hastily, wiping a sudsy bubble from her sleeve. "He's taking a shower. Sara, stop splashing like that. You're drowning me and the floor, honey. See the front of my shirt? It's soaking wet."

Sara giggled.

Sam sniffed, rubbing his nose with a soapy finger. "I wish Aunt Dee would come back. I miss her."

"I know you do," Melissa responded gently, trying not to feel hurt by Sam's continued rejection of her.

"Her's married," Sara said to her brother. "Her's never coming back."

Melissa took Sara's rag and wiped the rose-flushed skin. "Not to live, but she'll be back to visit you, I'm sure." Then turning to Sam, she said, "Don't forget to wash behind your ears."

"Will you read us a bedtime story, Lissa?" Sara asked suddenly.

"Mmm, maybe, but only if you hurry and get finished with your bath."

Sam cut his eyes to her, interested in spite of himself. "Would you read the *Little Engine That Could*?"

Melissa smiled at him. "Sure will. That's one of my favorites, too. Now, both of you get out, and let's get dried off."

Several minutes later Sam was dressed in his *Star Wars*

pajamas and was on the other side of the room, playing with the boat on the carpet. Sara, in her gown, was standing in front of the mirror clutching her Cabbage Patch doll, while Melissa took her hair out of that adorable topknot.

"Did you know my mommie's in heaven with Jesus?"

Melissa's hand stilled at the same time Joshua appeared in the doorway. Had he heard? Of course, he had, she told herself, feeling her heart race. Why else would he have that stricken, haunted look on his face?

"Yes, honey," Melissa murmured, lowering her eyes, "I know."

"You kiddos about ready to hit the bed?" Joshua asked, striding into the room, his expression bland.

Her mother forgotten for the moment, Sara twisted around. "Lissa's going to read us a story first."

Joshua quirked a brow. "Lissa, huh?"

"Thanks to your daughter," Melissa said, feeling slightly uncomfortable.

"Yeah, I named her that, Daddy," Sara announced proudly, running to Joshua and lifting her arms. Once there, she gave him a wet kiss on the lips.

"Oh, gross," Sam said, shaking his head.

Melissa laughed.

Joshua smiled and motioned for Sam to come to him. "I'll make you think gross, young man." With Sara still in his arms, he leaned over and planted a kiss on top of Sam's curls.

Melissa, standing silently by, was suddenly struck by a sense of pathos; something in Joshua's attitude, the way the children were looking at him with adoring eyes, gripped her heart with the queerest pang. She could not define what she felt; she only knew she found something touching in their relationship and longed to be part of it.

"Lissa's gonna read us a story," Sara said, ending the short silence.

Melissa nodded. "Pile on my bed, both of you."

"Can Daddy come, too?" Sara asked innocently.

For a moment another silence fell over the room—a deeper, longer silence than before.

Then a slow smile lit Joshua's hard features. "Somehow I don't think Lissa's bed is big enough for the four of us." He paused, his grin widening at Melissa's obvious discomfort. "But I'll come and kiss you good-night."

Satisfied, they scampered down the hall, holding hands.

Melissa, aware of Joshua's presence with every nerve in her body, walked stiffly to the tub, where she leaned over and snapped the drain open.

When she stood a second later and turned around, Joshua was behind her, staring at her. She saw his gaze pause in the proximity of her breasts, which the damp cotton blouse did little to conceal.

The silence grew, and with it tension. With Joshua's direct gaze holding hers, she felt a curious paralysis in her limbs.

"You have soap on your face," he said huskily.

She swallowed. "I...do?"

Without answering, he reached out and scooped it off her nose.

She started as if she had inadvertently touched a live wire.

His eyes darkened. "You're afraid of me, aren't you?" He paused. The sound of his breathing was like a second pulse. "Or is it yourself you're afraid of?"

Eight

Melissa yawned, then stretched. Still she couldn't seem to wake up, even though she'd brushed her teeth and taken a quick shower.

Naked, she slipped into the robe hanging on the back of the door and belted it around her. Then turning, she stared at her reflection in the mirror. Her eyelids were faintly taupe, accentuating her dark eyes, and there was a blush heightening her cheekbones; her dark hair brushed back from her face fell around her head in casual curls.

Not bad for someone who hadn't fallen asleep until the wee hours of the morning, she thought cynically. But looks in her case were deceptive. While she might not look tired, she was.

After she'd read the twins the *Little Engine That Could* twice, she had put them to bed. Sleep, however, had eluded her. She hadn't been able to shake Joshua's softly spoken taunts—*You're afraid of me, aren't you? Or is it yourself you're afraid of?*—neither of which she had bothered to answer.

Instead she'd turned her back on him and gone straight to her room where the twins were waiting, his deep-bellied chuckle following her all the way.

Suddenly disgusted with herself for letting him dominate her thoughts, she flipped off the light and strode out of the bathroom.

Since it was too early to awaken the twins and knowing that Joshua would have long ago left for work, she made her way toward the kitchen, desperate for a cup of coffee.

She had barely gotten into the room when she froze. Joshua was sitting at the table, drinking a cup of coffee.

"Good morning," he drawled, eyeing her carefully.

She pulled her robe tighter around her. "I thought you'd be at work by now." The words came out in a rush, as if she couldn't check them.

"Should've been."

A silence followed.

His blue eyes leveled on her, and for a moment they gazed at each other. His rising color answered hers.

Melissa's lips parted on a terrified breath. She was the first to recover. Averting her eyes, she said inanely, "I thought I'd have some coffee before I woke the twins."

"Melissa..."

Suddenly a chill rippled up her spine, signaling danger. She felt exposed, naked of protection against his presence, his potent masculinity.

On legs that weren't quite steady, Melissa made her way to the cabinet, located a cup and reached for the coffeepot. As she leaned over, unbeknownst to her the top of her robe gaped and exposed her right breast.

His sharp intake of breath brought Melissa's head up and

around. Tracking his eyes, she found them focused on a creamy breast. Crimson-faced, she straightened abruptly.

In a heartbeat, he was out of his chair and next to her.

She took an awkward, frantic step backward. "Joshua... no."

"Yes, Melissa," he countered softly, inching still closer.

She could smell his scent. Not his cologne, but his essence. Unconsciously she breathed him in. He was clean shaven. The dark stubble that had covered his jaw last night was gone. Wet hair lay shaggily against the back of his neck. Crispy brown hairs curled along his forearms.

He began moving his hands across her shoulders to the sides of her robe. There was something about the way he was looking at her, touching her that made her unable to move. She experienced a familiar warmth, felt herself slipping, momentarily losing control. It seemed almost as if he had cast a spell in the vacant shadows where they stood. Everything was as if in a dream. Perhaps she had never fully awakened.

"Don't," she gasped, thinking she might faint. "Please don't."

He had been right. She *was* afraid for him to touch her again, afraid of the feeling that was building inside her, threatening to consume her.

"I have to or die," he said thickly, his eyes intent upon his hands as he caught the fabric with his fingers and easily opened the robe down to the waist, baring her breasts.

"No!" she said again, quivering, but her protests were as unconvincing as her response was positive. Her nipples became hard points under his fingers.

An intense heat rose in his body. Joshua groaned. "You want this as much as I do." He leaned forward then, and touched his lips to hers, his arm holding her fast, his large hand molded over a breast.

Suddenly nothing mattered, only his touch. Her fear dissolved, leaving only an all-consuming desire for more.

Instinctively she opened her mouth, accepting his tongue, responding without knowing why. Unable to think, she merely responded to being touched and kissed. Her senses soared, her limbs felt weightless. She was sky-rocketing into a fantasy land filled with warmth and well-being, where all that mattered was that he should go on drugging her with his mouth, his hands.

When he moved his hand off her breast, her eyes fluttered open.

"Oh, Melissa," he whispered, "I want you so much." From her breast, his hand slid down her back. He gripped her bottom, crushing her against the hard pressure of his body.

Maybe it was the ragged note in his voice or the way he was touching her, or maybe it was the coffeepot gurgling at that particular moment that brought her back to reality.

With a half-strangled cry, she tore herself out of his arms and stumbled backward, her face seemingly all eyes as she stared up at him in stunned amazement.

For a moment he, too, seemed lost for words, returning her stare. He looked as if someone had hit him in the head with a baseball bat.

She began to shiver, averting her eyes while nursing her swollen lips with her tongue. She couldn't believe what had just happened, though his actions came as no surprise. What stunned and frightened her was what *she* had done. Nothing like this had ever happened to her before. When Martin had kissed her, her emotions had been unaffected. Joshua quite simply made her ache.

She had been worried she might be frigid after all. Well, if it had been true, then to her dismay, Joshua Malone had thawed her out.

"Pretty potent stuff, huh," Joshua said at last, managing a rallying grin, which went a long way in relieving the strain around his mouth.

But Melissa wasn't fooled; the smile had not reached his eyes, and his breathing was still fragmented.

"Joshua...maybe I'd better—"

"Damn, I've got to get the hell outa here," he cut in, as if sensing what she was about to say.

With a trembling hand, she pushed the hair from her face, fully aware of her flushed, damp cheeks, aware of the warm, minty taste of his lips.

When she didn't respond, he leaned over and retrieved his hat from the buffet, then set it on his head.

"You'll...be here when I get home." His eyes, barely visible below the rim of his hat, were dark and unreadable.

"Yes," she said on a sigh, relieved that her voice was steady. The moment of madness had passed.

"I'll see you then."

He looked at her for what seemed an interminable length of time, an artery pulsing in his neck, then he spun around and walked out the door.

Darkness had fallen, and he still hadn't gone home. Using the hanging light as his guide, he hit the nail, kept hitting it until it had completely disappeared inside the wood.

"You just had to do it, didn't you?" he spat out, fishing another nail out of his pocket and treating it with the same lack of respect. "You just had to kiss her!"

When that second nail was finally buried, he dropped the hammer and stood to his full height. Thank God, no one was within hearing distance, he thought ruefully, looking around. The men, including his foreman, had left for the day. Joshua should've been gone, too, but he hadn't wanted to face Melissa.

With another burst of frustrated energy, he jumped off the ladder and stalked toward the temporary building. God, but he was in a foul mood.

He didn't notice the damp, chilly room as he sat down and leaned back, propping his feet on the corner of the desk. He hadn't bothered to turn on the overhead light, watching disinterestedly as the moon created shadows on the walls.

If she had packed her bags and was gone when he finally did get home, he wouldn't be at all surprised. And he would have no one to blame but himself.

Dammit, he'd intended only to tease her, flirt with her a little, try to get through that shell of hers. She always seemed so uptight, so in control.

But when her robe had parted and her overfull breast appeared before his eyes... Still that didn't excuse his behavior. Not only had his actions been foolish, but they might have cost him the best housekeeper he'd had.

Shoving his hand through his hair, he raised his eyes heavenward and let out a deep breath. Yet the picture of Melissa's lovely face and body remained imprinted on his mind.

Her skin made him think of velvet and the petals of a rose, and the instant she had gazed up at him with eyes so deep that he could drown in them, he'd wanted her like hell. And nothing at that moment could have stopped him from tasting those trembling lips or caressing that creamy breast.

Even now he could hear her silent pleas in his mind, soft pleas that stabbed him with red-hot longing. It was crazy, but no other woman had affected him this way, certainly not his wife.

The feel of Melissa, the sight of her, the scent of her, all combined to drive him mad.

How deeply was he going to get involved with this woman? he wondered. It was a meaningless question, as the answer was already painstakingly clear.

Nine

"**I**'m gonna tell Daddy on you 'cause you were bad."

Sam glared at his sister. "Was not."

"Was, too. You had to sit in the time-out chair."

"So what."

Sara grinned, the gap in her teeth standing out like a neon sign. "That means the teacher doesn't like you, 'cause you told something you weren't 'posed to."

Sam's lips twisted sullenly. "I don't like her, either."

"Daddy's going to spank your butt."

Sam covered his mouth. "Hmm. You said a bad word. If you tell on me, I'm gonna tell on you."

"But you'll get in more trouble than me, 'cause you told that Daddy..."

Melissa hadn't been paying much attention to the twins' conversation, which was taking place outside Joshua's bedroom, until Sara accused her brother of being bad. Immediately she had ceased placing Joshua's underwear in his drawer and listened. It was a lovely, mild afternoon, and the French doors were open off Joshua's bedroom. The twins were playing on the patio close by.

However, when Sara blurted what Sam had said, Melissa's hand flew to her mouth just in time to stifle her horrified cry. She shouldn't have been surprised; she had been expecting it before now. Maybe not this, but something. While Sara was adjusting to her, Sam was not. He continued to be one unhappy little boy, and no matter what Melissa said or did, she couldn't seem to get through to him.

Hastily she finished her task, determined to call a halt to the verbal skirmish before it developed into a physical one. Anyway, it was time for gymnastics and soccer practices.

Melissa went to the door and in her most calming voice said, "Okay, kids, it's time to wash your hands and faces, get ready to go."

"Yippee!" they cried in unison, dashing by her, their disagreement completely forgotten.

But Melissa hadn't forgotten. In fact, it was so much on her mind that once the twins had been dropped off, she decided to stop off at the job site and talk to Joshua.

Now, as she turned off the loop onto the construction-site parking lot and brought the car to a halt, she remained behind the wheel, faced with sudden doubts, uncertain as to the reception she would receive.

Yet she had no choice. If she wanted to talk to him about anything important, it would have to be here; for the past week he had made it a point not to come home until after she and the children had gone to bed.

He was avoiding her, which was fine by her. She hadn't wanted to see or think about him, either. Immediately after those mind-boggling moments when he'd kissed her, she had played a game with herself; she had convinced herself that Joshua had made it impossible for her to resist him. While the memory of that morning remained as vivid as ever in her mind, it had become distorted.

She had succeeded in making herself believe that Joshua had been the one at fault. What other explanation could there be for her behavior?

But later, after allowing every detail of what had happened to resurrect itself, Melissa could no longer harbor such a delusion. It was demeaning and two-faced of her to blame Joshua entirely. She had been as much at fault as he, maybe more.

Now, as she got from behind the wheel, she straightened the belt on her turquoise jumpsuit and surveyed her surroundings.

Bulldozers, cranes, large trucks and men in hard hats were scattered about the area. She hesitated, as she knew it wouldn't be wise to stray much farther on her own or she might get hurt.

Pausing, she looked around for Joshua. She had parked near his truck, so it was safe to guess he was somewhere on the premises. The moment she spotted the temporary building, she headed that way, making sure she kept a wide berth between her and the workers.

However, she noticed several had stopped what they were doing and stared at her. One even whistled. Ignoring him, she trudged on, trying her best not to get her white tennis shoes dirty. She was nearing her destination when a man appeared in front of her.

"May I help you, ma'am?" he asked in a gruff but polite voice. He had dark eyes, dark hair and heavy dark beard, which went a long way in hiding the scar zigzagging down his right cheek.

"Yes, I'm looking for Joshua Malone."

"And you're...?"

"Melissa Banning, his housekeeper."

"Ah..." He grinned. "I'm Tom Wingate, foreman on the job."

"Pleasure, Mr. Wingate," Melissa said with a sincere smile.

"You'll forgive me, won't you, if I don't shake your hand; mine are awfully dirty."

Melissa's smile widened. She liked this dark, burly man on sight. "Don't apologize; after all, you're working."

Tom Wingate yanked off a soiled blue baseball cap, smoothed his thick hair back from his forehead with a beefy hand and resettled his cap with the bill just above his eyes. "Why don't you wait in there—" he nodded toward the building "—and I'll get the boss. There's fresh coffee if you're interested."

"Thanks," she said, making no move to leave. "Is he busy?" Her tone was hesitant. "I mean...it's not important. It can wait," she added hastily, noticing that more of the men had stopped working and were watching her and Wingate.

Wingate grinned. "Oh, he's busy all right. That's him on top of that steel frame."

Melissa's eyes followed Wingate's pointed finger. She gasped. "But why is he up there? Doesn't he have men who do that? I thought he was the contractor."

Wingate cocked his head to one side. "He is, but he works as hard or harder than any of the men." He removed his cap again and scratched his head. "Doesn't believe in asking them to do anything he won't do himself."

Melissa shook her head. "While that might be admirable, it's terribly dangerous."

"Oh, it's that, all right. In fact, Josh took a tumble on a job very similar to this one. Banged his head pretty hard."

Her heart lurched. "Oh, God."

"He was lucky, really," Wingate went on as though on

a roll. "He has some bad headaches now and then, but other than that, he's okay." Then, as if realizing he was talking too much, Wingate shifted his feet and added hurriedly, "Well, I've taken up enough of your time. I'll get Josh. Nice meetin' you."

Melissa smiled. "Nice to meet you, too."

She watched as the foreman's big stride took him to the building itself, where he cupped his hands around his mouth and hollered up at Joshua.

"Hey, boss, someone's here to see you."

Rather than wait inside as Wingate had suggested, Melissa chose to remain outside, keeping a close eye on Joshua as he got down from the floor of the steel-framed building and headed in her direction.

It wasn't until Joshua was nearly upon her that he raised his head. He pulled up short, a surprised look on his face. However, concern instantly replaced the surprise, and he upped his pace.

"Hey, boss, she your latest?"

Illicit laughter erupted, followed by several wolf whistles.

Although Joshua behaved as if he hadn't heard a word, Melissa could not. She felt her face turn scarlet, and she wished the ground would open up and swallow her.

They thought she was one of his...his *women*, for God's sake!

"Yeah, man, she's much better-looking than the blonde, even if her—"

Joshua stopped and twisted around, his eyes and his voice cold as chips of ice. "Shut your mouth, Townsend. If you want to finish out the hour, you'd best haul your butt back to work."

When he stopped in front of her, Melissa's breathing had still not returned to normal.

"Sorry about that," he said, his tone still as grim as his features.

"Don't be," she said tightly, still furious that she was taken for one of his women. "You don't have to apologize for entertaining your women here."

Suddenly, his lips parted in a mocking grin, and she knew that once again her quick tongue had backfired on her.

A tiny fire leaped into his eyes. "Why, I believe you're jealous."

A brave smile deepened the lines on Melissa's face. "Don't be ridiculous! Of course, I'm not jealous."

"Of course not," he repeated softly.

"I can see coming here was a mistake."

"Let's go into the office," he said abruptly. "I could use a cup of coffee."

Assuming she would follow, he stomped up the steps, thrust open the door and stepped aside for her to enter. With her mouth set in a thin line, she skirted past him.

The office was furnished with a scarred desk, a chair, a small couch and makeshift coffee bar. A window, located behind the desk, was open, filling the room with fresh air and sunshine.

Melissa removed her sunglasses, perched on the edge of the couch and watched as Joshua poured two cups of coffee.

He looked tired, she thought irrationally. The lines around his eyes and mouth seemed deeper, more pronounced. But neither of those slight imperfections detracted from his rough, good looks. Dressed in his usual work garb of worn jeans and cotton shirt, his aura of masculinity was a power to be reckoned with. In spite of herself, she felt her heart give a skip behind her ribs.

"You're here about the twins." His voice broke into the heavy silence that had descended over the room. "Right?"

He had handed her a cup of coffee and was now leaning against the desk, his eyes moving slowly over her. There was another moment of sizzling silence as their eyes met and held, his unwavering stare sending an extended series of shocks through her. Then his concentration shifted from her mouth to her neckline in such a way as to make her terribly uncomfortable.

She had never met a man who concentrated on a woman with such intensity, as if every other human being had ceased to exist for him. She felt again that peculiar combination of uneasiness and excitement at being the focal point of his attention.

Giving a good imitation of a nonchalant shrug, Melissa exhaled slowly, broke the hold of his eyes and said, "As a matter of fact I did come about the twins—about Sam specifically."

"Oh?"

"I overheard Sam and Sara talking—" She broke off as he lowered his head and placed his lips to the cup. For an instant she became fascinated with his mouth.

"Go on," he said suddenly.

She hid the stormy emotions inside her with a cool smile. "To make a long story short, Sam got in trouble at school and had to sit in the time-out chair."

He chuckled. "What's he done this time?"

"You won't think it's funny when I tell you what he did."

"So why keep me in suspense?" His smile had long disappeared. "Let's have it."

Melissa didn't flinch. "Your son told the class at show-and-tell that his daddy slept without any clothes on."

"What!"

Even though it was really not funny, she was hard-pressed to keeping from laughing herself. However, she couldn't keep her lips from twitching. "You heard me."

"You mean he told the entire class I slept bare-assed?" When she didn't answer right off, he threw back his head and laughed. "Why that little bugger, I'll bust his—"

"Sara told him that's exactly what you'd do."

"Smart kid, that daughter of mine."

"What about your son? Don't you think you should talk to him?"

"Oh, I'll talk to him, all right."

"It's obvious he said that in order to get attention."

There was a second of absolute silence.

"From me?" A hard edge had crept into his voice.

She refused to back down. "Who else?"

"Are you saying that I'm not giving him the attention he needs?"

"I think you know the answer to that yourself." When he didn't say anything, she went on before she lost her nerve. "I know this job is important to you—"

"You're damn right it's important," he cut in, "but not more important than Sam and Sara. I've already told you that," he added curtly.

"Then why haven't you come home early enough to spend time with them?"

"I think you know the answer to that."

Instantly she tensed. "Then if that's the case, maybe I should—"

"No, dammit, you shouldn't." He raked a hand through his hair. "Look, I don't want you to leave, okay? The kids are doing much better than they've done in ages, and in spite of what you think, I don't want to lose you."

I don't want to lose you. For a moment those words raced through her mind, making speech impossible. Had he meant...? No, of course, he hadn't. God, what was wrong with her? It was just a figure of speech, nothing more, nothing less.

"Melissa?" He was looking at her strangely.

When her heart settled back to normal, she stammered, "Then...then please, don't make me the heavy in this. Come home, spend time with the twins."

His eyes held hers for a long moment, then clearing his throat, he said, "About the other morning, I owe—"

"Forget it."

"Have you?"

"Yes," she said, looking down. "I know you have a stable of women to choose from and that you're not interested in me."

His lips curved into a cynical smile. "Mmm. A stable of women. Now, that's a new one on me."

She raised her chin a trifle. "It's true, isn't it?"

"Look, I know what you're thinking."

"No, you don't."

"You're thinking all I've been wanting ever since you fell headlong into my arms the other day has been to get you in the sack. Am I right?"

"No!"

"And you think that all I care about is my work and my women and that I'm not worth a damn for the long haul—"

"I *said* no!"

"Okay, so I'm wrong." He paused. "But just in case I'm not, I want you to know that I haven't touched..." He broke off with a sharp expletive, as if realizing what he was about to say. Yet he couldn't seem to draw his eyes away from her.

The smoldering desire in that blue stare put an even sharper edge to her tone. "Damn you, Joshua, stop looking at me like that."

"Like how?" His voice seemed to come from a long way off.

Flustered again, she snapped, "You know."

As if suddenly tired of the game they were playing, he changed the subject. "You look tired," he said, drawing in a deep breath. "You've been working too hard. But I have to admit, the house looks great."

"Thanks," she said huskily, his praise as unexpected as it was pleasant. Would this man and his ever-changing moods forever remain an enigma to her? "I've been trying."

"It shows."

"Will you be home for dinner?" she asked, her voice controlled but still husky.

He seemed to hold his breath for a moment. "Yes, I'll be home."

She stood. "I need to go. It's time to pick up the kids."

"I'll take care of Sam. Don't worry."

She nodded, then turned her back and walked to the door. Her hand was on the knob when he called her name.

She turned back around. "Yes."

"You have freckles, you know. Across your nose."

A trembling began in the pit of her stomach. "I know."

"I love freckles."

The air was thick while she stood poised in a silent battle, desire and fear warring inside her—desire for him, fear for that desire.

She bit her moist red underlip. "Thanks...again."

"You're welcome." His smile spread through his voice.

While she still could, Melissa jerked open the door, and only after the cool, fresh air slapped her in the face, restoring her senses, did she breathe a sigh of relief.

Ten

Melissa cut off the water and stepped out of the shower. In the full-length mirror behind the door, she regarded herself critically. She was proud of her body.

She watched her muscles ripple as she worked the thick towel over her wet nipples. Her eyes fluttered shut, and she imagined what it would be like to have Joshua's lips there.

Then suddenly realizing what she was doing, what she was *thinking*, Melissa flung the towel aside in total frustration and padded into the bedroom where she slipped into a robe.

Before she walked out of the room, she glanced at the clock. It was after ten. But knowing sleep was a luxury that was sure to elude her, she headed down the hall to check on the twins, who she hoped were sleeping soundly.

When she eased open Sam's door, the night-light allowed her access to his small form on the bed. And beside him was Sara, clutching her Cabbage Patch doll against her chest.

A smile softened Melissa's face, and for some unknown reason tears welled up in her eyes. While she was in the shower, Sara must have wandered into Sam's room again. She wasn't surprised, as Sara did it quite often, always saying a bugger bear was after her.

But it was Sam who garnered her immediate attention. He was tossing and tumbling as though he might be feverish. The carpet soaked up the sound of her feet as she crossed to the bed. Just as her knee came in contact with the bed, Sam's eyes popped open.

He rubbed one eye, then stared up at Melissa.

"Honey, what's the matter?" Melissa whispered, lowering herself onto the side of the bed. "You having a bad dream?"

He turned his head away, but not before Melissa saw his lower lip begin to quiver.

Swallowing a sigh, she tried again. "Want me to sit with you a while?"

He twisted his head back around. "Daddy...Daddy's gonna spank me if I'm bad again."

Without thinking, Melissa reached over and gently pushed the hair off his forehead, only to then wait, panic-stricken, for his withdrawal. He didn't move a muscle; he continued to stare up at her with his green eyes wide and pain-filled.

Melissa's heart turned over, and it was all she could do not to grab him and hold him close. Instead, she said, "Is that what your daddy told you?"

He shook his head. "Sara's a tattletale. She told on me."

"No, Sam, Sara didn't tell your daddy, I did."

He kicked at the sheet and turned his head away, burying it in the pillow.

"I overheard you tell your sister about getting in trouble at school. I told your dad because it's wrong to tell personal things about your family at show-and-tell."

"That's what Daddy said," he muttered, twisting the edge of the sheet into a knot.

"Your daddy's right, you know," Melissa stressed gently. "And even though he had to punish you, he loves you very much."

"I know, but—"

"But what?" she prodded lightly.

"I wish I had a mommy like all my friends."

Melissa bit her lip and stared at the ceiling, trying to maintain control. But it was hard when her heart was breaking. When she felt that she could answer him without bursting into tears, she said, "I wish you did, too, honey, but you have your daddy, and you have me," she added tentatively. "And I love you, too."

He didn't say anything, so she went on, "How about if tomorrow afternoon we look for something really neat for you to tell about in class?"

"What?" he asked on a half sob.

"Oh, maybe we could catch a few tiny toads. I noticed some in the flower bed the other day." She smiled. "In fact, the little critters got in my way when I was pulling out the weeds."

His eyes widened. "Can Sara catch some, too?"

"Sure."

He smiled then, and in that moment he was a tiny replica of Joshua, Melissa thought with a pang.

"Okay."

"Feeling better now?"

"Uh-huh."

"Suppose you close your eyes and try to go back to sleep. Night, night."

"Night, night," he whispered, his eyelids easing downward.

How long she sat there fighting back the tears, Melissa didn't know. It was only after her right leg began to tingle that she forced her limbs to move. Careful not to disturb either child, she slowly walked out of the room, closing the door behind her.

Minutes later she settled on the couch in the den with a cup of hot decaffeinated tea in hand. After taking several sips, she put it down on the table beside her and leaned her head against the soft cushion.

Joshua was right; she was exhausted. Bone weary. She'd picked up the twins at gymnastics and soccer, and while they were busy playing outside, she had tackled the kitchen floor, getting down on her hands and knees and scrubbing until it was sparkling clean.

She had persuaded herself that such strenuous work would help clear her mind and set her to thinking clearly and rationally again. But it hadn't. Joshua was still on her mind as much as ever, especially after that exchange in his office. To make matters worse, she had felt his gaze on her until he had disappeared behind closed doors after dinner with Sam. Then following their talk, he had left for his office, or so he had said.

Pausing in her thoughts, Melissa reached for the cup of tea and brought it to her lips. What difference did it make to her if he went to his office or not? she asked herself. So what if he went to visit the blonde instead? She couldn't care less.

Only that wasn't quite true.

She had spent the majority of her adult life striving toward proper, professional achievements—nursing her final goal. She had become successful when the bottom suddenly dropped out of her life—first Martin betrayed her, then she lost her family, and last but not least, she had become disillusioned with her work.

And when she had hopes of getting her life back together, she ran headlong into Joshua Malone. If she ever gave into those feelings he aroused in her, when she returned home to Houston, she would be bereft, emptier than she'd been over her family's deaths and Martin's betrayal. So she had to forget the burning passion in Joshua's eyes, forget the way his hard, solid body had pressed so intimately against hers.

He had no intention of remarrying, and she had no intention of letting him or any other man hurt her ever again.

For a while longer her thoughts stayed on the same track, always coming back to the same conclusion. Since she could not order him to stop looking at her with his hot blue eyes that mirrored graphic thoughts, and since she was not about to desert the twins, she'd do her best to keep him at arm's length. Soon the attraction would wear itself out. It was only a matter of time.

Tired of her thoughts, she forced herself to relax. It wasn't long, then, until she grew drowsy. Her last coherent thought was that if she refused to let him hurt her, then he could not.

"How 'bout calling it a night and going for a beer?"

At the sound of his foreman's voice, Joshua swiveled around in his chair. "Tom, what the hell are you doing out stumbling around this time of night?" Joshua grinned. "What happened, did Hazel kick you out of the house?"

"Naw," Tom said with an answering grin, still holding the door open to the office. "Neither of us was ready to go to sleep, so she sent me to the store to get some milk. Of all the crazy things, she got it in her head to make some chocolate-chip cookies. When I drove by, I saw the light and your truck and wondered what the hell you were doing here so late.''

Joshua stood and stretched his back. ''Thanks for the offer of the beer, but you'd best get that milk home. Anyway, it's time I headed there myself.''

''Did you work out the problem with the subcontractor?''

''Hope so, but I won't know till tomorrow.''

''Guess I'll see you in the morning then.''

''Oh, before you go, tell Hazel I'll dance at her next wedding if she'll send me some cookies tomorrow.''

Tom took his hat off and rubbed his ear. ''What about your housekeeper?''

''What about her?'' Joshua's tone was guarded.

''You mean that sweet thing doesn't make you cookies?''

''Are you kiddin'? She can hardly boil water.''

Wingate chuckled. ''With legs like that, who cares?''

''You're right, who cares?''

Wingate laughed outright this time. ''I'll tell my old lady about the cookies.''

''Thanks. Good night.''

When Joshua let himself into the house minutes later, it was as silent as a tomb. For some unexplained reason, though, it didn't feel empty, not as it had those first few months after Gwen's death.

So as not to awaken anyone, he strode lightly into the den, where he came to a sudden halt, his eyes taking in Melissa's sleeping figure on the couch.

God, but she was beautiful, he thought foolishly, his limbs too heavy to move. But then he wasn't interested in moving. He guessed he could stand there forever and stare at her. She was just that easy on the eyes. But there was so much more to her than mere physical beauty. Not only was she warm-hearted, but she was extremely intelligent and competent.

Not wanting to disturb her, he eased closer, all the while wondering if he should wake her so that she could go to bed. Yet he hated to, because she looked so relaxed, so at peace. And Lord, if anyone needed to relax, it was she.

He'd meant it this afternoon in the office when he'd told her she was working too hard, though he hadn't expected her to pay any attention to him. From the beginning she had taken the house by storm and hadn't let up.

Joshua's gaze circled the room, a room that was mellow in the lamplight. It was also spotlessly clean and smelled good. Although he couldn't identify the smell that tickled his senses, he knew he liked it.

Now, as his eyes drifted back to her and locked on the gentle rise and fall of her chest, he felt the involuntary response of his body. What a difference she had made in their lives, and in just a few weeks' time. She was the best thing that had ever happened to them. The thought of her leaving...

Lord in heaven, but he was thinking crazy thoughts that didn't bear thinking about. Still he couldn't tear his gaze away or stop his mind from churning. Unwittingly he moved his eyes down her delectable body, feeling a sudden rush of heat charge through him as he envisioned her lying under him on the bed, naked.

Dammit, he knew it was a mistake to keep her here, just about the most stupid thing he'd ever done, especially when he'd go to bed at night and wonder what it would be like to have her beside him.

But she wasn't interested in one-night stands—if ever there was a woman who wasn't cut out for them, it was this one in front of him—and he wasn't interested in anything else. Besides, he was nobody's fool. It was inevitable that she would sooner or later go back to the bright lights, back to nursing, and he and the twins would become only a memory.

Following a guttural expletive, Joshua moved closer, determined to wake her up, thereby easing the ache inside him that was becoming unbearable by the minute.

But when he leaned over her and she didn't move a muscle, he didn't have the heart to disturb her. Suppressing a deep sigh, he very tenderly eased his arms under her knees and her shoulders and scooped her up.

Although he tried not to notice the way she moaned or the way she cuddled next to him or the way she smelled like a bouquet of roses, he couldn't help it. By the time he laid her down on her bed, he was sweating as though he'd just run five miles.

But instead of covering her with the blanket on the foot of the bed and getting the hell out of there, he paused a moment, thinking how uncomfortable she looked with her robe tangled under her.

With unsteady hands, he removed the garment. It was only after he'd completed the task that he realized she was wearing nothing underneath. She was gloriously, wonderfully naked.

He sucked in his breath. Blood pounded in his head. His tongue felt twice its size. He couldn't have moved if he'd wanted to. He was near enough to see the tips of her long lashes, the light spray of freckles across her nose. Wisps of hair had fallen from the loose knot on top of her head, curling around her face like a halo.

And her skin. God, her skin—it was sleek and unblemished. Her neck was long and slender, her shoulders as delicate as a china doll's.

Her tilted breasts were ripe and firm, the nipples pink and small. Her waist was narrow; her hips flared gently.

But it was her legs that he thought were superior. They were long and firm, the muscles taut and supple, the ankles narrow, her feet small.

With the blood pounding harder in his head, he bent toward her, then stopped. Dammit, he couldn't do it. Things were already complicated enough as it was. Blindly he grabbed the blanket, and after spreading it over her, he stalked out of the room without a backward glance.

He didn't alter his gait until he had the bottle of bourbon out of the cabinet.

Eleven

When Melissa's eyes popped open and she gazed at the lighted digital clock beside the bed, she was completely disoriented. Some sixth sense told her something was wrong. Leaning over, she flipped on the lamp and, after blinking several times, realized she was in her own bed, that her imagination had played tricks on her.

Her body relaxed instantly, but a second later, after tossing the covers aside, she froze. She was completely nude. Surprise mixed with shock drained every ounce of color from her face. Her heart slammed violently against her ribs. Her body turned hot, then cold.

How had…? Suddenly it all came back to her. She had fallen asleep on the couch, exhausted. And there was only one possible explanation as to how she could have gotten to bed. Damn him! He had gone too far this time.

Thinking she might possibly catch him before he left for work, she flounced off the bed and jerked on her robe, which she'd found discarded on the floor. After quickly brushing her teeth and slapping water on her face, she stormed out of the room, humiliation causing her temperature to rise. Confrontations had never been enjoyable or easy for her, but this was one she was going to savor.

Furious, she marched down the hall into the kitchen. Luck was on her side. Joshua was still there, but just barely. His Stetson was on his head, and his hand was on the doorknob.

As if he sensed her presence behind him, he whipped around. "Ah, good morning," he said with warm ease. "You're up mighty early."

Stiffly she crossed the room, head high, shoulders back, eyes icy. "How dare you?" she said, her voice shaking.

His gaze never flickered. With maddening slowness, he removed his Stetson, tossed it on the chair and smiled. "Let's just say I couldn't resist the temptation."

"You're despicable!"

His grin slipped. "Oh?"

"Don't play innocent with me."

"Just what do you think happened?" His tone had dropped five degrees and was almost as cold as hers.

"I think you took…took advantage of me, that's what."

Silence fell between them. Together they made the most of the moment, both recognizing it as the calm before the storm.

"Nothing happened," he said flatly.

"Nothing happened!" She could feel the hysteria in her voice, but again she could not control it.

"Calm down, for God's sake. You'll wake up the twins."

Although she lowered her voice, none of the hysteria was deleted from it. "How…how can you say nothing happened when...when I woke up..." She paused, the word sticking in her throat.

"Naked. The word's naked."

"All right, when I woke up *naked*! That in itself says something happened."

He leaned casually against the door facing, that devilish grin she had come to associate exclusively with him easing the tension around his lips. "You know, you're beautiful when you get all riled, especially with your hair mussed up and your eyes flashing fire."

"Damn you, Joshua, I'm serious." Her tone was icier than ever.

"You're too serious. That's your whole problem."

"We're not talking about *my* problems. We're talking about you and what happened between us last night."

"I told you nothing happened."

"You...you undressed me."

"But that's all I did."

She should have taken heed of the way his voice had dropped to that dangerous level once again, but she didn't. She was too upset.

"I don't believe you."

"Oh, believe me, sweetheart," he drawled. "If I'd made love to you, you'd have known it. There wouldn't be any doubt in your mind."

The red color rose even brighter in her cheeks. "You have the morals of an alley cat," she spat.

Before she could gauge his intentions, he clamped a strong callused hand around her wrist, yanking her against him. "And what about you? You're a supposedly grown woman behaving like an outraged virgin."

"Let go of me!" she cried, staring up into eyes that revealed nothing. "I don't want you to touch me ever again."

"Oh, that's not true, and you know it. You want me to touch you all right. You want me to touch you right now as much as I wanted to touch *you* last night. I wanted you so badly my gut ached," he said roughly, "but I didn't take you."

He had been drawing nearer to her during the arousing speech. "However, I intend to make up for that error in judgment right now."

Before Melissa could respond, his mouth came down on hers, hard. The instant he pressured her lips apart and probed greedily with his tongue, Melissa whimpered, felt herself lose ground, felt a delicious pleasure swimming along her veins.

But when he moved a hand to cover a breast and began to squeeze, to knead it, she came to her senses. With a cry she tore out of his arms.

"Stop it!" she demanded, her breathing coming in gulps.

He made an aggravated sound in his throat. "Why don't you grow up?"

"Why don't you go to hell!"

He blanched, and his jaw muscles jumped reflexively. "I think I've finally figured you out."

"I doubt that."

"You'll only go so far, then you freeze up like an icicle."

"Not only is that ridiculous, but it's unfounded."

"Oh, is it, now? Well, I think not."

His eyes, burning with passion only seconds before, were now hard and condemning. "What's the matter, Melissa, did someone leave you standing at the altar?"

Her face turned noticeably pale. "That's none of your business."

He looked at her for a long moment, the tension visible in the way his fierce eyebrows clamped together at a savage angle, the way his lips thinned to an almost invisible line. "I'll let you off the hook for now, but you can't run forever. Remember that."

After gathering the last of the threadbare underwear together and placing it in the sewing basket, Melissa walked back into the kitchen.

"Are you about through?" She spoke to both Sam and Sara, who were sitting at the table eating Oreo cookies and drinking milk.

It was after three in the afternoon, and they had just awakened from their naps.

Sara looked up at her and grinned, a white mustache staining her upper lip. "Can I have some more, Lissa?"

"May I."

"May I have some more?"

Melissa leaned down and kissed her petal-soft cheek. "How many have you had?"

"She's had five," Sam put in.

Melissa switched her gaze to Sam and smiled. "And you, Mr. Malone, how many have you had?"

"I've had six."

"That figures," Melissa said dryly. "All right, Sara, you can have one more, than I want you both to wash your face and hands."

"Then I'm gonna go outside and ride my bike," Sam announced enthusiastically.

"Me, too," Sara added, scrambling down from her chair and running after her brother.

"Hey, you two," Melissa called after them, raising her voice, "stay in the yard."

After cleaning up their mess and putting the finishing touches on dinner, Melissa once again grabbed the sewing basket and wandered into the den.

Today had not been one of her better days, she thought, sinking down into a chair by the French doors, which gave her a clear view of the twins now playing rambunctiously in the backyard.

The scene earlier with Joshua had upset her. As a result, she hadn't wanted to do anything. She'd been restless and irritable. And worried, knowing that each time he made another assault on her senses, she weakened. What would happen if she finally gave in to his hungry demands? Would the game be over? The challenge gone?

Before she could answer those questions, the phone rang. With her thoughts still in chaos, Melissa answered it, listening with only half an ear while a young woman tried to sell her aluminum siding.

"I'm sorry," she said when she could finally get a word in edgewise, "but I'm not interested." And with a "thank you," she hung up.

Suddenly deciding that the afternoon was much too beautiful to sit inside brooding, she made a quick decision. She would take the kids and go to the mall. The underwear would be impossible to fix, so why not buy new ones? she thought.

Moments later, with a spring in her step for the first time that day, she opened the French doors and stuck her head outside.

"Sam. Sara," she called.

Silence.

Frowning, she stepped onto the patio and gazed around the yard. They were nowhere in sight.

"Okay, kiddos, you can come out of hiding now. The game's up."

No response.

Telling herself not to get alarmed, Melissa walked to the edge of the house and stopped. Placing her hand on her forehead to shield her eyes from the glare, she scanned as far as she could see. Still no sight of the twins.

"Sam. Sara," she called again, only louder.

Another silence.

Don't panic, she told herself. In a few minutes time they couldn't have gone far. Yet no amount of talking could dispel her mounting fear. Like a stain, it kept spreading.

Whipping around, she raced toward the front yard, and after covering every inch of it, came up empty-handed there as well.

"Sam! Sam! Where are you? Answer me!" Her voice was now ragged.

When she got no response, she found herself standing reed straight in the backyard again, desperate to get her bearings, to decide where to look next.

There was a soft sighing in the trees above as a breeze passed through the leaves. But she was aware of nothing except her own hammering heart and the wave of panic seizing her.

Where were they?

Suddenly it hit her. The creek! Oh, God, the creek. The thought took her breath away, and she knew without looking in a mirror that her face had lost its color. She opened her mouth to cry out, but her tongue seemed glued to the roof of her mouth; she couldn't utter a word.

She was finally able to move. She tore off across the yard toward the slope that would eventually take her to the free-flowing creek edging Joshua's land. All the while she refused to give into the nausea that had only moments before rendered her useless.

Surely they couldn't have—have what? she cried inwardly. *Drowned!* No! That was impossible. They weren't even supposed to go near the creek, much less play in it.

How many times had she heard Joshua lecture them on that? But they were children; anything was possible.

Stark fear made her move quickly. Her panting seemed loud enough to be heard a block away. She tried to curb it by taking long, deep breaths. It didn't work. By the time she reached the creek bed, her lungs were burning.

"Sam! Sara!" she shouted, running alongside the water with the speed of a ferret, her heart beating in her chest like a gong.

Nothing. The twins were nowhere in evidence.

Clambering up the hill, she suppressed an outcry. It was as though something had a hold on her voice. She barely reached the middle of the backyard, still in a dead run, when she heard the phone ring.

Even in the daylight, its sound was like a silent scream. It rang ten times before her reflexes took over and she dashed inside.

With heart in her throat, she lifted the receiver.

"Hello."

"Melissa, Alice. Are you missing two cotton-topped children?"

Melissa latched on to the back of the chair for support, her stomach heaving. "Are they...at your house?" she asked through stiff lips.

"They're here."

"Thank God," Melissa wheezed. "I turned my back on them for half a second to get the phone, and they were gone."

Alice sighed. "I figured as much. When I questioned them about being here, they hung their heads."

"I'll be right there, Alice. And thank you."

But instead of heading out the door as planned, Melissa

went to the bathroom where she hung her head over the commode and lost the contents of her stomach.

What a day! And it wasn't over yet.

Twelve

Twelve

"Thanks again, Alice. I know you think—"

"Don't say it. Don't even think it. I know you weren't neglecting Sam and Sara. The Lord only knows how many times my girls did the same thing, just slipped out of the yard for no reason."

Melissa and Alice were standing on Alice's front porch, while the twins stood at the end of the sidewalk, watching Melissa with wide, uncertain eyes.

"I know," Melissa said, "but that's still no excuse. What if something terrible had happened?"

"It didn't, so forget it. Just make sure it doesn't happen again."

"Oh, I will. You can count on that."

Alice hid a smile. "I know it's not funny, but when you marched up that walk a few minutes ago, there was no mistaking your temper."

"Well, those two are in trouble, that's for sure."

"Oh, before you go, mark Friday night on your calendar. We're having a fish fry at the lake, and we want you to come. Be sure to tell Joshua."

Melissa smiled. "Sounds like fun. I'll tell him. And thanks again."

"You gonna spank us, Lissa?" Sara whispered between sobs.

The three of them were sitting in the den, the twins on the couch and Melissa on an ottoman in front of them.

"No, Sara, I'm not going to spank you," Melissa said with a sigh, "but you are going to be punished."

"We...we didn't mean to be bad," Sara went on, great tears rolling down her cheeks.

"But you were naughty, Sara. You were very naughty, because I told you not to leave the yard. Remember me telling you that?"

"Yes, ma'am," she whispered.

Ignoring Sara for the moment, Melissa switched her attention to Sam, who had kept his head down and hadn't said a word.

"Sam," she said quietly, "look at me."

Although he did as he was told, there was a defiant slant to his shoulders and a mutinous expression in his eyes.

"Was it your idea or Sara's to go to Alice's?"

Silence.

Melissa took a deep breath and prayed silently for guidance. Dear Lord, this was all so new to her, so frightening. How had she ever thought this would be an easy job, with no cares, no responsibilities?

"Sam, answer me."

"Both of us wanted to go," he blurted finally. "Mitzi got some new fish in her aquarium, and we wanted to go see them."

"All you had to do was ask me and I would have taken you."

"We didn't want you to go," Sam answered sullenly.

"That's not nice, Sam," Sara scolded before Melissa could say a word, but then Melissa wasn't sure she was capable of saying anything. Sam's continued rejection of her was like a sore that wouldn't heal.

"I don't care," he spat at his sister.

"Hush, both of you," Melissa said softly but firmly. "As far as I'm concerned, you were both to blame, but because you disobeyed me for no apparent reason, I'm not going to let either of you go to Ben's birthday party tomorrow.

Sam sprang off the couch, his small face pinched. "You're not my mommy!" he cried. "I don't have to mind you."

His words hit Melissa like a blow. The lump in her throat was so big, it was hard to get words past it. "Sara, honey," she said, "go to your room. I want to talk to your brother alone."

For a moment Sara hesitated, a new onslaught of tears gushing down her unblemished face.

"Go on," Melissa urged, forcing what she hoped was a reassuring smile. "It's all right."

As soon as she heard the door to Sara's room close, Melissa faced Sam once again, all the while wishing she could leave this house and never come back.

"Of course, I'm not your mommy, Sam," she said gently, striving to keep her voice even while fighting off her tears. "But I love you very much just the same. And because I do love you, I'm determined to do the job your daddy hired me to do, and that's take care of you and Sara, which means you have to mind me. Can you understand that?"

"Yes, ma'am," he muttered, shifting from one leg to the other, his lower lip beginning to tremble now.

"I want to be your friend, you know," she whispered, her heart aching.

He thought for a moment, then looked at her through anxious eyes. "You gonna tell my daddy?"

Melissa expelled a breath. "No, Sam, I'm not. This is going to be our secret."

He tilted his head and looked at her another long moment and then said, "Lissa, wanna come to my room and see my shell collection?"

The road that led off the highway toward the lake was a beautiful one. Tall pines, sweet gums and oaks grew side by side along its edge, each robed in the brilliant colors of fall.

They came upon the camp suddenly. One moment the car was surrounded by trees and in the next, the view across the lake was unimpeded. The lake itself was a deep blue, while the log cabin tucked close to the forest behind it looked homey and inviting.

"Oh, what a lovely place," Melissa said, facing Joshua, her eyes shining with excitement.

She had been looking forward to this outing ever since Alice had mentioned it. They all needed it, needed the rest and relaxation. As usual, Joshua had continued to work much too hard, but she would have to admit he had been coming home earlier, making an effort to spend more time with Sam and Sara. The twins blossomed under his attention, and because of it, Melissa's job had been easier.

The fact that she had opted not to tell Joshua about them running off had helped tremendously. It had earned her a few points, especially with Sam. She could tell his little heart was thawing toward her, and she was thrilled.

But Joshua was a different matter altogether. Though he had not made any effort to reopen their heated conversation of the other morning nor made any more advances toward her, she was nevertheless uneasy when he was around.

And today was no exception. She felt herself flush under his close scrutiny. She knew he wanted her. She could see it in the smoldering glances he cast her way when he thought she wasn't looking. The sexual tension building inside troubled her.

Chink by chink Joshua Malone was chipping away at her barricade, making her more determined not to give in. Yet, at the same time, she was saddened that she couldn't allow herself to trust again.

"Not a bad layout, I agree," Joshua was saying. "I envy Travis. Wish I'd been smart enough to invest here when he did."

"Is it too late—too late to buy, I mean?" Melissa asked, forcing her mind back on track.

"Yeah, Daddy, why don't you buy us a house here," Sara chanted from the back seat, bouncing up and down. "We love to come here, don't we, Sam?"

"Yeah," Sam said, "it's real neat."

"Well, we'll see," Joshua drawled, bringing the Bronco to a stop beside several vehicles. "Maybe when I get though with this job, I'll have time to do some checking."

"Oh, boy," Sam shouted, hitting Sara playfully on the arm.

"Stop it," she whined, hitting him back.

Joshua looked at Melissa and grinned. "Shall we leave these two in the car and enjoy ourselves without them?"

"We'll be good, Daddy," they cried, opening the door and climbing out just as the Sinclairs came into view.

Seconds later Melissa and Joshua got out of the car. Travis wiped perspiration from his face with a large handkerchief and grinned at them. "Greetings. Running kinda late, aren't you? Thought maybe you'd changed your mind."

Joshua pulled Alice into the circle of his arm while giving Melissa another wink. "I got your number a long time ago, Sinclair. You wanted me here early so I'd do all the work."

"All right, you two," Alice said, "don't start. You're worse than the kids." Then turning to Melissa, she added, "Come on, I'll introduce you to our other guests."

There were two other couples present, and after introductions were made, the men gathered at one end of a large cemented area where a table held two large cooking utensils and two heaping platters of uncooked fish, while the women remained on the deck.

Though Alice and the two other women included her in the conversation, Melissa was content just to relax and listen to their lighthearted exchange. Leaning her head back, she looked up at the huge pine trees that made an umbrella overhead. It was a gorgeous fall afternoon, the temperature so mild that they could remain outdoors until long after the sun lost its sting.

"Hey, can you get your head out of the clouds long enough to help me with the salad?"

Melissa jerked her head around. Alice was standing, looking down at her with a wide grin on her face.

"I told her I'd help," the long-haired blonde introduced as Lucy said with a smile.

"I offered, too," Maxine, a tall, lanky brunette said.

Melissa pushed her hair behind her ear on one side and smiled. "I don't mind."

Once Melissa and Alice reached the kitchen, Alice faced her. "I hope you didn't mind helping me. I thought maybe you could make the salad while I mixed the hush puppies."

"Of course, I don't mind, silly. Just show me where everything is and I'll get to work."

They worked in companionable silence for a minute, then Alice glanced at her slyly and said, "Are you happy working for Joshua?"

Melissa didn't reply immediately, and when she did, it was with reservations. "Yes, I guess I am, though it has its moments."

Alice chuckled. "Like when those two imps ran off."

"Exactly."

"The reason I'm curious is that it's hard for me to understand why someone who's a nurse would chuck it all to become a housekeeper and baby-sitter." She looked embarrassed. "I've been dying to ask, only I haven't had nerve enough until now."

"Oh, Alice, it's a long story. Maybe one of these days I'll share it with you. For now let's just say, I needed something different."

"Well, I for one am glad you're here. And I know Joshua is, too, even though I'm sure he's not all that easy to work for."

Melissa averted her eyes, but not before she saw the strange glint in Alice's eyes. "You can say that again."

"Well, just don't let him get the best of you."

Melissa smiled tremulously. "I'm trying, Alice. Believe me, I'm trying."

A short time later they gathered around the picnic tables and ate the delicious fish, fried golden brown, hush puppies and salad.

Once the dinner had been consumed and the tables and kitchen tidied, the adults sat in lawn chairs on the deck, the men drinking beer, the women coffee. Melissa, so full she couldn't move, watched as the kids played a short distance away.

"A penny for your thoughts."

Melissa jerked her head around to collide with Joshua's intense gaze. "Unfortunately, they're not worth even that," she said, suddenly short of breath.

"Oh, really," he responded, easing down in the chair next to her, only to jump back up as Sam came running toward them.

"Daddy, Daddy!"

He came to an abrupt halt in front of Joshua, his little chest heaving.

Joshua pulled him between his legs and brushed his hair out of his eyes. "Hey, get your breath before you try to talk."

"What'sa matter, young fellow?" one of the men asked. "Those girls giving you a hard time?" Sam was the only boy among five girls.

Finally when Sam's breathing was back to normal and all eyes were on him, he gazed up at Joshua and asked, "Daddy, what do the birds do to the bees?"

For a moment no one said a word, then everyone laughed, except Joshua.

He gaped at Sam. "What?"

More laughter.

Basking in the attention he was getting, Sam turned innocent eyes on Melissa. "Do you know, Lissa?"

That brought still another howl of laughter and a flush to Melissa's face. "I think you'd better let your daddy explain that."

"Did the girls put you up to this?" Alice asked.

"They were giggling about it," Sam said.

Fully recovered now, Joshua sat him on his knees. "We'll talk about it later, son," he said hastily, though a smile toyed with the corner of his lips. "Right now you go back and play...and tell the girls I said to button up."

"Okay," Sam said, seemingly satisfied, scooting off as fast as his legs could carry him.

"Well, let's hear it, Malone. What are you going to tell him?"

"Yeah, Malone," Lucy's husband chimed in, "let's hear it."

"Aw, go to hell, both of you," Joshua muttered good-naturedly.

The conversation had long ago switched to more mundane channels, and now bored with it, Joshua leaned toward Melissa and said, "Come on, I'll show you around."

"Sure, why not?"

Once they had excused themselves, they walked in silence toward the lake. Although the sun was beginning to lose its sting, the evening was still mild.

"Do you really like it here?" Joshua asked, ending the silence.

She glanced at him. "I take it you find that hard to believe."

He shrugged. "Well, after all, you're city born and bred. You said so yourself."

"True, but still I can appreciate these gorgeous trees and the clean fresh air."

"Do you think I ought to buy a lot here?"

Her response was slow in coming. "The kids would love it, I know."

"That's not what I asked."

She drew in a shuddering breath. "It doesn't really matter about what I think, does it? After all—"

"After all, you're not going to be around forever," he finished for her, his tone having plunged several degrees.

"Nothing's forever, Joshua," she said quietly, looking at him warily.

"Tell me something I don't know."

They had stopped at the water's edge, and he watched Melissa covertly. Her beauty almost robbed him of his breath. She was wearing an oversize gold shirt knotted at the waist and a pair of jeans. His gaze fell on the tight curve of her buttocks. He could see them flex as she leaned over and picked up a rock and tossed it in the water.

Before he did something foolish like grab her and haul her into his arms, he looked away and said, "For what it's worth, I want you to know again how much I appreciate what you've done, especially for the twins."

Melissa eyed him speculatively, as if caught off guard by his compliment. "You sound as if I'm leaving now," she said, her face pale.

He massaged his temple. "Maybe you should."

Melissa sucked in her breath. "Are you firing me, Joshua? Is this what this conversation is all about?"

"Of course not." A dark flush stained his face. "It's just that…" He broke off in confusion, knowing he should have kept his mouth shut.

"It's just what?" Melissa was saying, her voice sounding as tight as a new rubber band.

"Forget it," he said tersely. "Forget I said a word." Then grabbing her by the arm, he added, "Come on, we'd better be getting back. It's getting late."

The walk back was carried out in total silence. He knew his words had hurt her. That threadbare look was still on her face. He cursed silently with every step he took. Why he'd brought up the subject of her leaving again, he'd never know.

He couldn't deny any longer this woman's power over him. In the weeks she had been here, her presence had driven away the loneliness, the helpless feeling that had driven him like a master. He knew now he could never willingly let her go.

Walking beside him, she looked forlorn and withdrawn. He ached to place his arm around her. He didn't.

It was only after they walked up to where the children were still playing that the silence was broken.

"Daddy, Lissa," Sara cried, "look at Sam. Him's playing Superman."

"Where, honey?" Melissa asked.

"Over there," Sara responded, pointing a finger.

Melissa and Joshua followed that finger, only to suddenly freeze.

Sam was standing on the top of the brick barbecue pit with a towel tied around his shoulders, arms outstretched.

"Oh, my God, Joshua!" Melissa dug her fingernails into his arm.

"Sam, no! Get down!" Joshua shouted.

Too late. Their cries were in vain. By the time they reached Sam, he was lying unconscious on the concrete, blood streaming down the side of his face.

Thirteen

"**I**s my brother going to die like my mommy did, Lissa?"

"Oh, darling," Melissa said, kneeling down in front of the child and hugging her, "of course, he's not going to die. His cut looked worse than it was because it was on the head where you bleed so much."

Sara cut her tear-filled eyes to Joshua. "Lissa took care of him, didn't she, Daddy? 'Cause she's a nurse."

"That's right, sweetheart," Joshua replied, dropping down on one knee so that he, too, was level with the child. "She took very good care of him."

The second Melissa saw Sam leap off the brick ledge, she had charged forward, racing up the hill with Joshua behind her.

Joshua's startled shout had alerted the other adults, and they, too, had run toward Sam. But it had been Melissa's professional attitude and her training as a nurse that had kept panic from spreading and enabled her to administer to Sam.

Though he'd cut a gash on his head, it was his arm that had been the problem; it was broken, the bone protruding through his skin.

After she and Joshua had wrapped him in a blanket and gotten him into the Bronco, Joshua drove like a madman to the hospital. The Sinclairs had kept Sara, so all Melissa had to do was cradle a conscious but sobbing Sam in her arms, thankful that he hadn't gone into shock.

"My arms hurts, Lissa," he'd cried.

Struggling to keep her own tears at bay, she'd comforted him as best she could. "I know, darling, but soon we'll be at the hospital and the doctor will make you feel better."

"But he'll hurt me more," he wailed.

"No, darling, I promise he won't. Your daddy and I'll be right there with you. We won't leave you."

The gash on Sam's head hadn't required any stitches, and in spite of the bad break, his arm had been easy to set. As promised, neither Melissa nor Joshua had left the boy's side, and when the doctor had finished, he told them that since there was no sign of a concussion, they could take Sam home, especially since Melissa was a nurse.

Instead of leaving Sara with the Sinclairs, Joshua, after helping Melissa get Sam into bed, had gone after her, knowing how upset she'd be.

Now, hours later, Joshua kissed Sara's soft cheek and slowly got to his feet, but not before his gaze rested softly on Melissa for a long moment.

Melissa was the first to look away, unable to bear the haunted pain she saw on his face. It seemed the accident had aged him ten years, but then she felt the strain, as well. She hated to see children and animals suffer, because more often than not, they were unable to tell you where they hurt.

"Sara, honey, would you like to see your brother before I tuck you into bed?" Melissa asked at length.

Sara's eyes lighted. "I promise I won't wake him up."

"You don't have to worry about that, sweetheart," Joshua said. "The doctor gave him something to make him sleep."

Moments later the three of them were in Sam's room, standing beside the bed.

Sam was lying on his back, his small face deathly pale, the color heightened by the white pillowcase on which his head rested. The side of his head was bandaged, and the broken arm, encased in a new fiberglass cast, lay across his stomach.

Melissa once again fought back tears as she peered at him closely. He looked so defenseless, so fragile, so sweet....

She uttered a choking sound, and without looking at Joshua—knowing the same emotions, the same thoughts were tearing at him as well—she pulled Sara, who stood between them, closer to her side.

"Are you sure he's...he's not in heaven?" Sara whispered, her head soft against Melissa's thigh.

Joshua cleared his throat. "Watch his chest, sweetheart. See the way it's pumping up and down. That means he's breathing."

Her eyes were wide. "I see, Daddy, I see."

"He's going to be just fine," Joshua said.

Even though his words were firmly spoken, Melissa heard the uncertainty. Just as she opened her mouth to reassure him, he spoke again, directly to her. "Isn't that right, Lissa?"

At the abbreviated use of her name, her heart fluttered and she dared not return his gaze.

Keeping her eyes on Sam, she said, "That's right. In a few days he'll be as good as new."

"Is him going to get a spanking, Daddy, 'cause he tried to fly?" Sara asked.

Despite the seriousness of the question, Joshua cracked a smile. "No, but I am going to talk to him."

"Oh, goody," she said, her curls in sad disorder. "I tried to tell him that only birds can fly, but he didn't listen."

"I'm sure you did, Sara my girl. But we both know that brother of yours is hardheaded."

"I wanna kiss him night, night. Is it all right?"

Joshua looked toward Melissa, silently asking for permission. This time she responded. "Go ahead," she said softly.

"Easy does it then, honey," Joshua cautioned as Sara leaned over her brother and grazed his cheek with her lips.

"I love you, Sammy," she whispered.

Sara had only just lifted her head and stepped back against Joshua when Sam's eyes blinked, then opened on Melissa.

"Lissa."

The tiny, satisfied cry stabbed at Melissa's heart. She thought she couldn't stand it. "I'm here, darling," she said, laying the back of her hand on his cheek and gently caressing it. "I'm right here."

By the time she removed her hand, he was once again fast asleep.

"He looks so...so small, so helpless...." Joshua's voice broke off as if he were unable to go on.

Twisting around, Melissa looked up into blue eyes that were dark with tears. Oh, God, she thought, lowering her head quickly. I can't bear this; I can't bear to see him cry.

It was all she could do to keep from flinging her arms around him and cradling him against her breasts, as she did Sara and yearned to do to Sam.

Joshua coughed, then said roughly, "I'm going to put Sara to bed."

"Fine. I'll sit with Sam a little while longer." Then turning to Sara, who was already in her daddy's arms, Melissa brushed her lips against the child's crimson cheek, all the while conscious of Joshua's labored breathing. "Night, night, honey. I love you."

"I love you, too, Lissa."

Fifteen minutes later, secure in the knowledge that Sam was indeed sleeping peacefully and in no danger of waking any time soon, Melissa pulled his door shut and made her way into the den.

Although, there was no light on, Melissa could see Joshua standing in front of the French doors, his hands jammed into his pockets. The moon, in all its glory, flooded the room, wrapping Joshua in its ethereal glow.

She paused inside the door and stared at his ramrod-straight back for a moment.

Then as if sensing he was not alone, he turned around. "Is he still sleeping?"

She moved toward him, smiling. "Like a baby."

"It's a sad fact, but I'm not worth a damn around a sick bed."

"It's nothing to be ashamed of. Most men aren't."

"But I did the best I could with Gwen," he added fervently, as if he had to get that off his chest.

"I never doubted that."

"If it hadn't been for you…"

She gestured with her hand, cutting him off. "You could've handled it. I have no doubts about that, either."

Her voice was low and steady. "But I'm glad I was there, nevertheless."

"You're a born nurse, you know."

"So I'm told."

"You miss it, don't you?"

"What makes you say that?" Her tone was cautious.

"I saw it in your eyes," he said dully, "at the hospital."

She felt as if a cold hand had suddenly invaded her stomach. Here it comes again, she thought. He was going to bring up the subject of her leaving again.

Though her throat was achingly dry, she managed to ask, "Is...is this the continuation of this afternoon's conversation? I know you were hinting for me to leave, but..." This time it was her voice that broke.

Joshua crossed the room in record time, stopping just short of touching her. For the longest time, they delved into each other's eyes, the air between them seeming to quiver.

Then suddenly he reached up and rubbed his head, and the moment was shattered.

"Are you okay?" she asked, thinking about what Tom Wingate had told her about the headaches he sometimes had.

"No, I'm not," he said, drawing a savage breath.

"Sam's going to be all right, really he is."

"I know," he said thickly, "and may God forgive me, but that's not what's driving me crazy at the moment."

"What...what is it, then?"

His eyes fastened hungrily on her face. "I think you know."

"Joshua." Her voice had a high-pitched, alien sound to it.

"If you're going to bed alone, I suggest you go now."

She didn't move. She knew she wanted him no matter what tomorrow brought, no matter the consequences.

"I swear, Melissa, if you don't stop looking at me like that..."

She leaned toward him. "When I was ten, my brother swung me so high in a hammock that I fell out. The ground knocked the breath out of me. I remember opening my eyes and seeing stars, and I struggled to breathe. And it sounded like sirens were going off in my head."

He stood as if transfixed.

"And that's the way I feel right now, the way I feel every time you come near me, every time you touch me...." The muscles in her throat suddenly constricted, making further speech impossible. She stood shaking, drowning in her own emotions.

"What are you saying?" His voice had grown so hoarse, she barely recognized it. "I have to know."

"Do I have to say it?" she asked huskily.

The distance between them had narrowed, though neither could say who made the first move.

"Say it," he whispered. "Say it."

Her legs were no longer able to support her. She wasn't good at this sort of thing. Feeling so dizzy she thought she was going to faint, yet with a burning need inside her, she reached out and touched him.

"I want you to make love to me," she said achingly, gazing up at him.

With a cry resembling pain, he pulled her into his arms and simply held her.

"Are you sure?" he whispered at last, his mouth buried in the scented sweetness of her neck.

Pushing herself to arm's length, she gazed up at him, her heart in her eyes.

"Yes, I'm sure."

Fourteen

As if fighting some inner battle, Joshua hesitated for perhaps a second, then with a groan he once again pulled her into his arms.

Lips hot and wet overtook hers, and she tasted his scent as she felt the dart of his tongue into her mouth. She clung to him.

"Oh, Melissa," he whispered, his voice unrecognizable, "what you do to me."

Before she could respond, he dropped his arms under her knees, lifted her and without hesitation carried her into his bedroom. Easing her down onto the side of the bed, they sat facing each other, his eyes never leaving hers.

An orange light, compliments of the full moon, descended into the room and flickered across his face, a face that held incredible tenderness.

Feeling desire twist inside her like a hot knife, Melissa leaned into him, aching to feel his hands on her body, his lips on hers. A strand of hair fell across his forehead. She reached up and brushed it away. She wanted this man with an intensity and yearning that shocked her.

"I want to touch you everywhere," he said at last. "Every perfect part of you."

She felt herself stiffen.

"Melissa." He tilted her chin slightly. "Don't be afraid of me. I won't hurt you."

"I know," she whispered, "but what if—"

"What if what?"

"What if..." She stopped again, struggling to get the words past her lips.

"Say it," he coaxed. "Don't be afraid."

"What if I can't, won't please you? Maybe...maybe I'm not capable."

He chuckled. "Oh, honey, believe me, you're capable. You're more than capable. And I intend to prove it to you right now."

He kissed her then, and she felt herself soaring into a vast liquid space. His hands tugged at her shirt, while his lips were at her ear, his tongue delving with heady intensity.

She dug her fingers into his shoulders and whispered, "Oh, please..."

"Please what?"

"I—I don't know, just please."

"Anything you say." His voice was rough and sexy.

In one smooth motion, he raised her arms; her shirt, along with her bra, was peeled away. He caressed her spine then, running his fingers up and down the narrow indentation. She shivered and moaned as he turned his mouth into the side of her neck where he nibbled, then moved to take her full breasts, the nipples already stone hard and protruding.

She reached to unfasten the snap on his jeans, but he was already ahead of her. Stilling her hand, he stood, and in one rough quick gesture, discarded his clothes. He sat back down, his lips finding and covering the upper slopes of her breasts.

"Please," she whispered again, angling so that she could feel him, already stiff, and stroke him into pulsating hardness as he suckled on her nipples.

They sank as one onto the bed, shaking in anticipation. She knew at that precise moment that there was no turning back. All her doubts, her fears, her control vanished.

Her perfectly shaped legs were straight, and lowering his head, Joshua kissed her knees, ran his hands down her calves, before gliding gently to her breasts, touching, savoring her as if she were the only woman he had ever made love to.

"Oh, Joshua," she whimpered as he gathered her breasts with his big hand, laving each nipple until they glistened.

She shut her eyes against the hot tightness that made her insides feel as if they were disintegrating. She skimmed her hands along his body. Naked, he was more perfect than she had dreamed. His lips, his tongue, his fingertips—his worshiping filled her with a longing that burned like fire. She was ready. Wet and throbbing.

When she would have removed her silk panties, he again stilled her hand, moving between her open legs, his lips seeking their inner softness, slowly moving into her silk-sheathed moistness.

"Oh, please...Joshua!" Her fingers, stiff and white as strips of chalk, squeezed the edges of the pillow, while her taut muscles contracted the instant his tongue found its silken target. She moaned pitifully, her back arching. He swiftly eliminated the obstacle with one finger and then his tongue touched her there until, pulsating, shivering, she cried out.

"Come here," she whispered, drawing him to her, her fingers seeking him, her lips wild on his. "Now!" she cried, her thighs hot, clamping around his.

"Yes," he rasped, "oh, yes."

His mouth sought hers again. Ferocious and tender, she sank her fingers into his shoulders, urging him toward the slickness of her body. He thrust deep into her, then, barely moving at first, then upping his pace, only to slow again.

She met him stroke for stroke. She felt his vitality, his stamina, the craving he seemed no longer able to contain. She couldn't be sure if the muted cries that followed came from her mouth or his as the climax rocked her suddenly, fiercely, filling her with fire all the way to her throat.

When Joshua came back from checking on Sam, he knew Melissa was awake. The second he lay back down beside her, he felt her shake, troubled by thoughts he couldn't imagine. Suddenly something stirred in him he hadn't known he possessed, causing him to gape at her in total awe. A nipple, a curved leg, both in profile, were lovely.

With a murmured groan, he folded her in his arms. Her hair hung over his arm like a silk curtain. Again feeling the stirrings of passion between his thighs, he began to stroke her.

In the years since Gwen's death, he'd known his share of women. But few had stirred his interest, much less set him thinking about lasting commitments.

But this woman, this dismayingly lovely woman with her hot words of denial and her conflicting emotions, struck an unfamiliar chord within him that went far deeper than desire.

As he continued to hold her, feeling her trembling gradually subside, he pushed the hair back from her ear and whispered, "Why were you afraid you couldn't please me?"

"Please, I don't want to talk about it," she said.

He could feel the muscles in her back and shoulders tense.

"It's been a long time since you've made love," he said softly. "Hasn't it?"

She rolled out of his arms and hid her face in the pillow.

"Yes," she said finally.

"I thought as much." How could this woman with such a great capacity for loving go so long without touching, without being touched? "Tell me about the man who hurt you, who formed that layer of ice around your heart?"

"I don't want to talk about…him, either." Her voice was as soft as the night air.

"Maybe if you talked about it…" He trailed off helplessly as she turned over, eyes blazing.

"Why? What possible difference could it make to you?"

For several moments their eyes sparred. He simply looked at her, wondering just what in the hell he was trying to prove. But he couldn't back away, not now, not when he'd found the one woman he wanted.

"I'd been seeing him for quite some time," she said at last, when Joshua had given up hope of her ever speaking to him again. "Tall, dark and handsome, every woman's dream." Her tone was filled with bitterness. "On top of that, he was a successful attorney."

"But he was married."

"How did you know?"

"It wasn't hard to figure out."

"He wasn't only married, he had a three-year-old son."

"So you told him it was over, and he tried to talk you out of it."

"No, I told him it was over, and he tried to rape me."

Her words cut like a whiplash through the silence, and while Joshua was groping for the right words to say, she went on in a lifeless, methodical voice. "When he finally admitted he was married with a child, I told him to get the hell out.

"We—we argued. He wouldn't listen to reason. Before I knew what was happening, he—he had me pinned on the couch with the intention of making love to me, thinking that would solve everything. When I refused, he tried to force me, raising his hand to hit me. It was then that I shoved him. He lost his balance, and I got away."

Suddenly Joshua's eyes turned into shafts of blue steel, his muscles bunched, his mouth became a grim line. He wanted to hit something, anything. But most of all, he wanted get his hands on the sonofabitch who'd hurt her and knock him into the next century.

"So now you know," she said wearily, her face devoid of color.

"If I ever find him, I'll kill him."

"He isn't worth it, Joshua. Anyway, it happened a long time ago."

For a moment they were both quiet, each battling their own tormenting thoughts.

Then Melissa said, "Tell me about you."

"What do you want to know?"

"Did...you love her a lot?"

"Yes, in the beginning I loved her very much. But then, when the twins were born, they became her whole life. And I found myself on the outside looking in."

"How did you handle it?"

"I kept on trying." His voice was pitched low. "God knows how hard I tried because I didn't want to fail."

"That's understandable," she said almost inaudibly.

"But I failed nevertheless. Maybe if I hadn't stopped loving her…"

"Don't," she pleaded softly. "Playing the what-if game will only bring more pain and heartache."

Her eyes were luminous in the dark. The heat of her body, its essence penetrated him.

"Yeah, I know. And another thing I know is that you and I do have something in common. We're a pair of walking wounded."

She shivered, then wrapped her arms across her chest, hiding her distended nipples from his view.

"Oh, Lissa," he whispered, "come here, let me hold you." Uncrossing her arms, he drew her against him, clasping the cheeks of her buttocks so that her entire body rested against his. Her flesh felt chilled as he moved his hands over her. When he tilted her head back and their eyes met, her lips parted.

"You have a lovely mouth," he whispered, brushing his lips against hers. "In fact everything about you is lovely, the way you kiss, the way you're so small inside, so hot, and the way you taste—ah, a man couldn't ask for more."

"Don't." Her voice sounded strangled.

"Don't say those things to you, right?" He smiled, his mouth very close to hers.

She struggled for breath. "You have no right…"

He smiled. "Why does it embarrass you? You don't turn red when I touch you, only when I talk about it."

"This is…" Her voice broke as she looked up at him glassy-eyed. "This is insane."

"I know, but isn't it wonderful," he said, closing his lips on hers.

Eagerly, yet slowly, they began to reexplore each other, like two blind people whose sight had been restored. They kissed as lovers often do, filled with pleasures and emotions too myriad to name.

The moment was his. He felt alive. He felt free. And if he never drew another breath, he would die fulfilled and happy.

It was very early when Melissa awoke for the second time. The dew had formed a web of moisture over the yard. And her limbs were hopelessly entangled with Joshua's.

Dear Lord, Joshua was beside her. Naked. Cautiously she twisted her head to one side to look at him. She felt a throbbing ache deep inside that had nothing to do with regret. He was lying on his side, facing her, asleep. His hair was a mess, his cheeks stubbled with a day's worth of beard. He looked wonderful, incredibly sexy.

But what was she doing in his bed? She didn't know, yet she didn't feel guilty. Concerned, yes. Sorry, no.

Then, with her heart beating in her inner ear like thunder, with the press of his hard limbs against hers, she knew she loved him. She loved him with her heart, her soul, her mind.

Oh, God, what now? she thought, feeling panic rise in her. Very gingerly, she tried to extricate herself, moving his hand from her waist first. But it was when she pulled her legs from his that his breathing changed and his eyes opened.

"No need to rush off," he grumbled.

Heat suffused her face. "I have to see about Sam."

"Good idea," he agreed softly.

The entire time she groped for her shirt, and even after it was covering her nudity, she could feel his unwavering gaze on her. Her skin tingled as though every nerve in her body was exposed. Silently she cursed herself.

She had just reached the door when he stopped her.

"Melissa."

She turned around. "Yes."

"Are you sorry?"

She drew a steadying breath. "No...no, I'm not sorry."

His mouth twisted in a lazy, seductive smile. "If you had said yes, I think I'd gladly have strangled you."

Fifteen

She loved him. A week later she was still having trouble coming to terms with that shocking revelation.

It had left her feeling confused, lost because she'd had no idea where it was going to lead. Part of her insecurity, she reasoned, stemmed from the reality that Joshua had not touched her since. Yet a part of her knew that was only temporary. His smoldering glances filled with a yearning he didn't bother to disguise followed her every move.

She could only assume that by keeping his distance, he was giving her time, time to make adjustment to the sudden and volatile change in their relationship. Instead of finding fault with that, she could be thankful.

Despite all the unanswered questions and the feelings of insecurity raging inside her, Melissa was happy, happier than she'd been in years. She had made a success of her job, and the nightmares were gone, replaced by pleasant dreams. She was eating better, had actually gained weight.

But most important, she was part of a family again, which added to the glow inside her.

The twins had accepted her and no longer resented her presence. In fact they seemed to take her presence for granted. Just the thought of leaving them broke her heart.

But she didn't dwell on that sad aspect. Instead she dwelled on the moment, leaving the future to take care of itself.

"A penny for your thoughts?"

Joshua's unexpected presence beside Melissa gave her a start.

"You really ought to come up with a more original line, you know," she said, smiling warmly, watching as he plopped down beside her on the towel.

They were at the beach in Galveston on a gorgeous Monday morning and practically had the beach to themselves. In honor of the last day of their Aunt Dee's visit, Joshua had let the twins miss kindergarten. Joshua had taken off from work, and together they had opted for a day at the beach. Though it was October, the weather was still warm, unseasonably so even for east Texas.

A teasing glint danced in his eyes. "Think so, huh?"

"What brings you out of the water?" Melissa asked, changing the subject. She settled her brown eyes on his wet hair, gleaming in the sun, and on the whipcord strength of his shoulders and flat stomach. Suddenly a renewed surge of love rushed through her that was potent and distinct and distressing.

"Thought you looked like you needed some company."

"Well, it is kinda boring not being able to get out in the water," she said forlornly.

"Why not chance it?" His grin was persuasive. "You know I'd love to smear that suntan goop all over you."

She laughed a delightful laugh. "I'm sure you would,

but even with that goop, I'd still turn red as a lobster. Then later I'd be so sorry." She paused with a shudder. "I know. I've been there. Once I came here with a church group and stayed in the water all day. When I got home that evening, I had clear blisters the size of dimes on my back and shoulders."

"Ouch!"

"Ouch was right. I promised myself then and there I'd never do that again." She leaned back, propped herself on her elbows and looked at him. "But don't let me stop you from enjoying the water. Believe me, I'm perfectly content just watching all of you have a good time."

Even as she spoke, squeals of laughter reached them from the water. Melissa shook her head and smiled as she saw Dee lift Sara onto her shoulders, while Sam, holding his arm out of the water, looked on, laughing.

"It's been great having your sister here," Melissa said, turning her attention back to Joshua.

"Yeah, it has been nice. It's too bad she can't stay another day."

"The kids are crazy about her."

Joshua had leaned over her and tweaked her nose. "But not as crazy as they are about you."

Her pulse quickened at his nearness. "Oh, I don't know so much about that."

"I do, especially Sam. Ever since he broke his arm, you've been fussing over him. He thinks you hung the moon."

She removed her glasses so she could see his eyes. "You really think so?"

"Know so." He bent close to her lips. "And you're beautiful."

The air was suddenly charged with electricity.

He groaned weakly. "You have a habit of that, you know."

"What?" she asked.

"Looking at me like that."

She smiled coyly. "So what are you going to do about it?"

"How 'bout this?"

Suddenly he pressed a hard kiss on her open mouth, then drew back to look down at her, his elbows braced on either side of her head. The bantering glint in his eyes was gone, replaced now by something she couldn't read, but something that sent tremors through her.

She blinked, and when she looked again, he was lowering his head, certain to finish what he had started.

"Lissa, Daddy, looky what Aunt Dee found!"

Joshua muttered a curse, and there was a frown on his face as he tore his gaze from Melissa and looked on as his daughter came running toward them as fast as her chubby legs would carry her.

Melissa chuckled and punched him in the ribs. "Get that frown off your face. Sara'll think something's wrong."

"Something is wrong. I'm hotter than—"

"Joshua, behave!"

He flashed an indulgent smile. "Yes, ma'am."

"That's better."

"Later?" His eyes were filled with promises.

"Later," she whispered.

"Oh, Dee, it was so good to meet you. We've all enjoyed your visit so much."

Dee Johnson, her petite features wrinkled in a smile, returned Melissa's exuberant hug. They were standing on the porch while the kids and Joshua were stuffing Dee's car trunk with various items she had left behind when she'd moved.

It was just before dark, and Dee was anxious to get on the highway.

"I guess I'd better be going," Dee said, pulling away from Melissa, "but I do hate to leave. It's been such fun."

"Don't wait so long to come back."

Dee colored. "I would've come sooner, but I hate to leave Tommy even for a day."

"No need to apologize." Melissa gave her a knowing look. "After all, you're a newlywed."

"Well, I won't apologize from now on, because it's obvious I don't have to worry about Joshua and the kids any longer. You're in control. The house, the yard, everything looks just great."

"Well, let's put it this way—I've tried."

"But more than that, you've worked wonders with my brother. There's a marked difference in him...." She shrugged and let her voice trail off, all the while eyeing Melissa closely. "I'm not sure what it is yet, but it's there. Maybe it's that he's more at ease, less uptight."

This time it was Melissa who colored. "Maybe it's because he's getting two square meals a day," she said off the top of her head, only to then blush deeper.

Dee grinned, as if reading her mind. "No offense taken. I never made any pretense of being a good cook." Her grin widened. "But then, from what I hear, neither are you. No, I don't think food had anything to do with it, not by a long shot. And you, Ms. Banning, have that same look. Is anything going on I oughta know about?"

"Did he really say I couldn't cook?" Melissa asked, pretending to be outraged in an effort to hide her confusion. Dear Lord, was it obvious she was crazy about Joshua?

"Sure did," Dee quipped, obviously deciding not to

push her point. "But I wouldn't worry about it, if I were you."

Relaxed now that the uncomfortable moment had passed, Melissa's lips twitched. "I'm not. Just between you and me, I hate to cook."

Dee's laughter was still ringing in Melissa's ears minutes later as she stood with Joshua and the twins, arms linked, and watched Dee's car disappear behind a cloud of dust.

"Did you check on the twins?"

Joshua didn't answer her immediately. Instead he unsnapped his jeans and let them pool around his ankles, then stepped out of them.

"No problem. They're sound asleep."

Melissa's breath caught in her throat. While she had touched and kissed every part of his body during that one marathon night of lovemaking, it had been in the dark, with only the moon to guide her. She had not seen him nude in the light. Now as her eyes traveled over him, she felt herself melting on the inside.

"Your body's beautiful," she whispered at last, the lamplight casting him in a glow that made him look like an untouchable Greek god.

He chuckled and tossed the covers back, leisurely taking in her body clad only in a transparent lace gown. "Isn't that supposed to be my line?"

"Only if you don't believe in women's lib," she returned saucily, watching as he eased himself down beside her.

He pressed her against him, then switched off the lamp. "Oh, I'm a believer, all right. You can do anything to me your little heart desires."

"Anything," she said, moving her mouth across his chest.

"Anything," he muttered harshly.

"Mmm," was all Melissa was capable of saying as she continued her assault on his senses.

Seconds later he ground out against her lips, "Forgive me, but I can't wait."

He caressed her thighs, then with his finger made sure she was ready. With an urgency to match his, she twined her hands around his neck, begging for him to come inside her. When she felt him hard and insistent against her, she caressed him with her hands.

"Oh, Melissa!"

His strangled cry gave her the courage she needed. With heady excitement, she guided him into her, feeling herself unfold like the petals of a morning glory.

She awoke to the delicious smell of bacon frying. Smiling, she stretched her sore limbs languorously, only to suddenly flop over onto her side and stare at the clock. Seven-thirty!

Minutes later, wearing a cream-colored jogging suit, she made an appearance in the door of the kitchen. Three pairs of eyes turned toward her.

"Morning," Joshua said easily, standing in front of the stove, a long fork in his hand.

The twins were sitting at the table, dressed for school, calmly munching on eggs and toast.

"I'm sorry...I overslept," she said.

"Are you sick, Lissa?" Sam asked, using the back of his hand to wipe his mouth.

Melissa winced. "Sam, honey, please use your napkin."

"Okay," he said. "But are you sick?"

Melissa blushed hotly. "No, honey, I'm not sick. I didn't...er...sleep much last night."

"How come?" Sara asked innocently.

"That's enough, both of you." Joshua's tone was brisk, but his eyes were dancing with mirth. "Finish your breakfast."

"Thanks for getting the kids up," Melissa said, looking up into warm blue eyes that were closely scrutinizing her.

He grinned. "You're welcome. Now, how about some coffee?"

She had just taken the cup from his hand and sat down when the phone rang.

"Keep your seat," Joshua said. "I'll get it."

Seconds later he was holding the phone out to her. She must have looked puzzled because he said, "It's a man. He wants to talk to you."

She rose, accepting the phone. "Hello," she said tentatively.

"This is Dr. Broughton," a gruff voice said. "Remember me?"

Her heart skipped a beat. "Of course, Doctor. How are you?" She saw Joshua's eyebrows rise.

"I'm fine, and you?"

"Fine, thanks," she murmured.

He chuckled. "Now that we've gotten the polite small talk behind us, I'm going to get right to the point."

"Please do."

She listened for a minute, then finally said, "All right, Doctor. Yes, and thank you very much."

The instant she hung up, Joshua's eyes met hers.

"What was that all about?" he asked.

She looked at him critically. Outwardly his manner appeared calm, his voice even, but his features suddenly looked as though they were carved out of granite. No, he was far from calm.

Sighing, she clasped her hands tightly in front of her. "That was Dr. Broughton, the hospital administrator."

"What'd he want?"

Cutting her eyes toward the twins, who hung on to their every word as if sensing the sudden and radical change in the atmosphere, she asked, "Can't we discuss this later, Joshua?"

Without taking his eyes off her, he said, "You kiddos go brush your teeth and finish getting ready for school."

"Aw, Dad," Sam pouted.

"Now."

Instantly they vacated their seats and hurried out of the room.

"Melissa." He smiled, but there was no echo in his eyes.

The rich color faded from her face. "He...he wanted to know if I'd be interested in talking to him about a teaching position at the hospital. It wouldn't be as demanding as IC, but would be equally as challenging, with the same amount of money."

A heavy silence fell over the room.

One corner of his mouth lifted. "So what are you going to do?"

Sixteen

Melissa was torn. Shortly after she had accepted this unlikely job as housekeeper, she was certain she had made a mistake, that she was not domestic, could never be domestic and that she could never cope with the twins, much less win them over. But more than that, she had been convinced that she would miss the hustle and bustle of the big city hospital, would still crave the pressures that went along with it.

Now she knew better. Her love for Joshua had changed her goals, had changed her. She knew she could stay here with him forever and be content. But how could she turn the hospital down when she had no commitment from him? He had never said he loved her, only that he wanted her. In order to protect herself and her future, she had no choice but to return to Houston, to at least listen to the doctor's offer.

"Dr. Broughton wants me to visit with him in the next

few days." She paused and searched Joshua's face, looking for some sign of what he was thinking. His face was as blank as an empty page.

"Go on."

Melissa began to breathe as if she had been running. "I told him yes."

His features drained of color, and for a second Melissa thought she saw raw agony reflected in his eyes. Then his head snapped up arrogantly, his jaw stiffened. "What's wrong with today?"

"Pardon?"

"I said, what's wrong with today?"

Melissa shivered as if a chill had passed over her. "What...? I mean, I don't understand."

"I think I made myself quite plain." His voice was an icy sneer.

Struggling to comprehend what he was trying to say, she stammered, "W-what about the twins, the house?" She spread her hands.

"What about them?"

"I can't just walk out right now without—"

"Yes, you can. We'll do just fine."

She licked her suddenly parched lips. "Are you saying you don't need me any longer, that you want me to go?"

"Yes, that's what I'm saying." His words were cold, clipped.

She gasped, feeling as if he had thrust a knife straight into her heart. "You can't mean—"

"Oh, but I do. You don't belong here, and we both know it."

"How dare you say that!" she cried, feeling as if she were dying, as if drops of blood were seeping from her wound. "I've put my heart and soul into this job."

"And now you have the hots to go back to civilization, to a new challenge."

His words bit into her heart, and she flinched as if he had physically struck her. She had no difficulty deciphering what was stamped across his hard face: anger, cold anger.

When she didn't think she could stand the silence another second, he spoke again, "Just go, Melissa. Get your things and don't..."

"Bother to come back."

"Right. You can't just waltz into our lives and back out again at the slightest whim."

She went rigid with fury and humiliation.

"Yeah, I think it's best you go," he added, his face grim, white lines etching his mouth, "both for your sake and mine."

Before Melissa could respond, she heard a sound behind her, followed by a small voice.

"You gonna go away, Lissa?"

Both Melissa and Joshua whipped around. The twins were standing in the doorway, holding hands, staring up at them, confusion and fear mirrored in their eyes.

With a muted cry, Melissa went to them, dropped to her knees so that she was at eye level and embraced both of them around the waist. "Yes, I'm leaving," she said brokenly.

"But we don't want you to go," Sam wailed, his mouth in a tight, straight line. "Why do you havta?"

Before she could answer, Sara reached out and placed her soft palm against Melissa's cheek. "We don't ever want you to go away, Lissa, 'cause we love you."

"Yeah," Sam added. "Why can't you stay forever and be our new mommy?"

Joshua's strangled curse was the only sound in the room.

Then letting go of a harsh breath, he spoke directly to the twins. "You two run along and get in the car."

"But Daddy..." Sara began.

"I'll be there in a minute," he said gently. "Run on."

Hot tears filled Melissa's eyes, the small faces swimming before her. She clung to them for a moment longer, then rose unsteadily to her feet. "Go ahead, do like your daddy told you." She smiled through her tears. "I'll see you later, okay?"

They nodded, their heads hanging over their chests.

Melissa bit down hard on her lower lip to keep from crying as she stood helplessly and watched them walk away, their little shoulders slumped in dejection.

The instant they were out of hearing distance, she turned back around. "Joshua...damn you."

Blatantly ignoring her, he began making his way slowly toward the door, his stance unyielding. "I gotta get the kids to school. Don't be here when I get back."

The door slammed shut behind him.

Suddenly her anger drained away, and a dull sickness took its place. The tears were free-flowing now, scalding her cheeks. Do something, anything, she told herself as she died inside. But what could she do? He'd made it plain she was no longer welcome there, and it wasn't in her nature to stay where she wasn't wanted. But more than that, he'd proved that she had been right all along—he did not love her. And because he didn't, it was easy to let her go.

Behind tightly closed lids, hot, painful tears continued to gush. She pressed a hand to her heart; it was beating so fast it hurt.

How long she stood there, she didn't know. She knew she should move. But then she wondered how she was going to do that when her heart was shattered into a million pieces.

During the following weeks, Melissa buried herself in her new job. Yet she felt as if she were existing in a vacuum. Nothing seemed real, though she carried out her duties to perfection, or so she was told by her superiors.

She had never worked harder. When she wasn't in the classroom or in her office, she was in the library. She spent as little time as possible in her condo, and outside the hospital she had no social life, telling herself that the empty, dead feeling would pass more quickly if she kept herself busy.

Still, thoughts of Joshua and the twins would push their way to the forefront of her mind in spite of her efforts to keep them at bay. Automatically, she would try to work even harder.

Her diligence had paid off, until she got sick. For two days she'd been at home with a cold and a sick stomach.

After lunch on the second day, she was lying on the couch when the doorbell rang. She opened the door to Laurie's smiling face.

But the smile swiftly disappeared from her friend's face, and a frown took its place. "God, you look like hell."

Melissa gave her a twisted smile. "Thanks, friend, you sure know how to cheer up a person. But come on in, anyway," she said. "I'd love to hug you, but I don't want to give you what I've got."

Once inside the den, Laurie hung her purse on the back of a chair before sitting in it. "You're not just worked to death, then? You're really sick?"

"I picked up some kind of bug."

Laurie eyed her carefully. "For heaven's sake, sit down before you fall down."

Melissa smiled again and followed orders. "Gee, it's good to see you," she said warmly. "But what on earth brings you to Houston?"

"Two things," Laurie replied with a grin and a careless shrug. "You—and the guy I'm dating. He's attending an insurance seminar at the Houstonian, and he wanted me to join him. And since it's Saturday…" She let her voice fade.

"Well, you're a sight for sore eyes, that's for sure."

"If that's so, why haven't you answered my messages? God knows, I've left enough on your machine."

"I called and left a message on your machine that I was back in Houston."

"Instead of calling, why didn't you stop by the apartment or my office before you left Nacogdoches?"

Melissa wiped her suddenly clammy hands on her robe and looked away. "I was too upset, that's why."

"What happened?" Laurie asked softly.

"Joshua sent me packing." Melissa didn't bother to hide her bitterness.

Laurie's eyebrow shot up. "Why on earth would he do that? I thought everything was going great."

"It was, until Tom Broughton called."

"He wanted you to come back to work, right?"

"Right."

"So what'd Joshua say?"

Melissa told her. When she finished, the room was quiet. Then Laurie reached over and squeezed Melissa's hands. "You love him, don't you?"

Melissa swallowed with difficulty, but when she spoke, her voice was calm and clear. "Yes, God help me, I do. However, he doesn't feel the same about me."

"How do you know? Maybe he was scared. Ever thought about that? Maybe he thought once you got back to Houston you wouldn't come back to him and the kids."

Melissa stood up, only to then cling to the arm of the couch for support.

"Hey, take it easy," Laurie said.

"I'm okay." Melissa faked a smile. "My cold's nearly gone, but this darn queasy stomach and dizziness just keep hanging on."

"What does the doctor say?"

"I'm going to see him tomorrow. I'll know more then."

"You want a Coke or something?"

Melissa sat back down and laid her head against the cushion. "A Coke sounds wonderful. There's some cold in the fridge."

By the time Laurie returned with two glasses of Coke, Melissa's latest bout of dizziness had passed, though it left her feeling as weak as dirty dish water.

Smiling her thanks, she took a healthy drink from the glass Laurie handed her. "Mmm, this hits the spot."

"Kinda thought it would."

They sipped in silence for a while longer, then Laurie said, "You haven't heard from him." It was a statement, not a question.

Melissa made a big deal of setting her glass on the table beside her. "No," she said dully, "I haven't heard from him. Or anyone connected with him, for that matter."

Laurie's gray eyes were troubled as they sought Melissa's. "That's what I thought. And while I hate to be the one to tell you this, I see I have no choice."

Melissa's heart skipped a beat. "Tell me what?"

"Joshua got hurt on the job."

Melissa's throat froze up solid, and then a cry split her lips.

"You're not going to faint on me?" Laurie asked anxiously, her eyes fixed on Melissa's pale, stricken face.

Melissa sat rigid, unmoving. Joshua hurt. It didn't bear thinking about.

"There's more, honey, but this time it's good news,"

Laurie said hurriedly. "He's already out of the hospital and back home. At least that's what the article said."

The sunlight was streaming through the window, creating weird shadows about the room, but neither noticed.

Melissa blinked in confusion. "Article?"

"Here, read it for yourself," Laurie said, reaching into the side pocket of her jeans and pulling out a folded piece of paper.

Melissa shook her head. "Please, just tell me what it says."

"An elevator cable on the job site broke and the car fell to the ground. Joshua was in it. He suffered a concussion and multiple bruises."

Melissa clutched her throat with her hand. "When... when did it happen?"

"Last week."

"But why didn't you tell me?"

"I tried, but you wouldn't answer my messages, remember? And I hated to leave something like that on the machine. Anyway, I thought maybe his sister might have called you."

"Oh, Laurie," Melissa cried, "what am I going to do?"

"What do you want to do?"

Melissa stood once again and crossed to the window.

When she didn't say anything, Laurie went on, "I can't tell you what to do, honey, you know that. But it's obvious you're miserable, and not just because you're sick. Or maybe it is because you're sick—sick at heart."

Melissa turned around just as the tears seeped from her eyes.

"Oh, honey, I hate to see you like this. Is there anything I can do?"

Melissa clasped her hands tightly in front of her and smiled through her tears, though when she spoke, her voice was wobbly. "I guess what I need is time by myself to think." *There's nothing to think about. I love him. That hasn't changed and never will.*

Laurie sighed. "I'll be at the Houstonian. You'll call if you need me?"

"I promise."

The instant Melissa closed the door behind Laurie, she leaned against the hard wood and did something she hadn't done since she packed her bags and walked out of Joshua's house. She bent over and sobbed.

When she had cried until there were no more tears, she felt no better. Just as Laurie had said, she was miserable. She'd admit it.

She missed the twins. She missed country life. She missed the trees. She missed the cool, invigorating air. She missed being part of a family.

But most of all she missed Joshua, missed his smile, missed his gruff voice, missed having his hands and lips on her body. She ached to see him, to see for herself that he was all right. But he didn't want to see her, she reminded herself painfully. He had sent her away.

Despite her weakness, she began to pace the floor, her thoughts keeping pace with her feet. Then, with a suddenness that was shattering, she realized that without Joshua and the twins, life wasn't worth living. And if they meant that much to her, then they were worth fighting for. Even if she gambled and lost, it would be worth it.

Seventeen

"**D**addy, when's Lissa gonna come back?" Sara asked, her lips turned downward in a pout.

Joshua sighed and didn't say anything for a moment. He and the twins were piled in the middle of his bed, Sara on one side, Sam on the other. For the past half hour, he had been reading them stories from their favorite books.

Before they traipsed into his room and crawled into his bed, Joshua had supervised their showers. Sara looked adorable in a pink Snoopy nightshirt with her rosy cheeks and her curls tumbling about her head. Sam also looked adorable in his blue Snoopy nightshirt.

For a moment Joshua feared his heart would burst with love and pride. It was hard for him to believe that he had fathered these two. Yet along with that pride, he felt a tremendous burden. He wanted to give them the best life had to offer. He wanted to give them Melissa.

"Mmm, Sara, my girl, you smell good enough to eat,"

Joshua said at last, struggling to come to grips with his own thoughts, at the same time hoping to divert his daughter's attention.

Sara giggled and snuggled closer to him. His arm tightened around her automatically.

"Lissa gave me some of her powder, Daddy. She said it smelled better on me than it did on her."

"She did, huh," he said lamely. Each time Melissa's name was mentioned, which was at least a hundred times a day, it was as though someone punched him in the gut. And this evening it was no different. It was worse. The doctor hadn't let him go back to work; as a result, he'd had plenty of time to think, think about Melissa and what might have been.

"Daddy, is your head hurting?"

This time it was Sam who was looking up at him with inquiring eyes.

Joshua tousled his curls. "No, son. Why?"

"'Cause you were making a funny face."

Joshua drew a long breath. "Well, don't you worry. I'm going to be okay, good as new, Doc Ramsey said. He also said I should be able to go back to work in a couple of days. And speaking of work, you guys need to haul it to bed. Tomorrow is a school day."

"I'm going to be in the school play, Daddy," Sara exclaimed.

"So what?" Sam responded nastily.

"Hey, boy, that's no way to talk to your sister. You should be proud of her."

"I don't care. I don't like school."

"Now, son, let's don't start that again."

"He hasn't gotted in trouble any more, Daddy," Sara chimed in, her voice low and sweet.

"It's 'he hasn't gotten,' young lady. Your language of

late leaves a lot to be desired.'' Then to Sam, he said, "Keep up the good work. I'm proud of you.''

"I still don't wanna go,'' he mumbled, pulling on the covers. "I wish Lissa was here.''

Joshua expelled a harsh breath, while giving into the terrible sense of loss and utter futility that possessed him.

Though both Sam and Sara missed Melissa, were lost without her, Sam was the one who missed her the most. Since she had left, he had gotten in trouble twice at school. The second time the principal had called and asked Joshua to come see her.

"Sit down, Mr. Malone,'' she'd said, when he'd walked into her office at the appointed time, his Stetson in his hand.

The minute he took a seat, she came straight to the point. "While playing in the block center yesterday, Sam said the D word.''

Joshua blinked. "The D word? I'm afraid I don't—''

"Your son said *damn*, Mr. Malone. And that's a word we don't allow them to say in the classroom.''

It was all Joshua could to do keep a straight face, but he managed. "I couldn't agree more, Ms. Clayton.''

"Instead of hitting the block, he hit his finger. That's when he said it. After his teacher brought him to me, I told him we didn't say words like that at school.'' She paused and eyed Joshua with disapproval. "Would you like to know what he said, Mr. Malone?''

Joshua shifted uncomfortably. "I have a good idea.''

"Well, to quote your son, 'when my dad hits his finger, he says *damn*.'''

That had taken place two days after Melissa left. Joshua had tried to bridge the gap that Melissa's absence had created, but he'd failed miserably, though he had tried harder than he'd ever tried before.

Yet he'd never felt as much a failure as he did at this

moment, when he gazed into his son's upturned face and
watched as tears trickled down his face.

Unable to bear the pain in the child's eyes, Joshua rested
his chin on the top of Sam's curls and hugged him. "I wish
Lissa was here, too, son."

"Why can't we go get her, Daddy?" Sara asked naively.

Joshua straightened. "I wish it were that simple, sweetheart."

"Why is she mad at us?"

"Oh, sweetheart, she's not mad at you," he said, feeling
a tightness in the back of his throat. "It's just that there
are things you and Sam are too young to understand."

Sara suddenly scrambled to her knees and placed her
palms on both sides of his cheeks as she was so fond of
doing. Her excited breath was warm on his face. "Can we
go see her, Daddy, and ask her to come home?"

Can we go see her, Daddy, and ask her to come home?
Long after he'd put the twins to bed, that question had
continued to spin in his head.

He hadn't known the answer to the question then, nor
did he now. All he knew was that he was dead tired, that
his head felt as though it were going to split in two and
that he should have been in bed long ago. Instead he had
trudged into his office, sat down and dropped his head in
his hands, letting Melissa dominate his thoughts.

He had known he loved her long before that fateful
morning when the phone had rung, only he hadn't wanted
to admit it even to himself. It was only after she'd hung up
that he'd almost blurted it, only it was too late.

The look in her eyes, the interest in her voice hadn't
escaped him. She wanted to go back to Houston; he'd been
sure of it. And when he'd asked her what she was going

to do and she'd told him, he'd wanted to grab her and never let her go.

So why hadn't he? Why hadn't he asked her to stay, begged her? Pride. Too much damn pride and fear of rejection.

After all, she'd never intended to make a life's career of this job. He'd known it when he'd hired her. So there was absolutely no excuse for letting his guard down, for falling in love with her.

He would have laughed if it wasn't so painful. Here he was nothing but a good ole boy from the wrong side of the tracks who had come up through the school of hard knocks, who was still rough around the edges, still uneducated, still mannerless.

Melissa was just the opposite. So beautiful, so educated. A winner. Lord, she was a nurse, with a bright, promising career ahead of her. Why would she want to live in the boonies, saddle herself with a man and two kids?

Aw, hell, he knew he was feeling sorry for himself, wallowing in his own self-pity, but he couldn't seem to stop.

Daylight was not far off. If he didn't get hold of himself, he wasn't going to be worth a damn to anyone. On the chance that he had been wrong, could he face her as Sara had begged him to do? Could he swallow his pride, go to her?

He didn't know; he honestly didn't know.

The house seemed deserted, but she knew it wasn't. His Bronco was in the garage, and so was the pickup. Anyway, she'd gone by the construction site, and he hadn't been there.

What was she going to say to him?

Feeling herself begin to perspire under her arms, she opened the door and got out.

The air was crisp, filled with the scent of burning leaves. Insects buzzed. Birds sang. But Melissa was oblivious to the sights and sounds around her, so intent was she on her mission. Yet the closer she got to the front door, the more her steps faltered.

God, this was insane. After all, they had only touched each other's lives briefly, had practically been two ships passing in the night.

With trembling fingers, she pushed a strand of hair out of her eyes and forced her stiff legs to move. She had made a commitment to see this through, and now that she had come this far, she wasn't about to back down.

If nothing else, she had to assure herself that he was all right. She had only the paper's word for it that his injury was not serious. As a nurse, she knew that too many licks on the head could cause permanent damage.

Dear Lord, what if he refused to talk to her?

At last she summoned the courage and pressed the doorbell. Its sound seemed unusually loud and demanding, and she felt meek, tense and insecure.

The door opened.

At the sight of him, she wanted to disappear. Instead she felt trapped.

"Melissa?"

The incredulity of his expression was such that she had to hang on to the door frame for support.

"Hello, Joshua," she said quietly. "May I come in?"

Eighteen

Without saying anything, he stood back, and she walked past him into the house. Her stomach was tightly knotted. She had feared that he wouldn't be glad to see her, but, dear Lord, how it hurt that he wasn't.

She didn't stop until she was in the den. A fire was hissing cheerfully in the fireplace, yet the metal curtain was drawn across it, as if he'd been about to leave. For a moment she inhaled the wood's rich aroma, struggling for composure. This was going to be much more difficult than she had ever imagined.

She put her purse down on the couch and turned to look at him. He was within arm's reach of her. His face was thin, shadowed—marred with suffering.

"I guess you're wondering why I'm here," she said at last, her throat so tightly constricted with emotion that she barely got the words out.

Veins stood out at the base of his neck, but he didn't say anything.

"How...how are the twins?"

"Fine."

"I'm glad."

Silence hung between them.

"Is that why you came back, to see the twins?"

"No."

His eyes were on her, as if he was waiting for her to continue. She studied them closely, but they revealed nothing.

"Laurie told me about your accident."

"I'm all right." His tone was harsh.

"You don't look all right," she whispered.

"Well, I am," he said flatly.

The urge to run was almost overwhelming, but she stood her ground. She would say what she came to say, even if it killed her.

"Is that why you came back?" he asked. "To check on my health?" There was agony in his voice and pain in his eyes, but Melissa didn't see it or hear it. Her head was bowed while she tried desperately to come up with the words that would tell him what was in her heart.

"Melissa," he said in a croaky whisper that tore at her heart. "Answer me."

Her resolve was weakening. She gripped the back of the couch for support. Who could say what he was feeling, and what he was thinking? More than likely it would take forever to figure that out. She only knew that she wanted to be part of that forever.

What should she do? This was the most important moment of her life, and still she stalled, certain the words needed to convince him they were right for each other were locked inside her.

Then suddenly, as if they had a will of their own, the words spilled from her lips. "I...love you, Joshua Malone, more than I've ever loved in my life. But it's...it's obvious you don't feel the same..." Her voice cracked, then broke, and she turned away, groping for the door through tear-filled eyes.

She never got there.

He yanked her against him and held her tightly. It was heaven. And though Melissa never wanted him to let her go, she pushed him away.

"Joshua, I..."

"Oh, God, Melissa, I love you, too...so much."

"Then why...why were you so cold, so—"

"Because I was scared," he said thickly, "scared that you had truly come back because of the accident and not because you loved me." He paused and took a deep breath. "And when you came through that door, I died a thousand deaths, because I knew this time, no matter what, I couldn't let you walk out again."

"Oh, Joshua," was all she was able to say before he bracketed her jaw with one strong hand, tilted her head back and looked deep into her eyes, his own burning with passion and something else. Love. She saw love.

She felt the slow crawl of hot tears as their lips crushed together, her mouth opening under his, her warm breath mingling with his.

When they finally broke apart, they were breathless.

He looked down at her. "I was on my way to Houston, you know."

"You were?"

"See for yourself. My jacket's on the other end of the couch and the screen's closed. I had just hung up from talking to Alice about the twins."

She stared up at him, her face registering concern. "But the concussion—you aren't supposed to drive yet."

"I was going to anyway. I'd decided that I couldn't go another day without telling you how I felt."

"Me, either," she whispered. "That's exactly why I'm here."

"Oh, Melissa, we've wasted so much precious time."

"A month," she said unsteadily. "But it seemed like a lifetime."

"Will you ever forgive me for being such a jerk?"

"Only if you'll forgive me."

He trembled, and she softly kissed his face.

"From the moment I set eyes on you, I wanted to hold you like this, kiss you." A rueful laugh escaped him. "I couldn't help thinking you were the brightest, loveliest creature I'd ever seen, and I just couldn't deny myself the pleasure of flirting with you."

"You devil."

"Yeah." He grinned. "I was, wasn't I? But when you pranced around the kitchen and—"

"I'll have you know I didn't—"

He kissed her suddenly, stopping her rebuttal. For a few seconds there was only silence in the room.

"Yes, you did." He grinned.

"Well, I will admit," she said coyly, "that I had never reacted to any man the way I reacted to you. When you touched me, I felt I'd been plugged in to a live wire."

Suddenly his expression turned serious. "But I never meant it go any further. I wouldn't admit my feelings even to myself until after you got that phone call."

"Oh, Joshua, darling, me neither. I didn't want the complications of a man in my life. I had enough problems with the grief over losing my family, a career in chaos—"

"Speaking of your career..." His voice held torment.

"Shh, don't say it, don't even think it. My career is no longer top priority. You and the twins are, though I'm sure that one of these days, I'll return to nursing."

"But here in Nacogdoches."

"That goes without saying. All I'm interested in now is being a wife and mother, being a part of a home and family again."

"That's what I want, too," he said, urging her down with him onto the soft rug in front of the fireplace.

"What about the twins? Will they want—"

He didn't let her finish the sentence. "Of course, they will. You have no idea how much they've missed you. In fact, all I've heard since you've been gone is Lissa this and Lissa that and when is Lissa going to come back."

Melissa smiled through her tears. "I can't wait to see them."

"We'll surprise them and pick them up at school. But first you and I have some unfinished business to attend to."

She whimpered his name as he caught her close and buried his face in her hair. He nibbled on her neck before finding her mouth. Her body immediately matched the heat rising from his, and she greedily returned his kisses, clinging to him.

"Darling, we shouldn't," she whispered.

He chuckled. "Honey, it was my head that was hurt. Believe me, there's nothing wrong with that part of my body." And to prove it, he reached for her hand and placed it on the throbbing hardness.

Her eyes widened. "You're right."

He chuckled again. "I love it when you blush."

"You're terrible!"

"But you love it."

She wrinkled her nose. "I know."

He lowered his head to her breasts, and in spite of her blouse, aroused a nipple. "Will you marry me?"

She squirmed underneath the sweet attack. "Oh, yes."

"When?" He unbuttoned her blouse, his lips settling on her soft, scented skin.

She tugged on his hair until he lifted his head. "Today, tomorrow, whenever."

He delved deeply into her eyes. "I love you more than life itself, but you're getting the raw end of this deal. No sense in pretending otherwise. I'm rude, crude and quick-tempered. Maybe worse."

She traced his face with her fingers, as if reacquainting herself with every plane, every angle as she lingered on his lower lip. "I'm willing to take my chances," she said, smiling contentedly. "And anyway, you're not half as tough as you think you are."

He nuzzled her neck. "You sure about that?"

"I'm sure."

"Think you can live with me?"

"Just try to stop me."

He grinned. "When my job is finished, I might be rich."

"Mmm, my mom always said it was just as easy to love a rich man as it was a poor one."

"Your mom was a smart lady."

They closed their minds to everything around them as they quickly disposed of their clothes. They faced each other, naked, the rug cushioning their knees. Groaning, he leaned forward, his mouth opening first on her lips, then enveloping one nipple.

Finally looking up, he whispered, "I was so afraid I'd never get to touch you, taste you ever again."

His panting was hot in her ear as she bent and kissed the skin of his stomach with such longing that she wasn't sure she could remove her lips from his flesh.

"Don't stop!" he cried. "Don't stop."

She didn't.

While he still could, he rolled back. When he was flat, he lifted her so that she straddled him, accepting all of him. Later, in the hot aftermath, their bodies drenched in perspiration, they lay side by side, satiated and weak.

"I love you," she said, tracing his lower lip with a fingernail.

"And I love you."

She kissed him again, then moved as if to get up.

He clamped an arm around her wrist. "Where're you going?"

"Nowhere," she murmured huskily. "I...there's something I have to tell you."

His eyes darkened. "You aren't sick, are you?"

"What makes you ask that?"

He studied her, his eyes filled with concern. "When you first came in the door, you looked peaked." He shrugged. "I meant to ask you then if you were all right, but..." His voice trailed off.

"Don't worry, I'm not sick." She smiled at him weakly. "I'm pregnant."

Joshua froze. "Pregnant."

She nodded, staring at him anxiously.

"When...when did you find out?"

"Yesterday. I thought I had a virus, but it turns out I didn't."

He grew very still. "Are you happy about it?"

"Are you?"

"Of course, I am." He grinned the widest grin she'd ever seen. "You're something, you know that?" His voice was low, warm and rich with love.

Once they were on their feet and dressed, she hid her face against his chest as his arms circled her. "Oh, Joshua,

I love you,'' she said again, ''and I'm so glad you're happy about the baby.''

''Oh, my love, don't you know, it will be just another added delight.''

And she was.

* * * * *

A Note from Marie Ferrarella

Dearest Reader,

If you've picked up this collection of stories, then you're of the same opinion as I am that Family Matters. Family always matters. But in this day and age family no longer always means the traditional Mommy, Daddy, two and a half children (where *is* this infamous half child, anyway?) and the dog. It can mean any combination represented by blood and/or by marriage and, most important of all, by the heart. Because it is the heart that brings people together and the heart that brings in the most important element within a family: love.

And so it is here, with Daisy and Drew. They both love their orphaned nephew, Jeremy, and both believe that they are the best suited to care for him. What they don't realize is each can only provide one half of what Jeremy needs. Together, they make a family unit, and together they can supply the love that is so necessary in providing the fertile ground in which a family can grow and flourish.

I hope, when you read this story, that it will remind you all over again what it was like to fall in love with that special someone and also help you remember that love doesn't always mean being in agreement. It just has to *be*.

I wish you love, joy and a quiet time now and then.

Marie Ferrarella

FAMILY MATTERS

Marie Ferrarella

To Valerie Hayward
With Love,
For Understanding
And Having Faith

Chapter One

Anastasia "Daisy" Channing sat on the window seat of the nursery she had helped her brother-in-law and older sister wallpaper five years ago. Five years ago, when Jonathan and Alyce had been so full of life, so vital, and the future had looked wonderfully promising.

A lifetime ago.

Cartoon-faced yellow suns played hide-and-seek with pink and blue lambs across green meadows. The wallpaper had been Jonathan's choice. Jonathan, who was light-years from the Jonathan he had been the day he had stepped into Alyce's life. Or more accurately, the day she had rushed into his. With the Mustang.

An accident had brought them together and now an accident had taken them away.

But at least they're together.

Daisy hugged herself as she struggled to contain tears, listening to their only child breathe peacefully in his bed as he slept. She leaned her head against the windowpane, the cool glass soothing her aching head. But what would soothe the ache she felt in her heart?

She watched the rain fall at a steady pace. Drops slid down the multi-paned window just the way tears slid down inside of her soul.

Why?

Why did it have to be them? Why not two other people? *Anyone* else. Even her and...and Jonathan's brother, Drew, she thought hopelessly as she knotted her fingers together. Alyce and Jonathan had had so much to live for, so much love to give.

And they had Jeremy.

She looked over toward the bunk bed. Jeremy had been so proud of selecting it. It had been his first "big boy" decision and Alyce and Jonathan had applauded it.

Daisy brushed the heel of her hand against her cheek, angry at the tears, angry at the world, angry at the waste.

Now she was the one who was responsible for Jeremy. Six months ago, Alyce and Jonathan had asked her to become Jeremy's legal guardian in the event that something unforeseen ever happened. She had felt spooked just signing the papers. They had said it was only a formality and not to let it bother her.

But the unforeseen had happened and Daisy hadn't the slightest idea about how to go on, how to relieve this awful emptiness inside that was gnawing away at every fiber of her being

Alyce had been her big sister, her rock. Her best friend. Alyce and Jonathan and then Jeremy had been her family. Now there was just Jeremy. Jeremy and her.

Oh, God.

Daisy dragged her hand through her long black hair and squeezed her eyes shut. The haunting words echoed in her head. The words she had heard three days ago that had shattered life as she knew it. She had been standing in the kitchen, singing along with the radio as she prepared lunch for Jeremy. The news came on and a deep-voiced newscaster stated that a single-engine Cessna had gone down on the western side of the Rockies. The man had no idea that he was forever changing her life, hers and Jeremy's, as he said that there appeared to be no survivors.

She had dropped the pot of soup all over the floor. Over and over again, Daisy had told herself not to panic. Alyce and Jonathan weren't the only ones with a single-engine Cessna. Southern California was full of them. The planes almost littered the grounds of every airport between LAX and John Wayne Airport. Damn, the whole country was full of them.

But she had known.

Even as she dialed the radio station to get any shred of information she could, Daisy had known. All four of them were supposed to have been on that plane, on their way to a vacation in the cabin in the Rockies. Jonathan had given the cabin to Alyce as a fifth wedding anniversary present. This was to be a celebration. But Jeremy had woken up with a cold and Daisy had volunteered to stay with him, urging Alyce and Jonathan to get away and have a second honeymoon.

New tears came, hot and stinging. She rubbed those angrily away, as well. Now her anger, fueled by guilt, was aimed at herself.

If I had kept my big mouth shut, they'd both still be here.

But they weren't here. Not any longer. And because of a twist of fate, she had a little soul to watch over. She pressed her lips together, digging deep for control. She couldn't think of herself now; couldn't dwell on her own grief. She had Jeremy to think of and he made all the difference in the world. From now on, she would have to be both mother and father to him.

She wasn't going to think, she told herself, just do. She had already taken care of all the funeral arrangements, seen to everything that needed handling. She'd even notified Drew.

She shifted uncomfortably, unconsciously bracing her shoulders as she remembered him.

She had first called his home, then his office as soon as she had gotten back from the site of the wreckage. As soon as she had gotten back the use of her voice. Drew couldn't be reached, so she had finally left a lengthy message with a secretary who sounded as if her last job had been with the British prime minister. The woman had softened considerably as she had listened to Daisy recount the details, her voice catching at times, making it difficult to go on.

Drew never returned her call. Instead his secretary had called, stating that he was catching the first flight out and would be there to take care of things.

As if he thought she couldn't. That was Drew for you, she thought.

It had been dislike at first sight.

At least, she was certain it was for him. Andrew Addison was too Ivy League, stick-in-the-mud, well-mannered to actually have said the words, but Daisy had seen it in his eyes, in the set of his jaw. It was as if it was written across his icy patrician face.

By the way Drew looked at Alyce it was easy to tell that he disapproved of her sister, disapproved of the way Alyce had turned his straitlaced brother Jonathan into someone who no longer lived and breathed Dow Jones, into someone who appreciated the world outside of the *Wall Street Journal* and corporate stocks.

Drew's censure had been there the moment he had murmured a subdued hello to Alyce when he had arrived at the house for Jeremy's christening. Having missed the wedding a year earlier, this had been Drew's first meeting with his brother's new wife. His displeasure was instantly evident to Daisy.

There was nothing that aroused Daisy's ire faster than someone being critical of Alyce. And so, though Daisy and Drew had been forced to stand next to one another at the baptismal font while the kindly looking priest had murmured the appropriate words over Jeremy Channing Addison's little head, there had been nothing but the hum of animosity between them.

Alyce and her obvious effect on Jonathan hadn't been the only thing Daisy and Drew disagreed upon. As the party wore on, each time they were within the confines of the same conversation—no matter how else or how many other people were involved—Daisy and Drew wound up being at loggerheads. There didn't seem to be a single thing that they saw in the same light.

Each had come away that day with a definite impression of the other. Drew thought she was a mindless, happy idiot who took maddening delight in arguing with him about everything under the sun. Daisy thought Drew was an opinionated, pompous jackass who had missed all of life while being trapped inside the glass of his forty-story building. He was like a fly captured in amber, well preserved, but not alive.

In Drew's case, Daisy doubted that he had ever *been* alive. It was with great relief that she saw him board the plane bound for New York the next day.

That had been four years ago last June. The handful of times Drew had come to Southern California for a visit, Daisy had tried her best, for the sake of family harmony, to crack the six-inch-thick wall of ice the man seemed to have around him. To no avail. Though he was Jonathan's younger brother, he lacked Jonathan's soul.

They probably forgot to issue him one at the corporation, she thought now, miserably.

Daisy pulled her knees up to her chest, wishing she was six again and didn't have to deal with anything. Life after that age had gotten complicated. But she had always had Alyce. Wonderful, sunny Alyce. No one could ever be unhappy around her. Jonathan had discovered that. Reserved and almost humorless when they'd first met, Jonathan had thawed out to become a warm, giving human being once Alyce got to work on him.

It was something Drew probably never forgave Alyce for.

Drew reminded Daisy of Uncle Warren. Uncle Warren had been her mother's older brother. Part of a rock band, her parents left Alyce and her in Warren's care under the pretext of giving the girls a stable home while they were on the road with their band. They were away three hundred out of three hundred sixty-five days almost every year. It would have been a lonely life for the girls if they hadn't had each other. Warren Baxter was not unkind, just never actually kind, either. He treated Alyce and Daisy as he treated everything in his life—fairly but without feeling. They had called him Warren the Warden behind his back.

And now there was no Alyce. Daisy looked over at the sleeping child again and silently swore to Jeremy that he would never lack for love, not even for a moment. Even if she didn't love the boy to distraction, she owed it to Alyce's memory.

Andrew Addison's hands tightened on the steering wheel of the full-size car he had rented at the airport less than half an hour ago. LAX was always difficult to negotiate out of. The fact that Drew wanted to accomplish that feat quickly made it next to impossible.

Nerves frayed and on edge because of the reason for his being here, Drew felt like ramming the cars in his way. For one insane moment, he wanted to maneuver the maroon

Lincoln onto the sidewalk and drive up to Bel Air at eighty miles an hour.

He wanted to outrace his feelings.

Drew felt his emotions churning within him, churning so violently, he felt sick. He hadn't had a moment's peace since his secretary had given him the message. Jonathan was dead. It seemed absolutely impossible. Drew had wanted to call back, to talk to Anastasia and demand that she admit this was all a hideous joke. Part of the macabre thing she called humor.

But he hadn't called back. He hadn't had the courage at that moment to hear the words. He knew it wasn't a joke; in his heart, he knew. It was that odd sixth sense he had about Jonathan, just as he had known, six years ago, that Jonathan wasn't returning from the coast. Though Drew's need to deny the situation was strong, he hadn't been able to talk to Anastasia. If he heard her voice, he was afraid that all his own well-restrained emotions would break down. Control was all he had to hang on to.

Impatient, Drew glared at his speedometer. The needle hovered jerkily around eleven. They were moving at little more than eleven miles an hour. A crawl away from absolute gridlock he thought, biting off a curse as he ran a hand through his dark blond hair. He should have followed through on his impulse to have a helicopter meet him at the airport. There was a large open field behind Jonathan's house that could accommodate a helicopter—

The image of a helicopter had him swallowing and remembering the message that had been so delicately relayed to him. His brother and sister-in-law had been killed. In a plane accident. A single-engine Cessna for God's sake. Jonathan hated flying. He had come out to the west coast via a cross-country train the first time.

It had been his last time, Drew thought ruefully. Because he had fallen in love with a pair of soft brown eyes. Alyce had a face like an angel. Poor Jonathan never knew what hit him. He had been in unfamiliar territory in Alyce's world and had never had a chance against her. It had been a business trip that had ended up in pleasure. And made Jonathan forsake all business.

No, that was unfair, Drew thought. Jonathan hadn't forsaken all business. He had started up a branch of the corporation out here in Bel Air. It had been just the tiniest of grains when the actual silo was back in New York. Jonathan had done it purely to placate him, to try to keep the peace. Drew knew that. And he knew why Jonathan had fallen so hard for Alyce. After Drew had set his initial animosity aside, he saw all the qualities that Jonathan had found so dear. If truth be known, perhaps Drew even envied his older brother a little because he seemed so happy. It wouldn't have been the kind of life Drew would have chosen for himself. To Drew it seemed like an irresponsible madness. But it seemed to make Jonathan happy and he loved his brother enough to want him to be happy.

Now he wasn't anything.

Damn, why had Jonathan ever come out here? If Jonathan had stayed in his office on the fortieth floor, he would still be alive today.

Drew leaned on his horn as a taxi advertising a local radio station in bold magenta letters cut in front of him, making him lose precious feet of space. He swore under his breath and punched the buttons on the dashboard to turn on the air conditioner.

Lukewarm air came in with a great deal of sound and fury, but did nothing to lower the unseasonably warm temperature that pervaded the car. The air conditioner was obviously in need of repair.

So was his life.

Drew scanned through the radio stations, searching for

something that would help calm his inner turmoil, knowing there was nothing that could.

He was going to miss Jonathan. God, he was going to miss him. It was one thing not to see him, knowing that Jonathan was somewhere else. Alive, vital, happy. A little crazy maybe, but alive. It was another thing knowing that he would never see his brother again.

Grief was an unfamiliar emotion for Drew. He had never allowed himself to experience it or to give in to its overwhelming, engulfing grip before, though there might have been occasion when his parents had each passed on. He had eluded it then, but he hadn't managed to elude heartbreak's scratchy, grasping fingers today.

He sought refuge in planning his next steps. He'd handle whatever needed to be done with Jonathan's estate. That scatterbrained sister-in-law of his undoubtedly wasn't up to doing anything. He had her pegged as the kind who fell apart easily, unable to deal with the real world. Why else would she always be so maddeningly cheerful each time he had the misfortune to be with her? He felt that people just shouldn't be cheerful as a general rule, not without concrete cause, and then only fleetingly. Lovely though she was, she had the IQ of a pair of shoes. Definitely not the type to shoulder responsibility.

After the funeral, he was going to take Jeremy back to New York with him. Jeremy needed a proper home. Drew hadn't the slightest idea of what to do with a four-year-old, but he could hire people for that. The best that money could buy for Jonathan's son. There would be nothing too good for the boy.

Damn it, Jonathan, why'd you have to come out here? Why'd you have to die?

Drew signaled his intent to change lanes. Surprisingly, the driver in the next lane slowed down to let him in. He had anticipated a battle, was actually hoping for one to

release some of the tension he was experiencing. This simple kind action depleted his sails. Another sudden rush of
sadness filled the void.

It had just begun to sprinkle. At the next corner, a young
boy stood, hawking carnations, waving bouquets at each
car that inched past him.

Hell of a way to make a few pennies, Drew thought
absently, his mind desperately searching for diversions of
any sort.

His thoughts returned to Anastasia. Why hadn't she
called him as soon as the accident had happened? Why had
she waited almost three days?

His full mouth tightened, thinking of her. The woman
looked like some misplaced Gypsy. Her dark, exotic col-
oring was like Alyce's, but on Anastasia, it was somehow
wilder. With her torrent of black hair and wide mouth, forever moving, forever spouting nonsense, she had struck him
as the craziest woman on the face of the earth.

A crazy woman, and she had his nephew. That Jeremy
was also her nephew didn't enter into the picture. She was
probably eager to get rid of him and go back to doing
whatever it was that she was currently doing.

A space opened up to his left and Drew aimed the hood
of his car toward it. A second later he was stomping on the
brake to keep from colliding with a beat-up, black 4×4
entering the same space from the other lane. Drew swore
again and carefully maneuvered back into his space, now
made smaller by the red sports car behind him that had
inched up. A horn blared as he wedged back in.

Drew fervently wished for the helicopter again.

More than that, he wished for his brother.

It was after ten o'clock that night when Drew finally
drove up his brother's driveway.

Daisy watched the big car come to a halt from Jeremy's

room, adrenaline suddenly pumping madly through her veins.

"Showtime," she murmured, uncurling her body. She wasn't looking forward to this by any means.

Barefoot, a flowing caftan billowing about her as it caught a draft, Daisy tiptoed out of Jeremy's room, carefully easing the door closed behind her. The doorbell was ringing by the time she got to the stairs. Long and loud. That had to be Drew all right. It was his type of ring. Impatient. She pressed her lips together.

Be kind, Daisy. He's lost somebody, too.

"I'll get it, Irene," she called out in case the housekeeper was still up. The doorbell pealed again.

Irene, her blue eyes still red-rimmed from three days of intermittent crying, bobbed her head as the two women met in the hallway. "I've been answering this door for six years, Miss Daisy, I'd feel better doing it now, if you don't mind."

Though the doorbell sounded for the third time in sharp staccato peals, Daisy placed her hand on the white-haired woman's slightly rounded shoulder. "You'd feel better with a nice hot cup of tea, in bed. Go ahead, now." She nodded toward the back bedroom. "I'll show Mr. Addison to his room."

Irene sighed and withdrew a frail, blue-veined hand from the doorknob. Since the news, she had aged a decade, her normally abundant supply of energy deserting her almost completely. She had no idea what she would have done if Daisy hadn't taken everything over. "If you say so."

"I say so." A frequent guest at the house, Daisy knew that the woman retired early, usually around eight. Irene was just waiting up for Drew to arrive. It was taking duty beyond its call, Daisy thought.

She watched the woman walk toward the rear of the house before she turned toward the door. "Geronimo,"

Daisy said under her breath, pulling it open. She was totally unprepared for the sight that greeted her.

Drew looked like a wet rat. A tall, handsome, angry wet rat in a near-ruined gray suit.

Words of condolence had been on the tip of Drew's tongue. He had meant to offer them as soon as he saw Daisy. After all, even though he didn't care for her, she had suffered a loss, as well.

But good manners had been nudged rudely aside while he had stood on the steps, jabbing relentlessly at the doorbell, enduring the rain and getting completely soaked.

Distraught, upset, Drew cloaked himself in a sharp retort. "It's raining out here," he snapped when she just stood in the doorway, a barefoot Gypsy in a vibrant caftan, looking at him with eyes that were too wide, too green. Too beautiful.

A whoosh of wind sent rain in through the opened door around Drew, sprinkling her toes. Daisy let out a little noise of surprise. "So I noticed."

Drew shifted his weight forward onto the balls of his feet. Was she just going to stand there all night? "Are you going to study the weather, or let me in?"

Well, grief apparently didn't change his disposition for the better. The sympathy she was feeling toward him was on shaky ground.

"Sorry, come on in." She stepped aside to let him pass.

As soon as the funeral was over and loose ends tied up, he and Jeremy would be gone, Drew promised himself. Setting down his overnight case close to the door, he began planning his escape.

Daisy looked at the small case. Good, he wasn't going to stay long. "You certainly didn't bring much," she said for lack of anything better to say.

He took off his jacket, then looked around the wide foyer for somewhere to hang it. He settled on an antique brass hat rack near the hall closet. A small puddle formed directly under it as the jacket dripped onto the light gray tile. "I don't need much."

Her mouth twisted into a smile. Stoic to the end.

He ran his hand through his hair, pushing it away from his face. He was waiting for her to offer him a towel. He should have known better.

"Look," he began tartly in a voice his subordinates recognized and cringed before, "Anastasia—"

She heard the edge in his voice and refused to rise to the bait. He might be ill-tempered, but she didn't have to be. Besides, he might be one of those people who didn't know how to handle grief except to bluster through it. She had cried an ocean in the past three days. It had helped, a little. Drew, she instinctively knew, didn't have that kind of an option open to him.

"Please call me Daisy," she said as she ducked into the powder room and returned with a mauve towel. "It's easier."

Nothing about this woman would ever be termed as easier, he thought darkly. The towel was only large enough to wipe his face, but he took it. He sidestepped the issue of her name altogether, not wanting to be any more familiar with her than was absolutely necessary.

He pulled off his tie and stuffed it into the pocket of his trousers. Because his collar suddenly irritated him, he opened the top two buttons of his custom-made shirt.

Now that he was here, he needed to know more. "The details my secretary gave me were rather sketchy."

She shrugged, looking incredibly frail for a moment. "I don't have much to add to what I told her." She walked into the family room. "Would you like a drink?"

What I'd like is my brother back. It was much too personal a thought to share with her. "Please. I'll have whiskey. Neat."

She nodded, reaching for the bottle behind the bar Jonathan had always kept stocked for company. After pouring Drew a glass, she mixed a gin and tonic for herself. She suddenly needed something to do with her hands, somewhere to look with her eyes. She didn't want to talk about what had happened three days ago, not ever again, yet she knew Drew deserved to hear. She settled down on the sofa, aware that Drew was still standing stiffly over her. "He was taking Alyce to the cabin—"

"What cabin?"

She backtracked, losing her momentum. "Their cabin. The one he bought her for their fifth anniversary."

Were they talking about the same person? "Jonathan hates the outdoors. Hated the outdoors," he corrected himself. Would he ever get used to talking about his brother in the past tense?

"He changed his mind. I heard about the plane crash over the radio. I called the station. They put me in touch with a ranger. As soon as I could, I made them take me up there. I identified them." Her voice hoarse, Daisy took a deep gulp of air as she pulled her hand through her hair. "I told Jeremy as gently as possible. I don't think he really understands yet."

She wet her lips and plunged ahead, jumping from one topic to the next. "Look, I know we've never exactly gotten along, but I want you to know that you can come and visit him here anytime you want to."

What the hell was she talking about now? She wasn't through giving him the details he wanted, needed, to put Jonathan to rest properly in his mind.

"Visit?"

He made it sound like a foreign word. Didn't he care about Jeremy at all? Daisy wondered, suddenly impatient with this man. She tried to put it in terms he would understand. "You know, whenever your schedule lets you."

She had completely lost him. "Why would I visit him here?"

For an intelligent man, he certainly was dense. Maybe it was the shock. "Because Jeremy's going to be living here, with me."

Drew stared at her, stunned. "The hell he is." The words fell from his lips, tense, harsh.

What did he think, that Jeremy was going to be shipped off to a foster home or some orphanage? "Where else would he live? I'm his legal guardian."

Drew held the chunky glass with both hands as he took a healthy-sized swallow. It didn't help. Daisy was still sitting there when he opened his eyes.

Chapter Two

The Scotch warmed him physically, but that was all. Mentally, if anything, it made him more melancholy. It heightened his feelings of sadness and made him acutely aware of his loss. Drew glanced around the room. The last time he'd been here, he had begun to get a slight inkling of what it was his brother had found. There had been warmth, life, here. Now it was bleak and barren.

His mood and then her comment about taking his brother's son had finally opened the floodgates of reality for Drew. Even so, he didn't want to be here. Didn't want to be discussing anything with this woman. The idea of her taking custody was so ludicrous, so patently ridiculous, that for a moment, it didn't fully register. Was this her idea of a joke? The child was an Addison and as such, belonged with him.

Drew refocused his thoughts and looked—really looked—at her. Looked into her eyes. And then the horror struck him. She was serious.

''And just whose idea was this?'' he asked.

The room was dark except for the lamp on the table next to the sofa where they were sitting. He carefully placed his glass on the coaster. Her reflection shimmered on the surface of the liquid within the glass, winking and blinking at him. Mocking him like some sort of fairy sprite mocked reality.

Drew waited, anticipating an incongruous reply. There was no way on God's green earth that he was about to leave that innocent child in her careless hands. Jonathan had told him all about her over the years. She'd turned her back on being a lawyer to do something with flowers, for God's sake. He owed it to Jonathan to take Jeremy with him. Besides, Jeremy was his only tie to Jonathan, and though Drew couldn't verbally express it, that connection was very, very important to him.

Their eyes held. She refused to be intimidated by his tone. Couldn't be intimidated, not after what she'd been through. ''It was Jonathan's and Alyce's decision.''

He didn't believe it for a minute. It was one thing for his brother to be in love with Alyce. She had turned out to be bright and funny, and most important, she had loved his brother dearly. A blind man wouldn't have been able to miss that. But it was quite another to entrust the welfare of Jonathan's only child to a whimsical bohemian who believed her flowers grew because she talked to them.

Drew looked at her, refusing to be taken in by that innocent expression that hovered so close to sensuality it should have been outlawed. ''Jonathan would never have done that.''

You didn't know him at all, did you? ''Alyce told me it was originally his idea.'' Daisy pushed her own glass aside. The drink tasted bitter on her tongue, just like this conversation. She didn't have the energy to continue it.

But there was a funeral to be faced together tomorrow

and Daisy searched for some sort of middle ground for them, at least for now. Later they could draw swords; right now she hadn't the heart for it.

"Look, I can tell by your expression that you're not happy about this—"

Not happy? He thought her assessment didn't begin to do justice to the situation. "I had no idea that understatement was within your grasp."

She had an angle, he thought, she had to. What did some untethered soul who flittered from job to job possibly want with the responsibility of raising his brother's child? The first thing Drew thought of was money. She was after the money that Jeremy would inherit.

Daisy blew out a breath between teeth that were clenched to prevent her from saying something she might regret. She felt she couldn't cope with anything further tonight. She was exhausted from having maintained a good facade for Jeremy's sake. The boy had clung to her when she had returned from the site of the crash as if he silently knew that he'd never see his parents again. She'd been brave and smiled as she spoke to him. And held her own tears in check until she was alone in her room. It had been a horrible, horrible day and she wasn't about to be pushed to the wall by this neanderthal in a designer suit and fifty-dollar haircut.

She looked at him, trying to remember that Jonathan cared about this man, although for the life of her she didn't know why. "I'm not really up to hashing this out with you tonight. Could we please wait until after the funeral is over?"

He was right, she was fishing for money. She wanted him to think it over carefully, give the idea time to play in his mind. Well, if it took money to buy her off, so be it. Jeremy was worth every cent he might have to pay out. His nephew was going to have a good home. With him.

"Fair enough," Drew agreed. "After the funeral."

For a moment, sparring with Anastasia had taken his mind away from Jonathan's funeral. The realization hit him like a fist to the solar plexis. He still couldn't get himself to actually accept it. It felt like a nightmare. Any minute now, he'd wake up and realize that it was just that, an awful nightmare. He would be in his room, alone—

He sighed, rising. What good did it do to pretend? Jonathan was gone. He'd have to face it. "I'll take care of the arrangements—"

"They've been taken care of," she said dully, trying not to dwell on what had transpired in the past twelve hours. The caskets would be closed. No wake. Only she and the rescue team had seen the condition of the bodies within them. It was going to take a while before she could really sleep again.

"By you."

Drew's voice brought Daisy back to the present. She looked at him, astonished and annoyed at his words and condescending tone.

"By me." For the barest second, her voice had an edge to it.

"I see." Drew was tired and overwrought and just wanted to be alone with his pain. He'd never experienced feelings as intense as these before. His entire life had been mapped out. He always knew what he wanted to do. All the details were planned. He was always somewhat remote, removed, and analytical of a given situation. He had to be, to make a rational decision. This was different. For the first time in his life, he didn't feel in control. He felt lost, unsettled, confused and angry. Especially angry. Anger hummed within his soul, like a ricocheting ball searching for the one opening that would set it free. He turned on the likeliest candidate. "Why didn't you call me three days ago?" he demanded.

The vibrating anger she heard startled Daisy. "Excuse me?"

Was she purposely trying to play dumb? "When you first found out that the plane had gone down, why didn't you call?" he demanded. He had gone on with his life for all that time, not knowing his brother lay dead or dying. "Why didn't you tell me?"

For two cents, she would have hit him, right there, in the family room. It would have felt good, releasing the frustration that was eating away at her. But it wouldn't have done any real good and she knew it. Venting her anger by hitting Drew wouldn't have brought either Alyce or Jonathan back to her.

She dragged a ragged breath into her lungs and told him the truth. "Because I was hoping there wasn't anything to call you about." She stared at the liquid in his glass, watched it catch the light and scatter it. Just like her life, she thought. "I was hoping, praying, that somehow they were alive."

He rose, too restless to sit. "I had a right to know," he insisted.

Tears shone in her eyes as she raised her head to look at him. "Look at it this way," she told him, her voice growing hoarse, "you had three more days than I did to think everything was fine."

"I—"

Drew clenched his hands at his sides. She was going to cry. Damn it, he couldn't handle a woman's tears. He had no words, no recourse, faced with that. Tears completely undid him, leaving him feeling even more frustrated, even more helpless. For a moment, he even wanted to take her into his arms and offer some sort of words of comfort.

Except he didn't know how.

Instead, Drew shoved his hands into his damp pockets and kept them clenched there. "Look, I—I'm sorry."

She nodded numbly. Maybe he was human after all. "So am I," Daisy whispered. "So am I." *About everything.*

Drew was about to say something, what he wasn't certain, when the noise stopped him. He turned his listen. A high-pitched, eerie wail was echoing from the recesses of the house. He looked at Daisy, his brow furrowed in confusion. "What's that?"

She shed her grief and was halfway toward the stairs. Jeremy needed her. How could Drew not recognize that? "It's called crying."

He followed her, not fully realizing that he was doing so. "Jeremy?"

Of course, Jeremy. "Unless Irene's found an old Bette Davis movie to watch," she tossed over her shoulder as she hurried up the stairs.

She hoped her wisecrack would make him forget what had happened in the family room just a moment ago. She hadn't meant to cry just then, not in front of him. He would point to it as a sign of weakness and somehow twist it to his advantage when it came to Jeremy. She didn't want him thinking she was the type of woman who crumbled, no matter what the situation.

He shouldn't have had the drink, not even one sip. It only compounded his physical and emotional exhaustion. His legs felt like lead. Drew gripped the banister. He thought of his jacket and suitcase, but was too tired to retrace his steps and retrieve them. The hell with it. He'd sleep nude. "You're going to him?"

He sounded surprised. She had been right. The man had no love, no concept of what it took to raise a child. There was no way he was getting his hands on Jeremy, if that was his actual aim. "Yes, I'm going to him. He's probably frightened."

"I figured that part out." What he hadn't figured out was why she was rushing to the boy. He'd had nightmares as a child and had been informed by his governess that he had to bear up to them. Facing his fears helped to build his character. Although he did recall how grateful he had been when Jonathan had offered to sleep in his bed. Until the governess had caught him and ordered him back to his own room.

Daisy resisted the temptation to say "bravo." Biting her tongue, she continued up the stairs.

Jeremy's door was ajar, just the way she had left it. Daisy pushed it opened and found Jeremy sitting up in the bunk bed, shaking, sobbing. Putting on a bright smile, she crossed to him.

"Hey, Tiger, what's the matter?" Sitting down on the boy's bed, Daisy gathered him close and stroked his hair. "Bad dream?"

Jeremy gulped sobs, nodding his head. He looked up at Drew and then back toward his aunt with huge questions in his eyes.

Daisy settled Jeremy against her as she turned her head toward Drew. Feeling somewhat awkward, Drew ran his hand along the bedpost. The boy was the spitting image of Jonathan as a child. A lump formed in Drew's throat. The lump dissipated with the sound of Daisy's next words to Jeremy.

"Sweetheart, I'd like you to meet your uncle." She leveled a gaze at Drew and thought of his intentions to take the boy away from the only home he knew. Away from her. *The grinch who stole Christmas,* she thought.

Drew scowled at her. He moved forward toward Jeremy. "He knows who I am."

The blank look on Jeremy's face testified otherwise. "I do?"

Drew smiled down at the small face. "Of course you do. I was here just last..." Drew searched his mind for a time and then remembered. "Year," he concluded quietly.

A year was a quarter of a lifetime to a child of four. "I rest my case," Daisy said simply, straightening Jeremy's light blanket. Cartoon characters from a popular Saturday morning program romped all over it in a barrage of colors.

He wanted to tell her that she *was* a case, but refrained from what he knew was a childish display. There was no denying his emotions were in a state of upheaval that he was completely unaccustomed to. He couldn't seem get a hold of them. Irrational thoughts and reactions kept bouncing through his mind. Such as the fact that he had been here a total of fifteen minutes and was vacillating between wanting to comfort Anastasia and wanting to strangle her. Strangling was quickly edging out the former.

Daisy rose and then tucked Jeremy in properly. "Uncle Drew's going to be staying with us for a while, honey. Would you like that?"

Drew noticed that she used the word "us." He pressed his lips together grimly. She had spun a tight, secure web around Jeremy. Poor little boy, at four he didn't have a chance against her. But that was where he came in, Drew thought. He might not have been around very much before, but he was here for Jeremy now and would find away to take the boy back home. There was no doubt in Drew's mind that Daisy would quickly tire of her little charade of playing the concerned aunt and direct her fleeting attention span to something else. It seemed a safe enough assumption to make about a woman who, in Jonathan's words, shed careers and relationships with the ease that other people shed an old pair of shoes.

Jeremy struggled manfully to come to terms with all the changes in his young life, changes he didn't understand or like very much. He was almost five and hurrying to be on his way to six. He looked down at his ever-present teddy bear, as if it was the bear and not the man standing near him that he was addressing. "I guess so."

The little face was still sad, still bewildered. Daisy's heart ached for him. She had done her best to explain to Jeremy that his mommy and daddy had gone to heaven together, but she knew that he was hurt because he couldn't see them any more. What hurt most was that they had left without him.

"Not by choice," she had whispered to him at the time, holding him to her. If she lived to be a hundred, she knew that there would never be anything more difficult for her to do than to tell Jeremy that his parents were gone.

"They won't come back, even for a visit?" he had asked, struggling to understand.

She had fought back tears, telling herself she had to stay strong for Jeremy. "Perhaps in your dreams. But they're watching out for you, sweetheart. And they still love you very, very much. And I'll always be here for you."

It had been a pitifully small thing to offer the boy, but it was all she had.

Daisy looked at Drew now. She knew that he was going to try to argue with her about Jeremy's legal guardianship. It didn't matter what he said or thought. She had the law on her side. And more important, at least to her, she had Jonathan's and Alyce's wishes backing her. "Your mommy and daddy would have wanted Uncle Drew to stay with us for a while, honey," she told Jeremy.

A small smile flittered over Jeremy's lips at the mention of his parents. "Then I guess it's okay." He settled back on his pillow and sighed, one hand tightly wound around the worn bear. "I'm sleepy now."

She patted his head. "Good."

Jeremy's other hand darted out quickly as he grabbed at her wrist. His dark eyes were wide with fear. "Will you stay with me?"

Daisy understood this. Jeremy was afraid of the dark, afraid of being alone. She'd been there herself once, when she and Alyce had first come to stay with Uncle Warren. Daisy ruffled his hair. "I'm not planning on going anywhere, Tiger."

Drew regarded them both in silence for a moment. When it became evident that Daisy was really going to stay with Jeremy until the boy fell asleep, Drew quietly left the room.

He could feel her watching him all the way to the door.

How did you figure a woman like that? he wondered. She apparently got diabolical pleasure out of disputing everything he said, yet she seemed to be putty around a small child. Up to a point, he supposed that meant she had some redeeming qualities.

That wouldn't, of course, keep him from gaining custody of Jeremy and taking him back east with him. Even if he had to take her to court, and he doubted that it would come to that.

He heard her humming as he closed the door behind him, a strange, melodic song without words that wafted through the air, seeping under his very skin, reminding him of a siren's song.

What an absurd notion. Absurd.

And that, he knew, was the word for Anastasia Channing as well. Absurd.

Concentrating on that and only that, Drew managed to stave off the bottomless depression he felt and had felt ever since eleven o'clock this morning.

He went to the room where he always stayed when he visited. The first time he had arrived after the christening, he had made reservations at a hotel, but Alyce had insisted that he stay with them. It seemed that Alyce always got her way, he thought as he entered the room. She had been a subtly persuasive woman, never asking outright, just somehow bending the corners, turning things in her direction. She had a knack for making the other person think that it was their idea.

She would have made a hell of a corporate executive, or corporate raider for that matter. Drew eventually came to understand why his brother had fallen in love with her. But it still didn't stop Drew from resenting the fact that it had happened, that Jonathan had met and married Alyce. For it had taken Jonathan out of his life. Permanently.

And now there was a void within him that would never be filled.

They had been as close as brothers could be. Eighteen months apart, they had done everything together, with Jonathan always paving the way. Jonathan had been ahead of him in school, in clubs, breaking ground for him, making the painful shyness that had racked Drew as a boy easier to deal with. Words had never really been necessary between them. They understood one another without ever having to express anything, although there were times when they had talked until dawn, laying plans, dreaming of what was waiting for them. They shared the same feelings, the same reactions and, until Alyce had come into Jonathan's life, the same goals.

Drew sighed as he crossed to the double bed. He didn't bother turning on the light. It would have been a harsh intruder on his grief. Somehow, he felt better in the dark. It matched the hollowness inside.

He needed sleep, he thought, toeing off his shoes, though he doubted it would come. He felt exhausted, restless, on edge. But he needed sleep to help him cope with tomorrow, with the funeral and the fight with Anastasia that he knew lay ahead of him. He meant to have Jeremy with him when he boarded the plane for the east coast. He would do whatever it took to have him. Jeremy had a heritage waiting for him in New York. He was an Addison. Addisons went to Bently Private School for Boys and, eventually, to Harvard. Taking Jeremy's strengths into consideration when the time came, Drew would map out his nephew's life for him in a beneficial, orderly manner. There'd be no chaos for the boy the way there'd be, Drew imagined, if Jeremy lived with Anastasia.

Drew's thoughts shifted to Anastasia. At the same time, something warm and odd shifted within him that he ignored. He didn't want to go exploring any more emotions right now. He felt too drained. Order was probably not a word Anastasia was familiar with, he thought, stripping off his shirt. He let it fall to the floor. For once he didn't bother to hang up his clothing. He was just too tired to care. The shirt was joined by his pants and finally, his briefs.

There was a slight chill in the room, but he welcomed it. He'd always preferred cool weather. Sitting on the edge of the bed, Drew had just begun to take off his socks when the door opened and light flooded the room from the hall, temporarily blinding him. But not before he saw the outline of a green caftan.

"Oh!"

Daisy looked quickly down to the floor, the suitcase she had brought up from the foyer dangling from her fingers. Amused, flustered, she felt a blush rising up from her neck to her cheeks.

"I, um, didn't think you were in here," she murmured. Which was the truth. Making sure the front door was locked, she'd seen the suitcase and had only meant to leave it in his room. She hadn't wanted to run into him again tonight. And definitely not like this.

Startled, Drew had the presence of mind to yank the edge of the bedspread over himself. The multicolored velvet cover pooled strategically onto his lap. She was doing this on purpose. The woman was utterly impossible. "Where the hell would I be?"

She shrugged, purposely staring at a pattern in the powder blue Oriental rug in front of the bed. She didn't like his tone. It had been an honest mistake on her part, but she supposed he was entitled to his reaction. "There was no light in the room, I thought that maybe you'd gone outside on the patio."

Was she out of her mind? "In the rain?"

"Some people like to watch the rain falling." But he wasn't like some people. Actually, she had wondered where he had gotten to. It was too soon for him to have gone to bed so quickly, but she didn't give it too much thought. "I wasn't thinking clearly."

He felt like an idiot, sitting here completely naked except for one sock. "Another understatement."

Her head jerked up. She was tired of finding excuses for his behavior. "I came to bring this up to your room." She gave the suitcase a slight shake, wishing it was his head instead. "You forgot it downstairs. I thought you might need something in it." Kindly inclinations vanished in the face of his reaction. "Now I realize what you need is a muzzle and a book on manners."

"Manners?" he echoed incredulously. His eyes opened wide and he nearly rose before he remembered that he couldn't. "I'm not the one who came barging into your room unannounced with you stark naked."

"Sorry, next time I'll have the housekeeper announce me. Besides, you're not naked. You're wearing a sock." She bit back the giddy desire to laugh. And to stare. For a corporate executive, he had an incredibly toned and muscular build. "And I already told you it was an honest mistake." She lifted the suitcase higher. "Where do you want this?" *I know where I'd like to put it.*

He was the most ill-mannered man she had ever met. Sure he'd been through a lot, but so had she. At least he hadn't had to explain the tragedy to a four-year-old boy. Or identify the bodies.

"On the floor," he said coldly, "on your way out would be nice."

She let the suitcase slip from her fingers and it dropped to the floor with a thud. She hoped there was something inside that was breakable. It would have served him right. Just to irritate him, she let her eyes drift over him in a slow, appraising glance.

"No problem." She grasped the doorknob, then turned to give him one final look. "Oh, and Drew?"

"Andrew," he corrected shortly, wishing she'd leave. "What?"

"For an ill-mannered, stuffed shirt, you have nice legs. Good night, Drew."

Daisy closed the door, feeling just a tad better than when she had opened it. For just the briefest of moments, she'd managed to get away from the sad, lonely feeling that surrounded her.

But as she walked to her room, on the other side of Jeremy's, her smile faded. The feeling was back. Daisy searched vainly for the humor, the optimism, the childlike faith in tomorrow that had always sustained her before and had seen her through the years.

It wasn't there.

It was too soon, she told herself, too soon. But it would return. After tomorrow was over, it would return. Slowly, perhaps, but it would be there. It had to be. She'd be no good to Jeremy any other way. Or to herself.

She looked in on him one last time to make sure he was still sleeping. He had held on to her hand so tightly until he had dropped off to sleep, as if afraid that she would disappear, too, just like his parents.

"Never happen, Jeremy," she whispered. "I'm yours forever."

She planned to be there for him for as long as he needed her. And no humorless, straitlaced uncle was going to change that, she thought, glancing over her shoulder toward Drew's room. No matter how good he looked wrapped in a bedspread. She and Jeremy belonged together. She was just going to have to find a way to convince Drew of that. The man *had* to have a heart somewhere. It was her job to find it and make it work.

Chapter Three

The rain gradually subsided the next morning until it was just a light, occasional sprinkle, wetting the land. But the clouds remained, ominously hovering over the area. It seemed somehow appropriate.

Daisy managed to get through the ordeal of the funeral by placing one foot in front of the other. And tightly holding on to Jeremy's hand. She had initially debated leaving the boy home with Irene. Weighing everything carefully, Daisy decided that it was important for Jeremy to attend the service. He had to be able to say goodbye in his own way.

She also thought it important that he feel the outpouring of love for his parents, which came from all directions as people who had known Jonathan and Alyce attended the services and offered their condolences.

Daisy smiled and nodded and talked. And cried silently inside. It hurt like hell, being there.

She was vaguely aware that Drew remained at her side throughout it all. That it had been his hand on her elbow, helping her into the limousine. That he had been there during that moment in the church when things had gotten just the slightest bit dark and she thought she was going to faint.

Drew felt rather than saw her sway slightly against him. His hand went around her shoulders automatically. "Are you all right?"

Because she wasn't, she didn't know if that was concern or irritation in his voice. Probably the latter. She took in two deep gulps of air, leaning against him though she hated being weak. "Yes, it's just hot in here," she muttered.

"There are a lot of people here," he commented. She saw that Drew didn't really believe her excuse, but for once, he didn't pursue it. She was grateful to him. It was a kindness she hadn't expected.

His expression was so stoic throughout the morning, Daisy didn't know what he was feeling or *if* he was feeling at all. In her heart, she chose to believe that everyone was susceptible to the same emotions. Everyone felt love, hate, grief and joy. But the expression of these emotions took on different forms with different people.

Some people, she thought, glancing at Drew's face, were embarrassed by their feelings, though she couldn't for the life of her fathom why. She ascribed the latter behavior to Drew. He reminded her a lot of Jonathan when they had first met. It was inconceivable to her that he wasn't saddened by his brother's death, that he wasn't silently grieving along with everyone else in the church.

But she wished he could show it. It would have made her feel that he was human and heartened her about the duel that was just ahead.

It was finally over. The ceremony, the people crowding Jonathan and Alyce's house—now her house she thought ruefully, for that had been part of the agreement, that she raise Jeremy in familiar surroundings—it was all over. Everyone had gone to his or her home to continue with their lives.

Now it was time for her to pick up the pieces of hers and attempt to place them into some kind of order. They had to fit together somehow, she thought, although she didn't know how. At least Jeremy was taken care of for the time being. She had made it a point to invite some of his friends over for the afternoon. They were all now playing in his room, under Irene's watchful eye. It gave them both, Daisy mused, a slight diversion. Something to do.

She watched as the rain began to fall heavily again, beating against the window. If only she knew what to do with herself.

Drew walked into the den looking for Anastasia. He found her standing by the window, just staring out. Pausing, he studied her, the set of her shoulders, the delicate profile. She looked lost, he thought, and for the first time, he knew what she was feeling. There was a small feeling of empathy, but it was gone in the next minute.

Daisy saw his reflection in the window and turned. Well, here they were, she thought. Now what? "It was a nice funeral, wasn't it?" she murmured vaguely.

He crossed the threshold, trying to banish the awkward feeling permeating through him. "Funerals are never nice."

"No," she agreed, combing her fingers through the fringe on the window shade, "they're not. But it gives the living something to cling to, I suppose."

Not me. He shrugged, not wanting her to launch into something chipper and cheerful and totally inane. He just wasn't in the mood to listen to anything like that. "We need to talk."

Here it comes. Daisy gestured to the sofa. "All right, about what?"

She felt a tenseness setting in her shoulders. She knew what he had in mind. He was taking her at her word, when she had said they'd discuss Jeremy's situation after the funeral. She had hoped that he'd give her more than an hour to pull herself together. She should have known better, she thought, sitting on the sofa. All business, that was Drew.

Was that Drew? Wasn't there a glimmer of something else, something more inside? Something she could work with? There *had* to be.

Why was she playing dumb? "It's Jeremy." Drew sat down, although he would have preferred to stand. "I want to take him home with me."

She knotted her hands together over her knee. "I already told you, I'm his legal guardian."

Which proves that justice really is blind. "All right, we'll play it your way for a minute." He proceeded to explain the matter as if he was talking to a very young, very naive person. "As his legal guardian, you can see that I have the most to offer the boy."

This emotionless robot? The hell he had. Her promise to herself to stay calm flew out the window. "The most to offer? You must be joking."

Unlike you, I'm not a happy idiot. "I never joke."

And there, she was certain, he was being honest with her. More's the pity. She looked almost sad as she said, "No, I don't suppose you do. Which is just another reason why I wouldn't let Jeremy live with you."

He expected this sort of reasoning from her. It made absolutely no sense at all. But then, neither did she. "Because I don't tell jokes?"

Missing the forest for the trees, she thought. "Because you don't know how to laugh."

She was babbling. "Since when is laughter a prerequisite for raising a child?" Annoyed, he rose and stood looking down at her.

She let out a long sigh. He sounded just like Uncle Warren had. In all those years with him, she didn't remember one instance when he had really laughed. "You really mean that, don't you? Laughter's right up there next to love and understanding." She saw that Drew didn't see her point at all. "Or don't you think those are prerequisites, either?"

He tried to figure out what exactly she was driving at. He said the only thing he thought she might remotely understand. "I love Jeremy."

She smiled. Deep down, she had always hoped that. It gave her an ace card. Maybe. "Then you'll leave him with me?" she asked hopefully.

For a moment the look on her face made him lose his train of thought. He had already acknowledged that she was a very physically attractive woman. When she smiled that way, there was something magnetic about her, something almost innocent and sweet, and though he knew it had to be an act, it was dangerously appealing.

It took him a second to pull himself free. His thoughts were becoming jumbled. It wasn't like him. "I have no intentions of letting my nephew be raised by the prototype for Auntie Mame."

It was becoming increasingly clear that the man didn't understand *anything*. "As I recall, Patrick turned out pretty well in that story."

"A fortunate accident," he concluded. "No thanks to Mame's bohemian ways. The woman was an unorthodox lunatic." He turned to look at her, his meaning clear in his eyes.

She wasn't going to get angry. She wasn't. It wouldn't help the situation one bit.

"You do know how to make the most of your words, don't you?" She set her mouth firmly as she rose to face him. It was only a little better than sitting. The man was too tall. "Jeremy's staying with me." Daisy saw the stubborn look enter his eyes. They'd be nice eyes if it weren't for that, she thought. Maybe not unduly kind, but gorgeous nonetheless. What a waste. "You'll fight me on this, won't you?"

She wasn't quite as scatterbrained as he'd first thought. "Only if I have to." Maybe she'd be open to reason. "I'd rather just take Jeremy quietly. He's obviously been through enough."

She nodded. "My thoughts exactly."

Success? It felt too easy. "Then you'll give up custody?"

"No."

He nearly threw up his hands, but that would have been too emotional a gesture. Too much like her, he realized. "You are an infuriating woman."

He did frazzle easily, she thought. That would work to her advantage. She licked her lips and plunged ahead hopefully. "But I'll make a deal with you."

Drew lifted his brow. Here it comes, he thought. The money part. "Yes?"

Good, he almost sounded reasonable. "I don't want to drag Jeremy through a court fight. He deserves better than that."

Drew began to write out the check mentally. He wondered how much she'd settle for. "I agree."

So far, so good. "Here's my proposition. You stay here with us at the house for...say, three months. Until New Year's Day." On a roll, she began to talk faster, afraid that he would interrupt. "Let me see what kind of a guardian you'd make for him. If he takes to you, if I see that he's really better off with you than me, and that's a big 'if'—" she drew a breath before finishing "—I won't stop you from taking him."

Drew stared at her. This was the last thing he would have expected her to say. "What?"

He looked at her as if she were speaking in tongues, she thought. "What part would you like me to explain?" she asked patiently.

"All of it," he muttered, then to his horror realized that she was going to launch into another explanation. "No, wait."

He held up his hand, stalling for time while he regrouped mentally. She sat quietly, waiting. How could someone who looked so innocent one moment, be such a source of trouble the next? he wondered. "Let me get this straight," he began slowly. "We're both supposed to live here."

"Yes." It would never work, she thought gleefully. He'd be gone, happily, within two weeks. Three, tops. He wasn't cut out to be a parent. It was what she was banking on. But if all else failed, she had no intentions of living up to her part of the bargain. She couldn't. Jeremy would be devastated. What she was really praying for was a miracle, a transformation on Drew's part just as there had been on Jonathan's. He'd realize that Jeremy belonged with her.

"Together." The word was etched in disbelief. She had to be crazier than even he had thought if she imagined that this had a prayer of working.

The smile she gave him could have been termed as sweet, he thought, if he didn't know any better. "It's nice to see your Harvard education paid off so well." Daisy took a deep breath, her smile fading. "Don't you see? This is the only way that will give Jeremy the opportunity to decide—"

Drew cut her short. "He's four years old. He can't possibly decide something of this magnitude for himself. Which toy to play with, yes," he conceded. "But not which relative to live with." She had to be insane to even think so.

Daisy held on to her temper, her voice deceptively soft. "He knows who he loves."

Finally. Drew had had a feeling that Anastasia would fight dirty. It was just a matter of time. "That's only because you've always been around."

She held up a finger, victorious. "My point exactly. Now you have to be around so he can learn to be comfortable with you. There's no way in the world I'm just going to hand him over to you now, when you're almost a stranger to him."

"I am not a stranger."

"He didn't recognize you," she reminded him.

Daisy dragged a hand through her tangled black hair and roamed to the window. That was the term for it, he thought, not walked, not crossed, but roamed. Like some wild, fascinating animal someone had had the good sense not to imprison yet. Not that they'd be able to, he realized. Unless she wanted them to.

She turned around to look at him, deadly serious. "It's the only way I won't fight you for custody. And I warn you, I fight to win."

He didn't doubt it for a minute. She might look small and frail, but he knew that was just her deceptive camouflage. He'd probably have his hands full in court, fighting her. Looking the way she did, she might just turn the judge in her favor. Then where would he be? And throughout it all, Jeremy would be the one to suffer.

Daisy wanted to tell Drew to pack up and go, but if she did, as sure as the sun rose in the morning, she knew that there would be papers served. Above all, she had to think of what all this would do to Jeremy. If Drew agreed to the bargain, she knew she could get him to see things her way. The possibility of anything else resulting was inconceivable to her.

She smiled at him sweetly, laying a gentling hand on his arm. "Look, just because we disagree about every topic under the sun doesn't mean we can't live under the same roof for three months."

He didn't trust her or her smile. "Prisoners do it all the time. Speaking of doing time..." He moved toward the doorway, signaling an end to the ridiculous discussion. "My staying here is unacceptable."

This was easier than she thought. He was giving in already. For the first time in three days, happiness began to bud within her. "Then you're giving up?"

Whatever gave her that idea? "No, of course not. I want you to."

So much for tidy, happy endings. She shook her head, dark hair sweeping along her shoulders like storm clouds. "No way. Over my dead body."

There was something almost stirring, he realized, about the way her eyes flashed just then. It was the kind of look that sent poets to their desks and artists to their easels. And corporate men to their antacids. He refused to be intimidated by it. Or aroused. He had less control over the latter than he would have liked. "You're only sweetening the pot."

All right, the gloves were off, she thought. She jabbed a finger at his chest and met with a good deal more physical resistance than she would have thought. A flash of the way he had looked last night when she had walked in on him crossed her mind. And warmed her even though she was braced for battle. There was an electricity here she would have liked to explore if the stakes weren't so high.

"Now listen to this. Alyce and I were raised by someone exactly like you. Our Uncle Warren. He was a topflight corporate lawyer who had blue chips instead of blood running through his veins. Our parents were always away on some road tour or other. We had about as much love passed on to us as a pair of lepers in a vacation colony. And I won't have the same thing happening to Jeremy!"

She poked his chest again for emphasis. This time, Drew grabbed her finger in his hand and pushed it firmly aside, his eyes warning her that he was not about to be backed into a corner. She dropped her hand to her side, but the look on her face remained unchanged.

God she was beautiful, he thought completely against his will. "Are you possibly suggesting that I'd be that way toward him?"

She wasn't about to back off. "No, I'm not suggesting it. I'm flat out saying it." She gave him a knowing look. "You'd send him to boarding school, wouldn't you?"

He didn't answer her directly. "And what's wrong with that?"

She answered with a question of her own. "How much time do you have?"

She was maddening, utterly maddening. Even more maddening was the fact that, in the midst of all this, he kept finding himself reacting to her in a completely emotional as well as physical manner. And he didn't like it. It wasn't like him at all. Part witch. The Channing women were all part witch, he decided, thinking of the spell Alyce had woven over his brother.

And just who the hell did Anastasia think she was, judging him? He felt his normally cool manner hovering uncomfortably close to meltdown. "So, Jeremy'd be better off living with a woman who talks to flowers and drifts aimlessly through life than going to boarding school?"

He seemed to know just enough details to cloud the issue and not enough to clear it, she thought angrily. She had her own business now and talking to flowers had turned out very well for her, thank you very much. But she wasn't going to get into an argument over his opinion of her. If he thought of her as some flighty, flaky creature with unorthodox views, that was his problem, not hers.

For the first time in her life, she wished she was taller.

She didn't like the way he loomed over her. "Yes, because with me he'd have the kind of love and nurturing support that he both needs and deserves."

She was spouting emotional gibberish, but he had expected as much. What he hadn't expected was to lose his temper. But it was getting dangerously frayed around the edges. "I want to see him raised properly."

Like a little wind-up soldier, she thought bitterly. She had heard sentiments such as Drew's voiced before. In her childhood. Then they had been applied to Alyce and her. She could feel her blood run cold at the very thought of it. "I want to see him well adjusted."

He saw the impassioned look on her face and thought, quite against his will, that it made her look beautiful. "Why does it sound like we want the same thing for him when it's really not?"

Daisy let out a long breath. It helped take some of the edge off her animosity. She was willing to give the Ivy League jerk the benefit of the doubt for Jonathan's sake. "Because we both love him." She squared her shoulders. "Now, I gave you my offer. My only offer. Take it or leave it."

Drew frowned. To the untrained ear, she sounded noble, but Drew was well acquainted with deviousness. The corporate world was full of it. He wasn't fooled by her words. He trusted this woman as far as he could throw her. Less. Besides, she was only making this proposition because she knew remaining here was impossible for him.

"You can afford to play all the games you want. You're not tied down by a career."

"I own a business," she informed him, her pride wounded even though she told herself that what he thought of her didn't count. If she had gone from one thing to another, it was because she hadn't found her proper place in life before and had no problem with abandoning something that made her miserable.

She had found her niche last year.

"Doing what?" Drew asked. He couldn't quiet help the condescending tone that came into his voice.

"I own a nursery."

He thought of the boy on the corner he had seen yesterday, hawking flowers. He could see her doing the same with ease. She'd probably enjoy it, he thought, unconsciously smiling.

She had no idea why he looked so amused. She did know that she had a sudden urge to plant the heel of her shoe somewhere on his muscular torso.

"We do landscape consulting." Her anger dissipated at her next words, because of the memory that was attached to them. "I just finished redoing Alyce and Jonathan's backyard."

Drew let out a little huff, unable to picture anything that had to do with his brother without feeling pain. "Be that as it may, you're still located here. My headquarters, as you know," he said pointedly, "is on the other side of the continent."

That, too, was his problem, not hers. "They have telephones now. Work pretty well, they tell me."

Drew opened his mouth to respond, but she went on. It was what he was afraid of. The woman had a rapid-fire delivery second only to a discharging machine gun. He'd hardly formed the first syllable of the first word and she was already completing a full sentence.

"And you've heard of flying, I assume, for the business you can't conduct from here." She looked at him innocently, her eyes open wide.

Sexy. Standing there that way, he had to admit that the woman looked definitely sexy. And was a definite royal pain. "Don't patronize me."

Her eyes darkened. "Then don't be so stuffy. It's not as if you were a factory worker with a time card to punch every day. According to Jonathan, you're the boss of a major conglomerate that's spread out throughout the world. With telecommunication and fax machines that can bring the board meeting right into your living room, you're all set. You can work anywhere you want to." A smile lifted the corners of her mouth as she raised herself upon her toes to be closer to him. "What's the matter? Afraid of spending three months with me?"

He caught the faintest whiff of a cologne that brought an image of white lace and old-fashioned porch swings to his mind. How absolutely incongruous with the woman who was standing in front of him, challenging every fiber of his being. "Terrified out of my mind. But someone has to save Jeremy from your influence. And there's no one else but me."

Her smile softened, making her mouth look tempting. He bent his head, almost giving in to the sudden surge of desire before he caught himself. Drew decided that the stress of the funeral had him practically hallucinating.

Daisy's heart was hammering. My God, he had almost kissed her. In the middle of an argument? There was hope for the man yet.

She dropped onto the arm of the sofa and looked up at Drew, studying him.

From the set of his jaw, she guessed that he at least thought he was in for the duration, hoping, no doubt, to somehow outsmart her and outlast her. He had a surprise coming, she mused. She wasn't about to be outsmarted. But if they were going to be under one roof for a total of ninety days, the air had to be cleared. She knew he didn't like her. But his antagonism toward Alyce was a different matter. Alyce had been sweet, loving, kind. It irked Daisy that this man held anything but the greatest regard for a woman whose shoes he wasn't fit to clean.

"Tell me something. Why were you so horribly hostile toward my sister? She made your brother very happy." There were a thousand and one different instances Daisy could have cited for him to substantiate her statement.

He thought back to his initial feelings about Alyce. They had changed, but there was no reason to tell Anastasia that. He would have sounded as if he was backing off. So he gave her the bottom line.

"Your sister changed Jonathan. She took a highly motivated businessman and turned him into a laid-back individual who puttered in the garden."

Which was true. The last time he had been here, Jonathan had tried to get him involved in his roses. *Roses*. Though he had tried his best to be understanding, he drew the line there. There were gardeners for things such as that. Jonathan hadn't graduated at the top of his class with a degree in business from Harvard to spread mulch and manure around.

Daisy shook her head. "Horrible thing, making living things grow and thrive."

He closed his eyes. Trust her to miss the point. "That's not what I meant. He was wasting talent."

She shrugged carelessly, her silk blouse rustling against her shoulders. She didn't think Drew would understand. Absently, she ran the tip of her finger along a petal of one of the roses in the vase. The petal fell to the oak desk. The flowers she had picked at the beginning of the week, just before she had heard the news, were dying. Soon, they'd be gone, too.

Daisy roused herself. "Your idea of talent might not have been his."

It had been once, he thought. "You know, you have a way of twisting words."

She raised her eyes to his. Green eyes met gray for a moment and held. Was he totally dead behind those eyes? She refused to believe that. "I have a way of seeing the truth."

He let out a long breath. "You haven't changed any."

She struggled to hold on to her temper. She was just about out of patience and endurance. Even a saint had a breaking point and she had never considered herself particularly saintly.

"From when? You only met me a handful of times. You don't know me."

"I know all I need to know." More than enough, he added silently.

Daisy scowled at Drew. With a huff, she pushed away her hair with the back of her hand.

"Made up your steel-trap little mind, didn't you? Just like that." She snapped her fingers. "Without all the facts. Just some sort of emotional response. No, excuse me—" she held up her hand to forestall any words of correction that might be coming "—mechanical response. You don't have any emotions." Her eyes narrowed. "I really do think I frighten you."

He caught a whiff of cologne again, or maybe it was the flowers this time. It was strange that something so nebulous, so feminine, should snare his attention just now. He wished he could stop winking in and out this way and just concentrate on the fact that she was the most annoying woman God ever created. It helped to hang on to his anger at a time such as this. If he didn't, then he'd have to face the wrenching fire of emptiness that hovered, threatening to tear at his insides. And something else, equally as powerfully, waiting just beyond. Something he refused to give substance to.

"Yes, you do. I'm always afraid of crazy people, especially those in vivid colors." He waved a hand at her.

"Why did you wear that to the funeral, for God's sake?" Didn't she know how to show respect?

She was wearing a lavender suit. "It was Jonathan's favorite color," she answered quietly. "And you're not afraid of me because you think I'm crazy. You're afraid because you think I'm right and you're wrong."

That would be the day. "See, crazy, completely crazy." A beat passed and she said nothing. It was like waiting for the other shoe to fall. "All right, right and wrong about what?"

"Life. My approach to it."

Her approach. "Like a bull in a china shop?" he asked archly.

She turned her eyes toward him. The vividness of her clothes paled in comparison to the brightness of her eyes. They seemed almost electrifying as she gazed at him.

"No. Like someone who wants to savor every damn last minute." *Before there was no more life left to savor,* she thought sadly. "Who wants to try everything." He obviously wanted to try nothing, she thought. Nothing that had a risk attached to it. She wondered if he knew that.

"That's a euphemism for unstable in my book."

"Your book," she echoed, then nodded her head knowingly. "Ah, yes, that would be the 1955 YMCA version of 'The Facts of Life.'"

He had no idea why he was even trying to reason with her. Emotionally, he was about as drained as any man could be. Arguing with her wasn't helping matters any. "I'm not going to go on talking to you when you're babbling."

She watched him cross back to the doorway. He was a fairly good-looking man, she thought. What a shame he was so pigheaded.

She crossed her arms in front of her. "So, where does that leave us?"

"At each other's throats?" he guessed archly. At least, it looked that way to him.

"It doesn't have to be that way." There was a child's happiness at stake. She had to give this her best shot.

"Why? Having a personality transplant?"

Maybe the shot should be aimed at him. "No, investing in a silver bullet." *Down, Daisy. The man can't help being a jerk. It's probably something genetic.* She touched his arm, surprising him. She could tell by the way he looked at her. "All this bickering isn't going to help, or be good for Jeremy. Now we're both agreed that he's what's important here, right?" She dared him to dispute that.

He hated conceding a point to her, even if it was the truth. "Right."

She found it fascinating that he could talk through clenched teeth. "Neither one of us wants to drag him through court, right?"

"Right."

Two for two, not bad. "Yet neither one of us wants the other to raise him."

"Right," he agreed emphatically.

Then it was simple. Couldn't he see that? She smiled beatifically, tossing her hair over her shoulder, a sultry dark wave. "Then we have to try it my way. There is no other way."

There was one. He hesitated just a fraction of a second before he tried it. "Could you be bought off?"

Drew couldn't remember ever seeing eyes turn so dark so fast before. Dark and dangerous. The word magnificent whispered around the perimeters of his mind.

She couldn't tell if he was serious or not, but by his own admission, he didn't joke. That made what he suggested reprehensible. She chalked it off to stupidity. "Don't even suggest it," she said quietly, her tone all the more underscored because of it. "I don't want to have a reason to hate you."

So, she really wasn't doing this for the money. "Maybe I did misjudge you."

She arched a brow. "Maybe?"

"All right," he relented. "I misjudged you."

Daisy shook her head. He was difficult, no two ways about it. But she could handle difficult if it meant keeping Jeremy. "Like pulling teeth, Drew, but I guess you'll come around."

He didn't know just how she meant that, but he was taking no chances. "Don't hold your breath."

"So—" she stuck out her hand "—we have a bargain?"

He looked at her hand for a long moment. It was true, what she had said earlier. If necessary, he could arrange things so that he could work out of the L.A. office temporarily. And he could fly to New York for meetings that were unavoidable and couldn't be attended through the miracle of a visual hook-up. If Jeremy's welfare really depended on it, then he would have to stay.

Reluctantly, Drew took her hand. It felt small and delicate in his. Delicate. And the moon was made of green cheese. "We have a bargain."

He had the distinct image of Daniel Webster shaking hands with the devil just before the trial began. But Daniel had won that case, he reminded himself. And Drew fully intended to win this one.

Chapter Four

Margaret Reilly looked over the tops of her reading glasses as Daisy tossed her sweater carelessly in the direction of the chair. The back office of the nursery was small and crammed full of books, reports, a desk and a computer. But the morning sun filled it and made it appear somehow homey.

"Are you sure you should be back, Daisy?" She tucked away her morning newspaper, but not the box of doughnuts that was in front of her. She swallowed the bite in her mouth. "The funeral was just yesterday."

Daisy broke off a piece of the doughnut in Margaret's hand and realized that she had struck pay dirt, or raspberry jelly as it was. She quickly licked it from her fingers, savoring the sweet taste. She was fighting her way back among the living, she thought, and recovery involved all her senses.

"I've been away for four days, Margaret. I'm sure."

Daisy popped the rest of the piece into her mouth. "Besides, I can't have you doing everything."

Margaret dusted the sugar from her fingers with a napkin, then took off her glasses. "Normally, I'd heartily agree. But this isn't exactly normal." She gave Daisy a huge hug. "How are you holding up?"

Daisy was grateful for the concern. It helped. "I need to work."

"Well, God knows you have it." Margaret ran a hand through her tangled blond hair. Hair that made her resemble, Daisy had affectionately pointed out, a mature Orphan Annie. "It seems like everyone in creation has been calling since you've been gone."

Margaret gestured toward a stack of order forms in the In box on the scarred desk. The desk had been a gift from Alyce, rescued from a thrift shop. It had turned out to be an unappreciated antique. Everywhere she looked, Daisy thought, there were going to be reminders of Alyce. For the rest of her life, there would be reminders. She'd have to find a way to deal with that.

"Word about us has gotten around." Margaret picked up the top two forms as she reached for another doughnut with her other hand. "I've had calls for everything from African violets to full-grown palm trees."

Daisy took the forms from Margaret. Friends since college, Margaret was more her partner than her assistant, though the mortgage papers only contained Daisy's name. The company, begun on a whim, had evolved from a simple florist shop to a landscaping consultant service with a small nursery in the back. The shop was a potpourri, like Daisy herself.

Daisy perused the first form. Indigo Company. Big time. "Palm trees?"

Margaret nodded. "The Indigo Company said they need instant landscaping for a mall they're putting up in Bedford.

Seems the man in charge knew Jonathan and...'' Margaret's voice trailed off. She looked at Daisy hesitantly. ''Sorry.''

''No reason to be,'' Daisy assured her, forcing her voice to sound bright. ''Jonathan lent me the money to get started in this business and his connections have always brought us a lot of clients.'' She replaced the order forms on top of the stack. ''Did you call Keeline?'' she asked, referring to the largest wholesale nursery they dealt with.

''Not yet.'' Margaret eyed another doughnut. That would make three this morning. ''The call came in yesterday afternoon.''

Daisy took the order forms and secured them on her clipboard. She'd have to go over them today to make sure the proper calls were made. And check the delivery forms, as well. It wasn't that she didn't trust Margaret, it was just that Margaret tended to be easily distracted. Food or a good-looking man did it every time. ''But you told them yes.''

Margaret took out a third doughnut from the box and plopped it on the white napkin. A deep red stain oozed onto it.

''I told them yes. No order too large, no order too small, right?'' She parroted the slogan beneath the Showers of Flowers...and Things logo outside the door and on their business card.

Daisy glanced at an invoice. Good, the five-gallon cypresses she had ordered had been delivered. Daisy checked off the form, making a note to take a look at them before having them delivered to her customer. ''Right.''

Margaret sighed contentedly as the doughnut plugged up the remaining space in her stomach. She fixed her attention on Daisy. ''So, who was that hunk I saw standing next to you at the service?'' She flashed an apologetic grin. ''I didn't think it was right to ask yesterday.''

Daisy had to stop and think for a minute before she realized that Margaret was referring to Drew. "That was Jonathan's brother." She thought of the way he had corrected her the night of his arrival. "'Andrew.'"

Margaret sighed deeply. "What is he?"

"Annoying." Daisy reached for the pot of coffee Margaret had made. It was weak, but it was better than nothing. At least it was hot and she needed something to get her engine started.

Margaret shook her head. Her tight curls bobbed up and down like tiny blond springs. "No, I mean, what does he do?"

Daisy took a sip of the coffee and then frowned. She could have gotten the same results, tastewise, if she had stuck a brown crayon into boiled water. At that moment, she would have paid a king's ransom for some old-fashioned, strong caffeine.

"I told you, annoy me." At least it felt as if that was his principle occupation in life since he had driven up her driveway two days ago. "He's in the same company Jonathan was in. Heads it, actually."

Margaret cocked her head, peering at Daisy's face. "Sounds like the beginnings of a wonderful relationship."

Margaret, Daisy thought, had to stop going to those old movie revivals. She downed the rest of the coffee and frowned again. Hot and terrible, no question about it. "No relationship. More like a war."

"Want to clarify that?" Margaret took the cup from Daisy and replaced it with a doughnut. To Margaret, Daisy knew, sugar solved everything.

Daisy carefully turned up the side filled with jelly so that it wouldn't leak out. "Drew *thinks* he's come to take Jeremy back with him to New York."

Daisy had Margaret's undivided attention. "Uh-oh. Does he know that you've got legal guardianship?"

Daisy nodded and set her mouth grimly.

"And?" It seemed to Margaret that that would be the end of the matter.

Daisy's eyes darkened again, just as they had yesterday when it had happened. "He tried to buy me off."

Margaret groped behind her for a clear spot on the desk and leaned against it. "How many stitches did they have to give him in the emergency room?"

The image tickled Daisy and she laughed. "None. He remained unscarred, but it wasn't easy for me."

"I'll bet. On behalf of the female population, we thank you." The teasing grin faded as Margaret momentarily became serious. "You're not giving Jeremy to him, are you?" It was actually a rhetorical question. Daisy loved Jeremy as much as she had loved her sister and brother-in-law. If there was anything the woman was, it was fiercely loyal. Jeremy was going nowhere.

Daisy thought of the discussion they had had last night and Drew's reaction. "We have an arrangement."

Margaret leaned forward. "Sounds interesting." The grin had returned. "And he's without stitches. Hmm."

Daisy gave her a warning look. Margaret thought that everyone should be paired up. "Don't 'hmm' me. The arrangement is that he has to stay at the house for three months—"

"Better and better."

"—And in that time," Daisy pressed on doggedly, "if Jeremy grows to really love him, then I'll give Drew custody."

Margaret's grin faded and her jaw sagged in surprise. She was staring at her as if she had just declared that the world was really flat, Daisy thought. "You'd give him up?" Margaret finally said.

"In a pig's eye I will," Daisy declared firmly. "What I'm banking on is melting Mr. Ice-Water-For-Blood Addison so that he understands that Jeremy is better off staying with me. All I need," she concluded with a sigh, "is a blow torch."

"Alyce did it with Jonathan," Margaret reminded her. "As I recall, he was pretty stiff upper lipped when she first met him."

"I know, but I'm not Alyce," Daisy said wistfully.

"True." Margaret patted Daisy's hand. "But you work a lot quicker than anyone else I ever met. My money's on you, kid."

Daisy frowned as she toyed with a doughnut. "I don't know. I keep hoping that I'll find a way to make him come around, but what if I'm wrong? Right now, the man seems like an utter cold fish."

Except, Daisy amended silently, for that one moment when he looked as if he wanted to kiss her. But that could have just been her imagination.

Margaret scooted some crumbs off the desk and into the doughnut box. "If he's such a cold fish, what does he want with Jeremy?"

Daisy lifted a shoulder and let it drop. "I don't know." She would have liked to believe it was because Drew loved the boy, but she sincerely doubted that love came into the matter. Or, if it did, that Drew even realized it. She had her work cut out for her all right. "It has something to do with heritage and last names and things like that." She didn't want to waste any more time thinking about Andrew Addison and his motives. She had work to catch up on. "Come on, let's tackle these orders that came in." She gave her clipboard a little shake for emphasis. "I have a date for lunch this afternoon."

"With Mr. Wall Street?"

"Don't be silly. With my favorite short person." Daisy smiled. She hated leaving Jeremy this morning, but she assuaged the guilt by promising lunch at his favorite place.

"I'm taking Jeremy to Hamburger Delight. They've just remodeled their play area and I know he's dying to break it in."

Daisy settled in behind the desk and began to divide the forms according to which wholesale nursery she would have to deal with to fill the request.

Margaret poured another cup of coffee and placed it within Daisy's reach. Daisy pointedly ignored it. "How's he taking it? Jeremy, I mean."

"Remarkably well for a four-year-old." Daisy stopped sorting to consider. "Almost too well. There seems to be a lot more of his father in him than I thought." Maybe that was for the best after all, she thought. She looked at Margaret, who was puttering around by the coffee machine. She knew procrastination when she saw it. "Come on, less talk, more work," she prodded affectionately.

Margaret pulled up a chair next to Daisy's desk. "Nice to know you haven't changed." Impulsively, Margaret gave Daisy's hand a squeeze. "Welcome back, Boss."

Daisy smiled her thanks, then looked at the forms again. There was a lot of planting here. Showers of Flowers...and Things wasn't just contracted to deliver the small orders, but to plant them, as well. And one-third of their crew on the premises had quit to go back to school full time last week. That put them in a bind. "Have we filled Eric's position, yet?"

Margaret sucked on her lower lip, suddenly chagrined. "Oh."

Daisy sighed as she looked at Margaret. She was afraid of what was coming. "What's 'oh'?"

Margaret made a comical face. "I forgot to place the ad in the newspaper."

Terrific. Daisy turned in her swivel chair and studied the bulletin board on the wall behind her desk. All the specifics of what went where and when were detailed on the spread sheet posted on it. "The Samuelsons are expecting to have three *Ligustrum* delivered and planted in their front yard today."

Margaret shook her head. "Doesn't look likely. Simon's got a bad back and Pablo's out with the flu. That just leaves you and me. The job's too small to call in a contracting crew," she pointed out.

When it rained, it poured. But, as everything else, it could be handled. Daisy squared her shoulders. "All right." She rose. "Help me load the shrubs and some bags of leaf mold and manure on the back of the truck."

"Me?"

Margaret was as sturdy-looking as Daisy was fragile. "You don't think I hired you just for your looks, do you?" Affectionately, Daisy patted Margaret's forearm. Despite Margaret's love affair with food, the woman never gained an ounce. "I knew I needed strong peasant stock to help me load things."

"Tote that barge, lift that bale."

"Now you've got the picture." Daisy laughed. She had been right about getting back to work. Being around Margaret always made her feel better. "I'll drop the shrubs off at the Samuelsons and start digging the holes myself after I have lunch with Jeremy." She paused. "Maybe I'll swing by Keeline and pick out the palm trees, too." She glanced at the form to see how many. Eight. Thank God she wasn't going to handle planting those. Keeline did its own delivering and planting. She just did the contracting. "Jeremy might get a kick out of helping me select them. It makes him feel important."

"You're not really planning on planting the Samuelson's shrubs yourself, are you?" Margaret asked as she followed Daisy out the door.

"You have a better idea?"

"Sure." She walked out to the back of the nursery with Daisy. "Stall them."

She was going to need several bags of leaf mold and manure, Daisy thought as she made her way to the rear of the yard where she had the shrubs set aside.

"That's not how a reputation gets built." Daisy began to mentally reshuffle her day, making certain that Jeremy wouldn't feel short-changed. "When I leave, you stay here in the shop and handle the walk-ins. Simon can help. I'll take care of the shrubs." She went to back their truck up to the delivery area of the nursery. "And make sure the ad for a nurseryman is in tomorrow's paper, okay?"

Margaret saluted. *"Oui, mon capitaine."*

Drew glanced at his watch as he entered the neatly tiled kitchen. Eight o'clock and no sign of her. She was probably sleeping in, he thought. It figured.

He had no patience with laid-back people. He'd been up for more than an hour already. He had showered, shaved and dressed, then called New York and informed them that he would be staying in Bel Air for a while. He didn't specify the exact length of time he would be gone. He hoped that it would ultimately be considerably less than the three months Anastasia had irrationally insisted on. With luck, he would get her to come to her senses and realize that Jeremy was better off with him before the month was out.

The CEOs hadn't been very happy about the news. He could tell by the response he had received during the three-way conversation. But he was head of the company and that put an end to the matter. At least, he had thought, hanging up, for now.

His father had inherited Addison Corporation from his father, but it had taken Drew and Jonathan to turn it into the vast conglomerate it was today. Initially begun in the 1940s as a simple electronics company, Addison Corporation had diversified to include a whole range of technology. They were now a holding company for several companies in a number of major fields. The array spanned the spectrum from television monitors to sophisticated optical imaging and sensing devices used on the latest space shuttles. And ever since Jonathan had eased away, Drew had been in charge of it all. The corporation occupied most of his waking hours, but it provided him with an enormous sense of accomplishment. It wasn't even the money. He lived basically a simple life. It was seeing something so large and diverse prospering because of him.

Consequently, Drew had no idea how to relax, how to function in a home with time on his hands. But he didn't see that as a liability. For him home was a place where he brought his work if he didn't get a chance to finish it in the office. A place where his live-in valet prepared his meals and where he slept when he wasn't on a business trip in Europe or parts of the U.S.

Without work, he felt restless, at loose ends. To just sit back and do nothing productive wasn't in his nature, even for a day. There were things he could be accomplishing. Why waste precious time?

Because he couldn't operate without a detailed daily schedule, Drew had made mental plans while he'd showered. He was going to see about creating a temporary headquarters at the small research operation Jonathan had begun in Bel Air. It was more of a scientific think tank than an actual branch office. They paid top-notch scientists to work free-form, developing ideas that might someday fuel an entire new technological field, the way PCs and VCRs once had.

Addison Corporation's actual west coast building was located in San Francisco, but Jonathan had set up an annex in Southern California because he hadn't wanted to move. Undoubtedly, it had been Alyce's idea, but Jonathan had remained adamant when discussing the matter with Drew. It was Bel Air or nothing. And so, Bel Air it was.

Drew had just begun to address the problem of the coffeemaker and how it worked when Irene walked in, followed by Jeremy.

"Good morning, Mr. Addison," Irene said crisply. "Breakfast?"

"Good morning." Drew searched his memory, trying to remember the woman's name. "Irene," he added belatedly. "Coffee."

The white head nodded once without bothering to make a confirming reply. Drew turned his attention toward Jeremy. Though he wanted the boy to live with him and knew that he loved the boy as much as he was capable of loving anyone, Drew still felt ill-at-ease in Jeremy's presence. He had little to no idea how to make idle conversation with adults, much less a child.

Drew forced a smile to his lips. "Hi, Jeremy, how are you today?"

"I'm okay." Jeremy pulled out a kitchen chair and scrambled onto it. Seated slightly askew, he stretched his feet out in front of him. The sneakers were new and almost scuff free, with large, bright blue, droopy laces. Jeremy surveyed them proudly. He was learning how to tie them himself.

Abruptly, he looked up at Drew. "Are you gonna come, too?"

Behind him, Irene was busy doing whatever she normally did. Drew decided to join Jeremy at the table for a minute while he waited for his coffee. "Come? Come where?"

"To Hamburger Delight." The "of course" was silent but implied nonetheless. The word "precocious" presented itself to Drew. "Aunt Daisy's taking me."

It sounded like the kind of establishment she would be partial to, Drew thought. "I wasn't invited." Thank God for small favors. He could just imagine the kind of food served there. Besides, he wasn't going to have time for any outings today. There was just too much to do. He was already behind by two days.

Drew half turned in his seat as Irene approached, ready to take his coffee from her. He saw that she was holding a bowl of cereal and a container of milk. Self-consciously, he let his empty hand drop as she placed both items in front of Jeremy.

The boy grasped the milk container in both hands and doused his cereal liberally. A white stream came pouring out. Drops of milk ricocheted off round, colored balls and then fell on the tablecloth. Drew squelched the impulse to brush them off with his napkin.

"You can come if you like," Jeremy said as he tried to sink pink, yellow and purple tiny balls beneath his milk. He looked up hopefully at his uncle.

Drew didn't like the way Jeremy's expectant expression made him feel. An unfamiliar tinge of guilt sliced through him, almost making him squirm. "I don't think your aunt would like me tagging along."

"Sure she would." Jeremy grinned at him, his lips already outlined in milk after one sampling. "Aunt Daisy likes everybody."

Well, he had his suspicions that the woman didn't like him and that made him a member of a very exclusive club, according to Jeremy.

"No, I really don't think that I can make—"

Drew stopped, aware that Irene was watching him and there was just the slightest frown of disapproval on her lips. Was he going to have to contend with her while he was here as well? He wasn't used to living in a house with women. His mother had divorced his father and left when he was ten, not that she had been much of an influence in his life before then. He had spent most of his youth in all-boys boarding schools. Reckoning with the female sensibility was something completely foreign to Drew.

Still, the disapproving, maternal look made him uncomfortable. He looked at Jeremy and relented ever so slightly.

"Well, maybe. I have some things to take care of first." The boy would probably forget all about having him come along as soon as he was out of sight. Children weren't known for their lengthy attention spans, or so he had been told.

Jeremy wriggled happily. "We're going at 'leban-thirty. That's when Aunt Daisy told me she'd be back."

"Back?" Drew echoed, surprised. He glanced unconsciously toward the ceiling. She wasn't in bed? "Back from where?"

Jeremy was finally winning his battle against the cereal balls. Growing soggy, they were beginning to sink. "The flower place."

Drew glanced at his watch. No, it hadn't stopped. It was only eight-fifteen. "You mean that she's at work now?" That didn't fit the irresponsible image he had of her.

Jeremy bobbed his head up as he gleefully shoved another colorful spoonful into his mouth. The cereal still crunched.

"It smells good there. Sometimes she takes me and lets me play hide-and-seek," Jeremy confided, lowering his voice just a fraction. He smiled proudly. "She even let me help pick flowers for the backyard." Some of the exuberance left his eyes as his expression grew solemn. "Mama's backyard."

Oh, God, Drew thought, the boy was going to cry. Now what? He was as lost with a child's tears as he was with a woman's. Not relishing the prospect, Drew sought to divert Jeremy's mind. "Where is Hamburger Delight? I'd like to come."

The small shoulders rose and fell as Jeremy searched his

memory. "I dunno. Over there." He pointed vaguely past Drew's head.

East. That didn't exactly narrow things down.

Irene finally brought him his coffee, freshly brewed. It smelled like heaven. "Third and Rosencrans. On the corner. Can't miss it. Unless you're not looking." She placed the cup down near his elbow, then set a creamer next to it. There was a small ceramic bowl of sugar cubes in the middle of the table. Irene moved it toward Drew.

"Not you," she warned Jeremy when his hand darted out to take one.

Drew took his coffee black and eye opening. Irene's was. He waited a beat until the hot fluid burned its way through his system, jarring everything to attention as it went.

"Thank you," he murmured in Irene's general direction. He remembered that he didn't really know his way around the area that well. "Do you have a map of the city somewhere?" he asked Irene. "I have to get to the office and set up some things."

"Are you going to eat with me?" Jeremy asked suddenly before Irene could reply.

"Sure, at Hamburger Delight." Just as he thought, no attention span whatsoever. Boarding school would quickly cure that.

The brown hair fanned out as Jeremy shook his head fiercely. "No, I mean now." Jeremy looked at the empty space on Drew's place mat. "Daddy always ate breakfast with me."

There it was again, guilt. He didn't care for it at all. "That's because Daddy didn't work very much," Drew pointed out.

The words had no effect on Jeremy. "My daddy was fun," Jeremy said wistfully.

Fun. Drew doubted very much if he could be *fun*. But he had enlisted in this war for Jeremy and knew that he was going to have to score some direct hits. Otherwise he had no hope of gaining Jeremy's approval. Without that, the boy wouldn't come willingly with him to New York. And then he'd have an even worse war on his hands. With Anastasia.

Drew looked at the open, upturned face. "Just what was it that your dad did to be fun?"

Jeremy chewed quickly so he could answer without a mouthful of cereal getting in the way. "He played trains. Can you play trains?"

"I don't know," Drew answered honestly. "I never tried." He couldn't really remember playing when it came down to it. There was a vague recollection of a set of toy soldiers in gray and blue uniforms, but he couldn't actually remember ever playing with them. They had stood at attention, lined up on a shelf. He had no childhood to draw on.

Cereal forgotten, Jeremy was out of his seat and grabbing Drew by the hand. "I gotta set o' trains in the playroom. Daddy put 'em up." He was tugging Drew out of his chair urgently. "C'mon and see."

"What about your breakfast?" Drew pointed toward the bowl. He had absolutely no desire to "play trains." He had an office to set up.

"Breakfast first, young man," Irene said sternly.

For the life of him, Drew wasn't certain if she was just addressing Jeremy or if he was included in the reprimand. To further confound him, Irene placed a plate of bacon and eggs in front of him.

"I don't eat breakfast," Drew told Irene. "Just toast."

His statement fell on deaf, unsympathetic ears. Irene eyed the plate. "Shame to let it go to waste." She made absolutely no attempt to remove the dish.

"C'mon," Jeremy urged, wiggling back onto his seat. "Hurry up and eat so we can go and play."

"I can't go and play, Jeremy, I—"

Drew saw a look of disappointment paint the small features. Features that echoed Jonathan's. "All right," he sighed. "You show me the trains and we'll make them go around once, fair enough?"

Jeremy was wolfing down the rest of his breakfast. More milk joined the spots on the tablecloth as the spoon flew. "What's that mean?"

Drew searched for an explanation Jeremy would understand. He wasn't used to trying to simplify things. "That means we compromise."

"Huh?" The dark eyes stared at him blankly.

Drew heard Irene chuckle in the background. She was obviously going to let him work this out on his own. What the hell was a synonym for compromise? "I do something that you want and then you let me do something that I have to do."

"Oh." Jeremy's face lit up as he understood. "Sure. Fair enough," he sang out. He grinned at Drew as he repeated the new phrase.

Drew had a sneaking suspicion that there was a lot more of Anastasia in the little boy than first met the eye. Oh, well, he supposed he could spare half an hour. He ate his breakfast quickly and estimated that he could get to the office at around nine if traffic was light.

Chapter Five

The best laid estimates of mice and men often went awry, Drew decided sometime later. He was down on his hands and knees, attempting to successfully mount a derailed steam engine back on the track. He discovered that it was a lot more difficult than it looked. It took Drew three attempts before all eight stationary and two front mobile wheels made proper contact with the tracks.

The layout in the room was surprisingly elaborate. Jonathan had obviously been a railroad enthusiast. All those years they had spent growing up, and he had never known, Drew thought. The entire floor of the recreation room was covered with tracks, trestles and two complete villages with various people and animals populating the imaginary world. Jeremy had happily told Drew as much history about the growth of the two villages as he could remember while they ran the engines on alternating tracks.

Drew sat back on his heels, unconsciously tugging at the

engineer's cap Jeremy had insisted he wear. That this had all been lovingly arranged by his brother left Drew totally in awe.

What else didn't I know about you, Jonathan?

"Can we run it yet?" Jeremy asked. He was wearing a smaller version of Drew's cap and lay sprawled on his stomach on the floor. He tapped the toes of his new sneakers impatiently against the indoor-outdoor carpeting.

Drew nodded, hoping that the engine would work this time. It had made the most feeble attempt at traversing the tracks the other two times. During both tries, the train had moved about three lengths of track forward, falling over at the first curve it encountered.

"One last time around and then I have to leave, or I won't be able to make lunch," he warned Jeremy.

As it was, Drew didn't think he really had a prayer of making it to the restaurant. Setting up his office was going to take the better part of a day. Which was just as well. He hadn't had a hamburger in years and hated anything that came under the heading of "fast food."

Jeremy solemnly took in the information. His hand hovered over the transformer. There were passengers waiting in the little station for the green and black engine to arrive. "Ready?"

Drew gave the signal. "Turn it on." He felt a certain surge of accomplishment when the train sped smoothly by him, even though he knew it was absolutely absurd to feel that way about a toy train. Still, he watched as it traveled by a tiny herd of black and white cattle on its way into the first village.

"You did it!" Jeremy cheered.

Drew was totally absorbed in the train's progress. So absorbed, he didn't hear the door behind him opening. He heard her laughter before he managed to turn around. Anastasia. She *would* catch him like this, he thought in embarrassed disgust. Her laugh was low and throaty, and made him think of a dark, smoky room where people drank whiskey and exchanged secret stories that no one bothered to remember.

He quickly got to his feet to face her. She had an amused expression and was staring at his head. He realized that she was looking at the hat Jeremy had given him. Belatedly, Drew snatched it off, crumpling it self-consciously. The indignant look he gave her had absolutely no effect.

"I guess you're surprised," he muttered.

He looked so adorably silly. And it touched her heart to find him this way because of Jeremy. She wished now she hadn't laughed so that she could have observed them a little longer. *Yes, Virginia, the man is human after all.* "Speechless."

Drew thrust the hat to Jeremy. "I sincerely doubt that." The woman probably even talked in her sleep. The sudden urge to find out utterly mystified him.

Daisy took the hat from Jeremy and turned it around in her hand, as if to study it. "It makes a very interesting statement." She raised her eyes to Drew. "Complements your suit."

Jeremy had no idea what they were talking about. But he knew that Daisy's appearance meant that she was going to keep her promise. Since his parents had gone away, he was nervous about other people disappearing out of his life. No one was more important to him than Daisy. He tugged on her hand until she bent down. When she did, he pressed petal-soft lips to her cheek.

"Hi, Aunt Daisy."

She gave him a proper kiss back and then pulled the brim of his hat down over his eyes.

"Hi, yourself." She rose so that she could face Drew. "So, what have you two men been up to?" She still couldn't believe that she had actually caught Drew playing

with the trains. Jonathan had sometimes holed up here for
hours, drifting off into another, simpler world with his son.
But Drew wasn't Jonathan. Yet.

Drew saw the laughter lingering in her eyes. They crinkled slightly on the sides and seemed to glow, lighting up
her face. It was an enticing picture. That still didn't mean
he appreciated being the source of her amusement.

"We were playing trains, Aunt Daisy." Jeremy tucked
his hand into hers easily, trustingly. She closed her fingers
over his, thinking how warm it felt, having a child look to
her for security. "Uncle Drew plays trains pretty good. I
teached him how."

"Taught, baby, you taught him," she corrected affectionately. Daisy took Jeremy's hat off his head and tousled
his hair. "We'd better get going."

The boy cocked his head quizzically, glancing at the
clock on the wall. It was big, with a white face and black
numbers, resembling the clocks found in old railroad stations. Jeremy was just learning to tell time and once in a
while, the numbers became jumbled. "Is it 'leban-thirty
already?"

"No. It's ten-thirty." She pointed out the numbers.
"See?" The small face turned toward hers, waiting for an
explanation. "I thought we'd go out a little sooner. I've
got to deliver some shrubs early this afternoon. Is that okay
by you, Tiger?" She began to walk toward the doorway.

Jeremy loved being consulted and nodded vigorously as
he followed. "Sure. He's coming, too," Jeremy added as
an afterthought.

She turned from the door. "Who?" Daisy looked at
Drew. Jeremy had to be talking about one of his friends.
He couldn't possibly mean Drew. The man was dressed for
a power meeting, not lunch at Hamburger Delight surrounded by screaming children.

Sometimes he wondered how grown-ups kept track of

anything at all. "Uncle Drew," Jeremy told her patiently. Who else would he be talking about?

Time to make an exit. "Well I——" Drew saw the way Daisy lifted a brow knowingly as she looked at him. Her laughter might be enticing, but her smug look had him wanting to strangle her again.

Think you know all the answers, don't you? Something perverse had Drew taking up the challenge. "Yes, Jeremy invited me along."

"He has to go to an office," Jeremy told Daisy quickly, holding her hand as they went down the stairs. He looked over his shoulder at Drew. "What's an office? Is it like Aunt Daisy's flower shop?"

Drew could just envision her shop. Chaos in a rectangular box with bills haphazardly scattered throughout. "Hardly."

"No, sweetie," Daisy said cheerfully as she opened the front door. She let Jeremy go out first. "Nothing living thrives there, I'm sure."

Definitely strangle, Drew thought. First chance he got. They didn't prosecute justifiable homicide and anyone who knew her knew it was justifiable.

Lost in thought, Drew was unprepared for the frontal attack.

"But you'll go to the office later, right?" It was a hopeful question, voiced by a boy who didn't appear as if he was going to graciously accept no for an answer. Jeremy took Drew's hand in his, linking small fingers through long, artistic ones. He smiled brightly up at Drew. "'Cause Aunt Daisy's here now."

Drew looked at Daisy over Jeremy's head. "Your timing is off." *As always.*

"On the contrary." She turned and walked toward her truck. "I think my timing is marvelous. You can follow us in your car if you like."

He was struck speechless as he examined the large, brightly painted truck. It was a flatbed with large lavender flowers painted on a field of white. Across the side was the logo. She belonged behind the wheel of a cabriolet convertible coupe or something equally as diminutive. Not a large truck used to haul who-knew-what. "You're going to drive this?"

"Sure, why not?" Next, he was going to criticize the clothes she wore. The man was a chauvinist. She dug deep for patience. "What's wrong with it? It's the company truck." She attempted to maintain a cheerful attitude, but he was making it difficult.

Drew circled the vehicle slowly and stopped at the rear. There were shrubs in it. Large ones secured with a chain to prevent them from falling over. "What are you carrying around with you?"

"*Ligustrum* for the Samuelsons," she said matter-of-factly, joining him at the rear of the truck. "I was planning to go to lunch with Jeremy, then swing by the Samuelson's house and plant their shrubs." She took Jeremy's face in her hand and gave it just the slightest affectionate squeeze. Jeremy pretended to make a face and she made a sillier one in return. "You can help me water them when I'm done."

"When *you're* done?" Drew looked at her. She made it sound as if she was actually doing the job herself. "Don't you have any help?"

She didn't care for his condescending manner. Did he think he could just walk in and take over her life as well as Jeremy's?

"Yes, I have help. I have lots of help. Normally. But Pablo's sick, Simon strained his back and can't do heavy labor for a while, and Eric has admirably gone back to college full time." She walked to the front of the truck and boosted Jeremy inside the cab, then secured the seat belt. "Unfortunately, that leaves me in a bind."

He didn't see a problem. "Why don't you hire someone else?"

Daisy got into the truck and closed the door. She leaned her elbow out of the open window. "I'm trying. But in the meantime—" she nodded toward the shrubs "—work has to get done."

Every time he gave her the benefit of the doubt, his original assessment returned. Crazy, completely, irresponsibly crazy. "You can't possibly lift those things."

Her annoyance gave way to amusement again. He did look cute when he got so worked up. "Why can't I possibly?" she asked, echoing his words.

She had to ask? "You're too…too…" He waved his hands in frustration. Didn't she realize she could get hurt? "Too damn stubborn is what you are."

Daisy nodded solemnly. "Maybe that's how I got them on the truck in the first place. By being too damn stubborn." She grinned at him, conveniently omitting the fact that she had had help.

He should just let her go and do the work. What did it matter to him if she hurt her back or wound up in the hospital? It would get her out of the way that much sooner and he could go home with Jeremy. No, not his concern, no, sir.

"Where is this place?" His tone was gruff.

"Three miles from Hamburger Delight. West." For good measure, she pointed, curious to see what Drew would say next.

He turned the situation over in his mind. The woman needed a keeper. How could she possibly believe she was equipped to take care of a four-year-old when she couldn't even take care of herself?

"All right, I'll help you." He bit the words off as if he had just agreed to a death sentence.

Daisy sat back in her seat, studying him. *Why* was he offering to help? "You'll get your suit all dirty."

She was mocking him, he thought. "Let me worry about my suit."

"Fine." Daisy raised her hands, palms up, in surrender. Far be it from her to turn down free help. She hadn't looked forward to doing the job and she had absolutely no problem about needing to do things on her own. Help was fine. Terrific. Even better if it came from him. If nothing else, it meant that there was a little bit of Jonathan lurking somewhere within that single-breasted suit.

She indicated his car. "Now, if you'll just follow me." She turned on her engine and watched Drew walk toward his car and get in. He looked as if he was muttering to himself. She couldn't keep the smile from her lips and didn't bother to try as she fastened her seat belt.

Jeremy leaned over as far as he could, held back by the massive seat belt that restrained him in two places. "How come you're grinning?"

"I think that Uncle Drew might just be a nicer man under all that gruff talk than he wants everyone to believe." And nice men, she thought, could ultimately be gotten to see things her way. Especially when it came to the care of a sensitive child who was attached to her.

Jeremy tried to puzzle that out for a moment and failed. "Why doesn't he want us to know he's nice?" It made no sense to him.

Daisy looked in her passenger mirror, making sure not to lose Drew. "I don't think he knows it himself."

Carrying a tray overflowing with French fries, hamburgers, sodas and one token black coffee for Drew, Daisy made her way into the outdoor portion of the restaurant. Drew followed silently while Jeremy had already blazed a trail for them. She found an empty table in the shape of a flattened mushroom and sat down on the closest toadstool. Drew looked uncertain whether or not to sit down at all.

"It doesn't bite," she assured him with a grin.

He scowled and then sat, careful to avoid a small, damp lime-green spot that had once been part of a Popsicle.

An enclosed pen with multicolored balls and a curved, royal blue slide leading into it provided the main source of entertainment for anyone under four feet tall. Squeals came from beneath the balls, belonging to children who had dive-bombed into the pen ahead of Jeremy.

Jeremy took one bite of his hamburger, then went barreling into the center of the pen.

There was no back to the toadstool and it was uncomfortably small. Drew realized that there was no right way to sit on a toadstool. He watched as Jeremy went clambering up the ladder on the other side of the slide. He was right about wanting to take Jeremy with him. The boy had no discipline.

"You should make him sit down and eat. It's better for digestion."

She shrugged, watching Jeremy enjoy himself. She was relieved that he wasn't sitting around, moping, although she knew it had to come someday. It was like waiting for the other shoe to drop.

"He's having fun. His digestion's taking care of itself." She pulled a French fry out of the paper container and ate it.

"It's a bad example."

She chewed slowly, her eyes on Drew's face. "Having fun?"

Why did she always insist on twisting things? "You know what I mean."

"Yes, I do." Her eyes held his as she wondered what was behind them. She was relieved that her initial wish was true. Deep down, so far down he probably wasn't aware of it, Drew really wasn't as cold, as strict as he liked to portray. Now it wasn't just a matter of keeping Jeremy safe with her. It was also turning into a matter of trying to pull this self-contained man out of the prison he had voluntarily walked into years ago. "Do you know what I mean?"

"Never."

She sighed and ate two fries before continuing. "Right now, Jeremy needs fun. He needs fun and love a lot more than he needs proper table manners." She watched Jeremy jump into the pen, balls flying everywhere, then scramble out for another turn. "We'll work that part out later."

Drew looked at the amount of fat and cholesterol represented by the items on the tray and frowned. "Along with nutrition?"

His attitude tickled her. This was a man who needed fun in his life as much as Jeremy did. He desperately needed to loosen up. "You don't like French fries and hamburgers?"

How could she be so blissfully uninformed? Everyone knew what junk food was. Poison in an appealing wrapper. "Do you have any idea what they're doing to your body right now?"

Because it irritated him, she bit into another fry. "Making it happy?" she guessed.

He tried not to watch the slow, sensuous movement of her mouth. She was doing this on purpose. "You're incorrigible, you know that?"

She sighed, dragging her hand through her hair. "If I didn't, you'd keep reminding me." She looked at the paper coffee cup. He had left it untouched. Probably needs a French name attached to the coffee bean before he'd deign to sip it. "You obviously hate the food and you look like you're ready to be shot out of a cannon at any minute. What are you doing here, anyway?"

"Jeremy asked me to come."

She sighed, stretching out her long legs before her, the heels of her worn boots resting on the black, scarred asphalt. For a short woman, she seemed to be all leg, he observed.

Daisy told herself to keep a rein on her temper. The man was trying. Pathetically, but he was trying. And you didn't encourage a flower to grow by hitting it. "I supposed that means you're not all bad."

"Thank you."

She sat up again, as if some mysterious force had suddenly energized her. "But with some effort, I'm sure you'll get there." Maybe it was time for a serious talk, without the boxing gloves on. This seemed like an innocuous enough place to do it, surrounded with children and their mothers. "Why do you want to take Jeremy away, Drew? You can see he's happy here."

She really didn't understand, did she? All she seemed to think of was playing and having fun. Those traits didn't go very far in the real world, not if you intended to make something of yourself. He ducked as a bright red ball went sailing overhead. Damn, this place was hazardous. "I want to see him reach his full potential. Happiness alone isn't everything."

"It is if you don't have it." She thought of how frightened she had felt those first few nights at Uncle Warren's house. And then at the boarding school when even Warren had shipped them away. "It plugs up an awful lot of holes."

She looked as if she were speaking from experience. He felt a vague curiosity as to what had caused that faraway look in her eyes, but he dismissed it. The less he knew about her, the simpler things remained. Jonathan had told him more than he wanted to know as it was. "The holes get larger if you don't have the proper education to face the world."

"I don't see a conflict here." She broke off a piece of a French fry and tossed it to a scavenging starling that had wandered into the play area. "You can have happiness and get an education." The small bird struggled with the piece as he tried to fly and eat at the same time.

The sound of her delighted laughter curled through Drew's system like sweet potent wine. If he didn't know any better, he would say it had a drugging effect on him.

Two more birds hovered hesitantly a few feet away and she broke the remainder of the fry in two and tossed it to them.

She seemed to be more interested in throwing her food away than in eating it. "What are you doing?"

It was an odd question. "I'm feeding a bird." She stopped and realized why he might have asked. "Didn't you ever feed pigeons as a kid in New York?"

"No."

She wasn't surprised, just saddened. He had probably never done a single carefree thing in his life. She suddenly felt sorry for him, even though he was still the man who wanted to take Jeremy out of her life and turn him into a robot.

"Ducks?" she pressed. "Birds? Stray cat?" Had he even had a pet? "Anything?"

There was pity in her eyes and he couldn't for the life of him understand why. Why should she feel sorry for him because he never threw food at an animal? "You make it sound like a crime that I didn't."

"No, just a shame."

"Why?" It made no sense to him but he wanted to understand. Why, he didn't know and didn't try to explore. Knowing would make him as flaky as she was. "Because I didn't clog a bird's arteries?"

She stopped feeding the starlings and looked at him, a French fry dangling from her fingertips. "Are you always such a wet blanket, or do I get special treatment?'' She turned all the way around on the toadstool to face him. ''You can't possibly be as single-mindedly bleak and morose as you paint yourself out to be. This has to be an act, right?''

He wasn't going to get into an argument with her in a public place. Drew tried to turn away from her but found that when he turned sideways, he was in the way. A legion of small children kept running into him on their way to the pen's slide. He shifted around.

''You're babbling again.''

He didn't fool her. ''I think I'm coming damn near close to the truth and you don't like it. Emotions frighten you, don't they?'' His expression darkened and she knew she was right. The man couldn't show any emotion except anger. She supposed it was a start.

He was about to tell her that it was none of her business, then stopped as Jeremy came running over for another bite of his hamburger. The boy barely broke stride as he turned to hurry back to the slide.

''Careful, Jeremy,'' Drew called after him. ''You're going to throw up.''

''No, he won't.''

How did he know she was going to say that?

''Jeremy never throws up. He has a cast-iron stomach.'' She started to throw another piece to the one lone bird that remained, then decided not to.

''Even iron cracks.''

She looked at him. Was he talking about himself, or her? ''I'm counting on it. Here—'' she held up the French fry in front of his mouth ''—have one.''

He lifted a brow. ''Run out of birds to feed?''

She shook her head, her eyes on his. He did have beautiful eyes. Soulful eyes. Was there a soul behind them? ''Found something that needs charity more.''

Drew grabbed her hand in his to move it away. For some reason, he didn't. He left his fingers laced lightly around the small wrist. Her pulse was scrambling against his thumb. He watched the smile spread on her lips as she slowly fed him the slender strip of potato.

"Good?"

He wasn't even aware of chewing. All he was aware of was her, the light fragrance that wafted to him, the sensuous smile on her full lips. He was eating a French fry, for God's sake. Why did it feel like an erotic experience?

"Greasy," he murmured.

"There's something to be said for that, too." The words were hardly a whisper as his lips grazed the tips of her fingers, finishing the tiny bit of food.

She had felt something, Daisy thought. Something strange and powerful and just the slightest bit dangerous. It intrigued her.

The tingling sensation on her fingertips wouldn't go away.

A shout jarred their attention away from one another and toward Jeremy. The boy was standing on top of the last rung on the slide, waving to them.

"Watch me!" he crowed importantly just before he did a half gainer into the center of the balls two feet below. A barrage of balls went flying in all directions again as other children squealed with delight or indignation at being displaced.

"Jeremy, careful!" Daisy called out, half rising. "You don't want to squash anyone."

The warning brought only giggles from Jeremy and the children around him.

She had no idea how to go about disciplining a child. "That's it, make it sound like fun."

Her pulses still humming, Daisy sat a little straighter, a little more removed from Drew. "It *is* fun. Your trouble,

Mr. Addison, is that you don't know the first thing about having fun."

"My trouble," Drew corrected her, "is sitting right next to me." He had never meant anything so wholeheartedly in his life.

Jeremy was exhausted, but they still had to drag him away from the play area.

"Are you really going to go through with this?" Drew nodded at the shrubs in back of her truck.

"This isn't a challenge, Drew." She bent inside the cab to secure Jeremy's seat belt. "This is my work. I'm sure you understand what work is."

"I understand." He closed the door on Jeremy, then walked around the front of the truck. "I just never expected to hear the word coming from you."

"Don't start," she warned.

Too late for that, he thought as he got into his own car. Something *had* started and for the life of him, he didn't know what to do about it, other than ignore it and hope it would go away.

Drew had no idea why he bothered to follow her. Anastasia was a damn stubborn woman who deserved to reap the consequences of her actions. But she was dragging his nephew around, so that meant that he had to keep an eye on them both.

The Samuelsons lived in a ranch-style house that was sprawled out on a third of an acre and looked far too large for them to be living in alone. They were an elderly, retired couple. They had the look of people who had weathered a good many storms in their lifetime and had been together forever.

They were both out front when Daisy pulled up in her truck. It looked as if they had been waiting for her. Mrs.

Samuelson hurried to the rear of the truck before Daisy had even parked.

"Oh, these will look so lovely out front, my dear." Daisy joined her with Jeremy following in her wake. All signs of exhaustion had vanished in the short trip. "Are you sure you can handle this?" Mrs. Samuelson looked at her dubiously. Though they were the same height, the older woman was a great deal more sturdy-looking. "Maybe Mr. Samuelson could—"

The last thing in the world Daisy wanted was to have the older man sweating and possibly working himself up to a heart attack. She was more than capable of planting the shrubs by herself. She had done it before.

"I'm fine, really. You two just go inside and I'll call you when I'm finished." She looked at the bags of manure and leaf mold leaning against the inside of the flatbed. "It's going to take me a while."

Drew pulled the car up behind her, parking by the curb. When he got out, he was greeted with a broad smile and a warm handshake. Mrs. Samuelson had his hand in both of hers.

"You must be Daisy's husband," Mrs. Samuelson said warmly.

"God forbid," Drew and Daisy said at the same time.

Mrs. Samuelson looked completely confused.

"This is my brother-in-law, Drew Addison." Daisy hooked her arm through the woman's and gently led her toward her front door.

"You'll call if you need anything?" Mrs. Samuelson asked. "Water, iced tea, lunch?"

":I promise." Daisy turned around to catch the amused look on Drew's face.

"You're not half bad when you smile, you know?" she observed, passing him.

He had no response for that. He watched the way Jeremy

shadowed her every move. At the very least, the boy would be in her way and he could get hurt. "Why don't I take Jeremy home?" Drew suggested.

"I don't wanna go home." Jeremy stuck his hands in his back pockets the way Daisy did as she surveyed the front yard. "Aunt Daisy needs help."

Truer words were never spoken. "I fully agree."

Daisy looked over her shoulder and quirked her lips into a fraction of a smile before bracing herself to tug the first bag of dirt from the truck.

Stupid, that's what she was. She didn't have the brains that God gave a gnat. Drew elbowed her out of the way. "I'll do it."

She looked at him. She was wearing jeans and a pink pullover while he was attired to address the chairman of the board. "You'll get your suit all dirty," she reminded him.

"I'll send you the cleaning bill."

Maybe there was hope for him yet. "Fair enough."

"Hey, I know 'bout that. Uncle Drew teached—taught—me," Jeremy said eagerly.

Daisy smiled at Drew before climbing onto the truck. "See, happy kids absorb things more quickly."

As he slid the second bag from the flatbed, Drew refrained from answering. Daisy worked the first container to the edge of the truck.

"I've got it." Drew yanked the container down, setting it on the driveway. He climbed on the back of the truck and pulled over the other two containers, then placed them next to the first one. Sweat was beginning to trickle down his back by the time he finished.

He frowned, taking off his jacket. He should have done that in the first place. "And now you're going to dig?"

She rolled up her sleeves and hid a smile as she saw

Jeremy do the same. "Unless you know a better way to get them into the ground."

"Yeah, hired help." Drew let out along breath. "How many shovels did you bring?"

"One." She took it off the truck and turned to look at him, a lopsided grin on her face. "I'm not a two-fisted digger."

He attempted to take the shovel from her by placing his hand over hers on the handle. "We'll take turns."

She surrendered the shovel, wondering how long it would be before Drew gave up. Men who sat behind a desk for a living didn't tend to have much stamina as a rule. "Far be it from me to argue."

"Ha!" He stripped off his shirt, tossing it on top of the jacket.

Daisy's breath backed up in her lungs as she saw the ridge of muscles she had only glimpsed briefly the other night. His was not a body that came from a sedentary lifestyle. It was, in a word, gorgeous. She knew Margaret would be drooling right about now.

"Health club?" she guessed.

He dragged the first container over toward the front yard. Jeremy was holding on to the other side of the deep green plastic and running to try to keep up. "What?"

"The muscles." She tapped one finger at his biceps. "Work out at the health club?"

"No, I had them flown in."

She took the shovel from him and poked a hole in the center of the first bag of manure, preparing it. She poked a little harder than she might have. "Look, no one's asking you to do this."

He took the shovel from her. "Shut up before I find another use for this thing."

She stood back, her arms folded before her. "Are you

always this testy, doing good deeds? There—" she pointed "—start there."

He broke ground. "I don't know. I'm not in the habit of doing good deeds."

And why he was doing one now was totally beyond him.

Chapter Six

Daisy watched Drew as he dug, wrestling with the almost impenetrable ground. His muscles rippled from the effort. Sweat glistened on his body and ran down his back in twisting, winding rivulets, creating an ache in Daisy that completely surprised her. This was Drew she was reacting to. For a moment, the realization took Daisy's breath away.

Except for the trousers, which were quickly losing their crease and gaining stains created by dirt and sweat in their stead, no one seeing him now would have ever taken Drew to be a high-powered executive. He looked like a laborer, one who could have easily caused, she thought, more than one female's heart to arrest. Fortunately hers was working just fine. Perhaps beating a little faster than normal, but it was almost eighty-five degrees and she *was* working. At least it was an excuse.

Daisy tried very hard not to stare as she dragged the five bags of leaf mold and manure into the yard. It wasn't easy. Whatever else he was, Drew was magnificent.

Drew felt his arms aching. He had met with annoying resistance each time he tried to push the shovel into the ground. The earth in Bel Air had a lot in common with Anastasia, he thought.

The shovel resounded with a tinny clunk as it hit something even harder than the earth. Drew bent to take out what looked to be a rusted length of pipe in the hole he was digging. He tossed it to the side.

Wiping his forehead with the back of his hand, he glared at Daisy. "What do you people have out here for soil, rock?"

Daisy dropped the last bag next to the others, then came up behind Drew and peered into the hole. It wasn't deep enough yet. "Close. It's clay that oozes and sucks your shoes right off if you try to walk on it when it's wet. It turns into cement when it's dry."

Difficult, he thought. Definitely like her. He shook his head in disbelief as he crossed his arms over the shovel and took a breather.

"It's surprising that anything grows here at all." He had begun to regret volunteering for this the moment he had taken the shovel from Daisy. Nothing was happening to make him change his mind.

"That's why I brought all these soil additives." She knew he wasn't going to be happy with what she was about to tell him. "It has to be deeper than that." She pointed to the hole. "Close to four feet."

Drew had never planted anything before but his own two feet on the ground. He had no idea if she was being unreasonable, but it would have been like her. He glanced at the shrub closest to him. While he had been battling the soil, she had worked the shrub free of its container and had methodically untangled some of the roots. "You're going to bury the whole thing?"

She smiled patiently and it annoyed the hell out of him.

"The roots have to spread out if the shrub is going to grow. They need good soil. Actually, this soil is exceedingly nutritious, but it tends to be too hard for the roots on first contact." She indicated the mixture of leaf mold and manure she had been preparing. "We mix about twenty-five percent of that to the existing soil to help the roots along."

She took a step toward him. "You're obviously tired." Daisy reached for the shovel. "I can—"

Drew pulled the shovel toward him. "I'll do it." It sounded faintly like a growl. Digging these holes had turned into a matter of pride.

Daisy raised her hands. "Fine with me."

Shifting to stretch his back, he allowed himself an additional moment and then began to dig again. He could feel muscles straining from his forearms up to his neck and down his back. He was a good foot taller than she and probably had seventy-five pounds on her. The idea of her digging in this soil was ludicrous.

"How could you possibly think that you could dig in this soil?" he demanded. The woman was an airhead.

Daisy started mixing the second batch for the next bush. "I'm a lot stronger than I look."

He almost snorted, his eyes skimming her body. "Yeah. I hear barbed wire usually is."

She didn't bristle at the comment. "I did a lot of weight training when I was preparing for the Olympics. The three thousand meter run," she added. "I never really stopped."

Drew left the shovel where it was, stuck upright in the dirt, and turned around to stare at her. "You were in the Olympics?"

"No."

Just as he thought. She was spinning stories. He wondered how many she had told Jeremy and hoped that the boy didn't take after her.

"I did make the try-outs, though," she said matter-of-factly, sprinkling the dark soil into the powder-light brown leaf mold she had brought with her. She was aware that Drew had stopped digging and was staring at her. "A broken ankle kept me out of the actual competition." She sighed. It would have been nice, being able to compete, and possibly winning. "By the time I had healed enough to practice for the next games, I lost interest."

"I see." The woman should be a fiction writer, not a landscape consultant. She certainly had one hell of an imagination.

Daisy rose, dusting off her hands on her jeans. "What I didn't lose interest in was the weight training part of it. It only make good sense, keeping your body in shape. Don't you agree?"

"Yeah, sure."

He glanced in her direction again as she bent over to open the third sack of leaf mold and felt something twist sharply in his stomach. At least she hadn't exaggerated that part of her story. She had managed to keep in phenomenal shape—for a chronic pain in the neck.

It was hot and almost eerily quiet. Jeremy was inside the house, watching television with Mrs. Samuelson and scarfing down her homemade cookies. Because he could use the diversion, Drew decided to see how far Daisy would go with her fabrication. "So, how does an Olympic hopeful wind up planting shrubs?"

"I decided that I didn't want to be a lawyer." She worked out the proper ratio again, then sifted the mixture with her hands. The bright red garden gloves she wore clashed with her pink shirt. "I went into it with great dreams, but it turned out to be too cold for me, too bogged down in nasty technicalities that don't have anything to do with justice. I didn't like being concerned with the strict letter of the law and not the people whose lives it affected."

She shrugged, dismissing a whole way of life as if it

were nothing more than an unappealing meal. "I tried a few other things, but this was what I liked best." She cocked her head as she looked at the shrubs. She could visualize them in a year's time, flowering, bright and green. It gave her a good feeling. "Planting things, making them grow. There's something very simple and beautiful about that. Besides, I like nurturing things."

"Whoa." Drew held up a hand to stop her before she went meandering down another twisting verbal road. He pinned her with a look meant to make her confess that she was lying. She looked at him innocently. "A lawyer?" Right, and he was a basketball player for the New York Knicks. Jonathan had never mentioned that she was a lawyer. Drew assumed the information would have been passed on if it were true. Wouldn't it? "You passed the bar exam?" He waited for her to say no.

"Yes." She looked at him as if she had done nothing more outrageous than state the ingredients of an angel food cake.

She was one cool customer. He could almost admire, in an odd sort of way, the way she let things roll off her tongue, if it wasn't for Jeremy. His nephew had been handed over to be raised by a pathological liar. What the hell had Jonathan been thinking of, agreeing to let her have custody?

"You passed the bar exam," he repeated. "While you were single-handedly saving the rain forest and simultaneously performing open-heart surgery?"

Rather than look indignant or offended, she simply smiled. It was a Mona Lisa kind of smile that drove him crazy. "You don't believe me."

He laughed as he turned his attention back to the hole in the ground. Shovel met dirt with an accompanying grunt. "That's putting it mildly." He thought he saw her shrug carelessly out of the corner of his eye.

An olympic hopeful/lawyer who spent her time feeding birds at Hamburger Delight and planting shrubs for elderly people. Who was she kidding? He threw the dirt over his shoulder and pushed the shovel in again. Did she actually expect him to believe her? She might be crazy, but he wasn't.

He looked at the shovel in his hands. He was digging and she wasn't. Maybe something had to be reevaluated here. Later, when he had time.

Three hours had never moved so slowly or with such agony. But at last, at the end of that time, all three shrubs stood neatly lined up behind one another, evergreen sentries between the two adjacent gardens.

Drew thought they looked a lot smaller in the ground than they had in the containers. He stood for a moment, just looking at them. Not out of a sense of pride or accomplishment but because he needed a breather. He was beginning to have grave doubts that he could make it to his car unassisted. And he wasn't about to have Anastasia help him. Death before dishonor.

But he had done it. He hadn't let her dig so much as a single shovelful of dirt. Why, he didn't know. Maybe he had had something to prove—to her, to himself.

Or maybe she was contagious and he was going crazy. He was too tired to think about it.

Moving very carefully, Drew bent over and picked up his shirt and jacket from the grass where he had thrown them. He debated putting them on and decided against it. He couldn't bear the thought of anything against his hot, wet skin right now. Instead he slung both over his shoulder and turned to look at his car. It was parked behind her truck, a good fifteen feet away.

One foot in front of the other, Andrew. You can do it.

Daisy was busy loading the empty containers and bags

onto the back of the truck. Drew passed her slowly as he walked to his car. She felt awful for him, but he had insisted on doing it himself.

She tossed the shovel on last, then wiped off her hands. "Are you going to the house?"

He nodded, dropping the jacket into the car. He needed a shower, he thought. Badly. "To change."

The way he said it, he made it sound as if he had plans. "And then what?" She shoved her hands into her back pockets as she leaned against the hood of his car.

"I still have an office to set up," he said doggedly. An office that he would have been getting well under way if it hadn't been for obstacles she kept providing.

Daisy looked at her wristwatch. "But it's after two-thirty." He couldn't get much done now, especially not in his condition. "Why don't you just call it a day and go soak in a hot tub?"

God, it did sound tempting. He could almost feel the water surrounding his aching body. Drew tried to make it a point to work out on a regular basis no matter where he happened to be in the world. But the workouts were nothing compared to the three hours' worth of digging he had just put in. He must have lost five pounds of water alone, despite the five glasses of lemonade Mrs. Samuelson had brought out for him.

But he couldn't give in. He was already behind, he reminded himself. "Later," he told Daisy as he dropped into the driver's seat. It took effort to pull his feet into the car. "After I get back." It hurt just to tilt back his head as he looked up at Daisy. "You?"

Why couldn't he just admit that he was exhausted and stop trying to be the man of steel? She shrugged in answer to his question. "I still have palm trees to pick out at the nursery."

He slumped back in his seat. "Don't tell me, you're planning to plant those, too?"

Well, she'd have to do those by herself. He was through being a good scout. He had no idea what possessed him to do it in the first place, except that she had looked so damn frail. Now she looked damn rested, while he probably looked as if he had spent the day in a coal mine.

"Relax." She laid a comforting hand on his shoulder. Her fingers were slippery from the perspiration she found there. Rather than wipe her hand, she slowly rubbed her thumb over her fingers. Drew had no idea why he found that extremely sensual. But he did.

"The wholesale nursery I do business with will take care of getting them into the ground. They had a full crew available. I just want to pick out the best specimens."

Like you, she couldn't help thinking. Even perspired and grumpy-looking, she had to admit that she had never seen a man with a build as good as his. At least not up close. Yes, Margaret would definitely be drooling right about now if she were here. If she were inclined to drool, which she wasn't, Daisy would have done so herself.

Daisy glanced over her shoulder and saw Jeremy running toward her. "Jeremy's going to help me pick them out." She stretched her hand out toward the boy. He moved into the pocket it created, like a small kitten seeking its mother's warmth. "Aren't you, Jeremy?"

After spending the better part of the past three hours inside the house with Mrs. Samuelson, watching cartoons and eating cookies, Jeremy was well rested and raring to go. "You bet."

Drew looked toward the Samuelson's house, unable at the moment to will his body into action. Just a few seconds more, he promised himself, then he'd turn on the ignition. He realized that Daisy was looking at him. There was just the slightest touch of sympathy in her eyes. The last thing he wanted was for her to ask him if there was anything wrong.

He sought to divert her attention away from him. "Why do they need such a big house? There's just the two of them, isn't there?"

Daisy curled her arm around Jeremy's small shoulders. "She likes to have room for the all grandchildren when they come to visit." It sounded like a greeting card type of life. One she had never had. Still, she was optimistic. "I hope I wind up like that someday. In a nice, comfortable marriage, looking forward to having my grandchildren come over to spend the weekend."

She sounded wistful, he thought. "First you have to get someone daring enough to marry you." He had almost said "foolhardy" instead.

Drew positioned himself carefully and pressed down on the gas as he turned on the ignition. Every bone in his body told him that he was going to regret this afternoon long before nightfall.

The man was a born romantic. "What a lovely thing to say." She straightened away from the car as it rumbled to life. She had no doubt if she remained, he'd probably use it as an excuse to run her over. Still, she owed him one. "What time do you think you'll be home?"

"Later."

The word hung in the air as he pulled away from the curb and drove down the street.

He was heading in the wrong direction, she thought, wondering how long it would take him to find out. She was grateful that she wouldn't be there when he discovered his mistake.

She gave Jeremy a squeeze. "There goes a very stubborn man, Jeremy. Come on." She turned toward the house. "Let's go tell Mrs. Samuelson we're finished."

He thought of the cookies. And the way Mrs. Samuelson

had laughed over the cartoons. Not like a grown-up at all. "Can we come back and visit her sometime, Aunt Daisy? She's nice."

"Count on it." Daisy was rewarded with a very broad grin.

Daisy had just begun to lose the battle with her drooping eyelids. The book she was reading was slipping from her grasp when she heard the front door being opened and then closed.

Drew was home.

The thought telegraphed itself through her body, waking her up. She glanced at the digital clock on her nightstand. Eleven o'clock. He was a stubborn man all right. She shook her head and rose from her bed, the hem of her light blue nightgown floating down around her legs. She slipped her arms into the matching robe and tied the single ribbon at her breast. She had almost given up on him.

The stairs were a challenge.

They spread before him like a towering Mount Everest, daring him to climb and conquer. Swallowing an oath that encompassed both his fatigue and Daisy's existence on earth, Drew gripped the banister with sore, aching fingers and slowly made his way up. He was dragging himself up more than walking. It felt as if he had been shot through with lead and it was only a matter of time, perhaps minutes, before he would turn completely immobile.

Immobile but not numb. True to his prediction, every single bone in his body was aching wretchedly. There were blisters on his hands. One had broken open on the way home as he had gripped the steering wheel. It made holding on to the banister almost impossible. But if he didn't hold on, Drew wouldn't make it up to his room at all.

He briefly flirted with the idea of simply collapsing on

the sofa and spending the night there. He was exhausted enough to do it. Except for the fact that Anastasia would find him there in the morning and probably gloat or cluck sympathetically, which was probably even more irritating. He wasn't about to give her the opportunity.

Five minutes later Drew stood on the landing and let out a sigh of relief. He had successfully negotiated the stairs, despite the fact that there seemed to be twice as many steps now as there had been when he had left this morning.

He looked down the hall toward his door. Just a few more feet and he'd be in his room. Mecca. Once inside, he planned to do nothing more strenuous than fall face down on the bed. He knew he hadn't the will or the strength to even undress. He was going to have to call his valet in New York and have the man express mail more suits and shirts out to him. Tomorrow.

Tomorrow was much too far away for him to even contemplate.

Miraculously reaching his door, he placed his hand on the doorknob, turned it and all but fell into the room.

He blinked. The lights were on. Had he forgotten to turn them off this morning? He would have scratched his head if the effort required to do so hadn't been too much for him. He looked toward the bed. There was a covered silver tray on it. Was he in the right room?

Right room or not, he was going to bed. Sitting on his bed, he stared at the tray. Whatever was under the lid, he hadn't the strength to eat it. He was about to push it aside when the fragrance drifted his way. He knew immediately that Anastasia was in the room.

She stood in the doorway, framed by the light from the hall. She looked a little like a wood nymph, come to plague him. Or were those banshees?

He looked about two yards past exhausted, she thought,

feeling sorry for him. "You weren't kidding about later," she said as she walked in.

He was beginning to recognize that tone. "I'm tired, Anastasia. Could I have a reprieve tonight?"

She sat on the bed, keeping the tray between them. "From what?"

He was tired, but he wasn't dead. He couldn't help noticing that the robe was just the slightest bit opaque. All he saw was the nightgown beneath, but it was enough to stir an imagination he thought had gone to sleep. "You. I'm not up to sparring with you."

Daisy smiled and held up her hands. "No sparring. No gloves." She turned her hands front to back for his benefit. "See?"

He looked at her suspiciously. Was she about to offer some compromise in hopes that he was too tired to think? "Then what are you doing here?"

The man had a lot to learn about trust. "Returning a kindness for a kindness." She lifted the silver lid to expose a platter of food she had prepared herself. "Cold fried chicken." She thought of his lecture at Hamburger Delight. "Or don't you eat that, either?"

He loved fried chicken, but not at this moment. All he wanted to do was sink into a pillow and ignore the thousand pulsating points on his body. "I'm too tired to eat. All I want to do is go to sleep. Preferably not sitting up." It was a blatant hint.

She looked at the platter regretfully before replacing the lid. "You have to eat to keep your strength up."

Yes, against you. He tried not to watch the way the material moved against her breasts as she shifted. It was like trying to pull himself out of quicksand. The more he tried, the worse it became.

"I don't think I can chew. Everything hurts but my teeth." Right now he couldn't have tasted anything even if he wasn't exhausted. There were other appetites suddenly waking up.

Oh, my God, not with her.

"I'm prepared for that, too."

He hadn't the slightest idea what she was talking about. With effort, he rose from the bed. "Aren't Boy Scouts the ones who are supposed to be prepared?"

Daisy loosened his tie and then slipped it from his collar. "So are Girl Scouts."

The words, he was trying to keep his mind on the words, he told himself. "You were a Girl Scout?"

"Senior Girl Scout." She rose and removed his jacket, one sleeve at a time. He could only stand there and let her. Sudden movements were not advisable for him at the moment. For a number of reasons.

"Of course. I forgot. You went through vocations like some people go through tissues. Just how many vocations have you had?"

Placing his jacket neatly on a chair, Daisy removed the tray from his bed. "Three—no, four." She shrugged as she placed the tray on the bureau. "Enough to know I had found the right one when I came to it."

He couldn't turn his head, he couldn't move. Any movement would start up the pain again. "Isn't that just a tad unstable?"

"What, looking for happiness? I don't think so."

She was standing in front of him. As she considered his question, she undid the top button on his shirt. "Happiness again," he muttered. Damn, his throat was going dry. "Is that all you can think about?"

She eased the second button free. "What else is there?"

Drew opened his mouth, but couldn't think of a single answer for her. His brain had completely overloaded and was in the process of shutting down. The only thing he could focus on was her fingers as they slowly glided down his chest. He felt his skin heating. "What are you doing?"

"Can't you tell?"

He could tell. He could tell all right, and it wasn't going to work. She wasn't going to seduce him into relinquishing his claim to Jeremy. Even if she had the softest body, the firmest breasts he had ever seen. Not even if his hands ached now for a new reason.

"Anastasia, it isn't going to work."

"No," she agreed readily, "not if you keep your clothes on." She began to tug his shirt out of the waistband of his trousers.

He caught her hand. "I have no intentions of taking off my clothes. Any more of my clothes," he corrected.

"Suit yourself," she said, "but liniment is more effective if you don't apply it through material."

What was she talking about? "Liniment?" He blinked, trying to clear his head. She was muddling everything inside it. "What liniment?"

"This liniment." She held up the small bottle she had had tucked in the pocket of her robe. "It's what the coach used when our muscles were too sore."

"Coach," he echoed. "That would be the Olympic coach, right?" She never gave up, did she? But he was too tired to argue over this.

"Yes." She grinned, knowing exactly what had crossed his mind. She finished pulling his shirt free and pushed it off his shoulders. She saw something flame in his eyes then disappear just as quickly. She shut away her own tingle of excitement. It wasn't her intention to entice either one of them. "Sit."

"I'm not a dog." Drew's protest was not as forceful as he'd meant it to be. Surrendering, he sat.

Daisy climbed on the bed and positioned herself behind him on her knees. He was aware of every movement, every breath. His fatigue, his pain, faded behind a haze. He was aware of only her.

Daisy cupped her hand and poured liniment into it, then quickly rubbed it into his skin as she began to knead his tense muscles.

"Oh, God." He didn't know if he groaned the words or if they just echoed in his mind. He wasn't sure of very much anymore.

He wasn't relaxing, but that, she figured, took time. He had knots in his shoulders the size of hand balls.

"Good?" She grinned to herself when he didn't answer. Stoic to the end. *But you'll come around eventually.* "It's all right, you can admit it. I'll still respect you in the morning."

He leaned back slightly, into her hands, into her touch. He didn't know if he was responding to her massage or to her, or a combination of both, but it felt like heaven. He was on his way to becoming human again.

He turned and his bare arm brushed against her thigh. Sparks tap danced all through him. Maybe too human. Survival instincts erupted. "Do you ever shut up?"

She wondered if she was crazy, feeling sorry for him. "It's been known to happen." She squeezed his shoulder just a little too hard and enjoyed watching him wince. Served him right. "Are you asking me to stop talking?"

He knew that would bring on another debate. "My aspirations aren't quite that high at the moment." This was beginning to feel too good. Alarms went off all through him. "You don't have to do that." He moved his shoulders against her hand.

"Yes, I do." God, he was tense. "Unlike you, the milk of human kindness has not curdled in my veins." She leaned over him and he could smell her. Almost taste her, damn her. "I do appreciate what you did today, for whatever reason it was that you did it."

He wanted to keep it as simple as possible. For both of them. "You didn't look as if you could handle digging all those holes, that's all."

She poured more liniment and enjoyed watching him shiver involuntarily as she applied it to his back. "Since when are you concerned about me?"

"I wasn't concerned. I was just—" She was doing it again, making him trip over his own tongue. She had an uncanny knack for that. "Crazy, all right? I don't know what came over me."

Annoyed, he turned around so suddenly that she lost her balance and tumbled forward. Without thinking, Drew caught her in his arms.

Startled, she stared at Drew. "Well, this is an interesting position." She kept her voice deliberately flippant to hide the fact that her heart was suddenly threatening to leap out of her chest. "What do we do about it?"

He felt the muscles in his stomach contract into a tight fist. "I could just drop you on the floor."

She shook her head slowly, her eyes never leaving his. "Too violent. You're not given to violence."

He thought about his earlier urge to strangle her. It was still a viable choice for what she was doing to him. "I don't know about that."

Daisy raised herself up ever so slightly so that her mouth was just inches away from his. "I do," she whispered.

Her breath was sweet, tempting, and any resistance he might have had, had long since evaporated in the strong California sun. Without realizing what he was doing, or perhaps not wanting to realize what he was doing, Drew cupped the back of her head, threading his fingers through her hair.

He brought her lips to his.

He shouldn't be doing this when he was tired. He shouldn't ever do it, he emphasized, but definitely not when he was so exhausted, when his guard was nonexistent. It felt as if everything within him was completely, instantly undone. Something overwhelming was happening and he had no control over it, no control over his own reaction. It was as if his body had been invaded by an alien force.

The kiss deepened. He wasn't even certain if he was responsible for that or if she was. He did know that his arms tightened around her as he drew her body even closer to him.

Inexplicably, suddenly, he was transported into another world, a world of flashing lights and heat and sounds that buzzed in his ears. A world filled with needs, incredible, insatiable needs.

He wanted to make love with her.

His body hadn't an ounce of strength in it. There was no one single place where he didn't ache. And yet all he wanted to do was take her to bed with him and try to explore what it was that she was doing to him. He didn't even like her, for God's sake. Why would he want to make love with her?

He knew why, damn it.

Her head was spinning. She had wondered, in between the bickering, what it would be like to kiss him. Pleasant, interesting, arousing. Perhaps even boring. All these words had presented themselves to her.

Now she knew there was no word for it. What was happening right at this moment defied description. All she knew was that she wanted more. Much more. But not now. Not until she was prepared to handle it.

Heart pounding, she braced her hands against his chest and pushed until there was a wedge between them. She drew air into her lungs, trying to find her voice. And then she heard the noise.

Her mouth curved. "Should I take that as a compliment?"

Dazed, he looked at her. "What?"

"Your pants." She pointed toward his pocket. "They're ringing."

Chapter Seven

"Oh." Drew fought through the haze that had encapsulated his brain. He felt the phone vibrate ever so slightly against his thigh as it rang again. "That's my private line to New York."

At that moment they both stood up. Drew fumbled for the phone and took it out of his pocket. It looked like a small, elaborate calculator, Daisy thought.

She looked at the folded black object in Drew's hand. Daisy knew without being told that the incoming call wasn't personal. Nothing about this man was personal. "It's almost three in the morning in New York. Who would be calling you from there, the night watchman?"

"I've got someone patching me through on a three-way, conference call to Japan. Tokyo, actually." He had forgotten that, Drew realized. It wasn't like him to forget. He was not forgiving of mistakes, especially his own. He had to get a better grip on things. This woman had him sliding in directions he had no desire to go in.

"Tokyo. Of course." She took a step away from him, testing the strength in her legs. They still worked. Sort of. She suppressed a sigh of relief. Saved by the bell. At least for now.

He just held the phone in his hand without lifting the cover, thinking of what he had nearly done. He must have been crazy, really crazy, to lose control that way.

"Better answer it before they decide to trade with someone else," Daisy advised. She glanced at the tray on the bureau as she began to retreat. "I'll leave this here in case you get a second wind." She ran the tip of her finger over her lip and remembered.... "Or a third one."

Drew extended the antenna and opened the phone before he was tempted to drag her back and do something he knew was utterly stupid, utterly out of character and utterly risky to his very way of life. He watched her as she left the room and wished that his pulse would stop jumping around so erratically. He looked away, but the sway of her hips beneath the light material was irrevocably burned into his mind.

"Hello?" he mumbled into the receiver.

Daisy eased the door closed and then leaned against it for a moment until she was sure she had regained full control over her knees. Right now, they felt as if they were going to buckle.

Who would have thought?

Who would have *ever* thought that the Iceman could kiss like that? Kiss her until her blood was boiling, her body was turning to fluid, and her head was spinning dizzily like some child's toy? Not in a million years would she have foreseen that happening. Daisy liked surprises, but this was an exception.

Or at least the verdict was still out on her ultimate reaction to the fact that the touch of Drew's mouth made her

forget her name, her rank and her serial number, and had
her wanting to throw all caution to the wind.

Well, this was probably as composed as she supposed
she'd be for the rest of the night, Daisy thought. She
straightened, moving away from the door, and slowly went
to her room. She couldn't help wondering if this was what
Alyce had felt the first time she had kissed Jonathan. If so,
the Addison men were lethal.

Life returned to as normal a routine as was possible,
given the circumstances. Jeremy returned to his pre-school
the following Monday. Daisy moved her belongings from
her apartment into the house and went to Showers of Flowers…and Things. And Drew went into hiding.

At least, that was the way Daisy saw it. Drew came down
to breakfast every morning punctually at seven. He would
consume two cups of black coffee and, occasionally, a
piece of toast. When he spoke, it was to Jeremy or to Irene.
Daisy noted that he avoided speaking to her as if she were
the personification of the Black Plague. For the time being,
she played along, wondering how long it would go on.
Drew would leave for work long before they were finished
eating.

And then they wouldn't see him again until the following
morning, at which point the ritual was repeated. It went on
like this for four days. When it looked as though the routine
would continue indefinitely, Daisy made up her mind to
wait up for Drew and beard the lion in his den. Or, more
precisely, at the front door.

The man obviously had to be told what he was doing
wrong since he was apparently too blind to see it for himself.

She had spent the better part of the morning working on
the nursery's monthly inventory and the afternoon helping
Simon plant the Applegate's azaleas. When Daisy arrived

home, it was to spend the evening playing with a very active Jeremy. There had been a party at the pre-school and Jeremy was wired on chocolate cake and red fruit punch. It had taken her awhile to get him into bed. By nine she was ready for bed herself. But she was absolutely determined to talk to Drew when he got home.

If he got home, she amended, staring at the grandfather clock that stood majestically guarding the foyer. It faced the front door. Daisy had dragged over a chair so that she was catty-corner to it. She wanted to be the first thing Drew saw when he came in. If she fell asleep, she knew the noise he'd make as he opened the door would wake her.

Ten-twenty-one.

What the hell did a man do "at the office" until ten-twenty-one at night? she wondered irritably. Maybe they'd have this talk early tomorrow morning. She debated calling it a night when she heard a car in the driveway. Speak of the devil.

It hadn't been one of his easiest days, but it had certainly been one of the better ones, Drew thought as he pulled up in the driveway. He had gotten inside information that there was a takeover being planned for one of his subsidiary companies. Normally he would have flown to the site, but there hadn't been enough time. The miracle of telecommunications had enabled him to stop the takeover before it had actually had a chance to gain any momentum and roll right over him.

Yes, he thought, getting out and slamming the car door, a very good day. He was tired, bone-tired, and looked forward to going to bed and sleeping the sleep of the victorious.

And then he saw her and triumph did an immediate about-face.

Ever since what he had mentally termed as "the unfortunate incident'' in his room, Drew had been purposely avoiding Daisy. Work had been a handy excuse to hide behind. He hadn't liked his reaction to her, nor had he cared for the weakness that flowed over him when he had kissed her. Like a flash flood that had come from nowhere. And had nowhere to go.

She had something on her mind, he thought as he closed the door behind him, still facing her. "Loaded for bear," he believed the expression was. Was he the bear?

"Staking out new territory?" Drew gestured to the foyer, keeping his voice mild as he began to walk toward the stairs.

She was on her feet instantly, just as he knew she would be, following him up the stairs. He decided he was cursed, or doomed, or whatever word it was that meant he was destined to make one hell of a mistake. And probably very soon.

He kept walking. She was wearing that perfume again, the one that swept through his senses and scrambled his thinking processes. He wondered if he could buy the company and have the perfume banned from the market.

Daisy tried to stay calm, although waiting had made her agitated. "You've been working awfully late this week."

He responded without turning around. His room was within reach now. Maybe he could just shut the door on her, once inside.

"I work awfully late every week." She was making noises like a neglected wife and all he had done was kiss her once. There was a reason, he mused, why he had never bothered getting married. To avoid scenes such as this one.

He opened his door, but she had anticipated him. She was in the doorway before he could shut it. "So this is normal for you?" she asked.

He didn't care for her tone. "Yes."

All right, he thought, he was stretching it just a little. He did work long hours and felt exhilarated by it. But this time he was working longer hours to get the job done *and* to avoid her.

Drew would rather have had his tongue cut out than to tell her that she had him on the run. Why, of all the women who were available in the world, did he have to be attracted to a sharp-tongued, overly perky flake who had the annoying ability of turning his words inside out while simultaneously doing a number on his male hormones? What was worse, he had a feeling that she could very capably crack the very foundations of his nice, safe world—a world where the only risks he was asked to make involved business transactions. Emotions never came into play.

Lately, around her, nothing else *but* emotions seemed to be stirring. There was no justice in the world.

She leaned against the doorjamb, as leery of entering the room as he was of having her there. She crossed her arms in front of her, trying to look nonchalant. "So far, you're not making a very good case for yourself."

He turned and looked at her. Now what? "What do you mean, case?"

He was too busy to even remember why he was supposedly here, she thought. Typical. "You're never home. What kind of a life is that supposed to be for Jeremy?"

"A comfortable one." What did she want from him? "Look, real fathers go to work all the time." Unlike the Bohemian she had probably had as a father. Drew could envision her being raised by two misplaced hippies living in the last of the communes. That seemed to fit with the aura she gave off. Sitting cross-legged on the floor, weaving blankets, making pottery and doing nothing. That might suit her, but that wasn't him.

"Yes, they go to work, but they don't live there." How could this be the same man who had kissed her so passionately only a few days ago? Had he used up his entire supply of feelings in that one instance? For Jeremy's sake, she refused to believe that. "The important things are at home." She looked at him pointedly. "Or should be."

The woman didn't have a logical bone in her body. But then, he already knew that. It was why he was attracted to this life-threatening mass of contradictions and pulsating emotion that he didn't understand. "There are things that I have to take care of."

She blew out a breath, stifling an urge to beat on his hard head. "I appreciate that. But do you have to run the whole damn company?"

She didn't have the vaguest idea of what it took to run something like Addison Corporation. "What would you know about it?"

When he said something like that, she had no idea why she had reacted to him the way she had the other night. "I know that people in authority hire other people they trust and delegate responsibilities. They don't try to do it all themselves."

Oh, no, she didn't. She didn't use one set of rules and give him another. "Like plant shrubs?"

She knew he'd bring that up. "That was a temporary situation." She crossed to him and stood on her toes to face him. "I'm talking about a way of life."

The company *was* his life. Or had been. "The company is important."

"Of course it is." She threw up her hands. "But it's a thing, an entity." Didn't he understand anything? Was that man who had played trains with Jeremy in that ridiculous hat someone she had just dreamed up? No, it had happened. There *had* to be something inside of him she could work with, draw on. "We're talking about a small boy who won't always *be* a small boy and who needs memories built up now."

Drew sighed wearily. She could probably talk all night if he let her. "Where is this leading?"

There was nothing in his eyes, no spark of understanding. "Nowhere," she answered quietly, "if you're not listening."

This was what she wanted, wasn't it? Jeremy all to herself, by default. But if Drew didn't understand this, he wouldn't understand why she would fight his attempt to get custody of Jeremy and they'd be right back where they had started from. Square one. She was trying desperately to turn him into someone who would understand why Jeremy had to stay with her. She couldn't do that if Drew was in hiding.

Her eyes were like flames when she was angry, he thought. Damn it, he was getting distracted again. He had to exercise more control over himself. This shouldn't be happening, not if he didn't want it to. And he didn't.

"All right," he relented, "I'm listening."

Yes, but are you hearing? "Spend some time with Jeremy."

What was she talking about? "I see him every morning at breakfast."

Dead from the neck up. "You see the newspaper every morning," she fairly shouted then remembered that Jeremy was only two doors down the hall. She lowered her voice. "You don't have a relationship with that, either."

He should have known better than to try to conduct a rational, logical conversation with her. "You're babbling again."

The hours of waiting, of anticipating this conversation, took their toll. She simply reacted and took a swing at him, landing a punch on his arm. It didn't do any good. It didn't alleviate the frustration. It just hurt her knuckles. "I am making sense, you idiot. Can't you understand anything that's not printed on a spreadsheet or a legal document?"

He rubbed his arm, surprised. The blow had stung. "I

can't understand you," he admitted freely. And he doubted he ever would.

She shut her eyes for a moment, gathering strength. The man had a head like a rock. And she suddenly despaired that his heart wasn't far behind. "I'm not asking you to understand me. I don't matter. Jeremy does. You came barging in here, demanding him." She grew angrier at the very thought of his actions and the possible motives behind them. "He's not an acquisition, a takeover to crow about." Inadvertently, she had struck very close to home. "He's a little boy who needs a hell of a lot more attention than you've been giving him."

Because he knew he had been absent more than he normally would have, Drew conceded the point to her. "What do you want me to do?"

Finally. Exhausted from the effort, she sat on the edge of the bed. "Take him to the park."

"Park?" he echoed.

He looked so bewildered, she had to smile. "You know, the place where they have slides, green stuff, swings. Anything sound familiar here?"

Drew had never gone to a park as a child. He hadn't the vaguest idea why that would be a pleasant experience for anyone. "And exactly what am I supposed to do with him at the park?"

Was he serious? Maybe he *did* work all the time. Maybe he had been born working. "Anything he wants you to. That's the idea of taking him."

Maybe she had a point at that. He loosened his tie and undid his collar button. "I'll see."

He wasn't going to get out of it that easily. "Tomorrow."

If she wasn't the pushiest woman on the face of the earth, he'd hate to meet the woman who held the title. "I'm going to work tomorrow."

Why didn't that surprise her? "It's Saturday," she pointed out.

"So?" He began to take his jacket off and then thought better of it. Though they were arguing, on another plane, he was still reacting to her, reacting to the fact that she was sitting on the edge of his bed and he wanted her in it. With him.

She sighed. "You're absolutely hopeless." She gave up, angry with herself for having cared, angry with him for existing in her life and Jeremy's. "Go ahead. Go!" She waved her hand at him, rising. "Go to your office, to your meetings and to your ringing pants' phone—"

"Cellular phone." His voice was so damn patient she could have screamed.

Her eyes grew dark as her voice lowered. She began to speak slowly, with emphasis. The change, so unusual for her, made him pay attention. "But just remember this conversation when you try to get custody of Jeremy."

He was an insensitive brute and would always stay that way. He couldn't be made to change, or see reason. She would see him in court, she thought, and that would be that. Daisy turned on her heel and began to stalk out the door.

"What if it rains?"

She was an idiot for giving him another chance. Hands at her sides, she turned around.

"This is California. Haven't you heard the song? It never rains here. Except for the rainy season," she added, her lips quirking into a small smile. "And if it does, you'll play trains with him again, or see a movie, or watch cartoons—"

"Cartoons?" he asked incredulously, disdain dripping from his voice.

"Drawings that move," she felt bound to explain. "You must have heard of them." She couldn't help the grin that rose to her lips as she imagined him watching with Jeremy. That was something she might even videotape and save for posterity. "There're a lot of them on Saturday morning. You have your choice."

He picked the lesser of the evils, or so he hoped. "I'll go to the park."

Daisy nodded. "Smart move."

Not by along shot. "No, a smart move would have been if I had sent my lawyers out here instead of me." A lot smarter, he thought, feeling an ache forming just by being here, alone with her.

She smiled sweetly. "I would have carved them into little pieces and sent them back in a box. Figuratively speaking, of course."

"Of course." It sounded silly, but somehow, he could see her doing just that. "So why am I so lucky?"

She patted his face the way a mother did with a slightly slow child. "You're family."

No, I'm a hell of a lot more than that. And less than that. "Are you going to come along?"

The question surprised her. She wasn't certain which way he would have preferred it. "Do you want me to?"

No, I don't want you anywhere close by. He thought of being alone with Jeremy and how awkward that made him feel. Perhaps inadequate might have been a better word, but he didn't want to think about that now. "Yes."

The smile she gave him before she left the room haunted his dreams that night. "Then I'll come."

Margaret ran the nursery on Saturdays. Daisy wasn't thinking about work when she picked up the phone as it rang on their way out the door.

Margaret didn't bother saying hello. "You know that palm tree order for the mall?"

Daisy had an uneasy feeling in her stomach at Margaret's wording. "Yes?"

"Well, that's just it. They only got one. The order was for eight. They've got to get them put into the ground before the men can start on the brickwork. I can't reach anyone at the Keeline Nursery and the customer is screaming for blood. Or at least more palm trees. He keeps saying things about deadlines and forfeiting fees."

"I've got Steve's private number at his house." She noticed that Drew was listening and frowning ever so slightly. "I'll call him and get back to you."

"Steve?" Drew asked as she hung up. It was absurd to think she hadn't had a life before he appeared, yet the fact that she did irked him in a way he found troublesome. What was coming over him? He didn't care if she did cartwheels naked in the snow, so why did it matter if she had a man's private number?

"The owner of the wholesale nursery." She pulled her personal phonebook out of her purse and started thumbing through the pages. "We've got a little problem with an order."

Shoe on the other foot. "Surely that's not going to make you miss our outing to the park?" The sarcasm was three inches thick.

He was enjoying this, she thought. "No, I just need about a half an hour to unscramble this. You two go on ahead." She saw the dubious look enter Drew's eyes. Unless she missed her guess, he didn't want to go. "You can't miss it. It's just three blocks away." She pointed vaguely in the right direction. Drew didn't move. "A simple little playground," she persisted, "with sand and swings. I'll be there as soon as I can."

"We can wait." He leaned against the counter as she thumbed through her telephone book. Jeremy was restlessly moving from side to side.

"You might, but he can't." She ruffled Jeremy's hair. "Right, Jeremy?" She looked at Drew and wondered if he was afraid to be alone with Jeremy for some reason. Why else was he hesitating?

"But you'll come?" Jeremy looked uncertainly over his shoulder at Drew, then shifted his gaze anxiously to his aunt.

"Of course I'll come. I promise," she added when the anxious expression didn't leave Jeremy's face.

"You know," Drew drawled slowly, "work shouldn't just take over your life like that."

Rather than get annoyed, she laughed. Let him have his moment. It was harmless enough. "Shut up and go have fun, you two."

It took a little longer than she had hoped, necessitating a quick trip to Keeline itself. On the way back, she made a quick side trip on impulse. It was almost an hour later before she pulled up to the playground.

It was a mini-playland for children and had been one of the main reasons Alyce and Jonathan had decided to settle in this development as opposed to another. The play area was well equipped and well maintained. It had everything to fuel a child's imagination, from an elaborate swing set to a miniature old pirate ship for the children to explore.

It took her a few minutes to locate Drew and Jeremy. They were by the swings. Drew was absently pushing Jeremy with one hand. The momentum was dismally listless. In his other hand Drew held his cellular phone. The conversation he was engaged in held all of his attention.

Damn, wasn't he ever going to learn?

Daisy's good humor evaporated. She had to work at curbing her temper. She didn't want Jeremy to witness a testy confrontation. She managed to wait until Drew ended his conversation.

As Drew said goodbye, Daisy crossed to him. "Finished?"

She had startled him, appearing out of nowhere that way. "As a matter of fact, yes."

He stopped pushing Jeremy altogether as he retracted the antenna and flipped the phone closed. Just as Drew was about to put it in his pocket, Daisy snatched it out of his hand.

Now what had come over her? "Do you want to make a call?"

She shook her head as she dropped the offending object into her purse and then closed it.

"Just what do you think you're doing?"

"Freeing you," she said cheerfully. She nodded at Jeremy. "He needs your undivided attention, remember? Hi, Tiger." She kissed the top of the boy's head. "Are you having a good time?" One look at his solemn, bored face answered her question.

Now that she was here, Jeremy wriggled in his seat, holding on to the chains on either side of him. "Push me high, Aunt Daisy. Uncle Drew doesn't know how." The last statement was uttered with childish disgust.

It was difficult, but Daisy came to Drew's defense. "That's because he was only using one hand. He can do a lot better when he uses them both." She gestured Drew toward Jeremy. "All yours, Drew."

She stepped back, folding her arms. He had hoped that she'd take over instead of confiscating his telephone and utterly confounding him in the space of two minutes. He should have known better. He looked at her stance. Both feet were planted firmly on the ground and she looked as if she was monitoring him. "Are you going to rate me?"

"Just enjoying the view, Drew, just enjoying the view." She grinned to herself as he began to push Jeremy again. "By the way, next week's Halloween."

Why did he have this sinking feeling in his stomach that he wasn't going to like what was coming? "So?"

She shrugged. "So, I took the liberty of ordering your costume."

He stopped pushing. "My what?"

"Costume. The thing you put on your body when you go trick-or-treating. You're not pushing, Drew," she pointed out.

He didn't like having her watch his every move. He wasn't used to it. It had been a long time since he had felt himself accountable to anyone. "I'm also not going trick-or-treating."

"No, not technically," she agreed. "But I thought it would be fun to dress up when we took Jeremy around the neighborhood."

Jeremy twisted around in his swing and she could see by his broad grin that he approved of the idea. Alyce and Jonathan had dressed up and taken him last year. She felt this might help ease things a little for him.

But obviously not for Drew, she thought, seeing the disgruntled expression on his face. "You've got to be kidding."

She grinned. He wasn't getting out of this one. "Do I look like I'm kidding?"

Drew was beginning to believe there wasn't a reasonable bone in her body, but he was going to try to reason with her anyway. Something told him he would have gotten better results discussing philosophy with a shoe. "Halloween is...when?"

"October 31st. Same day it is every year."

He ignored the sarcasm. "It's a week night." And that should have been the end of it.

Daisy was unfazed. "I'll give you a note to take in to the office if you oversleep."

The woman did not live in the real world. "Why don't I just quit altogether?"

The sarcastic question appeared to go right over her head, as far as he could see. "That's entirely up to you, but it might not be such a bad idea to consider." She ignored the glare he gave her. "Jonathan used to only go in part-time."

Drew pushed a little too hard, but Jeremy only squealed with glee. "That's because I ran the business and besides, there was the money he inherited."

She looked at him innocently. "You didn't inherit any money?"

"Yes, but—" He gave up trying. "Never mind." He pushed silently for a few minutes, aware that she was still watching him. "You don't know my size," he pointed out triumphantly. And there was no way he was going in for a fitting.

She smiled, conjuring up a memory. "Oh, I had a pretty good idea."

She was referring to the night she had walked in on him, he could tell. Trust her to bring that up. Well, she could bring up anything she wanted. He wasn't going to put on a costume and he sure as hell wasn't about to go trick-or-treating. And that was the end of it.

Chapter Eight

The box was on his bed when he arrived home from the office. It was a large, retangular white box with bold red letters that read London's Better Costumes across the front. He eyed it for a moment, prepared to ignore it and Halloween altogether. But curiosity got the better of him and he finally opened the box. The situation was not unlike the one he found himself in with Anastasia, Drew thought. He was prepared to ignore her and somehow, he just couldn't.

But he was working on it.

An involuntary laugh exploded from him when he held the top half of the outfit up against himself. A long, green jersey. Fawn-colored leather trousers and a bow and arrows remained in the box. It took him a few minutes to figure out that it was a Robin Hood costume. She wanted him to be Robin Hood. She was out of her mind. Stark, raving, certifiably crazy. If Drew had had any lingering doubts before, they were certainly gone now.

"Like it?" Daisy had heard Drew come home and had purposely waited until he had gone up to his room. She had a feeling he wouldn't be able to resist looking into the box. Few people resisted innocent temptation. The next step was getting him into it. For that, she had enlisted Jeremy's aid, carefully coaching the boy in what to say.

Drew turned to tell her exactly what he thought of the costume and her in no uncertain terms and then stopped. She was wearing a floor-length forest green dress made of velvet. It was cinched at a waist so small that it begged for a man's hand to span it, to let his fingers dip down to the enticing swell of her hips. The color of the dress brought out her eyes so vividly Drew felt as if he were hypnotized. She had done something to her hair, too, something that made it look like a dark cloud storming around her shoulders. Her bare shoulders. They were a creamy white and tempted him to gently glide his fingers along them. He ached just to touch her.

He found his voice, but it wasn't as easy as it should have been. "Who are you supposed to be?"

The way he looked at her made her forget, for a brief second, that they were, at bottom, adversaries engaged in a mental war over the welfare of a child. The look in Drew's eyes made her feel warm, wanted.

She smiled at him. "Maid Marian, m'lord."

His eyes strayed to the bodice. It was cut deep and set off what he surmised was her best feature. Or one of them. He tried not to stare. "Maid Marian is going to catch a cold if she's not careful."

She had seen the appreciative look before he locked it away. *Gotcha.* "Robin wouldn't let that happen." She indicated the costume he was holding up against himself with her eyes.

"What?" He glanced down, forgetting for a moment that he was still holding the shirt in his hands. "Oh, no way.

No damn way am I going to put this on." To emphasize the point, he tossed the costume onto the bed behind him. It landed on top of the bow.

Her grin grew mischievous. "Why not? It's the realistic model." She pointed to the pants. "A rugged, manly costume if ever there was one. I could have gotten you the one based on the Errol Flynn interpretation of Robin Hood." Her eyes were teasing. "I did have a yen to see you in tights, but I suppressed it."

"Thank you." He wanted to wipe the smirk off her face. He wanted to kiss it away until her lips were too numb to form a smile. Or to talk. It was something, he thought, to aspire to for the good of the world as well as for reasons of his own reawakening lust. He refused to view his reaction to her in any other terms. It was lust, pure and simple. Or maybe not so pure or so simple, but lust nonetheless.

He tried to keep his mind on the topic. "I am not about to make a fool of myself, parading around in any sort of ridiculous—"

He never got a chance to finish. Jeremy fairly bounded into the doorway, circumventing his aunt's wide skirt. It occurred to Drew, belatedly, that Daisy was bringing in reinforcements. Dressed in Lincoln green, with a hat held jauntily in place on his head by means of an elastic band beneath his chin, Jeremy looked like a miniature citizen of Sherwood Forest. He was holding tightly onto a large plastic staff that was as tall as he was.

"You have to come, Robin," Jeremy informed Drew. Authority rang in his voice that went far beyond his few years.

Commanding people around ran in the family, Daisy thought. She placed her hands on Jeremy's shoulders and ushered him farther into the room. She had rehearsed him well. "This is Little John, Robin," she explained to Drew.

"He can't go anywhere unless you lead. After all, you are the leader."

Like hell he was. Drew folded his arms across his chest and regarded this general in crushed-velvet skirts. "I'm surprised *you* didn't want to be Robin Hood."

She grinned, and it did something to him, damn it, no matter how hard he didn't want it to. "I thought about it." She spread out the skirt. "But we're a set and you would have looked silly in this dress."

And she didn't, he thought. Not silly at all. Too damn arousing is what she looked.

"Look, I—" It was a valiant try that never got off the ground, doomed before its birth.

"Please?" Jeremy looked up at him. "My daddy and mommy used to dress up a long time ago when they took me trick-or-treating."

"Last year," Daisy corrected him with a fond smile. This part he was adding on his own, and her heart ached for him. She didn't want him to forget his parents, ever, but she was afraid that their memory would make him too sad.

The accuracy of details wasn't important to Jeremy. He kept his gaze steadily on his uncle, hopeful. Waiting.

Those were Jonathan's eyes looking at him, Drew thought with a pang. He looked toward the bed at the costume he had thrown aside. The Jonathan he knew, the Jonathan he *thought* he knew, wouldn't have had the time to wear costumes and go trick-or-treating, or play with trains or eat French fries at Hamburger Delight. But the Jonathan Jeremy had known obviously had.

She saw Drew wavering. *Good.*

"At least try it on," Daisy urged as she moved to the bed. She picked up the heap from the box and brought it to him, her skirts rustling enticingly as she moved. "Who knows? You might get lucky. It might not fit." Although she knew for a fact that it would. She had called his valet in New York and had gotten Drew's exact measurements. Drew might think of her as being scatterbrained, she mused, but there was very little Daisy liked to leave to chance. Not when things mattered.

Drew took the clothes from her and saw Jeremy grin. "What's the point, then?"

"At least you will have tried." Turning, she ushered Jeremy out of the room. "Hurry up and change. Irene has dinner waiting for you. We've already eaten."

Drew remained where he was, staring in disbelief at the costume, at the leather britches that were hanging from his hands.

He wasn't moving. "Hurry," Daisy urged as she began closing the door. She peered in and pointed to the costume. "Or I'll come up and dress you myself."

He wouldn't put it past her, he thought. All right, he wasn't going to be completely unreasonable about this. He'd try on the costume. What were the odds that it would really fit him? And then he'd be off the hook.

It fit.

Drew scowled at the image in the mirror. It fit as if it had been tailored for him. He should have realized she would do something underhanded like this. Well, he wasn't going out and that was that.

He began to unlace the front of his shirt when there was a knock on his door.

He knew without asking that it was Daisy. "Go away." He doubted that she would, but he did his best to sound unfriendly.

"You decent?"

He yanked the lacings and found that he had somehow tangled them. "That never stopped you before."

Taking a chance, Daisy opened the door. "Is that an invitation?"

He looked up, frustrated by the lacings, frustrated by her. Most of all, frustrated by the hodgepodge his emotional network had become in such a short time.

"No, that was a curse, I just stifled it." He stopped fighting with the black ties when he saw the look on her face. "What are you grinning at?"

He looked like a sculpture, waiting for a pedestal. "You." She tilted her head, allowing herself a fuller survey. "I was right. You do look good in that." She felt her pulse quicken and decided to enjoy it rather than attempt to fight it or explain it away. It was much more pleasant that way.

For the first time in his adult life, he felt something akin to embarrassment poking holes in him. "I'm not wearing this."

She crossed to him, the bottom of her skirt whispering over the threshold. "Yes, you are." With practiced ease, she untangled the ties.

He wished she'd stop fiddling around his chest. He didn't want to feel her fingers on his bare skin like that. "I'm a full grown man. I know if I'm going to wear something or not. Look, I played it your way. I tried it on, saw how ridiculous I look, and now I'm taking it off."

He waved away her hands and saw that she had redone the slender leather ties.

She took a step back and her expression became serious. "Jeremy's waiting."

He wasn't going to be talked into this. It was a stupid idea and he wanted no part of it. "You take him."

Her eyes held his. "Yes," Daisy said quietly. "I will."

He knew what she meant.

He supposed there was no harm in indulging Jeremy a

little, but he was going to feel like a first-class fool, walking around like this. With an annoyed huff, Drew gave in.

"Damn you, woman, do you always get your way?" He stalked out of the bedroom, wondering why he was *letting* her get her own way.

Her smile was broad, pleased and beguiling. Almost innocent, except that he knew better. "No, not always, but enough times to keep me trying for more." As he walked toward the stairs, Daisy—carrying Drew's bow—surprised him by linking her arm through his. "Your quiver of arrows is downstairs."

He lifted a brow before taking the first step down. "Don't tempt me to use them."

Her smile broadened. "I wouldn't dream of it."

The sound of her laughter was like a sexy, stirring melody against his ear. He liked hearing it. He just wished it wasn't at his expense. No, he amended. He wished she wasn't laughing at all. Because when she did, he forgot that he was angry, forgot that his ultimate goal was to show her how much better suited he was to raise Jeremy than she. He forgot everything except that she existed. And that he wanted her.

Irene looked up as they came down the stairs, her eyes growing huge.

"Not a word," Drew warned the woman as he descended. "Not a single word."

Jeremy was ready, eagerly shifting from foot to foot. He hadn't mastered waiting patiently very well. But he was four and allowed, Daisy thought. He looked so normal, so untouched by tragedy. With all her heart, she wished it was true.

Daisy glanced at Drew. "Can she at least smile?"

"No," Drew answered gruffly, yanking the bottom of the jersey down as far as it would go. "And neither can you. Let's get this over with."

"But dinner——" Daisy looked toward the kitchen. He was probably grumpier on an empty stomach and he was bad enough as it was. She didn't want him fine-tuned.

"I've already eaten at the office." He had stayed at the office a little longer in hopes that Daisy and Jeremy would leave without him. No such luck.

"Whatever you say," Daisy said sweetly.

Ha, that'll be the day, Drew thought.

"You'll have fun," Jeremy promised, eagerly linking his hand with Drew's.

He sincerely doubted that. He was going to feel like an idiot, but maybe it would be worth it, Drew thought, looking into the small face with its dancing dark eyes. Besides, he didn't know anyone here, except for Anastasia, and she didn't count.

Daisy moved to the hall table and picked up Drew's accessories. She curtsied deeply as she offered them to Drew. "Your weapon, m'lord."

There was a ready retort on his lips as Drew turned toward her. The retort evaporated, dried to dust. It matched the condition in his throat.

He looked down at her soft breasts, covered just enough with green velvet to stir his fantasies and make his blood run hot. To make him yearn the way he had never yearned before. Indulging physical urges was a matter that was very low on his list of priorities. While he wasn't exactly a monk, the term playboy could never have been applied to him and he was content that way. Relationships took too much time away from his work, too much effort. They involved risks he wasn't prepared to take. He didn't have patience for the niceties that were required, wasn't up to playing the social games that people were forced to play. He firmly believed that being in love tended to create havoc in a man's life. Though he had eventually grown to like his sister-in-law, Alyce had turned Jonathan's life upside down, thrown it off course. She had transformed Jonathan into someone Drew didn't know. That fact was becoming more obvious to him with each passing day.

And now this gypsy in green velvet and nerve-jangling décolleté was doing it to him. Messing with his mind until he couldn't hold on to a single thought and follow it to its conclusion. Until he couldn't make a stand and stay there if she wanted him to move. It had to stop.

He took the weapon from her, wrapping his fingers around the bow and quiver. "Thank you," he mumbled.

For self-preservation, he turned toward his nephew. In comparison, things were more simple if he thought only of Jeremy.

"Let's go, 'Little John.' We have some robbing of the rich to do." He ushered the boy out the front door a little quicker than he had intended. Jeremy giggled, fairly skipping out.

It was a warm evening for October, even by Southern California standards. The streets seemed to explode with ghosts and goblins, witches and warriors, and green turtles with nunchakus. There were creatures Drew didn't recognize, mingling with miniature rock stars and cartoon characters. Some of the trick-or-treaters were surprisingly tall. It wasn't a night just for children.

To Drew's surprise, he was not the only adult besides Daisy to be wearing a costume. There were a handful of other parents who were indulging in childhood fantasies for the space of an evening. Cowboys and space captains nodded at him as they passed on the street, herding costumed children in front of them.

Despite the company, Drew still felt incredibly stupid. He was doing this for Jeremy, he told himself. And to prove to this overly bubbly woman next to him that he was capable of going along with a child's request, although what that had to do with properly raising Jeremy was still beyond him.

He looked about as comfortable as a lambchop at a fox convention, she thought, watching Drew. Had he always been this way? What kind of a little boy was the father of the man who hung back on the street with her tonight?

She needed to know. For Jeremy's sake.

And for her own.

Jeremy came racing up to them, holding up his huge orange pumpkin with its newest bounty. He tripped on a raised crack in the sidewalk and would have fallen if Drew hadn't been quick enough to catch him.

Unfazed, Jeremy ran to the next house. Daisy trained her flashlight on the sidewalk just in front of the boy to illuminate his way. "You've never done this before, have you?" Daisy guessed.

She had an irritating habit of plucking topics out of the air. "What?"

"Gone trick-or-treating?"

"No." He didn't like the fact that she could read him so easily, not when he was having increasingly more difficulty accomplishing the same with her. She was a hell of a lot more complicated than he had first thought. "How could you tell?"

"It shows." She turned to him. The porch light from the house in front of them illuminated his eyes. Such sad eyes, she thought. "A lot of things show."

He didn't want her getting any closer than she was. On all counts. "Now Maid Marian claims to have x-ray vision, as well?"

He wasn't fooling her. In a way, she thought not for the first time, Drew was a lot like Jonathan had been at first. It's what gave her hope. "You keep backing away. Are you afraid of a relationship?"

He refused to look at her. The moonlight was highlighting her profile and made her look wanton and temptingly innocent at the same time. He didn't understand how that could be possible. Yet there she was, being both. She, and what she was doing to him, scared the hell out of him.

Drew stared at Jeremy instead. "I'm building one. With Jeremy, remember?"

The man required an awful lot of patience, she thought. "You know what I mean."

He watched ahead of where Jeremy was walking, making sure that the boy didn't trip again. Making sure he didn't trip up himself.

When Jeremy rang the bell, eerie laughter pierced the air. Jeremy jumped back, but then bravely held his ground. Drew didn't realize that the feeling he was experiencing was pride.

"Don't flatter me, Anastasia. I hardly *ever* know what you mean."

Then she'd explain it to him, though she knew she didn't have to. "Us," she said quietly. "You can't deny there's not something humming between us."

This time he did look at her, but he was careful to only look at her face. A lot of good that did him. The banshee had a face like an angel tonight.

"Nerves. Nerves are what's humming between us. You scare the hell out of me." He'd make her back away if she wasn't going to do it voluntarily. "I've never dealt with a female barracuda before."

The description hurt, but she refused to show him. "Is that how you see me?"

They were under a street lamp and he saw the flash of pain in her eyes. Guilt rose, sharp and bitter. "All right, maybe not a barracuda. Something a little more petite." He looked away. If he didn't look at her, he couldn't feel guilty. A least, it was a good working theory. "How tall is a shrew?"

"All right, you've made your point." There was a strange hollowness inside of her. But she'd get over it. She had gotten over a good many things before.

Daisy turned her face forward, grateful for the darkness. "But all I have is Jeremy's best interests at heart."

He might not see it, but he could hear the hurt. He told himself he didn't care. It was her own fault. But it didn't erase his guilt. "So do I."

She aimed the flashlight beam ahead of him as Jeremy and two clowns, one shorter than he, one taller, scampered up wooden railroad ties to the next door.

"I guess we still have two months left to hash out what those 'best interests' are supposed to be."

"Two months?" he echoed.

Why did he sound as if she had just said something strange? She was tempted to look at him, but didn't quite trust herself yet. "The bargain was for three months, remember? One month has already gone by, or haven't you noticed?"

He hadn't. It struck him as odd. He had expected to feel like a prisoner, marking time, yet the month had somehow escaped him, slipping away without his even realizing it.

The air was warm, the moon was shining, and he could only keep a tight rein on his thoughts for so long with her next to him, half wearing that dress. He wanted to go home. "Hasn't he had enough yet?" Drew asked gruffly.

The grinch was back. But at least he had been nice for a while. The lapses were going to have to be longer if she ever hoped to thaw Drew out and have him relinquish his claim for custody. "He'll tell us when he's had enough."

More of her unorthodox philosophy. It was comforting to find something to become annoyed about. Otherwise his thoughts left him wide open to things he had no intentions of succumbing to. "You're letting a four-year-old decide things for himself?"

No, he had never been a little boy, celebrating Halloween, sneaking foods he shouldn't have, enjoying stolen moments past appointed bedtimes. She hadn't been wrong in
her estimation of him. But she had to change him if she
had any hopes of keeping Jeremy from suffering a fate
she'd had to deal with. She had to make Drew sensitive
enough to understand that she was the only one who was
able to meet Jeremy's emotional needs.

"It's Halloween," she said simply. "And he knows
when he's tired."

Jeremy gleefully ran up to show them his pumpkin. It
was almost filled to the brim. "Here, hold this." He thrust
the staff at her. "I need both hands." In a flash, he was
running off to the next house.

There was enough candy in that pumpkin to make any
three children sick to their stomach. "You're not going to
let him eat all that, are you?"

She wondered if he really thought she was so lax, or if
he was just trying to bait her. "No, that I'll dole out to
him."

Maybe there was hope for her yet. "At last, one sensible
decision."

She curtsied and the light from the flashlight wavered on
the cement before Jeremy. "Thank you, m'lord, that's very
kind of you."

He took the flashlight from her and shone it on the path
for Jeremy. "Why do I keep hearing a mocking tone in
your voice?"

"Possibly because it's there," she answered with a
smile. "Loosen up, Drew. You'll live longer." Still holding
on to Jeremy's staff, she lifted her skirts and walked ahead
of Drew. "Right now, it'll only seem longer."

They were out for a total of two hours. When Jeremy's
pumpkin was filled, Drew thought that would be the end

of the excursion. But Daisy merely took off Jeremy's cap, turned it upside down and transferred candy into it. That left Jeremy more room in his pumpkin.

Just as Drew was giving up hope of the night ever ending, Jeremy's energy suddenly petered out. They were more than a mile away from the house.

Daisy took the boy's hand into hers and led him away from the last house. No longer bouncing along, Jeremy's steps were small and shuffling. "I think Little John is tired," she told Drew.

Drew shifted Jeremy's hat to his other side. A candy bar fell. "Just like that?" He retrieved the candy bar from the sidewalk before she could tell him to. He was beginning to anticipate some of her moves and found a vague comfort in that. "He was fine five minutes ago."

Daisy looked down at Jeremy. His eyes were drooping. "Five minutes is a long time when you're four."

She sounded as if she was speaking from first-hand experience. But that was impossible. "You remember?" he asked sarcastically.

There was almost childlike wonder in her face. "Don't you?"

"No, none of it." His entire childhood was a blur, with only tiny fragments of memories scattered throughout his mind, surfacing when something accidentally triggered them. "And you don't, either." She couldn't convince him that she did. She was just making it up, the way she probably did a lot of other things.

"I have a photographic memory. I remember *every-thing*," she said sweetly.

So did he, about her. And he didn't want to. But details seemed to haunt the recesses of his mind, ambushing his thoughts and diverting them at the oddest times. "Just my luck, you're a walking computer. But even computers have glitches."

"I don't." She knelt next to Jeremy and brushed his hair from his face. He looked completely exhausted. "Come here, Little John. I'll carry you back." She moved to pick him up when Drew placed his hand over hers. She looked up at him quizzically.

"You'll trip with that dress." He shoved the hatful of candy at her. "Here, take this. I'll take him."

She took the hat and inclined her head, as if submitting. "As you wish, m'lord."

"Yeah, right." Only when it went along with what she wanted.

Drew slung his bow over one shoulder, next to the quiver. With one swift movement, he swept the boy into his arms. Jeremy slipped his arms around Drew's neck and nestled against him.

Daisy felt something tug at her heart. "I wish I had a camera," she murmured.

Drew looked at her sharply. To blackmail him? The britches were beginning to itch. "Why?"

"Because you've got an expression on your face I'd like to capture on film. Then I could take out the photograph whenever I felt inclined to bash you over the head. It would make me pause." She smiled, then turned to lead the way back. "I think you're human, Drew Addison, no matter how hard you try not to be."

"I'm not trying not to be human," he insisted, talking to her back. Moonlight shimmered on it, making her skin silvery. "I'm being logical." Tucking the boy against him, he kept a protective arm around his shoulders and walked as quickly as he could.

It was getting chilly and she wished she had rented a cape with this costume. "Like I said, that's one of the reasons I didn't become a lawyer."

She was still sticking to that ridiculous story. "Because of the logic," he recalled.

"No, because the logic got in the way of mercy, in the way of people, of justice. In the way of all the important things. Logic is very low on my priority list."

He laughed shortly and Jeremy stirred against him. The boy had fallen asleep, Drew realized. "Why doesn't that surprise me?"

She merely shook her head. "Maybe it's because you're so astute. Let's go home, Robin, and put Little John to bed."

They walked quickly down a twisting sidewalk, pools of light from street lamps guiding their way. The populace on the streets had thinned down considerably. Only a few die-hard trick-or-treaters were still out. Here and there, dogs barked behind fences, guarding their families from the threat of fairy folk.

"So, this was it?" Drew asked, breaking the silence between them.

Lost in her own thoughts about Drew, his question left her completely disoriented. "What?"

"Halloween. This is it?"

What more did he want? It seemed full to her. "Yes, pretty much."

He had no idea what the attraction was. "They go from house to house, collect candy that'll rot their teeth and make them sick and then fall asleep before they eat any of it." It all sounded very illogical when he said it aloud. "I didn't miss much."

You missed childhood, Drew. "Oh, I wouldn't say that."

There was that tone again, as if she knew things he didn't. Though he knew the conviction had no foundation, he still couldn't help the fact that it annoyed him. "No, knowing you, you probably wouldn't."

She looked up at him just before she crossed the street to their block. "You don't know me at all, m'lord."

He felt something twist within him. This time he recognized it. It was that weakness again, that weakness he had felt kissing her, getting lost in her scent, her taste. He shut it away, grateful that his arms were filled with a sleeping boy. Otherwise he would have taken her into them. "I think it's best if we keep it that way."

She shrugged too nonchalantly to please him. "If you say so, m'lord."

He did. He just didn't know if he meant it.

Chapter Nine

Daisy had left the front porch ablaze with lights. They were there to guide the steps of small trick-or-treaters on the brick walk leading to the house. But the sidewalk was empty now. It looked like any other evening in Bel Air. The costumed children were in their homes, shifting through their loot and the magic was gone for another year.

Daisy hurried ahead of Drew and unlocked the door. She held it open for him as he walked through, carrying a fast asleep Little John.

Irene rose from the armchair where she had sat during respites between onslaughts of sugar-motivated children. On the coffee table in front of her was a large, clear bowl that had been filled to overflowing with miniature candy bars and lollipops. It was three-quarters empty now.

The housekeeper hurried over to the child she had taken care of since birth. "Is he all right?" Concerned, she placed a hand to Jeremy's forehead and sighed when she found it cool.

"He's fine," Drew assured her. He looked down at the boy's face. Asleep, Jeremy looked even younger than four years old. He was such a little guy, Drew thought, and this was way past his bedtime. "He's just put in ten miles on those snazzy new sneakers of his."

Out of the corner of his eye, Drew saw Daisy looking at him. She had an amused expression on her face. And then he realized why. Oh God, now he was exaggerating, just the way she always did. He was *talking* like her. Where was his own personality going? How did she keep infiltrating his soul this way when he kept shutting all the doors?

Daisy placed Jeremy's pumpkin and the excess candy he had gathered in his cap on the table next to the bowl. She had emptied eight bags of candy into that bowl. "Looks like you had a lot of trick-or-treaters."

"Not in the last half hour or so," Irene answered. "But before that, it was like a siege. I couldn't hand out candy fast enough."

Daisy looked at her watch. It was a few minutes past nine. "I think it's time to close up shop, Irene. Thanks for manning the door."

Irene nodded. "No problem." She eyed the remaining candy in the bowl. "Well, if there's no use for these almond coconut bars," she murmured, "I'll just take a couple or three." She slipped several miniature bars into her pocket. "Good night." Smiling, the older woman made her way to her bedroom.

"She's going to be up all night if she eats all of those," Drew observed. "Too much sugar."

Didn't the man *ever* loosen up? Daisy shut off the porch light and turned to him. "I suppose you don't eat candy, either."

He could smell another disagreement coming on. Better

that, he thought, his vision skimming her low neckline again, than the other. "No."

He couldn't be for real. If it hadn't been for that moment of weakness last week, if he hadn't kissed her the way he had, she would have been completely willing to believe that he had been born sitting behind a desk, managing the corporation. As it was, the memory of that kiss was beginning to fade a little around the edges. She found herself yearning for a refresher course.

"I'd like to take you in for a blood test."

He looked at her, befuddled. "Why?"

"To see if you have any." She unwrapped one tiny bit of chocolate and popped it into her mouth, savoring it as it melted against her tongue. "*Everybody* likes candy of some sort or another."

Another broad, sweeping statement that wasn't true. He shrugged as he turned toward the stairs, shifting Jeremy into a more comfortable position in his arms. "I never got into the habit."

At times it was like trying to have a conversation with a robot. She only sighed and shook her head as she lifted her skirts and followed him up the stairs. What kind of a life did he lead? How could he even call it a life? It sounded so black and white, so devoid of textures, of excitement. She was beginning to amend her initial assessment. Compared with Drew, Jonathan had been wild and reckless when she had first met him.

Drew eased open Jeremy's door with his shoulder.

"I can take it from here." Daisy started to take the sleeping boy from Drew.

But he shook his head and continued holding Jeremy. "I've carried him this far, I might as well put him to bed, too."

The truth of the matter was, he wanted to put the boy to bed, wanted that tiny personal act to call his own. He had no idea why he suddenly needed these sorts of things, even as he fought against what he felt was a flaw in his personality. Maybe it was Jonathan's death, maybe it was the sudden brush with mortality that Jonathan's death represented. Drew didn't know, didn't want to analyze his reasons. He just knew he needed to do it.

She smiled. This was definitely a good sign. Maybe Iceman meltdown was in sight yet.

"Sure." She crossed the threshold and pushed aside the covers on the bunk bed, then moved out of the way as Drew gently laid the boy down. Daisy slowly removed Jeremy's sneakers.

When she began to cover Jeremy, Drew placed his hand over hers. "Aren't you going to finish undressing him?"

She shook her head. "I don't want to wake him. Besides, once upon a time, there were no such things as nightclothes." She tucked the blanket securely around the boy, then placed his arms on top of the covers. "People slept in their clothing."

Drew watched her turn on the night-light, then followed her out into the hall. "Going back to the dark ages?"

Daisy closed Jeremy's door. "Just giving you a piece of history." She looked at him, amusement lifting the corners of her mouth. "In case you wanted to stay in those leather pants and that jersey."

The costume. He had forgotten he was wearing it. Drew scowled as he looked down at his outfit. "You owe me for this."

She turned, her skirt whirling softly in the muted hall light, brushing seductively against Drew's legs. As she turned, he moved forward. His arm made contact with her breast. They both felt the jolt.

"What," she asked in a soft whisper, "is it I owe you, Drew?"

He had been fighting this feeling all evening. Fighting

desire ever since he'd kissed her. And he knew that the battle was about to be lost. Royally. He didn't like losing, but in losing, would he win? Or would he only succeed in losing himself? He no longer had any answers, only questions. What would it be like to kiss her again, to hold her warm body next to his and make love with her all night? What would it be like to hear that smoky, silky voice cry out his name in ecstasy?

His eyes skimmed along the outline of her lips. "You've got a smart mouth, you know that?"

It curved as she tilted her head back. "So you keep telling me."

Unable to stop himself, Drew combed his hands through her hair. Silky black strands wound themselves around his fingers. He saw her eyes darken slightly as desire awoke. His own blood heated. "God only knows why I want to kiss it."

She could feel her pulse starting to throb. If he didn't kiss her soon, she was going to have to take matters into her own hands. "Maybe it's because you're a lot smarter than you let on."

Drew lowered his head, his throat hoarse. "This isn't smart." The words whispered against her lips. "It's stupid."

Daisy rose on her toes just enough to cut the distance between their lips to a fraction of an inch. "Whatever."

He didn't remember starting the kiss. He was just suddenly in it. Hopelessly, completely in it. Desire erupted within him instantly, throwing him off balance, leaving him confused, disoriented. A beggar in a land he neither knew nor understood. He had no frame of reference to draw on. He had never *wanted* a woman this way, with this intensity, never felt as if everything was melting around him. As if *he* was melting.

All from the heat of her mouth.

He had always done things slowly, methodically, with precision. He had always looked before he leaped. Not only looked, but surveyed and measured the terrain completely. All those hopelessly outmoded adages applied to the way he lived his life.

So what was this that was happening to him now? Why was he leaping along a tightrope without a net beneath him?

He wanted to absorb her, to have her wrap herself around him and never let go. He wanted morning to never come. And all he was doing was kissing her.

It wasn't all. It was everything. The beginning of everything. And the end.

Her blood sang as his kiss deepened, taking her to points uncharted. This was it. She knew it just the way she had known when she had settled on what she wanted to do with her life. No more meandering, no more sampling. No more wondering. This wasn't merely pleasant, or interesting, or diverting. This was everything. Pain, happiness, and complete and total enchantment.

This was it.

He was the one.

Startled, a bit frightened, Daisy pushed away, her eyes open wide as she looked at him. She was in love with him. Just like that. In love. The realization had her breath backing up in her lungs.

"What's the matter?" He had gotten carried away again, Drew thought. Thank God she had stopped it when she did. There was still time to retreat.

She kept her hands on his forearms. Her legs were the consistency of whipped cream and totally useless. "I don't think we should be doing this here," she murmured, trying to catch her breath. She didn't think she would, not ever again.

His breathing was ragged. He felt embarrassed by it and didn't reply. He just nodded, slowly filling his lungs. His head still spun a little, but he could navigate without humiliating himself. "I'll just go—"

She tightened her grip on his forearms. When Drew looked at her, confused, Daisy shook her head. "I didn't say I didn't think we should be doing this. I said we shouldn't be doing this *here*."

"Then—?" Was she saying what he thought she was saying? With Anastasia, he was never sure.

She wanted to laugh but didn't, knowing it would hurt his pride. He was so incredibly adorable when he was fumbling.

"Then," she said with a nod. There weren't any more words necessary. Her fingers linked with his, she turned toward her room.

He followed her, knowing he shouldn't. Knowing that what he should be doing was running like hell to his room and locking the door. Not to keep her out, but to keep himself in. He had a feeling that if they made love now, things would never be the same again. And he didn't want anything to change, not for him.

Yet he couldn't turn away, couldn't leave. He couldn't do anything at all but want her. It was like being addicted and not having the willpower to cut himself free.

Daisy pushed the door closed behind them. It clicked softly, but the sound echoed throughout the room and vibrated within their heads. Daisy looked at Drew, waiting. The next move was his.

He felt his throat growing dry again. "This is crazy, you know."

Her grin was warm, inviting and rimmed with mischief. Her eyes sparkled and teased. "Yeah."

It was crazy, but there was nothing else he could do. Drew gave in to the desire pumping through him, churning his adrenaline past endurable limits.

Needs ran headlong into needs as he crushed her body

to his. He was acting so far against type that he had no idea who or what he was anymore. All he knew was that he was thirsty, so terribly thirsty and her lips held the sustenance he needed to survive.

Holding her to him, his mouth greedily drank in what she had to offer. His hands roamed her back, her shoulders, while his heart pounded and roared in his ears.

Still waters, she thought. It was true what they said about them, absolutely true. She never would have dreamed this need existed within him. Never would have dreamed that its twin beat in her own breast.

He needed to regain control over himself before he went too quickly, before he hurt her. Dragging air into his lungs again, Drew held her at arm's length. She was still encased in her costume, but now he viewed it as a barrier. A very cumbersome barrier.

He traced the outline of her décolleté with his fingers, watching her irises grow smoky and blur, feeling her breath as it stilled within her.

"How did people manage in the old days?"

This time she did laugh, but there was delight in it and he was unoffended. "They took things off, just the way they do now. Irene helped me with my zipper." She turned her back to him slowly. "Would you mind?"

Mind? There wasn't anything he wanted to do more. With hands that had grown suddenly clumsy, he unfastened the hook and eye above the zipper. He felt the slight tremor that went through her and it excited him. Slowly, he slid the zipper to its base, savoring the sight of her exposed back as it came into view. She had perfect skin. Skin that begged to be touched, to be worshipped.

He'd stopped. "Something wrong?" she whispered, feeling as if jelly had replaced her limbs.

"No, something right," Drew answered, his voice low. "Something very right."

Still behind her, he lowered his lips to her shoulder as he slipped his hands inside her bodice. His fingers cupped her breasts gently and he heard her moan his name as she leaned back against his chest.

Daisy's breathing grew short as she tried vainly to absorb all the sensations that were wickedly dancing through her.

Drew pressed his lips to the slope of her neck, moving with excruciatingly slow increments to her shoulders, her back. She began to shiver, needing the warmth of his embrace. Turning, she sought his mouth. As he kissed her over and over again, Drew slipped the long, trailing sleeves from her arms until the gown rested precariously about her waist.

She burned to feel him against her.

"It would help a lot if Robin took off his shirt," Daisy murmured against his mouth, tugging at the jersey in mounting frustration.

Completely steeped in her, in what was happening within him because of her, it took Drew a moment to hear her voice. "What?"

"Your shirt," she prompted, humor mixing with passion in her eyes. "Take off your shirt."

All he could do was look at her, at the way the light from the single lamp in her room bathed her skin. She was nude from the waist up and seductively uninhibited about it.

She was talking to him, wasn't she? He hadn't heard a word. "I—"

"Never mind."

Trying to curb her eagerness, hands shaking ever so slightly, Daisy unfastened the belt at his waist. Fingers flying, she undid the leather lacings at the front of his shirt, then pushed it up his chest and off his shoulders. Never once did her eyes leave his.

"Better?" she asked, fitting herself against him.

Drew's arms tightened around her, holding her closer.

He could feel her breasts against his chest, feel the erotic sensation of her nipples as they hardened.

"Better." He smiled, brushing her hair from her face. Infinitely better. There were times, he had to admit, when she was actually right. So right.

Such as now.

He pushed the gown from her hips. It fell to the floor, gathering about her ankles like a dark green lake. All she had on was the smallest bit of nylon. Soft, dark green, opaque nylon.

She saw desire flame in his eyes as he looked down at her. "I wanted to match your shirt."

And then she grinned and he had a sudden urge to nibble on her lip and taste her smile. He began with her eyelids as they fluttered shut beneath his lips.

Her head fell back as everything sprang to life within her. "I've never made love with a man in leather britches before."

Drew moved back. His eyes held hers. "How many men have you made love with?" He had no idea he was going to ask the question until it was there, hanging in the air between them.

"Counting tonight?" Daisy asked in a breathless whisper.

"Yes." The word was stark, rigid. Yet he had to hear her answer.

"One." No one else mattered, not the way he did. She wove her fingers through his hair. "None before you." *And none after,* she added silently. *Not ever again.*

He didn't believe her. A woman like Anastasia, with her zest for life, with her way of breezing through everything, had to have had countless lovers, men who she brought down to their knees in mute supplication before allowing them to experience a moment in paradise. He hated everyone of the faceless legion.

And he didn't give a damn who she had loved before, so long as she loved him now.

"Make love with me, Anastasia." Drew breathed the words against her shoulder, letting them linger on her skin like a love song that enveloped her.

Her hands were already on his hips. They felt taut and firm beneath her palms and she felt a shiver of anticipation pass over her.

She nipped his lower lip, gliding the tip of her tongue over it. His groan aroused her even more. "I wasn't about to suggest another round of trick-or-treating." Her eyes laughed, but it was that warm, inviting laugh that beckoned to his soul.

And he was racing to meet her. Racing even though he knew it meant his doom.

He felt her hands glide over his hips, his thighs, warming a path down as she tugged the britches from him. His breathing became shallow, his desire demanding as he followed suit with the scrap of material she whimsically called underwear.

All the while, he was kissing her over and over again. Kissing her eyes, her throat, her lips, unable to sate himself. The hunger was ravaging him, raging within him, pushing him on to take more and more. And she gave it to him. Met him demand for demand. The bounty she offered without asking for anything in return was endless and it humbled him.

When he had made love to women before, he had never lost himself, never lost sight of who or what he was, where he was. The earth had never moved before. It moved now. But this was California. Earthquakes were common in California, weren't they? And she was responsible for every one of them.

Colors filled his head. Colors and sights and sounds without definition, beyond description. And they were all originating from her.

A frenzy overtook him that he had to fight back. He wanted to plunge himself into her, to claim her, to make her his. But he wanted to go slowly, to savor every moment as if it were his last. For perhaps it would be.

But when they tumbled onto the bed, too weak to stand, he had no resistance left. He had to take her now. As he tucked her beneath him, his body poised, his eyes on hers, he linked his fingers with hers one by one.

"You knew, didn't you?" he asked, anticipating the answer. She had known, somehow known from the start, that they would wind up this way, here in her room, on the brink of discovery. On the edge of disaster.

She smiled, her eyes caressing his face. She could see by his look that he could almost feel her touch. "Didn't you?"

Yes, damn it, he had known. Some faraway part of him had known. Known that she was his undoing, just as Alyce had been his brother's. Perhaps he had known even at the christening, when he had first met her.

But he didn't want to think where this was going, where it would ultimately lead. All he wanted to think of was this moment.

And to somehow make it last forever.

As Daisy moved to accept him, he knew he was undone. She wrapped her legs around his body, holding tight, and the journey began.

It wasn't peaceful, did nothing to soothe. That part of it was over. Instead, they rode, wild and sweating, destined for a land they had never been to before. And they rode together.

When they came, spent, near exhaustion, to the threshold, they cried out each other's name.

But only Daisy heard.

Drew raised his head from where he had it pillowed against her breasts. It seemed like an eternity later. Or perhaps a lifetime later. His lifetime.

Because he couldn't completely fathom the magnitude of what had happened, the entire experience was almost hazy for him.

"Was I too rough?" he asked, concerned. Her lips were blurred from the imprint of his and he was afraid there might even be bruises, ready to rise. He felt as if he had been possessed. There was no other term that could quite adequately cover what he had felt. She had been a madness that had filled his blood.

"No. It was wonderful," she assured him.

Even the words took effort to say as she breathed slowly, languidly. She saw the furrow on his brow and her heartbeat quickened. He was withdrawing. So soon?

No you don't, not yet.

Daisy propped herself up on her elbow. Her hair rained down on his shoulder, synthesizing his skin. Drew could only stare, wondering how it was possible to feel aroused again when he was half dead from exhaustion.

The smile began slowly, lifting the corners of her mouth then spreading to her eyes like the sunrise on a prairie. Maybe he was only a quarter dead, Drew amended.

"Want to do it again?"

He rubbed his hand along her hair. The spirit was willing, but the flesh was weak. "In about two days, maybe, if I recover."

Humor. Very good, she thought. She'd melt the Iceman yet.

Watching his eyes, she feathered her fingertips along the light sprinkling of hair on his chest. She saw something stir within the depths. "Maybe I can stretch this out for two days," she mused.

Then she lifted her hand and slowly traced the path her

fingers had taken, this time using the tip of her tongue. She felt his stomach muscles quiver beneath her breast.

Dingdong, the Iceman's dead.

She was doing it to him. He had no idea how, or where the sudden surge of stamina was coming from, but she was doing it to him. Arousing him, making him want her again. Making him crazy.

And madness, he had to admit, had never looked so inviting.

Reaching for her, he cupped her face in his hands. Daisy looked up, a question in her eyes.

"Come here," he urged her. "I think I've just recovered."

She grinned and began to oblige, sliding the length of her body along his. She felt his response as his body grew harder, more aroused. Her grin widened.

"It's a miracle," she murmured just before she covered his mouth with hers.

Chapter Ten

When Daisy woke up the next morning, she was alone in her bed. The imprint of Drew's body was still there, but the sheet was cold. He had obviously left her side some time ago.

Sitting up, she ran her hand through her hair and let it fall in a tangled wave against her bare shoulders. Had he gone to his own room during the night for form's sake, concerned that Jeremy might see them together? It would have gone a long way in comforting her if she could have believed that to be true. But Daisy knew that was crediting Drew with being a little too aware of the way a child's mind worked. Drew had some distance to go before he reached that point in his emotional development.

But he was definitely improving, she mused as she stretched her body, remembering the way his hands had felt, gliding along her skin last night. The way he had felt, loving her. He had already come a long way from the stuffed shirt who had stood on her doorstep four weeks ago.

Well, she was going to get no answers lying here, she thought. She rose and threw on the first robe she pulled out of the closet. It was pale yellow and floor length, and it felt sleek against her bare skin, reminding her that she was nude. She wasn't used to sleeping that way. Thoughts of last night brought a sensual smile to her lips.

Knotting the sash, she noted the time. Just barely six o'clock. But she doubted very much if Drew was asleep. If she knew him, he'd be awake, holding what had taken place between them last night under a microscope, scrutinizing it from every possible angle. Taking the magic out.

She knocked softly on his door. There was no answer. She knocked harder. Still nothing. Perplexed, Daisy raised her hand to knock once more before trying the door when she heard him say, "Come in."

He sounded impatient, as if she was intruding on his space.

The man was a bear the morning after. Something else to work on. Well, she hadn't believed that he was going to make a total transformation just because they had made love last night. Even she was more realistic than that, Daisy thought as she opened the door.

There was a suitcase laying open on his bed. He was packing.

Daisy stared, the happy glow she had been savoring vanishing like a puddle of water in the hot noon sun. She forced a nonchalant smile to her lips as she walked into the room. "Going somewhere?"

He felt every muscle in his body become taut. He didn't want to face her, not yet. Pretending to be preoccupied, he took fresh socks from the drawer and placed them into his suitcase.

"Um, yes. New York." Drew shut the drawer, then opened another. "There's a board meeting I have to attend. I—"

He turned, angry at himself for fumbling, angry at her for making him fumble. It was the truth, damn it. There was an emergency situation and he had to go. Why did it sound like a lie when he told her? Trying to regain some order in his life, he had checked in with the New York contact this morning. There was a major crisis going on that left unchecked would have far-reaching repercussions and yet it sounded like a pitiful excuse he was making up just to avoid her. Why?

Because he was going for more than one reason and he knew it. He was leaving because it was necessary and because he needed space. He needed time to clear his head, to find that rational person he had always been. And he couldn't do it here, not with her so close by.

He saw she was still waiting for him to complete his sentence. "Look, I can't miss it."

He was being too defensive. "I'm not saying anything," she said rather coolly. *Coward.*

He haphazardly threw in a handful of underwear on top of the socks, not bothering to fold them. "No, but your eyes are."

"You're not intuitive enough to read eyes yet, Drew." Still maintaining the smile she didn't feel, Daisy began to roll his underwear into neat little tubes and replace them in the suitcase.

"Don't."

She raised her eyes to his innocently. "I've seen what you have under these, I can pack them for you. Besides, one of my friends is a flight attendant. She showed me how to pack more efficiently."

She took the shirt from his hand and rolled it, as well. "When did all this happen?" She placed the shirt next to the underwear. "This sudden need for a meeting, I mean. Did you get a call from your pants' phone?"

She didn't believe him, he thought. Well, why should

she? It all sounded suspiciously convenient. Make love and run. "It came up this morning. I phoned." He pressed his lips together. "This morning," he repeated unnecessarily. Damn, what had she done to him? Why couldn't she have just left him alone? This was getting too tangled for him, too complicated. He could plow through a seventy-page legal document with ease, but emotions, especially *these* emotions, were something he was a novice at. And expert status was too far away to attempt.

Placing the last shirt into the suitcase, Daisy perched on the edge of the bed and folded her hands in her lap, resigned to the turn of events. "So, how long are you going to be gone?" *You say forever and I'll cut your heart out, here and now.*

He shrugged without looking at her. "A day, maybe two. Maybe longer. I'm not sure." He walked into the bathroom for his electric razor and a few other items.

She watched as he dropped them into the case. Again, he didn't bother to arrange them. He was definitely nervous, she thought. Or guilty. "Are board meetings always this uncertain?"

He didn't know how long this was going to take. That much was true. "The meeting's about a takeover. I thought I squelched it last week. Obviously not. This thing seems to have more heads than a Hydra."

Just like his feelings, he thought, looking at her. He no sooner shored up one front, getting things under control, than another one opened up. Even now, he was reacting to her. It was six in the morning. Why did she look so good? It didn't seem right.

"But you are coming back?" Daisy lifted a brow when he didn't reply immediately. "The bargain, remember? Jeremy," she prompted.

He remembered. He remembered very well. If he hadn't made the bargain, if there wasn't a child's future at stake,

Drew knew he wouldn't be returning. To return to the scene of the "crime" and voluntarily continue in this unsettling situation without the motivation that Jeremy provided would be nothing short of insane. If there was anything Drew hated, it was not being in control, not knowing exactly what it was that he was doing. And with Anastasia, there was only the unknown, the uncertain.

"Sure I'll be back," he said, his voice harsh. "Why shouldn't I be?"

She got up from the bed and shrugged, the robe sliding down her shoulder. She adjusted it, aware that he was watching her every move. Did he expect her to pounce on him? "I don't know. Maybe because you've got this fugitive look on your face, a little like Richard Kimble, running from the police."

He was fiddling with the lock and made himself stop. "Who?"

She shook her head. Why had she expected him to know? "You probably don't watch old reruns on T.V."

He let the lid drop on his suitcase. "I don't watch television."

She hung her head in mock defeat. "Boy, I sure can pick 'em."

He didn't hear her. "What?"

"Nothing." He couldn't help the way he was, she thought. That part was up to her. The least she could do was set his mind at ease. At least for now.

She laid both hands on his shoulders and waited until he looked into her eyes. "Don't worry, Drew, I'm not asking you to make an honest woman out of me. That's something that's passé." A small smile creased her lips. "Unless you believe in love and romance and silly things like that."

She might not be asking him to marry her, but she was asking for something. Something he couldn't give. Commitment. "Um, Anastasia, what happened last night—"

"Was beautiful," she said quickly, "and I'm not going to let you spoil it by dissecting it, or looking for the logic in it—"

Logic? "There wasn't any." Making love with her had to be the most illogical thing he had ever done in his life. And the most exciting.

"Exactly." She dropped her hands from his shoulders. "And that's just the way I like it."

He didn't begin to understand her. Not on a conscious level at any rate. Unconsciously he could ascribe a dozen meanings to what she was saying, all of them confusing as hell. He dragged a hand through his hair. "God, you are the most frustrating woman—"

She turned from the doorway, looking over her shoulder. "Got you stirred up, don't I?" She smiled wickedly. He'd be back and that was all she needed to know right now. "It's a start."

She paused, wondering if it was necessary to remind him. She took a chance. "Don't forget to say goodbye to Jeremy."

Drew looked at his watch. It was too early. "He's sleeping."

It *was* necessary to remind him, she thought with an inward sigh. Just when she thought he was learning. "So, wake him up. He needs to hear goodbye followed by hello in his life."

The woman definitely needed to come with an instruction manual. "Can that be translated into something someone with a logical mind can follow?"

She crossed to him again. "You can't just slip out of his life conveniently for days at a time." *The way you seem to be able to do out of mine.* "He needs to know where you're going and that you'll be back. He's still on very shaky ground, emotionally."

Drew saw no evidence to substantiate what she was saying. Jeremy appeared to be as cheerful as any other four-year-old. She was creating problems where there weren't any. "He seems fine."

Daisy wasn't convinced of that. There was something in Jeremy's eyes, something that told her the worst was yet to come. He had accepted his parents' death too easily after the initial shock had faded. She wished with all her heart that Drew was right, but she had a feeling that she was.

"People are full of surprises when you lift the lid. Even little people." She touched Drew's arm, imploring. "Wake him up. Trust me on this."

Trust her.

How could he trust her? About this, perhaps, if he stretched it. But not about anything else. She was the one who brought total chaos into his orderly mind, into his orderly life. How could he trust someone like that about anything? The only thing he could trust her for was to do more of the same.

He snapped the locks on his suitcase closed one at a time. "All right. And when I get back, we'll talk." Gripping the handle, he began to walk out of his room.

"Or avoid each other," she murmured as she followed close behind him.

He heard and pretended not to. Because she was probably right. Drew didn't want to talk, didn't want to think, didn't want to feel until the serenity returned. Well, he amended, not serenity exactly, but a kind of peace. A lack of personal turbulence at the very least.

"By the way, why are you taking a suitcase?" she asked just before he went into Jeremy's room.

"Carrying clothes in my teeth is cumbersome."

He wasn't prepared for the pure delight that he heard in her laughter. For a moment he felt his tension abating, as if he wasn't really running for his life. As if all he was doing was simply going to a meeting in another city for a short while with every intention of returning. Willingly and eagerly.

"I meant, if you're going to New York, you have an apartment there. With clothes and a razor. Why was it necessary for you to pack anything at all?"

She was right. He didn't know why he had packed, except that perhaps it symbolized something to him. A neat, orderly withdrawal. "Maybe I just wanted something to hold on to."

"Fine." She took the suitcase from him and placed it on the floor. As he looked at her, almost spellbound, she placed his hands on her waist, rose on her toes and took his face in her hands. "Hold on to this until you get back."

And she kissed him, effectively disintegrating what was left of his functioning mind.

Drew sat in his penthouse apartment, looking down on the city. From the twenty-second floor, it didn't look dirty, or cold, or disinterested. It looked like a city of shining lights and tall buildings that stretched to touch the sky. A twinkling jewel-studded necklace for him to appreciate. Alone.

He missed her.

Damn it, he missed her, missed the sound of her voice, the smell of her hair, the sight of her quirky smile. The taste of her mouth.

He'd been gone only four days and he felt as if it was an eternity. What was happening to him?

He had hoped by returning to New York that everything that had happened in California would become a blur, a memory that would slowly fade. That's the way he had always reacted to traveling before. All his trips to Japan, to London, to Paris seemed like trips that had happened to someone else after a few days back. Reality was here, at Addison Corporation. And on the twenty-second floor of the Templeton Building where he had lived for the last eight years.

Or at least it had been. A little more than a month ago.

The Hydra had been completely beheaded yesterday. The takeover was permanently terminated. He could have caught a plane for the west coast last night, but he didn't. He had purposely remained another day, trying to recapture the old feeling. The feeling of belonging. It eluded him like a whimsical butterfly fluttering through a field of wildflowers.

He banged a fist on the coffee table and his coffee cup shook dangerously. What had she done to him?

He had only been gone from the New York office a month, an insignificant month. In that time he had been in daily contact with the people he normally dealt with via telecommunication hook-ups and fax machines, as well as constant calls on his "pants' phone."

The term had him smiling despite himself. It was supposed to be as if he were still there, in New York. As if, by maintaining this sort of visual contact, he could fool himself into believing that he hadn't actually left at all.

But he had left. He hadn't been in New York. He'd been in a house in Bel Air, living with a woman who seemed bent on redecorating the interior of his soul. Escaping, it should have given him a sense of overwhelming relief to be here, safe and sane in his apartment.

It should have.

But it didn't.

He took a sip of his coffee and pushed it aside, dissatisfied. As dissatisfied as he was with being in New York. He felt as if he had left a piece of himself behind in Bel Air. Part of his sanity, no doubt. He rose and walked to the huge bay window. The city lay at his feet, a beguiling panorama. What more could he want?

He knew the answer but refused to admit it to himself.

He pressed his hand against the cool glass and looked out. Right now, what was she doing? What was Jeremy doing?

When he had reluctantly woken the boy up before he left, Drew had been surprised by a display of tears. Still sleepy, Jeremy had thrown his arms around Drew's neck and just held on, without saying anything at all, only crying. And then he had let go and quietly said goodbye. It had been almost spooky for Drew. Did four-year-olds act that adult?

Drew turned his back to the city and eyed the telephone on his clear coffee table.

No, he wasn't going to call. He was stronger than that.

He hadn't a clue how four-year-olds were supposed to behave, really. He hadn't a clue about anything anymore. Why else would he feel, absurdly so, that he didn't belong in the very place where he *did* belong? The restless feeling threw him off balance completely. It was like trying on a favorite pair of shoes that had worked their way to the back of the closet and discovering that after all this time, they pinched.

He was going crazy, he thought, and would probably reach that destination soon since he was flying back tomorrow morning.

Searching for a diversion, Drew looked around his apartment and tried to picture Jeremy amid the white austere furnishings, the pristine white rug. Maybe he'd redecorate. White wasn't practical around children. Drew had no doubts that when the three months ended, Anastasia would give him custody of Jeremy. After all, she had to have seen how the boy held on to him. The boy loved him. That had been her point, hadn't it, for this enforced living arrangement? To see how Jeremy reacted to him. Jeremy was going to be his, just the way he had wanted. Drew was confident that he had everything going for him. The family name, money and the boy's affection.

He trailed his fingers along the top of the sofa. The day after New Year's he'd be back here permanently with Jeremy.

Just the two of them.

Drew had no idea where this strange, dissatisfied feeling was coming from. He'd be getting exactly what he wanted. What was the problem?

With a sigh, he picked up the telephone receiver, suddenly wanting desperately to talk to "the problem." He didn't know why, he only knew he had to. It was as if he was half sleepwalking through his life.

The telephone rang four times before there was an answer. He stayed on, waiting it out. He had no choice in the matter. He was even willing to settle for listening to the voice on her answering machine. In a way, it would have been almost preferable. At least that way, she wouldn't know he had called.

The receiver on the other end lifted and a sleepy voice murmured "Hello?" breathlessly against his ear. He felt something twist inside. He was beginning to recognize it for what it was. Raw desire.

Drew wrapped his fingers around a pencil so tightly he almost snapped it in two.

"Hello?" This time Daisy's voice was clearer, more alert.

"Hello, Anastasia. It's Andrew. Um, Drew. I just wanted to tell you that I was flying out tomorrow." Too tense suddenly to sit, Drew perched on the back of the sofa.

"You're coming home?"

Home. She made it sound as if the house in Bel Air was his home as well as hers. This was home. Here. In New York, not California.

If that was true, why was he arguing with himself about

it? God, when he had flown out to L.A., he had had all the answers. Now he had all the questions instead and none of the answers fit.

He didn't respond to her question directly. "I'm taking the eight o'clock flight."

"A.m.? P.m.? In or out?"

She sounded awake now and her questions chagrined him. They shouldn't have been necessary. It wasn't like him not to give details like that automatically.

"A.m. I'm leaving JFK at eight in the morning." The ticket his secretary had purchased for him was on the coffee table. He flipped it open for the fifth time since this morning, checking to see if it was still there. Staring at it, Drew told her which airline he was taking.

"Fine. Then I'll meet you at LAX at ten o'clock, my time."

"You don't have to do that." He hadn't called to ask her to meet him. Had he? He wasn't certain anymore, but he didn't want her thinking he was asking. She might construe that to mean he was eager to be with her. "I know my way around."

There was a pause at the other end of the line and he thought he had lost the connection. And then she spoke again. "That's okay. You don't have to worry, Drew. My hands'll be on the wheel at all times."

"I wasn't worried about that." That sounded incredibly stupid. "I mean—"

Damn, what did he mean? He'd spent four days thinking about nothing else but her since he had gotten on the plane. There was three thousand miles between them. Three thousand miles between what he wanted and what he knew was wrong for him. All wrong. They had nothing in common except for the love of one child. Why couldn't he just be logical about this? He'd always been so logical before.

Logic had absolutely nothing to do with this. "I've

missed you, all right?" He fairly barked the admission into the receiver. "Satisfied?"

"Not if you're not."

"Now who's dissecting things?" He rose and began to pace about the apartment restlessly. The sound of her voice was making him want her again and making him feel trapped at the same time.

"Must be the company I've been keeping."

He heard the smile in her voice and could see it in his mind's eye. Spreading slowly, lifting the corners of her mouth. He felt himself getting aroused.

What the hell was he doing to himself?

"How's Jeremy?" It was a safe topic—Jeremy's welfare—one about which they were both in agreement, at least in theory.

"He's fine. He keeps asking me when you're coming home." It was a good sign, she thought, his asking about the boy. Now if Drew would only realized that they all belonged together as a unit, everything would work itself out well. But that, Daisy knew, was going to take some time. She only hoped that she'd have enough. New Year's Day was not that far away.

There were a hundred things Drew wanted to say to her, yet nothing would come. It was as if his brain had disengaged from his tongue. "So, I'll see you tomorrow, I guess. But don't bother picking me up at the airport. I'll grab a cab. I might want to stop at the office first."

"Tomorrow," she promised.

The last time he flew to California, only a month ago, anxiety and agitation had been his constant companions on the trip because of Jonathan's death. They were back at his side again, but for a whole different spectrum of reasons.

Drew stared out the window, watching the cloud formations in the distance without seeing them at all. He felt like a man who no longer knew his own mind. He couldn't wait to arrive in Los Angeles, yet he didn't want to go. It was a little like standing in line, waiting for a ride on a giant roller coaster. It was both exhilarating and frightening at the same time.

Just like Anastasia was. Just like his feelings for her were.

It was a smooth flight all the way, if he didn't count what was going on in his stomach. When Drew deplaned, he bypassed the groups of people clustered at the luggage carousel, grateful that he had brought along only one suitcase. He didn't need more things trying his patience. He was agitated enough as it was.

He had no idea why he was scanning the crowd, looking for her face. He had all but ordered her to stay home. There was no reason to expect her to be here.

And yet, he hoped.

Maybe he should have stayed away a little longer, he thought. He needed more time to get a better grip on himself. The takeover had been stopped once and for all, mainly due to his efforts. Why couldn't he be this efficient with his private life?

As he walked toward the doors that led outside the building and to the line of queued-up taxicabs, he felt his left arm being taken while someone was simultaneously tugging on his right.

"Hi, stranger." The sultry voice washed over him, awakening every nerve in his body.

He could only stare at her, and grin like an idiot, he thought helplessly. "You came."

She brushed a kiss all too quickly against his cheek. "Did you ever have any doubts?"

Any answer he might have given was interrupted by the bouncing child on his right. "Uncle Drew, Uncle Drew," Jeremy yelled excitedly, still tugging.

Without thinking, only reacting, Drew scooped the boy up into his arms and hugged him.

Well, well, well, Daisy thought, *more progress.* At least he was coming right along on one level.

Uninhibited, Jeremy planted a wet kiss on Drew's cheek. It landed somewhere just beneath his eye. The boy threaded both hands around his uncle's neck and grinned broadly, relieved. Aunt Daisy had said he was coming back, but Jeremy hadn't been altogether certain until this moment. "What d'you bring me?"

Uh-oh. "Me." Drew had a sinking feeling that it wasn't quite what Jeremy was hoping to hear. At least, not exclusively.

"Oh." Jeremy's smile faded a little around the edges, giving way to a touch of disappointment.

"Was I supposed to bring you something else?" Drew stalled, his mind racing around. Was there anything in his suitcase he could pass off as a gift? He should have thought of that, he realized, when he was leaving New York. But he had never had a small boy waiting for him before.

"Hey, look, Tiger." Daisy nudged Jeremy's arm to get his attention. "Look what Uncle Drew has in his pocket."

As Drew looked down at the pocket in question along with Jeremy, Daisy pulled her hand up with a flourish, holding a wrapped package aloft. Though the package was small, its dimensions wouldn't have allowed it to comfortably fit into Drew's pocket.

Jeremy seemed blissfully unaware of that fact as he eagerly grabbed for the gift. Securing it, he planted another kiss on Drew's cheek. One that made Drew feel warm and guilty at the same time.

Drew set the boy down and looked at Daisy. He hadn't seen her carrying anything except for her small purse. "One of your many careers involve being a magician?"

"Pickpocket," she corrected. Her eyes were dancing and

he had absolutely no idea if she was putting him on or not. After living with her for a month, he wouldn't put anything past her.

"You think of everything." He nodded toward the package.

"Not everything, but I'm working on it." And then her smile softened and he felt the sinewy strands of desire twist a little tighter in his belly. Daisy's lips brushed against his as she murmured, "Welcome home."

It wasn't his home, not really. But he no longer knew where he belonged. Except, perhaps, within the warmth of her kiss.

Jeremy was busy sending bits of wrapping paper flying as he unwrapped his gift, the latest action figure from a popular Saturday morning television program. That gave him a second, Drew thought.

Placing his suitcase on the ground next to him, Drew used both hands to secure Daisy in place. And then he kissed her the way he had been dreaming about kissing her since he had gotten on the plane to New York.

Time stopped. The world stopped. They were no longer in a crowded airport with people milling all around them and a little boy at their feet. They were at the beginning of the path that they had forged for themselves with the fires of passion.

Daisy looked a little stunned and very, very pleased when their lips parted. She touched his face in awe. "You really did miss me."

He held her for a moment longer, enjoying the way his fingers comfortably fit around her waist. "Yes, damn it, I really did."

"I've never been cursed at quite that way before," she told him, amusement highlighting her features. "I think I kind of like it."

She looked down at Jeremy. Typically the boy was making his figure do some tricks of derring-do he had recently seen on television. Beckoning, she took his hand in hers.

"Let's get out of everyone's way, Jeremy. It's time to go home." Ushering Jeremy toward the door, she linked her other arm through Drew's.

Drew knew he shouldn't let that sound as good as it did to him. His future lay in a totally different direction than hers did.

But at least, he thought as they walked to the parking lot, they had the present.

Chapter Eleven

At first glance, it seemed as if every parking space in the
immediate area was taken, but Daisy had managed to find
a spot not too far from the loading and unloading zone in
front of Drew's terminal. As they walked through the electronic doors, Drew felt as if the actual land was greeting
him. The air was warm, the sky sunny. A picture-perfect
day. Five hours away, in New York, he had left behind a
gray, overcast sky and temperatures in the thirties. An altogether nasty day. Somehow, it almost seemed like an
omen.

Except that he didn't believe in omens.

He had to set the tone without further delay. He'd already
lost precious ground by letting her know how much he had
missed her. There was no point in perpetuating something
that he knew had no future.

"I am going to have to stop at the office," Drew reminded Daisy as they reached her car.

She unlocked the passenger side and then walked around the hood to her side. "I never doubted it for a moment." Drew thought he detected a tinge of teasing sarcasm, or was that just his imagination? "We just wanted to see you before you went into hibernation again, didn't we, Jeremy?"

Jeremy was already in the backseat, orienting his new action figure to a world he had conjured up in his mind. He stopped and looked at his aunt quizzically as she got into the driver's seat. "What's hi-ber-na-tion mean?" He said the word very carefully, as if he was aware of forming each syllable.

Daisy strapped in, glancing at Drew out of the corner of her eye. "It's what bears do in the wintertime. Put your seat belt on, honey."

"It is on. You don't have to 'mind me. I'm not a baby." Jeremy cocked his head as he turned toward Drew. "And Uncle Drew's not a bear." Drew smiled at Jeremy for coming to his defense and Jeremy sat up straighter, proud of the recognition.

Daisy saw Jeremy's expression in her rearview mirror. A little male bonding going on here, she thought with a smile. "No," Daisy started the car, "not anymore."

Drew raised an amused brow. Daisy ignored him, concentrating instead on getting them out of the parking lot.

Several miles later, with the airport far behind them, they came to a stop at a red light. Major construction was all around them. A new community of one- and two-bedroom patio homes was going up, resting on the site of what had once been rows of decaying storefronts. On the corner was just the beginnings of a mini-mall to accommodate future residents' immediate needs.

Daisy scanned the area, then smiled to herself. Corner of Berekely and Yale. This was the place. The man at the Indigo company had been so pleased with her efficiency, not to mention her price, that he had recommended Showers of Flowers...to the man in charge of building this mini-mall.

"Look, Jeremy, there're your palm trees. They're going to be planting them in the ground by the end of the week." She pointed them out.

Jeremy scrambled forward, straining against his seat belt tether for a better view, his hands on the back of Drew's headrest. "Hey, yeah."

Four palms trees stood lined up in an uneven row near the curb. They were still in boxes, their long green fonds swaying in the breeze, combing the air like massive green spiders trying to climb up on smooth glass and succeeding only in sliding back down.

"I picked out those two," Jeremy told Drew proudly. "The ones over there." He jabbed a finger confidently toward the two palm trees on the far side.

There was no way Jeremy could possibly tell the trees apart, Drew thought. He was about to point this out when he saw the warning look on Daisy's face. The observation went unspoken.

"He did a good job, too, didn't he, Uncle Drew?" she prompted as the light began to change to green. She looked at Drew expectantly before stepping on the gas.

Drew half turned in his seat. "Couldn't have picked out better ones myself," he told Jeremy.

Jeremy puffed up his chest even further and then broke into pleased giggles.

Traffic was moderately light, despite the hour and the fact that half the area appeared to be under construction these days. Down with the old, up with the new. It seemed to Daisy as if large sections of Southern California were bent on getting a face-lift.

The construction had threaded its way haphazardly into the area where Jonathan had set up the Addison Corporation's annex branch office. Directly across the street, where once had stood a seventy-year-old, eight-story office building huddling over a dilapidated stationery store and a candy store that had long since been boarded up, a new fifteen-story building was being constructed. It was just in the beginning stages, with silvery steel girders glistening in the sun like a giant erector set creation in progress.

Daisy pulled the car up to the green section of the curb. Drew unbuckled his seat belt and opened the passenger door. "Don't forget where you live," she said as she watched him get out.

He closed the door shut. "Don't worry, I won't." That was just the problem. He knew where he lived. He knew, if he was being honest with himself, where he belonged. And it wasn't here.

"See you at seven," he told Jeremy.

"Make it five," Daisy advised amiably. Her voice hung in the air as she pulled away from the curb.

He made it at five.

He hadn't really meant to, it just worked out that way. Traveling in the air for five hours had made him extraordinarily tired.

Or at least that was what he told himself as he got out of the cab in front of the house. It had nothing whatsoever to do with the fact that he wanted to see her, nothing to do with the fact that the importance of work somehow had waned in comparison to the way he had felt when Jeremy had thrown his arms around him.

Or when he had kissed Anastasia.

He was just tired, that was all. A man had a right to be tired and come home, didn't he?

It was funny that he had never had these internal arguments with himself before he had set foot on California soil for more than a day at a time. Now it seemed to occur on a regular basis.

He was about to insert his key in the lock when the door opened.

"Right on time." She'd hoped that he wouldn't revert back to his old behavior of staying late at the office, but she hadn't been certain. Seeing him here heartened her immensely.

For a moment Drew could do nothing but just look at her. Instead of her usual jeans and pullover, she was wearing a soft, feminine peach dress, with a flared skirt that showed off her legs to a fault. It made him think of peach sherbet. It was a silly thought, likening a dress to food. But it did remind him of that. He also remembered that he had a particular fondness for peach sherbet and the way it tasted as it melted on his tongue.

"What were you doing, watching for me?" He turned to look at her as she closed the door. The skirt swirled, brushing against her thighs, making him want to do the same.

"No," she answered solemnly, making him feel like an idiot for assuming that she had been. Of course she had better things to occupy herself with than standing at a window, waiting for him to come home.

And then her eyes gave her away. "Jeremy was." Even as she said it, Jeremy was emerging from his post in the living room, joining them. "Make a good scout, too, don't you, Jeremy?"

He lifted his head high as he fairly strutted before his uncle. "The best."

Drew dropped his briefcase by the hall table, where it would undoubtedly remain, he thought, for the rest of the evening. He had no desire to crowd his head with dry details. Not tonight.

"That's right." He placed a hand on the boy's shoulder. "Always be the best."

Jeremy raised his brows and looked to Daisy for confirmation. Daisy winked at him, brushing his bottom and scooting him along to the dining room. "Trying is what counts. Always try your best."

Trying without succeeding had never been enough for Drew. Success was all that counted. The world was filled with runners-up whom no one remembered. "Why does there always seem to be a difference of opinion between us?" Drew wanted to know.

"Because you choose to be stubborn." The statement was said matter-of-factly, with more than a trace of fondness. Daisy linked both her arms through his as she led Drew to the dining room. "But that's okay. You're allowed."

He shook his head as he sat down at the head of the table. He felt like a salmon trying to swim upstream during a monsoon. It wasn't easy, no matter how intent his goal.

"Welcome home, Mr. Drew," Irene said as she set a roast leg of lamb in front of him.

Drew looked to Daisy, but she merely lifted her shoulders innocently. "How did you know?" Roast leg of lamb was his favorite meal.

She spread her linen napkin carefully on her lap, wondering if he would be pleased or annoyed that she had set foot into his private world. "Orlando told me."

"You spoke to my valet?" Why hadn't the man said anything to him when he was home?

"Yes. At the same time I asked for your measurements for the Robin Hood costume."

She was a lot more thorough than he had given her credit for. If she had been a rival competitor, he would have been very leery of her, Drew thought, grateful that she wasn't.

He glanced at Jeremy.

Or was she?

Dinner reminded him once more of everything that had been missing from his life as a child. When he was a young boy at home, dinner had been a quiet affair. He couldn't remember ever volunteering a single sentence, or ever hearing Jonathan relate a story. He and his brother spoke only when spoken to. Even his parents hardly ever said a word. The silence at the table each evening had been deafening.

After his mother had divorced his father, there had been boarding school. Dinner there had been a painful experience because he was so introverted. Jonathan had been there to protect him, to act as his shield, but dinner had never been anything pleasant to look forward to. Living on his own, dinner meant the consumption of fuel to keep going, or something that was going on while he was wooing a rival or getting a client to see things his way.

Dinner had never been like this, full of noise and laughter. Boyish laughter. Jeremy talked almost nonstop, filling Drew in on four days' worth of activities, predominantly his, although a few children at his pre-school did appear in the telling from time to time. With a wealth of information coming his way, Drew found he had difficulty keeping track of everything. Especially since Jeremy had a habit of backtracking to throw in yet another detail he had forgotten to mention.

Drew's head was swimming by the time Irene cleared away the dishes.

"Did you follow all of that?" Drew lowered his voice as they walked into the family room. Jeremy had a new electronic game he wanted to show Drew.

She grinned. Dinner had been a pleasurable experience for her, as well. Drew was still a little stiff, but he wasn't the solemn, restrained man he had been. She was confident that things would work themselves out to her satisfaction by the time the end of their bargain arrived.

"Every last word."

She had to be kidding, Drew thought. But, then, with her rapid-fire mouth, maybe she wasn't.

"Hurry, Uncle Drew, I want you to see this," Jeremy urged eagerly.

She gestured Drew into the room ahead of her. "Your public awaits."

Drew knew better than to groan.

Jeremy finally wound down around eight o'clock. Once in bed, he had insisted that Drew read a story to him. It had taken ten minutes to choose the proper book.

"It's called being selective," Daisy said to Drew, noting his bemused expression.

"It's called stalling tactics," he returned in a whisper to match hers. "I used them all the time myself."

She gave him a knowing look as he sat beside Jeremy's bed. "Yes, I know."

Drew said nothing. Instead he began to read. It amazed him that the live wire who had been fairly bouncing all over the family room just a few minutes earlier, fell asleep by the time he reached page three.

"I guess I didn't put enough inflection into it," Drew murmured with a smile as he closed the book.

Daisy took it from him and replaced it on the shelf. "He just ran out of steam." She tucked the cover around the little boy, thinking how much she loved him, how effortlessly he helped to fill the ache she had in her heart because of her sister's death. "It does happen."

Drew walked out with her. "It doesn't happen to you, not so's I've noticed."

She closed the door and turned around. "What have you noticed?"

Everything. Your fragrance, your hair, the way your hips move when you walk, calling to me. "That you smell good." Drew watched the smile curve her lips. "That you've got a wicked mouth—"

She couldn't help the laugh that rose to her lips. "You mean that in the best possible way, of course."

He fit his hands around her waist. He couldn't help himself. He didn't even remember doing it. It was just something that happened automatically. "Of course."

She let out a sigh. It was so good to have him here. "My wicked mouth has missed you."

He skimmed his knuckles along her cheek. "No one to be sarcastic with?"

"I'm never sarcastic. I just react." She brushed a kiss against his lips, savoring the taste she found there. Yearning flooded through her. "Like now," she said softly, her body swaying into his.

He was tempted, so sorely tempted. But it wasn't fair. Not to him, not to her. To let this go on really wasn't right. "Maybe we shouldn't."

She saw the war that raged within his eyes. The war between needs and doubts. She knew which side she wanted to win. "For an intelligent man, you certainly have some dumb ideas."

No, he wasn't going to allow himself to get carried away. She had to hear him out. He anchored her in place with his hands. "Daisy, as much as I want you—"

She tilted her head. He was much too serious. She was always in trouble when he became serious. "Go on, this sounds promising," she teased, hoping to nudge him out of his mood.

She'd found the right word to use. "That's exactly it, I can't promise."

Her eyes held his. Didn't he know anything about her

yet? "Have I asked you to? Have I asked you to promise me anything?"

No, she hadn't asked. But it wasn't fair to take from a woman this way and not give her something in return. And he couldn't, no matter how much he wanted to. He couldn't give her what she needed, what she deserved. It wasn't in him to give.

He took her hands in his, holding them still. If she touched him, if she placed her hands on his chest, he couldn't think straight. She had a way of destroying his thoughts, except those that centered on her.

"Don't you understand? I don't know how to be intimate with you. I can kiss you, touch you, make love with you. But I can't be intimate. It's all locked up inside."

What had happened to him to tie him in knots this way? Was it the way they had been raised? Of course it had, she thought. From what Jonathan had told Alyce, there been no warm, nurturing love for the two boys as they had been growing up. Not even the smallest drop.

She feathered her hand along his cheek and cupped it. "Then let me set it free," she whispered.

Something broke down within him. Resistance crumbled. Drew dragged her mouth to his, thrown off balance by how much he needed to feel her mouth against his, to hold her body against his own.

Her kiss was warm, giving, loving. There was no thought to herself, only of him. He wanted to drop to his knees and beg her to love him.

He wanted to take her here and now, without a thought to tomorrow. Now was all that mattered.

He did neither. He absorbed what she had to give and demanded more, his mouth plundering hers. His blood roared in his ears as he pressed her closer, ever closer to him. He kissed her as if his very life depended on it, for at this one moment in time, it did.

She never ceased to surprise him. Even thinking he knew what he was in for, he was woefully unprepared. Each time it was the same. Astounding. Each time, it was different. Stronger, better.

He had to catch his breath, or go completely under. With his heart racing, he leaned his forehead against hers. "You have a hell of a way of conducting an argument."

She felt herself glowing as anticipation licked at the edges of her nerves. "I never argue."

He laughed, enjoying the way the sensation rippled through him, like sunshine. "Ha!"

"I cajole." Straightening, she opened the first button on his shirt. "I coax." Another button came free. "I reason."

He covered her hands with his own, but didn't remove them. "You haven't even got a nodding acquaintance with reason."

"Sure I do." She smiled into his eyes. "You're the soul of reason. And I'm acquainted with your soul."

Still cupping her hand, he turned it over. "It's right there in the palm of your hand."

She knew better. And so did he. "No, it's not. You still have it safely tucked away. And I wouldn't reduce your soul to such paltry portions."

She undid the last button. Splaying her hand over his chest, she thrilled to the heartbeat she felt beneath her fingers. His heart was beating fast. For her. "Now, are you going to make love with me, or do I have to hit you over head and drag you to my room, caveman style?"

He wondered if she would. She was a free enough spirit to indulge that fantasy.

"No dragging necessary." Allowing himself one small, swift kiss, almost chaste by comparison to what had come before, Drew lifted Daisy into his arms and carried her to her room.

She closed her eyes, savoring the sensation of being

swept away. Her dress softly floated onto the gray-blue cover on her bed as he set her down.

The pace was slow this time, slow and lyrical. They both knew what was there, waiting for them. They took their time, deriving pleasure from the journey. Drew undressed her a layer at a time, his fingers exploring secrets he had just begun to discover the first time. She felt so delicate, almost fluid beneath his touch, yet he knew she was strong in the most subtlest of ways. She was just possibly the strongest willed person he had ever known, this woman who sighed beneath the lightest caress.

A series of flirtatious tiny buttons hid her from him. There must have been at least twenty of them running down the front of her dress. "How long did it take you to get into this?" he marveled.

"Longer, I hope, than it'll take to get me out."

He watched her eyes, thrilling in the way they clouded and darkened as he made his way patiently down to her waist, undoing the tiny pearl buttons one by one. The material finally parted, a silken peach curtain hanging on either side. She wasn't wearing a bra or camisole underneath.

His breath caught in his throat as he pressed a kiss to her breasts, first one, then the other. He'd been right. Peach sherbet was still a favorite with him.

"You're a mystery," he murmured, peeling another layer of clothing away. "A beautiful, tantalizing mystery."

He was learning, she thought, pleased. "Haven't you heard?" She arched to his touch as he slipped the dress from her shoulders. "Women like to be mysterious."

Slowly, ever so slowly, he removed the dress from her hips, down the long length of her legs, until he finally tossed it aside. She lay before him dressed in nothing more than panties and a smile. "I haven't noticed anything. Nothing but the sound of your voice, ever since I arrived in L.A."

She laughed, a soft, sexy, throaty laugh that hit him like a velvet-gloved punch straight to his abdomen.

The panties vanished, as did the remainder of his own clothing, forgotten obstacles as soon as they fell to the floor.

Drew caressed, reveled, dreamed, all the while heating her body as quickly as he did his own.

The kisses were deep and they both sank into them, into the darkness that was there just before the light.

It felt, she thought, arching into each gentle, sweeping stroke, as if he were memorizing every movement, preserving it for some future day when they would no longer be able to be this way together. A day when there was a continent between them.

She couldn't think of that, couldn't believe that it would happen. He was here with her now, and that was all she needed, all she wanted.

No, it was a lie. She wanted more. She wanted that soul he had flippantly said she had in the palm of her hand. She wanted it to open to her, to have him share more than his body with her. She wanted him to trust her enough to share his innermost feelings.

She was losing all orientation. The last time, when the lovemaking between them had been frenzied, she had hung on for the ride, exhilarating in the pace. Now that tempo was more indolent, more soothing, she fell in love with him all over again. There was gentleness here in his touch, compassion, thoughtfulness, all the things she *knew* he didn't know he possessed. She longed to make him understand. There was power in his graciousness.

She longed to stay lost with him forever.

The exquisite agony of wanting the rush to come, even while wanting to prolong the journey to that rush was once more warring within her. Within them both.

The urgency to pleasure one another increased.

She felt everything.

She felt only him, every caress, every shift of his fingers, every layer of his kiss.

Intrigued, empowered, he traced each one of her pulse points, sampling, watching as they throbbed. When he pressed a kiss to the soft skin inside of her elbow, he heard her moan and felt her shift insistently beneath him.

It brought a smile to his face. "I don't think there's any place where I can touch you that you won't react."

She laced her fingers behind his neck. "There isn't." Humor touched her eyes, rimming the passion. "Am I a science experiment now?"

There was no way to pigeonhole her. He'd learned that. "No, but you really are something."

She laughed, pleased at the simple compliment. "Very eloquent."

He trailed his fingers along the soft skin around her belly, watching in fascination as it quivered. "You chase the words right out of my head, Anastasia. You chase everything out of my head. All there is, is you, in broad, vivid colors."

"Why does that make you sound so sad?"

"Because it makes me realize what I've missed all my life. The colors. They were here all the time and I never saw them."

She offered herself to him. "Then stop missing them."

She made it sound so easy, so uncomplicated. She had an uncanny knack for reducing things to the smallest denominator. But it wasn't that simple. Not for him.

I'd probably scare you to death if I told you I loved you, she thought, aching to utter the words on her lips. To taste them and see how they felt before she pressed her mouth to his.

But she would wait and give him more time to discover what she already knew to be true. That he loved her. He just didn't know how to break down the barriers to reach her. They were barriers of his own making and he would have to be the one to dismantle them.

It was like making love to the wind. He could feel her against every part of his body, feel her essence vibrating within him, infiltrating, filling him. Holding him prisoner in its grasp.

The slow, steady pace evaporated as needs rose to a dangerous boiling point. His kisses became greedy, his caresses more possessive and she was there for him at every turn, wanting to be every woman he had ever loved, ever wanted. Wanting to be all things to him so that he would never turn away from her.

For if he did, she knew she would be lost. As lost as he had been when he had first arrived at her doorstep.

When they joined their hands, their mouths, their bodies, it was as if by some unspoken mutual agreement. And then they were speeding ahead, eagerly rushing to familiar territory, to the place where only they could enter. And only together.

She could hardly keep up. Opening to receive him, she felt his thrust as he filled her. She wanted him closer, closer; he couldn't be close enough. She would never get enough of him. Quickly, the explosions came, seizing them both and propelling them upward as if they were merely leaves caught up in a devil wind that blew in from the desert.

And when it was over, they could only hold on to each other, clinging to the sensations until they faded into mists.

"You know," she said in slow, measured words because she couldn't manage anything more, "for a man suffering from jet lag, you had an incredible amount of energy."

He felt the words rippling against his chest, felt the comfort of her warmth as her head rested there. Her cheek was just over his heart. A tranquilizing echo was passing between them. He allowed himself a moment to sift her hair through his fingers, glorying in the way it felt.

"You bring some unknown force out of me," Drew murmured has he watched her hair rain from his hand. The light from the lamp shone in it, trapped there, making it shimmer as if it were alive.

Daisy raised her head, keeping her hand on his chest. She liked feeling the beat of his heart, liked pretending it was doing it just for her. "Is the force up to another appearance?"

He lifted a brow. After what they'd been through, she could ask? "Tonight?"

She traced swirls along his chest, wiggling closer. "Tonight."

He grinned and let a sigh escape. "If you say so, but this time, *you* do the work."

She slipped easily on top of him and he could feel his fatigue melting away as if it had never been.

"Gladly."

But he didn't let her make the first move. His pride wouldn't let him.

Chapter Twelve

It had been busy from the moment they had opened their doors. Everyone, it appeared, wanted to have their landscaping completed before the holidays arrived. It wasn't until five o'clock that the hectic activity slowed. By six, Daisy had thanked her last customer, walked with him to the door and then quickly flipped the Open sign to Closed on the window.

"Ah, peace, ain't it grand?" Margaret murmured with a contented sigh. "Coffee's on me."

She went into the back office to pour them each a mug, leaving Daisy to transcribe the pile of order forms on the table into her order book. Later she would input them all into the computer to retain them on permanent file. But she didn't have time to wrestle with the temperamental machine now. Drew was coming.

At least she hoped so.

"Here." Margaret passed a blue mug with the words

Boss Lady inscribed in fire-engine red across it to Daisy. "Milk, no sugar, just like you like it."

Margaret eased herself into a chair where clients normally sat, poring through albums filled with photographs of gardens Showers of Flowers...had landscaped.

Daisy smiled her thanks and continued making notes in the book. Margaret took a sip, let the coffee wind its way through her, then looked thoughtfully at her friend. It was apparent to Daisy that she had been dying to discuss Daisy's relationship with Drew all week, but the opportunity had never presented itself.

"So how is it going with you and the Prince of Wall Street? You've hardly mentioned him at all since he got back from his business trip." Margaret leaned forward over the circular black marble table and peered at Daisy's face. "Is that a glow I detect?"

Daisy went on writing. "Could be the new rosebushes we got in this morning for the Monroes," she answered casually. "I think I'm allergic to them."

Margaret placed a hand on Daisy's hand, forcing her to stop writing and look up. "Hey, this is me. Margaret. You've talked to me about every man you've gone out with in the last seven years. The doctor, the airline pilot, the dance instructor, the—" Margaret stopped ticking off the different men on her fingers as the reason for Daisy's reticence suddenly seemed clear. She narrowed her eyes. "This one serious?"

Daisy gave up transcribing figures. She laid her pen down and picked up the coffee Margaret had brought her. It felt good going down. Margaret was getting better. "Andrew Addison, the First, is *very* serious."

As a rule, Daisy was never evasive. Margaret frowned. "You know what I mean."

Daisy held the mug with both hands, wishing the warmth would reach her soul. "He's not."

"But you are?"

Daisy nodded. "Very." She looked at Margaret. All her feelings were there in her eyes. "Margaret, I think he's the one."

For a second, all Margaret could do was gape. Daisy had always been so carefree, so blasé about her relationships before. It was almost impossible to believe that Daisy had actually fallen in love with anyone. It was usually the other way around.

"You're kidding. That's terrific!" Margaret gave Daisy a fierce hug. "Wow, this is more startling than when you finally decided what you wanted to be when you grew up—last year." The humor slowly left her face to be replaced with wistfulness as Margaret released Daisy. Margaret, Daisy knew, had been infatuated, but never in love, not really. "Tell me, I'm curious. How do you know you love him?"

That ranked right up there along with wanting to know the secret of life, Daisy thought. She didn't want to dissect why she loved him, though there were a hundred tiny pieces that went into it. The way he was with Jeremy. The way he held her. "How does anyone know? It's just there, that's all."

It was apparent by her expression that this wasn't what Margaret was hoping to hear. "Sounds like you're describing laundry detergent." She finished her coffee and set the mug down.

"Maybe." Daisy laughed. "During the spin cycle." That was what it was like, emotions all jumbled up, tumbling madly in a circle.

It was all the hint that Margaret needed. "You've been to bed with him."

To bed. That sounded much too mundane to express what had happened between them. Since he had returned, they had made love almost every night. "I've been to paradise and back."

Margaret had slid to the edge of her seat, her coffee forgotten. "So when are you getting married?"

They had made love, but she was still no closer to peering into his soul, to making him really open up to her, than she had been at the start.

"Married?" The word was followed by a short laugh outlined in sadness. "I don't even know if we're going to come to an amicable solution at the end of all this." *But I'm hoping for it.* She looked at the calendar on her desk. The days were flying by too fast. "I've got until New Year's Day to make the man see that Jeremy is better off with me—and so is he."

Margaret gave her hand a squeeze. "My money's on you, kid." She reached for her purse.

"Thanks." Daisy flashed her a smile. With a sigh, she closed her order book. "I need more than money, I need a miracle."

Margaret was rooting through her handbag, looking for her lipstick. "With me, it's a miracle if I have any money."

Daisy was more than happy to move on to another subject. The dilemma of Drew was causing her too many sleepless hours as it was. "Is that a hint for a raise?"

Margaret paused, an intrigued expression on her face. "Would it do me any good to ask?"

They both knew Margaret was kidding. Daisy paid her a generous salary. It was a known fact of life that had Margaret been earning twice the amount, she still wouldn't be able to hold on to a dime. She was too easily tempted. Margaret lived to shop.

"Asking's the easy part, Margaret." Absently Daisy glanced toward the window that looked out on the rear of nursery. "It's the getting that's hard."

Margaret applied the splash of color to her lips quickly. "We've stopped talking about my raise, haven't we?"

"Yes."

The bell over the front door jingled softly and Margaret frowned. "Can't people read?" And then she smiled. "Uh-oh, speak of the devil—or whatever."

Drew walked into the store and strode over to the table. He looked, Margaret observed, none too happy about being there.

"Well," he said to Daisy, "I'm here."

In contrast to his dour expression, Daisy grinned, relieved. "Yes, you are. I'll just go get my purse." She rose, taking the order book with her to deposit in the back office. "Close up for me, will you, Margaret?"

Drew shoved his hands into his pants' pockets and continued to look uncomfortable and restless.

"Going dancing?" Margaret finally asked when he said nothing.

He had no idea why he had listened to Daisy's behest. He had work to do. They were closed tomorrow. The entire building was closed tomorrow because of the holiday. He should be at the office now, tying up a few of the loose ends. Addison Corporation experienced its busiest season between now and the New Year. He didn't have time for foolishness.

And yet, he was here.

"Going to the grocery store," he answered.

Margaret looked at him a little oddly. "Is that what people do on dates in New York?"

He scowled, annoyed with the whole thing. Anastasia kept making the most inane demands on him. But he'd be lying if he didn't admit that a part, a very small part, he told himself, liked these traces of domesticity.

"I'm not taking her on a date. For some reason she's insisting that we shop for the damn Thanksgiving turkey together.'' He stared off toward the back office and wondered what was taking Anastasia so long. "Says it might be too heavy for her to carry.'' He snorted at the feeble lie. "I've seen her tote those fifteen-gallon things around.''

He was cute, Margaret thought, even when there was steam coming out of his ears. She bet Daisy had her hands filled with this one. But if she knew Daisy, and she did, Daisy was more than equal to the challenge. "Maybe she just likes the company.''

Drew took a look at Margaret for the first time. She didn't talk like any employee he had working for him. There was too much warmth in her voice when she spoke of Daisy. "Are all her employees this outspoken?''

"All her *friends*,'' she corrected him, "care about Daisy. She's a good person.'' The phrase "and you be good to her'' went unsaid, but was clearly implied. Margaret continued studying Drew as she elaborated. "We were all a little worried that she wasn't going to find her niche in life. What with the lawyer thing not suiting her and that fling she had as a flight attendant, not to mention—''

Drew sat down in the chair Daisy had vacated. "You mean it's true?''

"Which 'it' are you referring to?''

It didn't seem possible. Everyone he knew had had a goal in mind while attending school, and then had gone out and reached it. Or at least tried to.

"All those things she claimed she did.'' He was at a loss as how to word it. "She really did them?''

Margaret had to bite her lip not to laugh at the confusion on his face. If Daisy didn't know why she was in love with Drew, Margaret could have easily made out a list for her. Starting with incredible eyes and fantastic lips. "Yes.''

There had to be an explanation. "Oh, I suppose she told you she did all those things.''

"Yes.''

Ah-ha, Drew thought. And then Margaret continued and ruined it.

"But I was in college with her, at least one of the colleges she attended." She saw the skeptical look rise in Drew's eyes. "The one she graduated from. And I was there for the celebration when she passed her bar exam." A faraway smile creased her lips. She could go on and on, but didn't. He didn't look like the type of man you could do that with. She smiled knowingly. Daisy was unusual. "You didn't believe her, did you?"

"No," he said simply.

No, he hadn't. But Anastasia was obviously a lot more complex than she pretended to be if all this was true. Why did she seem so flighty? And being intelligent, knowing what life was like, how could she be so everlastingly cheerful?

Margaret pushed her chair way from the table. Reluctantly, she stood up, taking the empty coffee mugs with her. "Daisy graduated first in her class from U.C.L.A." There was a hint of vicarious pride in her voice. "She gave the valedictorian speech."

That he found impossible to believe. "The woman who just went to get her purse?"

"The very same. Daisy's always had so much going for her, she's never known which direction to take. I always thought she could be anything she wanted to be." She laughed fondly. "So did Daisy. That's why she dabbled so much, trying out things until she made up her mind." Her eyes narrowed. "Nothing wrong in that, is there?"

Was he mistaken, or had her voice taken on a judgmental tone? Was he on trial here for some reason? "Are you her press agent, too?"

"Like I said," Margaret answered amicably, "Daisy's friends care about her."

He leaned over the counter as Margaret began to walk

into the back room. "I appreciate the information, but what does this have to do with me?"

Dense. Handsome, but dense. Daisy did have her work cut out for her. "That's for you to figure out."

Daisy passed Margaret as she walked into the display area. "Has Margaret been talking off your ear?"

He was relieved to escape Margaret's close scrutiny. "Yes, but the woman doesn't hold a candle to you." He took her arm. "Ready?"

"Absolutely." She looked over her shoulder. "See you Monday morning, Margaret. Happy Thanksgiving."

Margaret leaned out of the back office, taking one last long look. They did make a very nice couple, she decided. "Have a nice Thanksgiving! And don't do anything I wouldn't do," she called after them as the glass door swung closed behind them.

Daisy smiled as they walked to the car. "That leaves us a very broad spectrum to choose from."

Drew had parked his car at the curb in the twenty-minute parking zone. She got in on the passenger side and buckled up.

Drew took the wheel. "I still don't see why you just don't go shopping by yourself." Why did he have to come along and suffer through this?

By now, his tone didn't faze her. Patience was needed. It probably always would be to a degree, but she didn't mind that, either. "Well, for one thing, I don't have a car, remember? It's in the shop."

Margaret had swung by the house early this morning to pick her up. Jeremy hadn't gone to pre-school. He hadn't been feeling well and had remained home with the housekeeper.

"For another, I thought this might be a good experience for you." She studied his profile. His was a bit more chiseled than Jonathan's had been, a little harder around the edges, the jaw set a little firmer, a little more stubbornly. She had already accepted the fact that she was facing a tougher challenge than her sister had. "Ever been grocery shopping?"

There had always been someone else to take care of that for him. In New York, Orlando did all the necessary shopping. Drew couldn't remember ever being inside a supermarket. "No, and I really haven't missed it."

Daisy leaned back, a smile playing on her lips. This should be interesting. "Never know until you try."

They had been going up and down the crowded aisles now for twenty minutes, Drew thought, while Anastasia debated the merits of one mushroom over another in the vegetable section, and agonized over which brand of cranberry sauce to use. Finally she pointed him toward the center of the store. Parallel rows of large, open freezers stood side by side in the center aisle. Cold air hovered mistily over a colorful montage of ice cream containers, frozen vegetables and meal entrées.

"So..." Drew looked at Daisy. "This is the frozen section." He folded his arms across his chest and rocked back on his heels. "Quite an eye-opening experience."

She led him to the meat department. "Sarcasm belongs at the check-out stands, not in the aisles."

The cart was already filled with all the items they would need for tomorrow's meal, except for the main one. It had taken some effort, but she had cajoled him into pushing the cart. With Thanksgiving one day away, Daisy was pleased to find that there were still plenty of turkeys to choose from.

She gestured him toward the rectangular freezer. "And now, sir, since it seems fitting, I'll let you choose the turkey."

He lifted a brow, eyeing her. "Is that some kind of a crack?"

"Only if you have a guilty conscience," she said sweetly. "Otherwise, it just refers to your being the head of the family." Both brows went up. "Don't turn pale on me, it's just a term to fit the oldest member of the family and since you're older than I am, you get the title."

His mind was on things other than turkeys. "How old are you?" He suddenly realized that he didn't know. It had never occurred to him to ask.

She pretended to look surprised. "Ah, a personal question."

When would he ever learn? He shook his head. "Never mind."

No, he wasn't going to shut the door, not when she'd waited so long to have him open one. She liked the fact that he wanted to know things about her, however indirectly the question had come up.

"I don't mind telling you how old I am. I'm twenty-nine." There was a woman behind him who was obviously trying to choose a turkey and Daisy and Drew were in her way. Daisy moved aside. "And you're thirty-two, so that makes you older."

He hadn't told her anything about himself, not even that. Privacy was something he guarded zealously. The less she knew, the less, he figured, she could use against him. And in this particular case, he had enough going against him, including his own willpower. "How do you know how old I am? Orlando?"

"Orlando had nothing to do with it. Jonathan mentioned it in passing once. As a matter of fact, he mentioned a lot of things." She grinned. "I probably know a great deal more about you than you'd want me to."

That's what he was afraid of. "Such as?"

She thought for a moment. "Such as you were afraid of the dark." She saw that he didn't like being reminded. But after all, he'd only been a child at the time. It was forgivable for children to be afraid of the dark. "Kids used to make fun of you and you cried—"

"I never cried," he said indignantly.

"I'd be very unhappy if I believed that," she told him quietly. "Besides," she continued, "there's nothing wrong with crying. It just means you're human." She smiled. "And I know for a fact that you're very, very human."

He murmured something unintelligible under his breath in reply.

There were things that would melt in a short amount of time in the cart. She nodded toward the freezer, pointing out one bird. "How's this one?"

He looked closer. The turkey was marked at twenty pounds and three ounces. "Isn't it rather large? Who else is coming?"

"No one, this time." She looked at a few turkeys, but decided her first choice was best. "Thanksgiving is for families."

"What do you mean, this time?" Drew asked suspiciously.

Was she planning a "next" time with a horde of people joining them? He didn't know anyone here. Besides, there wasn't going to be a "next time." He had made up his mind about that long ago. It was sticking to the decision that was becoming increasingly difficult.

Why was everything like pulling teeth with him? She was determined to thaw him out completely if it killed her. "I thought for Christmas Eve we'd invite some of Alyce's and Jonathan's friends and let you meet them."

Another shopper nudged them aside as she reached in for a turkey. Daisy kept a proprietary hand on the one she had selected. The cold hurt her fingertips, but she kept them there until the woman had made her selection and left.

"Why?" He wanted to know.

"Because you're supposed to be friendly around Christmas. It's the law. Besides, I thought you might want to meet some of the people who thought your brother was a terrific person." She frowned. "God, Drew, someone should have given you an instruction manual the day you were born. This should be inherent."

"What they should have done was given me one on you," he shot back.

Her mood dissipated and she laughed. "Then all the mystery'd be gone."

"And the confusion," he pointed out.

Daisy shrugged and turned to take out the turkey she had chosen. He knew perfectly well that she was more than capable of doing it, yet he still felt as if he should be the one taking it out. It looked unwieldy.

"Here," he said, nudging her aside, "I'll do that. You'll strain yourself."

She raised her hands, palms up, an amused smile on her lips. "That's why I brought you along."

No, she had brought him along to make him even more crazy than she already had. He dropped the turkey into the cart, squashing the bread beneath it. "Let's pay for this and get out of here."

She tugged the loaf out and frowned at it. "You're the boss."

He gave her a dark look, knowing she was laughing at him. "I guess we'd better get another loaf of bread."

"Good idea."

Yes, she was definitely laughing at him. He couldn't help thinking that it should have gotten him more annoyed than it did.

When they arrived home half an hour later, Irene met them at the door to help with the bags. "Jeremy's cold's gotten worse." She retrieved one sack out of the truck. "I've put him to bed."

"Thank you, Irene." Daisy picked up two of the bags.

Daisy looked remarkably unconcerned by the news, Drew thought. He hefted three bags, including the one with the turkey, out of the trunk and followed her into the house. "Shouldn't we call a doctor or something?"

"Not unless his cold gets really bad." She placed her bags on the kitchen table. "There're some children's cold remedies on hand in the medicine cabinet and there's still some cough medicine and decongestant left from the last time the doctor prescribed them." Irene was unpacking the groceries and putting them away, something Daisy always hated doing. "Let's go see the little patient."

The door to Jeremy's room was open. He looked absolutely miserable when they walked in. "I'm sick, Aunt Daisy."

She sat down on the bed next to him and stroked his hair. "Yes, I know, sweetheart."

"Does that mean I can't have the turkey tomorrow?"

"No, that means Uncle Drew'll carry you downstairs *to* the turkey. But think on the bright side. Maybe you'll be better by tomorrow."

He would have been disappointed, Drew thought, if she hadn't said that. It was nice to be able to predict some things about her, even small things.

Daisy kissed Jeremy's forehead. It was warm. "I'm afraid you've got a temperature, Jeremy."

Drew had always thought that was a ridiculous method to use. "Shouldn't you be using something more accurate than your lips?"

She turned to look at him. "I think they're pretty good at gauging things." Before Drew could say anything to dispute that, she looked at Jeremy. "It's my best tool, right, honey? Kisses away hurts, makes things better, takes temperatures."

Any second now, he was going to be nauseated. "Do

you have time to bend steel with your bare hands during all this?'' Drew asked.

She wasn't going to get drawn into an argument. He was still annoyed about being dragged to the supermarket. ''If the occasion calls for it.'' She stood up. ''Now, why don't you stay here with Jeremy while I see if I can find that medicine?''

''Will you play games with me?'' Jeremy asked Drew hopefully.

It occurred to Daisy that Jeremy's voice sounded just a tad more pathetic. A born manipulator, she thought.

''Games?'' she heard Drew echo uncomfortably as she left the room.

Daisy grinned to herself. Let him see that raising a child was no bed of roses, that it didn't go by the book, because what he was dealing with was a mass of exceptions with soft brown hair and big brown eyes. She'd be damned if he was going to send Jeremy to boarding school, and Drew couldn't raise Jeremy alone. He needed someone to help him. Preferably, someone who loved him.

When Drew came downstairs the next morning, he felt exhausted. It was his own fault, he thought. He had been the one to volunteer to stay up with Jeremy in case he needed something. The boy woke up every few hours, either completely stuffed up, unable to breathe, or coughing. Drew had swallowed his pride and woken Daisy up when he'd tried to put the vaporizer on and got nothing but sputtering hot water for his trouble. But the rest of the time he was determined to handle everything himself.

Consequently, it was eight in the morning, Jeremy was sleeping peacefully and Drew felt as if he had spent the night in a foxhole fending off enemy fire.

With a robe hanging open over his dark blue silk pajamas, Drew found his way into the kitchen. It wasn't easy when his eyes weren't focusing properly.

Daisy looked up from the turkey she was stuffing. She'd been up for more than two hours. There was a cherry pie baking in the oven to testify to that fact. Her heart softened as she watched Drew stumble in. "You look like hell."

Drew sank onto the closest stool at the breakfast counter. He propped his head up, afraid it would fall off if he didn't. "Last thing I need is a cheerful critic." He looked around halfheartedly. "Where's Irene?"

Satisfied that the turkey held all it should, she began to close up the bird. "I sent her home for Thanksgiving. She's staying at her sister's."

"Who's making dinner?"

She thought that fact was rather obvious. She gestured toward her handiwork. "I am."

"You cook?"

She looked at him incredulously before placing the turkey into the oven and setting the dials. "You have to ask?"

"Sorry, stupid question. I forgot I was talking to Superwoman."

He could be as sarcastic as he wanted to be. She was rather proud of her accomplishments, even if most of them had ultimately led her to a dead end. Knowledge was never wasted. "I spent six months at the Cordon Bleu." She had thought she wanted to be a chef at a fancy restaurant and eventually open up her own. But, as with other things, she had lost interest.

Drew's eyes were closing. "Naturally."

She began to clear off the counter, preparing for the next phase. "I got an A in everything, except for dessert."

Drew's eyes opened. Finally, something she didn't do well. "Everyone has to fail sometime."

She raised her eyes to his. "I got an A plus in that."

He blew out a breath, then got off the stool. "Why do I

even bother?'' he muttered. He crossed to the silent coffee-maker on the counter. It was empty. ''How does this thing make coffee?''

She'd been so busy, she hadn't had time to set it. ''Not at all if you don't put in the ingredients.'' Drying her hands, she left her work.

''Wise guy.'' He opened the cabinet overhead, not too sure what it was he was looking for, besides a can of coffee. Didn't these things take filters or something? ''I need help here.''

''Glad to hear you admit it.'' She turned him around and pushed him in the direction of the stool he had just vacated. ''Sit down and I'll make the coffee.'' She took out the filters that were next to the can of coffee. ''Jeremy still sleeping?''

She knew he was—she had looked in on the boy only fifteen minutes ago. Daisy had hated leaving Drew to take care of the boy on his own, but she felt that this was an excellent opportunity for him to see the worst side of parenting. She had stayed with Alyce and Jonathan so often, she felt like Jeremy's surrogate mother. But Drew had to be indoctrinated as to the difficulties involved with being a real parent. She wanted him to see what he was getting into. And that surviving it alone was even harder.

''Yes, which is more than I can say for me. God, I'm tired.''

''Poor baby,'' she murmured. But she was grinning.

Within moments, the coffeemaker was making noises and dark liquid was trickling into the glass pot. ''Want something to go with the coffee?''

''Yes.'' That had just slipped out. He hadn't even realized it was there, on his tongue, until he said it. He saw by the look on her face that she knew exactly what he was talking about. ''Never mind, I probably don't have enough energy for that.''

She slipped onto the stool next to him and smiled. He looked adorable with stubble on his face and dark smudges under his eyes. "You'd be surprised."

He didn't want to get himself started. It wasn't the lack of stamina. That would come. But he needed to exercise a little more self-control, starting now. They both knew this wasn't going to work out. "Don't you have to cook or something?"

She felt the hurt vibrating within her and told herself she was being too sensitive. But it still didn't go away.

"It was your idea." She got off the stool. The coffee was ready. She poured him a cup, then placed it on the counter in front of him.

He shrugged, trying to be nonchalant. "I've been known to have bad ideas occasionally."

She set her lips firmly. For the first time in weeks, she felt like hitting him. "I can think of one."

He knew what she was referring to, but he didn't want to talk about it. The time wasn't up yet. Later they would hash it out, but not now. Now all he wanted was a little peace and quiet.

She had resumed preparing dinner. He pointed to the bowl of potatoes she had peeled. They were bobbing in water. Why, he had no idea. "Need help with that?"

"That?" She looked at the bowl. "I'm going to make mashed potatoes later. Just what is it you would like to do?"

He shrugged. "Whatever you need me to do."

"Do you cook?"

He didn't answer her question. "I don't have a certificate from the Cordon Bleu, but any fool can mash potatoes."

She drained the potatoes and placed the bowl in front of him. The bottom made firm contact with the counter. "Fine, I guess that means you meet the job requirement. Here."

He stared at the potatoes for a moment. She hadn't given him a utensil. What was he supposed to use? "Um, Anastasia?"

She was busy washing lettuce. "Yes?"

"Do I just crush them?"

She laughed and the tension left her. With a twist of her wrist, she shut off the faucet. "Here, let me show you."

Chapter Thirteen

It seemed to Drew that the farther he attempted to retreat from Anastasia and his own confused, budding emotions, the farther she followed him into his world. There was no escaping her, or himself.

Thanksgiving turned out to be, as she had assured him, a family affair. And for perhaps the first time in his life, Drew felt as if he was part of a family. Until he had sat there, joining hands over the meal that included his contribution—incredibly liquidy mashed potatoes—saying grace, he had never felt as if he had really belonged to a unit. Up to that moment, Jonathan had been the only person he had ever felt close to. For the past ten years, the corporation had been his mother, father, wife, everything. If that seemed a little cold and bloodless at times, there were still deeply satisfying feelings to be garnered from watching the firm thrive and expand through his guidance at the helm.

Or at least there had been. Now he found himself not

quite so content, not quite so satisfied. And it was all her fault.

He hit a key on his keyboard and the screen on his computer momentarily blinked, then jumped to a new spreadsheet. It would be over soon, he thought. There was a calendar on his desk, marking time. A little more than one more month and he would be back in New York with Jeremy. Permanently. And she would remain here. Drew couldn't ask her to give up her business. He knew what that meant. She belonged out here. And he belonged on the east coast, with Addison Corporation. He sighed, hitting another key. The future didn't look very good, at least for him.

He knew he had to accept that, accept the inevitable. He always had before. It was time to act like a responsible adult, not like some adolescent, cutting classes.

Yet the more he hid from her, the more he buried himself in paperwork, the more he wanted to be with her. The situation was driving him crazy. He couldn't wait until this madness was over.

He wondered if there was a way to make time stop.

Insane, he was going absolutely insane, he thought.

There was a knock on his door and he looked up, welcoming the diversion. Anything to stop thinking about Daisy...er, Anastasia. It seemed he was having a change of heart toward her. He straightened in his chair, turning it so that he could face the door. "Come in."

She did. Like the warm Santa Ana winds that blew in from the desert, she swept into his office, enveloping everything around her. She pushed the door closed behind her without bothering to look. "Hi."

He supposed that it had been just a matter of time before her invasion campaign brought her here. Still, he had to ask. "What are you doing here?"

Daisy came around his desk and stood next to him. She

leaned a hip against the teakwood edge and her thigh brushed against his arm. The straight red skirt she was wearing was a good four inches above her knees, showing off legs that made his feel weak. She had topped off her outfit with a bulky black sweater that only hinted at what was beneath. But he knew. And desired.

"We are going Christmas shopping," she informed him blithely, as if they had spent the previous evening discussing the matter instead of her swooping out of the blue with this preposterous notion.

Drew sighed, pushed himself away from his desk and reached into his jacket breast pocket. Taking out his wallet, he flipped through until he came to a gleaming gold card. He removed it and held it up to her. "Here."

She looked at the plastic plate as if it was an eviction notice. With a shake of her head, Daisy pushed his hand away. "I don't want your charge card, Drew. I want you."

His brow furrowed. "Excuse me?"

"To go shopping with me," she clarified, knowing exactly what he was thinking. A look of mischievous pleasure filled her eyes. "Your other interpretation we can take up later."

Drew dealt with straight-talking people all day, or had, until he had come out to Los Angeles. But he certainly wasn't used to a woman being so direct about a matter he felt belonged behind closed doors. And with a tight rein around it, he reminded himself.

He tucked the card back into its slot and replaced his wallet. Every time he thought he knew her, he discovered something to blow apart his theory.

Daisy was determined to get him to go with her. She had left Margaret in charge of the shop and had reserved the rest of the day for shopping. "I have no idea how you shop in New York, but I require a personal appearance. Now let's go," she urged, straightening away from the desk. "The stores are jam-packed as it is."

He looked at his desk. Though orderly, it was piled high with work that needed to be taken care of. The computer was blinking, waiting for more input and there were reports that needed his signature. He couldn't possibly get away. "I'm too busy to go shopping."

She gave an encouraging tug on his arm. "That's the whole idea," she insisted. "Christmas shopping wouldn't be half as much fun if it wasn't hectic."

That made absolutely no sense. "Did anyone ever drop you on your head as a child?"

She laughed as she raised her chin. "No."

He placed a hand on top of hers to remove it from his arm, but the contact was pleasant and warmed him. He never seemed to be properly prepared for her. Drew left his hand where it was for a moment.

"They should have," he said. "Maybe it would have knocked some sense into it. But then, you probably would have thought happy thoughts and flown away."

Her eyes crinkled as she laughed again, delighted with the description and the fact that he had created it. "You're getting into the spirit of the season."

"I'm getting certifiably crazy is what I'm getting," he countered, but he was weakening. It should have surprised him, but it didn't.

"Whatever." Daisy tugged on his arm again, more insistently this time. "Now come on. You don't have any important meetings coming up today and nothing is due. This is the perfect day for you to take off and go shopping with me."

He stared at her. "How do you know that? How do you know I don't have anything due?" She'd said it with too much confidence for it to have been just a lucky guess on her part.

"I checked with your secretary." She winked and he felt himself responding. "I'm impulsive, but I'm not reckless."

"That is a matter of opinion."

He wondered what she would do if he dug in and absolutely refused to budge. But he was already leaning toward going with her. Why, he hadn't the slightest idea. He had always thought of the Christmas crowds as comprised of people who should have their heads examined for getting sucked into the retailers' paradise. On the other hand, as the president of a thriving corporation that supplied a good many things being purchased for the holidays, he had to condone it. It wasn't, however, a dilemma he normally found himself actively in the middle of.

He wasn't going to talk his way out of this. "You can leave the helm of your ship, Captain Kirk. The Klingons won't be attacking today. And don't tell me you don't know what I'm talking about," she warned quickly. "Leave me some illusions."

Drew had only a vague idea what she was referring to. Another television program he hadn't bothered watching. He liked the way she lifted her chin when she dug in. "If I refuse to go, you'll probably drag me."

Now he was getting the idea. She knew she'd wear him down. "By force, if necessary. Those are wheels on your chair, Drew. And I know how to use them."

He started to laugh. "How can I possibly be outnumbered by one woman?"

Daisy stopped tugging. Leaning over, she brushed a kiss on his lips. "Because that woman is me."

She had no idea, Drew thought as he rose to his feet, how true those words were. And how prophetic.

The mall seemed to be filled with Christmas decorations, wall to wall people and an incredible level of noise.

"How much longer?" Drew wanted to know.

He shifted packages and bags, searching for a comfortable position he knew in his heart didn't exist. They had already been to a bookstore and three separate sections in a department store. Shopping with her was like trying to mount a horse and getting only one foot in the stirrup before the horse began to gallop away. All he could do was run along beside her and try to keep up.

The next stop on her list was a confectionary store at the other end of the mall. She stepped up her pace, weaving in and out of tiny pockets of space in the crowd.

"Slacker." She laughed, tossing the word over her shoulder. "We've only been at this an hour. How do you do your shopping in New York?" She slowed down when she realized that he was falling behind. "Catalog or secretary?"

He didn't particularly care for the smug way she had hit the nail on the head. "The latter."

She waited until he had caught up before taking the escalator to the ground level of the mall. A long line of children and harried-looking parents curled around the base of the escalator, waiting to talk to the jovial Santa Claus seated in the center of the court.

"No grocery shopping, no Christmas shopping." She looked up at Drew and he could have sworn he saw just a dash of pity in her eyes. "What kind of a life did you lead, Drew?"

"A sane one." He got off behind her. Someone bumped into him, hitting his arm. He nearly dropped the packages he was carrying.

Daisy caught them before they had a chance to fall. They looked at one another, the packages braced between them. "That's your word for it. I call it dull." She straightened his packages, then turned to look around.

They were standing in front of a restaurant that served different kinds of crêpes. Despite the crowds in the mall,

Daisy saw that there were still two tables left unoccupied within the restaurant when she looked through the opaque window. "I tell you what—if I feed you, will you stop being so cranky?"

Without waiting for an answer, she went into the restaurant.

"I am not cranky. " He tried his best not to hit anyone with his packages as they were led to a table by a young girl dressed in a French peasant costume. Drew was relieved to sink down into a chair. He deposited the packages next to his feet. "I just honestly don't see the reason for all the excitement."

They ordered and were quickly served. "You mean that, don't you? About not understanding the excitement. Besides Jonathan, didn't you ever have anyone to buy things for? Gifts that you *wanted* to buy yourself because you wanted to give someone a present?"

Taking a bite of the crêpe, he suddenly realized how hungry he was. "Jonathan and I didn't exchange gifts."

How sad, she thought. "Alyce and I did. We'd make little homemade things and hide them from each other. I still have the village she made for me one year." Her lips curved fondly as she remembered how excited she had been when she had unwrapped the gift. "She made it all out of shoe boxes. Alyce spent months collecting them, decorating them, adding in tiny details to the inside. It was the grandest present I ever got. I was nine."

He stopped eating and looked at her in disbelief. "And you kept it?"

"Of course I kept it. You don't throw away things that are made with love." He probably thought she was being foolish, but he would learn in time. Or at least she sincerely hoped so.

Daisy looked at the crowds of shoppers just beyond the restaurant window. "I guess that's why I like this so much.'' She nodded in the general direction of the shoppers. ''I never got to do it as a child.''

She turned and saw Drew looking at her as if he was seeing her for the first time. ''You see, I do know what boarding school is all about, Drew. Alyce and I spent a couple of Christmases there. Just us and the maintenance crew.'' Separated from the memory by almost two decades, it still hurt. ''Our parents were too busy to come and get us, too busy performing to spend Christmas with us. And Uncle Warren always seemed to be somewhere else.''

It astounded Drew how this charging dynamo had suddenly transformed into a small, hurting child right before his eyes. ''What did your parents do?'' he asked gently.

''Avoided being parents, mostly.'' She picked at her food, her appetite gone. ''They were part of Tomorrow. The band,'' she added when he looked at her blankly. ''They had one hit record in '74 or '75. They spent the rest of their lives trying to get another one, I guess.''

He didn't know what to say. He had never been good in situations like this. ''What was the song called?''

''Pretty Dreams.'' Her lips curved in an ironic smile. ''Rather appropriate, don't you think?'' She realized that her voice had dropped to almost a whisper. She raised it, trying to sound as if talking about this part of her life didn't bother her. ''Anyway, having two daughters got in their way. The other band members didn't have any kids, so Joe and Annie left theirs with Uncle Warren.''

She lowered her eyes to her plate. Funny how painful things that she had accepted were when she verbalized them. She felt the same emotions haunting her now as had plagued her then.

''Except that Uncle Warren didn't know what to do with two little girls any more than Joe and Annie did, so he checked around and found a neat little boarding school in Boston. And we were shipped off like so much luggage for the second time in as many months." She closed her eyes, reliving it. "God, that place looked so big when I first saw it." She opened them again when she felt his hand over hers. The lonely feeling within her evaporated and she smiled at him.

"How old were you?"

"Seven. Alyce was eight. She took charge," Daisy remembered. "She became my big, brave protector. I never knew how frightened she was until years later when we were talking about it."

Enough of this. Daisy forced herself to shake off the memory. "See, we've got more in common than you thought."

They did, except that inexplicably, she had turned out one way, and he another. She had become bright, sunny, extroverted, and he had withdrawn. The world hadn't offered love, so he had become self-sufficient and hadn't required any. He gravitated toward order and furthering a company. Things that didn't demand emotion from him, because he had none to give.

"That's what I don't understand. Having that in your background, having parents who were distant, why would this all appeal to you?" He gestured toward the shoppers outside the restaurant.

She really didn't see what his problem was with comprehending her reaction. It seemed self-explanatory to her.

"Because I didn't have it." He didn't see, she could tell. Daisy leaned forward across the small table for two, shutting out the restaurant, shutting out everything but Drew. "It's like spending years wanting ice cream and not having it. And then waking up one morning to be told that you are the owner of an ice-cream parlor." Her eyes almost glowed as she spoke. He could see it even in the dim atmosphere of the restaurant. "With five hundred flavors. You want to sample them all."

He had no desire to sample all of them. All he wanted was the taste of one particular flavor. If she were an ice cream, she'd probably be called peppermint candy, or perhaps, cinnamon spice. Something that left a tangy flavor that lingered on the tongue and on the mind.

He was beginning to understand, just a little. It frightened him in a way. It meant he was on her wavelength. "Is that why you went from job to job?"

She toyed with the coffee the waitress had brought, thinking. "Probably. I never analyzed it, but you could have something there. I didn't want to settle in a niche until I was certain that niche was for me."

She watched him over the rim of her cup as she drank. *And I didn't want to love a man until I knew he was the one I really wanted.*

Daisy set down her cup on the saucer. Turnabout was only fair. "What about you? I've told you my story. Now it's your turn to tell me yours."

He didn't like talking about himself. "I thought you knew my story."

"I do."

Over the years, Jonathan had told Alyce bits and pieces of his life and so Daisy had eventually heard about his younger brother. But that was second-hand. She wanted to hear it from Drew. How had he felt when he was growing up? What had he thought the first time he had walked into the boarding school?

"But I'd like to hear it from your lips." Her eyes skimmed over them and she sighed unconsciously. "Reinforcement I think you might call it."

"I thought you bored easily."

He was being evasive, she thought. "I don't get bored with certain things, things that I enjoy. I've seen *It's a Wonderful Life* at least twenty times."

He finished his coffee. The waitress drifted by and re-filled it. He nodded his thanks. "Is that a new movie?"

He was kidding, wasn't he? No, she decided, looking at him, he wasn't. A smile bloomed on her face.

"Oh, have I got a treat for you." She laughed at the uncertain look on his face. He had the expression of the man who didn't know if he had picked the lady or the tiger. "Tonight, we're all going to watch a video. Thank you," she said to the waitress as the woman filled her cup.

Wrapping her hands around the warm cup, she leaned forward. It helped create an intimate atmosphere within the eye of a hurricane. "Now come on, talk."

Maybe they had been better off shopping. At least that had left little opportunity for conversation. "You've cornered the market on that."

If he wanted to banter, he was out of luck. "You're not getting out of this, Drew. Tell me about the boy you were."

He shrugged. "I don't remember." He saw her skeptical look. She obviously didn't believe him. "Honestly, it doesn't unfold for me the way it does for you. No sweeping scenes, no years seen in wide-screen technicolor. Just snatches of memories I'd rather not rehash. I can't," he added.

Don't shut me out again. Please. "Can't, or won't?"

She was juggling words again, but then, she was good at that. "There's a difference?"

"There is," she answered quietly.

Even if he wanted to talk about it, he couldn't. He had locked everything away so well, he had lost the key. "Don't you want to finish your shopping?"

All right, she'd let him retreat for now. But not forever. She finished the remainder of her coffee. "Okay, pay the check with your gold card and we'll get back to it."

"I knew it. You just brought me along for my money,"

he teased, glad that the conversation had taken on a lighter tone.

She didn't bother to deny it. "That, and I intend to have my way with you in the car on the way home."

That, he had to admit as he gathered the bags and packages she had purchased, sounded very promising.

That evening Daisy did as she promised. She rented *It's a Wonderful Life* and made him sit down and watch the movie with her. Jeremy was tucked in between them, his eyes wide, as the black and white movie flickered on the television monitor in the family room. Toward the end, despite his involvement, Jeremy's head began to droop.

Drew shifted the boy so that he would be more comfortable and saw the tear sliding down Daisy's cheek. "You're crying." Amazed, he took out his handkerchief and handed it to her.

She only nodded as she wiped away the tears. On the screen, people were pouring into George Bailey's house, offering their hard-earned money to help him in his time of need.

Drew could only stare at Daisy, mystified. "But you said you've already seen this movie."

She swallowed and nodded. The bell was ringing on the Christmas tree. Clarence had become an angel. "Yes."

Drew didn't understand. This, like everything else about the woman, made no sense. "How can you cry, then?"

She let out a huge, cleansing sigh as credits rolled up on the screen. Shutting off the VCR and the set, she turned to look at Drew.

"Don't you have a sentimental bone in your body?" She wiped away the last telltale trace of tears and handed the handkerchief back to him.

He pocketed it absently. "I have to admit, it was a touching movie, for what it was."

She wondered if she was hitting her head against a brick wall. "What it was, Drew, was a movie about feelings. It was about seeing the good in your life and being grateful for it." She was talking about him now, and not a fifty-year-old movie. Her tone grew urgent. "And realizing just how many people you touch in your life. How many you affect."

By his reckoning, he probably affected a great many people in the strictest sense of the word. "I make decisions every day that, in one way or another, have repercussions all over the world. That still doesn't make me want to cry."

She refused to give up on him. Somewhere in that health-club-earned chest beat a heart. And she was going to find it. "We'll work on it. Maybe after you've seen the movie a few more times, it'll sink in."

He wasn't about to sit through that again. At least, not tonight. "I think we lost someone." He nodded at Jeremy. The boy's body was curled up into his.

She brushed the hair away from Jeremy's face. "You want to do the honors and take him up to bed?"

She'd always hovered around him when he did it before. "Alone?"

He was teasing, she thought, pleased. Where there was a trace of humor, there was hope. She rose and took the tape out of the machine. "You're capable."

He moved Jeremy so that he could easily lift the boy into his arms. "I know I'm capable, but you always seem to want to supervise."

Daisy turned and looked at Drew with Jeremy. They made a nice picture together. "I think you're ready for your first solo flight."

It was silly to feel that her approval meant something. He was used to taking his own lead, making major decisions that affected thousands of employees. But there was a glow within him that he couldn't deny.

When Drew came downstairs several minutes later, he found Daisy in the dining room. The results of all their hours of shopping in the mall was spread all over the table, dripping from the chairs, onto the floor. Colored foil was flying every which way as she wrapped, oblivious to his return.

He leaned against the doorjamb for a moment, watching her and wondering if there was some way to harness all this energy. If there had been such a creature as Santa Claus, all his helpers should have looked like this, Drew decided, incredibly sexy and ethereal.

"Couldn't wait, could you?" he asked, amused.

She swung around, surprised, then threw a roll of foil, making it unfurl. A sheet of silver draped over the box on the table, catching the overhead light and winking it about the room like trapped stars.

Daisy looked at him accusingly. "You're not supposed to be down yet."

He straightened and crossed to the table. "I didn't know there was a prescribed length of time for putting a little boy to bed. What's this?" With the tip of his finger, he pretended to lift the edge of the foil. She slapped his hand away.

"That's your present." Daisy wedged herself between Drew and the table, blocking his access to the box. "You'll just have to wait until Christmas morning."

"Present?" He couldn't begin to describe it, but there was a strange feeling building inside of him. Almost a bittersweet sadness. It tugged at emotions he had no idea what to do with. "You bought me something?"

Why would that surprise him so much? she wondered. "Yes."

"When?"

He had been with her the whole time. She had shopped for Jeremy and gotten presents for Margaret and several other people whose names he didn't recall, though she had told him. There hadn't been anything in the purchases that remotely resembled something he might use. When had she had the opportunity to get him a gift?

Daisy grinned, well pleased with herself. "When I sent you off to the gift-wrapping department to get Margaret's present specially wrapped. Remember?"

He had thought it odd at the time, seeing as how she hadn't wanted any of the other gifts wrapped. But he had just chalked it off to Daisy being her usual confusing self.

The rectangular shape beneath the silver foil curtain intrigued him. "You actually bought something for me?"

Hadn't there ever been a Christmas for him filled with warmth and wonder? Not even once? "Hasn't anyone ever bought you anything?"

Embarrassed, he flushed. "Well, yes," he began to lie. "No—never mind."

She put down the scissors in her hand. He needed her. "I see I have my work cut out for me." She turned her body into his.

Without even thinking, Drew placed his hands on her waist. It was becoming a habit, he realized. "Daisy, don't get carried away." There was more he wanted to say, about the need to be careful, about being adult about the situation they found themselves in. About their being two very different people.

But he never managed to say any of that. The smile on her face was seeping into the corners of his soul, blotting words from his mind. "What?"

"You've never called me Daisy before." She laced her hands together behind his neck, fitting her body comfortably against his. "I think, Mr. Addison, that I am getting to you."

"Getting?" he murmured. Inclining his head, he nipped at her lower lip and heard her contented moan. Tomorrow would come soon enough, he thought. For now, he'd enjoy tonight. "I think we should be using the past tense in this case."

"Always so proper." She rose up on her toes, moving in closer still.

The rush was beginning, pulling him in. "No—" he lowered his mouth to hers, already losing himself in her "—not always."

It took Daisy a long time to get back to wrapping gifts.

Chapter Fourteen

It happened gradually, without his being consciously aware
of it. He had taken to cutting back the time he spent in the
office on Saturdays until it had dwindled down to a few
hours at most. He was on his way out this morning to put
in a couple of hours when he heard the commotion outside
the house. It sounded as if there was a truck pulling up the
driveway.

Daisy was at the front door, shouting a greeting to someone. Drew looked past her shoulder. There were two men
seated in the cab of a truck and they appeared to be making
a delivery. He thought he recognized them from her nursery. Looking closer, Drew could make out the contents on
the back of the truck from where he stood. They were
bringing a Christmas tree.

"It's a real tree." He'd been surprised that here it was,
three days before Christmas and she still hadn't put up a
tree. He had been waiting to see some artificial monstrosity

take root in the living room. After all, this was California. It never occurred to him that she would use a real tree.

"Yes, I know." About to wave the men into the house, she stopped and looked at the frown on Drew's face. "You don't approve of real trees?"

He eyed the bound specimen as one of the men—Simon, he thought—climbed onto the truck. The tree looked to be about ten feet tall. "I don't approve of fires."

Daisy opened the unlatched double door, then worked the stops on the stationary door. Both doors would have to be opened to accommodate the tree and its base. "I'm not planning to set it on fire, I'm planning to decorate it."

Slowly, Drew had been changing his mind about her, finding Daisy to be more stable and conscientious than he had originally believed. Maybe he'd been too hasty. "That's irresponsible."

The second door stuck and she gave it a whack with the flat of her hand. It wiggled. "It would be more irresponsible not to decorate it."

"You know what I mean." He waved at the tree. "Why can't you be like everyone else in Southern California and have a pink tree or a silver tree?"

She swung the door back, allowing the men enough room to carry the tree in without having to maneuver it. Looking at Drew, she fisted one hand on her waist. "Because, in case you haven't noticed, I'm not like everyone else."

Drew sighed. Without realizing it, he tightened his hand around the handle of his briefcase. "I've noticed, I've noticed."

She caught her breath as Simon stumbled when he lowered the tree down to Pablo. Pablo, wider, squarer than his partner, managed to right the tree without damage. "And with everything else being so artificial these days, we need a real tree. Jeremy needs a real tree."

He understood that, but he understood what taking needless risks meant more. "Don't you ever read the newspapers?"

He wasn't going to let up, was he? she thought with an inner sigh. Well, he might as well work this out of his system. "Faithfully."

She was being obtuse on purpose. Doggedly, he pushed on. "About how many homes are burned to the ground by Christmas trees?"

She curbed the urge to help as Simon and Pablo struggled with the unwieldy evergreen up the walk. "I think all the trees responsible have now been brought to justice and locked up."

Why had he expected to talk her out of this? He hadn't one shred of evidence to prove to himself that she was a rational human being. "You're not taking me seriously."

She looked up into his face, smiling brightly before turning back to the men. "I'm doing my best not to, yes." She gestured Simon and Pablo through the door. "This way." Pivoting on the balls of her feet, she led them into the living room.

Drew followed, his trip to the office temporarily abandoned. "I can't believe you'd sacrifice something living for a few days' pleasure."

She looked at him as the two sinewy men righted the tree in the center of the room. That would have been his way, she thought, two and a half months ago. Now he was championing defenseless trees. *Yes, Virginia, there is a Santa Claus and Christmas Eve is full of magic.*

"I'm not. Thanks, guys, I really appreciate this." She slipped Simon an envelope she knew he would split with Pablo and saw them to the door.

"But—" Drew ran out of steam as he looked down at the base of the tree. Rather than being mounted in a stand, the tree's base was surrounded by wood measuring approximately eighteen inches or so on all sides. "What's that?"

Daisy crossed to the tree again. "It's called a box." She tapped it with her toe. "The roots are in that. Once Christmas is over, I'm going to plant it in the backyard near Jeremy's tree house."

She placed a hand on Drew's shoulder, the contact conveying her feelings even more aptly than her words. "I always hated Hans Christian Anderson's 'Fir Tree.' Cutting down some beautiful, thriving thing just to string lights on it for a little while seemed horribly thoughtless to me." She ran her fingers over the tips of the green branches. It had just as much right to live as anything else. "But I do love the scent of real pine and Christmas trees. Don't worry about fires, I'm taking all the proper precautions."

There was no arguing with her, but he had to have his say. He had seen a tree burn once. It had gone up in flames in seconds. The sight had left a lasting impression. "You're not omnipresent."

She winked, kissing his cheek. "No, but I'm working on it." She knew in his gruff, blustery way, he meant well. He just hadn't learned how to express himself properly. Lucky for him she was learning how to read between the lines.

"Is it here? Is it here?" The excited cry pierced the air as Jeremy ran down the stairs, holding on to the banister with both hands as he flew.

"It's here." Daisy laughed as she stepped out of Jeremy's way. He came tearing into the room, then skidded to a halt in front of the tree. His head fell back as he tried to take it in from close up. The tree looked to be a hundred feet tall.

"Wow. It's so big!" Eagerness spilled out from every pore. "Can we decorate it? Can we, huh?"

Daisy tried to look solemn and failed. His excitement was infectious. She was so relieved at the way he was handling the holidays. She had been dreading that the first

Christmas without his parents would turn into a time of tears and sadness for the small boy. She could have saved herself a lot of grief and worry. Youth had a resilience that she wished she could share in. "I take it you mean now?"

Jeremy hopped from one foot to another. "Sure."

"Drew?" Daisy raised her eyes questioningly toward him.

For a moment, he didn't know what she was asking him. For permission? That certainly wasn't like her. And then it occurred to him. "You want me to help decorate it?"

She spread her hands wide. "It's the family tree. And you're family." She glanced at his briefcase. She was against his working on Saturdays. "You can send that thing on ahead to the office. It'll get a head start for you."

He had wanted to go over the latest reliability report on the satellite components his subsidiary company, G.L. Aerospace, was supplying to NASA. There was a problem according to the latest stats and he felt better being on top of everything.

Like her, a tiny voice whispered, coming out of nowhere. He banked away the thought. And the urge.

"Please, Uncle Drew, please?" Jeremy, his dark eyes dancing, pulled on Drew's arm, trying to steer him away from the front door and all the responsibilities he had always placed first in his life.

Helpless, Drew looked toward Daisy for a way out of this. He should have known better.

"I need someone tall for the lights. It's a large tree."

"If I wasn't here, you'd find a way." Drew was confident of that. Nothing got in this woman's way. Jeremy was still looking up at him in supplication. With a sigh, Drew let the briefcase drop from his hands. "All right, I guess I can stay and help for a little while."

He had changed, she thought with a smile. He was no longer a man who could, in good conscience, send off a little boy to boarding school. He wasn't locked up in his ivory tower on the fortieth floor any more, either.

"Come on," she told him, "you can help me fetch the decorations out of the rafters in the garage."

Jeremy kept a death grip on Drew's arm as they walked out. This was important, special, and he meant to have his Uncle Drew there.

Three hours later, Daisy leaned back and surveyed their handiwork. Jeremy was still tossing fistfuls of tinsel at the glittering tree, but for all intents and purposes, it was finished.

"I think it's the best tree ever." She looked at Jeremy. "What do you think?"

He pitched another fistful. Crinkled silver strands rained down. Most of them landed on the rug. He seemed blissfully unaware of that fact as he grabbed another handful. "It's gonna be," Jeremy answered with a secret smile.

Daisy cocked her head and studied the boy. "What are you up to?"

Dark eyes widened innocently as thin shoulders rose and fell elaborately. He couldn't tell. If you told, wishes didn't come true. His mother had taught him that. "Nothing."

Daisy laughed and gave him a little hug. More silver strands hit the rug. Irene was going to have a great time vacuuming the rug tomorrow. "That's the most potent 'nothing' I've ever heard."

Jeremy dusted his fingers off. His dark corduroy pants had tinsel attached everywhere. "It's a magic tree, right, Aunt Daisy?"

Her smile faded just a little as she wondered what he was thinking. "Yes," she said slowly, "it is if you want it to be."

"I do." Jeremy shut his eyes tight.

Having returned the ladder to its place in the garage,

Drew entered the living room. He had to admit that it was the best-looking tree he had ever seen. And the first he had ever decorated. That went without saying. She knew, he thought. It was part of the reason she had used the boy to help convince him. He was secretly glad she had.

He wondered why it was so hard for him to open up and why he had to be all but dragged to do things that he ultimately found enjoyable. Old habits, he supposed, died hard.

He took a look at Jeremy. The boy's eyes were practically screwed shut. "What are you doing?"

Jeremy opened his eyes again. He had shut them so tightly, for a moment it was hard to focus in. "Wishing."

"For what?" Drew asked. Whatever it was, he was certain Daisy had covered it. She had brought more toys into the house in the past week than were normally found in the warehouse of a toy factory. There he went, he thought, appalled, exaggerating again. She *was* getting to him. In more ways than one.

Jeremy shook his head. "It won't come true if I tell." He smiled confidently. "But it'll be here Christmas morning."

Daisy ruffled his hair, hoping that he wouldn't be disappointed. It would have helped if he had confided to her what he wanted for Christmas. "Santa'll do his best," she promised.

"And God?" Jeremy asked, suddenly solemn as he looked at the manger scene he had set up beneath the tree with only a little help from his aunt. Shepherds and wise men were lined up, kneeling before the Christ Child. "This is about God, too, right, Aunt Daisy?"

Daisy gathered him to her. He *was* missing his parents, she thought. "And God, too."

He wiggled out of her grasp, a wide smile on his face.

"Now we gotta set up the trains, Uncle Drew. Around the tree," he said when Drew looked at him blankly.

"I've never set up a track," Drew began, trying to ease his way out of this.

"That's okay." Jeremy took his hand in his own. "I'll show you."

Drew looked over his shoulder toward his briefcase. The fine Italian leather case was now buried beneath opened, gaping boxes that had contained the decorations. Oh, well, it would keep.

"Okay, but I'm going to need a lot of help," Drew told Jeremy.

"Not any more," Daisy murmured, taking his arm. He was coming along just fine.

Drew misunderstood. "You're helping?"

"I have been all along."

Drew wasn't certain if they were still in the same conversation as he allowed himself to be led away.

The house was filled to bursting. Drew looked around, fascinated. It looked as if Daisy had invited the whole town to her Christmas Eve party. She called it theirs, but it was clearly hers. Her party. He didn't know anyone here.

Which was why she kept insisting on introducing him to absolutely everyone. Every time he broke away from one group, there she was again, latching onto his arm and directing him toward someone else. The consummate party giver, he thought dryly.

He took temporary refuge by the punch bowl, needing to be alone for a minute. Names and faces swam through his mind. He knew Margaret, of course, and several faces looked familiar from the funeral. But the rest were all mingling together. He was never any good at parties when business wasn't the prime reason for gathering.

He sipped punch and wondered when he could be alone with Daisy.

As he scanned the room for her, he saw Jeremy sitting on the sofa near the tree. A sense of camaraderie filled him and, abandoning his glass of punch, Drew made his way over to the boy. He dropped down next to him on the sofa. Dressed in his party clothes, Jeremy seemed very intent as he stared at the lights on the tree. They were the old-fashioned kind that bubbled continuously, and apparently had mesmerized Jeremy.

Drew looked at them. They did have a hypnotic effect. He blinked and turned toward Jeremy. "Hi. What are you doing?"

Jeremy fidgeted a little. "Waiting."

He looked around. There were several other children close to Jeremy's age, but he was apparently ignoring them at the moment.

"Oh, for Santa Claus," Drew realized.

Jeremy started to say something, then closed his mouth again and nodded. "Yeah, for Santa Claus." He regarded his uncle for a moment, obviously puzzling over something. Finally, he asked. "Do you believe, Uncle Drew?"

"In Santa Claus?" No, he had never believed. There had been no one to perpetuate the myth for him or to make him believe. Reality was something that had been fed to him very early in life. There was no room for make-believe and wishes coming true. It had been a very stark childhood, he thought, suddenly feeling deprived.

Jeremy wriggled and scratched. The wool slacks were itchy. "Yeah, do you believe in Santa Claus?"

No, Drew thought. Jeremy wasn't going to have the kind of life he had had. "Sure, doesn't everyone?"

Jeremy looked heartened by his uncle's verification. "There's this girl at school, Shelly, and Shelly says it's just your mom and dad, not Santa."

Drew supposed that he could tell Jeremy the truth. He had the right opening to work with. But he looked at the small upturned face and decided that Jeremy would see his share of reality when he grew up. He had seen more than he should already. Childhood should be the time for magic. He smiled to himself, thinking that Daisy would approve of the thought.

"She's a very mean little girl," Drew answered. He was rewarded with a relieved smile. Drew tucked his arm around the small shoulders. "Santa's real." He leaned back, trying to put himself into Daisy's mind. What would she tell him? "He's a magic elf who's made up from all the goodness in your heart."

Jeremy frowned for a moment, thinking. "What if you've been bad?"

"Santa Claus always finds something to work with," Drew assured him. The answers were easy, he realized, if he just pretended to think like Daisy.

It was then that he saw her. Daisy was standing off to the side, listening to him. He saw a tear sliding down her cheek. He half rose in his seat. "What's wrong?"

She wiped it away with the heel of her hand. "This is better than Clarence becoming an angel."

Sometimes it was hard to keep up with her. "Who?" And then he remembered. "Oh, the movie." He shrugged, self-conscious at being caught acting sentimental. It wasn't something he saw himself doing well. He rose from the sofa. "I think I'll get some punch."

Margaret drifted over just as Drew left. "Hi, Jeremy, how are you doing?" She made herself comfortable beside the boy. "Excited about tomorrow morning?"

He liked Margaret, liked the way she smelled, all pretty, like flowers. He liked the funny way she talked sometimes. And she let him have doughnuts even when Aunt Daisy said he'd had too many. "You bet."

"Excuse me for a moment," Daisy said to Margaret. "Entertain her, Jeremy."

He wasn't getting away that easily, she thought, going after Drew. Daisy wove her way through the crowd, exchanging words in passing with several people. She noticed that a very vivacious-looking woman had cornered Drew. Daisy recognized her as the date of one of Jonathan's friends. From the look on her face, the woman had obviously decided that Drew was far more her type.

Wrong.

She had never been jealous before, never experienced even a twinge of the annoying emotion running through her. It was taking a healthy-size bite out of her now.

"Excuse me." Daisy elbowed the blonde aside, flashing the woman a smile as she took hold of Drew's arm. "I'm afraid I have to steal him away from you. His wife and twelve children are looking for him."

"When did I have time for twelve children?" he whispered, amused.

"What you should have had time for was learning about barracudas," she returned in the same tone of voice.

"That innocent-looking girl?" He knew he was baiting Daisy and he was enjoying himself immensely.

"Girl? She's older than I am." Or looked it, anyway, Daisy thought. "I have something to show you." Still holding his arm, she ushered him to a doorway.

"What is it you want to show me?" He looked around and saw nothing out of the ordinary. There were people in the dining room. People in the kitchen, from what he could glimpse. But nothing or no one unusual.

"That." Daisy pointed to the archway overhead. "Mistletoe, Drew."

He glanced up at the green sprig and then looked at her face. "You never struck me as an old-fashioned girl."

Easily, Drew cinched her waist with his hands. For a

moment, it felt as if she was wearing nothing beneath her glistening silver wrap-around dress. His imagination began to take flight and he had to work at harnessing it.

She let her head drop back slightly as she laughed. "That's because I want to keep you guessing."

"You've succeeded admirably. Do I get to kiss you now?"

She had done this to him, he realized, taken away his discomfort. Relaxed him. Melted him. While he was the last word in competence as far as heading a huge corporation went, his interaction with people limited itself only to business. The man he had been three months ago would have never wanted to kiss a woman in the middle of a crowded room. Now he wanted nothing else.

"Try not kissing me and see what happens."

His hands slipped up her back. No, no bra, either. She was nude under that, wasn't she? His pulse quickened. "I'm not brave enough."

She raised her mouth to his. "Smart man."

Because they were in a crowded room, it was a fleeting kiss, barely hinting at the passion that existed beneath. But it was enough to make her yearn.

She opened her eyes again, pulling herself back from brink of desire. But even now, her pulse was unsteady. She left her arms wrapped around his neck. "I can get rid of all these people," she murmured.

"With a wave of your hand?" He looked around the immediate area. He hadn't minded this party nearly as much as he thought he would. It was almost pleasant. But being alone with her would have been infinitely better. "I don't doubt it. I don't doubt that anything is possible with you."

I hope so, oh, I hope so.

If he felt that way, then perhaps he would stay, she thought. The way Jonathan had before him. But Jonathan had had a brother who could take things over. Drew didn't. He had to run the company himself. Besides, it meant a great deal to him.

She'd give up her business, she decided, if he asked her to. It would be hard. She was happy doing what she was doing. Being a landscape consultant was her calling. But she knew at that instant that she would give up everything just to be with him and Jeremy. Nothing else really mattered.

But he had to ask. It wasn't something she could volunteer.

He saw the sudden shift in her eyes and wondered at it. Was it something he had said? "You look sad."

She shook her head, wishing her emotions didn't show so readily. "I'm just thinking."

"About what?"

She didn't want to tell him. What if he didn't feel the same way about her as she did about him? Yes, he had changed, changed a great deal, but what if that really just involved Jeremy and not her? What if she was just a pleasant interlude, a phase, a ship in the night? For the first time in a long, long time, Daisy felt uncertain.

"Nothing." She linked her hand with his. "Come on, let's get you circulated."

He thought of the blood that had roared through his veins just at the merest touch of her body to his. He thought about the fact that he intended to find out if his impression that she wasn't wearing anything beneath her dress was accurate as soon as everyone left. "I think you've already accomplished that."

She could read his thoughts and she laughed. "I meant talking to people. You still haven't met Jonathan's poker buddies."

That took him by surprise. Jonathan had never liked card games. "Jonathan knew how to play poker?"

"No," she grinned, "but he played anyway. I think Jeremy could have beaten him. I know I did."

"Why doesn't that surprise me?"

"Maybe you're getting used to me."

"Never."

She wondered if he meant that the right way. She hoped so. Daisy ushered him in the direction of a group of men near the fireplace. Her lips still tingled, making her anticipate a night to remember.

"Well, that's all of it," Daisy muttered, placing the last gift she had for Jeremy under the tree. She sat back on her heels. It looked like a child's idea of paradise. The base of the tree was draped in white cloth and an explosion of gifts littered the area all around the perimeter.

She looked at Drew, who had dragged in the sackful of gifts from her hiding place in the garage. "You looked like you had a good time tonight."

"I did." The fact still astonished him. A room full of strangers and yet he had enjoyed himself. Daisy made it impossible not to. He took her hand and helped her to her feet. "Of course, it's nothing compared to the time I'm about to have."

She placed her hands on his forearms. She loved the way his muscles felt beneath her fingers. "Oh? With anyone in particular?"

"Someone very particular." He toyed with the bow at her hip. "I've been wondering all night. What happens when I pull this thing?"

A smile teased her lips. "Why don't we go up to my room and see?"

Impulsively, he kissed her, unable to resist. "That is the best idea you've had in a long time."

"I'll see if I can come up with a few more tonight."

With his arm around her, Drew walked up the stairs with

Daisy. There was another mistletoe at the head of the stairs. Drew took full advantage of it.

Her head was spinning as she pulled herself out of the deep kiss. "Do that again and I don't think I'll make it to my room."

He laughed and drew her closer, delighting in her, delighting in the evening.

She stopped to peek into Jeremy's room before entering her own. The boy's even breathing was the only sound in the room.

She thought again what an immense comfort it was, hearing that sound. She turned to Drew. "Probably dreaming of all the presents he's going to get."

Drew's hand rested comfortably on the swell of her hip as he peered in over Daisy's head. "I forgot to ask, did you leave any toys in the toy stores for other parents to buy?"

She closed the door softly. "You're exaggerating."

"I never exaggerate." He led her to her room, shutting the door behind them. "You, however, have this distinct tendency to do that."

She leaned into him, her body tempting his, her warm breath tantalizing his skin. "Would it be an exaggeration to say you've been driving me crazy all night?" she asked innocently.

He wrapped his arms around her. "I don't know, would it?"

"No." She shook her head slowly, her eyes on his face. "An understatement. A vast understatement." She placed his hand over the bow at her hip. "Want to unwrap one of your presents early?"

"I've been counting on it all evening." He tugged on the tie. As it came undone, the entire dress parted, seductively hanging open from her shoulders. Just as he had surmised, she was completely nude beneath it.

Desire came, full blooded and demanding as he ran his palms over her sleek body. "Isn't that a rather dangerous outfit to wear in public?"

She felt the glow beginning, growing as his hands stroked her body. "I had a sailor's knot on the tie earlier. I undid it while you were in the garage, getting Jeremy's presents."

"A sailor's knot," he echoed. "If you tell me that you were an admiral in the navy, I'll—"

She lifted her chin, her eyes teasing him. "You'll what?"

He laughed. "I'll probably believe you."

"You're coming along, Drew. You're definitely coming along."

He lifted a brow. "Not yet, but I plan to."

Drew tossed aside her dress and took her into his arms, fanning flames that had refused to be banked all evening.

New and different, but the same, that was the way he felt about the sensations that ripped through him each time they made love. He knew what to expect, yet there was always more, so much more. An entire treasure trove for him to get lost in. He had no doubts in his heart that it would always be that way.

Unless—

He stopped thinking. He refused to think about anything. All he wanted to do was feel the life-giving forces coursing through his blood the way they did each time he was with her.

He framed her face. "This is the best Christmas Eve I've ever had."

Daisy began to unhook his belt. "Oh, no, the best Christmas Eve you've ever had is yet to be."

And she was right.

Chapter Fifteen

Light was nudging its way past filmy white curtains into Daisy's bedroom. Reluctantly she opened her eyes and then blinked as she tried to make out the numbers on the clock next to her bed. It was a few minutes after six.

Christmas morning.

Why wasn't Jeremy knocking on her door, begging her to come down with him and see what Santa had brought? He'd been so anxious the night before. No, she thought, pensive would have been a better word. He had talked about waiting. Patient, she mused, like his father.

And his uncle.

Daisy smiled, remembering the way Jeremy had looked last night in his jacket and matching slacks. Like a little man. Her little man. She looked at the wall that separated her room from his. He was probably exhausted from staying up so late at the party.

Daisy turned and propped herself up on her elbow. Drew

was still asleep. It seemed to be a day for sleeping in, she mused, watching the way his chest rose and fell as he slept. He'd stopped slipping out of her bed before dawn a few days ago. She liked the feeling of waking up in the morning and finding him next to her.

But for how much longer?

It was exactly one week until the end of their bargain and he hadn't said a word about it, about the future. Not one word. Not a single hint of what was going to happen once the three months were up. She hadn't brought it up, either.

Maybe it was because neither of them wanted to hear the words, she thought, pressing her lips together. What if—?

No, today was Christmas. She wasn't going to spoil it by wondering and worrying over what was to be. It wouldn't help matters, anyway. She was content in the fact that he obviously loved Jeremy and understood his needs. He'd do what was best for the boy. They both would. If Drew had to return to the east coast because his career was there, so be it. She'd go, too. She knew she wouldn't be able to function very well here if her heart was three thousand miles away.

It would be nicer, she thought, if he'd ask her to go, but she'd made up her mind one way or another. Nothing in this world was going to separate her from Jeremy. Or from Drew.

Lightly, Daisy touched her lips to his, and Drew stirred. She did it again, with a little more feeling, and he opened his eyes, surprised. "Hey, sleepyhead. Wake up. It's Christmas morning."

He threaded his arm around her, holding Daisy against him. "So it is," he murmured, trying to clear the sleep from his brain. He shifted, stretching his body against hers. "Want to celebrate early?" He could hardly believe, even now, that the words were his own. He had seen her coming a mile away three months ago, a banshee bent on shaking up his very foundations. He'd been just as bent not to let her disturb one brick.

Now look at him. He'd plunged from his fortieth-floor office just as surely as Jonathan had. Without a net. And loved it.

She tugged teasingly on his lower lip with her teeth, then pulled away, laughing as he started to deepen the kiss.

"Later. First, we have a little boy to take care of." She slipped out of bed and picked up her robe. She saw desire flicker in Drew's eyes as he skimmed them over her nude body. Pushing her arms through the sleeves, she knotted the sash securely at her waist. "I think it's rather strange that he's still sleeping."

Drew glanced at the clock. "It's a good habit to get into at six in the morning."

"Christmas morning?"

Drew threw the covers off and planted his feet on the floor. "You're right, it is odd." He pulled his slacks on and followed her out into the hall. "I'm looking forward to seeing his expression when he unwraps that engine you bought him."

"*We* bought him" she corrected. "This isn't a competition."

Not any more. He'd won all the marbles. And she had gotten caught in her own trap. By trying to change Drew into the type of man who understood that Jeremy was a sensitive boy with needs, she had inadvertently fashioned someone she was now hopelessly in love with.

Drew took her hand. "Come on. I might get lucky and find some mistletoe along the way."

She kissed his mouth quickly. "You don't need mistletoe. Now let's wake him up before I get carried away."

"You?" Drew opened his eyes wide in wonder and surprise. "Never."

"Don't be wise," she murmured, opening Jeremy's door slowly. "Honey, are you asleep? It's Christmas. Santa's been here."

She stopped, her smile freezing. The covers on Jeremy's bed had been thrown back, as if a boy had recently risen in haste. His bed was empty.

A nervousness began to seep into her system. She wasn't completely sure why. Instinct. "Drew?"

He heard the slight note of anxiety in her voice and glossed over the situation for her benefit. "He probably didn't want to wake you and just snuck downstairs. Let's go."

He didn't need to urge her. There was something not right about this. She could sense it in her bones. Jeremy *always* wanted her to be part of things, especially since his parents had died. Daisy flew down the stairs, the hem of her robe trailing after her.

"Jeremy," she called out. "Jeremy, are you in the living room?"

He wasn't there. The gifts were exactly where she had placed them around the tree the night before, neatly wrapped and untouched. Panic began to build. Why wasn't he down here?

Though he knew it was useless, Drew circled the Christmas tree. The boy wasn't playing some sort of prank. He wasn't hiding behind the tree. Drew looked at Daisy. "Where is he?"

She shook her head, trying to think, squeezing back her fears as if they had depth and breadth. "I don't know. You check all the rooms upstairs. I'll look down here."

There was no reason why Jeremy should be hiding from them, she thought. Why wasn't he answering?

She went through the rooms quickly, calling. Irene's door opened before Daisy could knock.

"What's the matter?" the housekeeper asked, wrapping her robe about her thin body.

"It's Jeremy. I can't find him."

Lines of concern popped out on the older woman's brow. "Shall I call the police?"

"No, no, not yet." Daisy dragged her hand through her hair, trying desperately to think. Her thoughts were scattering frantically in all directions, dandelion seeds in the brisk fall wind. Where would he go? And why? He'd never done anything like this before. Why now? It didn't make sense to her.

With Irene on her heels, Daisy started to return to the living room. As she hurried by the sliding-glass door in the family room, she noticed that it was unlatched. She knew she had checked it last night when the guests left. It was locked then. Could Jeremy be in the yard at this hour?

"Wait here," she told Irene and then hurried out.

She looked around. The backyard was spacious with a miniature waterfall on one side and an elaborate swing set near the house. The trees that bordered the fence on all three sides provided shade, but were too close to the fence for Jeremy to play behind.

He was nowhere to be seen.

That left only one place to try. His tree house.

Holding her robe against her, she hurried barefoot over the wet grass. "Jeremy," she called up to the tree house. "Are you up there? Jeremy, answer me. Please."

There was no reply, only a soft noise that sounded like a distant mockingbird. Or a muffled sob. Instinct had her climbing up the wooden ties that Jonathan had nailed into the tree.

She found Jeremy huddled in the corner, his hands covering his face. He was crying.

She knew it. She had known that something was wrong from the moment she woke up. Crouching, she half crawled, half shuffled on her knees into the tree house to reach him. "Oh, baby, what's the matter?"

He had wanted to be alone, to cry his heart out and empty out the pain. Now that she was here, Jeremy threw himself into his aunt's arms and sought out her warmth. "They didn't come."

Rocking him against her body, she stroked his hair. His wet face dampened the front of her robe. "Who, baby? Who didn't come?"

His cheeks shone with tears as he raised his head and looked at her. "Mommy and Daddy. They were supposed to come back. It's Christmas and they were supposed to come back to me."

She could feel her heart breaking. This was why he had taken his parents' death so well. He'd been waiting for Christmas, waiting for them to return, because Christmas was the time for miracles. How could she make him understand something that she didn't completely accept herself?

She felt tears gathering in her own eyes as she tried to answer him. "Oh, darling, they can't. They want to, but they can't."

He pushed himself away from her, angry, hurt, confused. "I thought if I wished real hard, they'd come back. You know, like a present for me. Christmas is magic. You said so. Uncle Drew told me so."

He looked as if he felt that everyone was lying to him, Daisy thought. It was a horrible thing for a four-year-old to believe. "Some things are beyond magic."

Jeremy hung his head. Two tears fell from his eyes onto her robe. "No, they don't want to come back. They don't love me."

She took hold of his arms and forced him to look at her.

"They did love you. We all love you, sweetheart." Her voice was fierce, stern, as she tried to get through to him. She saw the hesitation, the desperate need to believe. To understand. "It has nothing to do with love. When people die, they can't come back, no matter how much they might want to." She gathered him to her and held on to him tightly. "You know that turnstile you got stuck in at the drugstore last month?"

Jeremy hiccuped, rubbing his fists against his eyes. He nodded. "'Cause it only went one way."

"That's right." She kept her voice soft, soothing, hoping to calm him down. "That's kind of what life is like." She stroked his head. "It only goes one way. Forward. And your mommy and daddy have gone forward to the next level. Heaven. And someday, when you're a lot older, you'll join them."

Jeremy's small eyes searched her face. "And you and Uncle Drew? You'll come, too?"

Her heart ached at the compliment he had just given to her. To her and Drew. "And Uncle Drew and I will come, too," Daisy assured him with a smile, blinking back her tears.

"Where are we going?"

When she turned around, Daisy saw Drew looking in trough the tree house window. She could see by the expression on his face that he had overheard everything. His tone had been inordinately gentle when he asked his question.

Jeremy wiped away the telltale tracks of his tears with his knuckles. "To heaven."

"Now?" Drew looked down at his robe. "I'm not dressed for it."

Jeremy sniffled and a half smile began to form on his lips.

"Besides," Drew continued, snaking inside the small

quarters, "there are all these presents under the tree and I'm not sure about what kind of postage to put on them so we can mail them to heaven after you." He grinned at Daisy, knowing he was crowding her into a corner with his frame and enjoying the contact. "What do you say that we go and open them now instead of sitting in this tiny house?"

Jeremy let out a big sigh, then manfully nodded his head. He was his father's child. Even at four, he understood that there was no use in crying over what couldn't be. "Okay."

Daisy turned her head away from Jeremy, into Drew's shoulder. "Nicely done," she murmured under her breath.

"I was going to say the same to you. Never thought of life as being a turnstile before." He raised his voice as he looked at his nephew. "Why don't you go on first and I'll help your aunt down?"

Jeremy was already clambering out of the window as Drew turned toward Daisy. "Or were you a sherpa guide in the Himalayas, too?"

She gave him a shove with the flat of her hand. "Just go, wiseguy. I can climb down." She began to move past him toward the opening, but he placed a hand on her shoulder to stop her.

"In that case, let me go down first." He purposely raised and lowered his eyebrows as he looked at her robe. "I might like the view from the ground."

She laughed, her own tears drying. "Just take Jeremy into the house, all right?"

"Will do." He lowered himself out the window and climbed down agilely. Jeremy was waiting for him at the base of the tree. As Daisy watched, Drew took the boy's hand in his and led him into the house.

It was going to be all right, she thought. The other shoe had dropped and the worst was over. Jeremy would start to heal now.

When Daisy entered the living room a few minutes later, ripped wrapping paper had just begun to pile up on the floor beside Jeremy. The boy still looked somewhat subdued, but the magic of Christmas morning was slowly beginning to penetrate and dissolve the aura of sadness.

Daisy sat on the sofa where she could have a good view of Jeremy as he opened his gifts. She noted the loving expression on Drew's face as he observed Jeremy. The man was a far cry from the Iceman who had come in out of the rain three months ago. She had melted him just as she had set out to do. The rest was going to work itself out now. She just knew it. They would take joint custody of Jeremy and she would move to New York. It wasn't simple, but it would work.

Satisfied that Jeremy was all right, Drew leaned a hip against the arm of the sofa, next to Daisy. "Are you going to open your presents?"

She shrugged. "Not right now. I'd rather watch him." She saw the surprise and the joy as Jeremy unwrapped an airplane for the action figure "Drew" had brought him from New York. "Besides, I have a pretty good idea what everyone gave me. You drop enough hints, you're bound to get some of the things you mentioned."

"Oh?" His tone was so innocent sounding, it had Daisy looking in Drew's direction. He was rummaging through the gifts farthest from Jeremy. "What about this box?" Rising, he brought over a rectangular box wrapped in scampering Santa Clauses.

Daisy stared at it. She didn't remember that one. It looked like a shoe box. "Shoes? I didn't hint for shoes." She turned the box around slowly. "There's no card on it."

Drew was back on the arm of the sofa. Perched, as if he was too agitated suddenly to sit properly. "Why don't you open it? Maybe there's one inside."

Intrigued, suddenly inexplicably nervous, Daisy unwrapped the paper. It *was* a shoe box. A decorated shoe box. Windows were cut out on all sides and there were trees drawn on the back. A tiny sign on the front proclaimed Showers of Flowers…and Things.

Pressing her lips together to keep from crying, she raised her eyes to his.

Drew slid from the arm of the sofa down next to her on the cushion. "For your collection. I thought maybe your village might need a nursery." He felt a little foolish as he shrugged. "It seemed appropriate."

Tears rose again, this time from sheer joy. "It's beautiful. You did this for me?"

"Had to. Couldn't find anyone else to do it without making it seem as if I was crazy."

"You are," she laughed. "Wonderfully crazy."

She started to set the box down, to hug him, but as she slid it from her lap, she heard something move inside, sliding from one end to the other. It made a tiny thud against the box. Her brow furrowed as she took the lid off. Inside there was another small box, wrapped in the same sort of paper.

"Oh, yes." Drew cleared his throat, devastatingly anxious, "I thought—hoped, actually—that you might like that, too."

Jeremy was busy trying out the electronic drum set she had gotten him, but all Daisy heard was the buzzing in her ears as she tore off the paper from the small box.

Holding her breath, she opened it. Inside was a ring with a single, exquisite, square-cut emerald.

He had addressed huge auditoriums filled with employees and never experienced a single twinge of agitation. Nerves were slicing through him now like butterflies with razors for wings. "I thought that since you liked green so much, Maid Marian, you might want an emerald instead of a diamond for your engagement ring."

Her hand shook as she held the box. She couldn't even take the ring out. "Engagement?" Daisy repeated, her voice low.

He was floundering, he thought. "Engagement. You know, the thing that happens before you marry someone?"

Her mouth felt dry as her palms became damp. Was he serious? "Marry?"

"There seems to be an echo in here. If I say yes, will I hear the same word in return?"

She was going to start babbling any second now. Daisy lowered her eyes and stared at the box in her hand. "I don't know what to say."

She was going to say no, Drew thought, feeling his stomach muscles tighten. "That's a first." He licked his lips nervously. "Do you want to think it over?"

Daisy shook her head emphatically. "No."

The word cut through him like a carving knife. "No, huh?"

"I don't have to think about it." The words dripped from her mouth almost in slow motion as disbelief gripped her. He wanted her. He really, really wanted her. Forever. It *was* working out. They'd have each other and Jeremy, as well. *Oh, Alyce, Jonathan, I wish you were here to see this. You made all this happen.* "I've been thinking about it for a long time already."

He wasn't going to let her say no. He *couldn't* let her say no. She had to marry him. He couldn't go back to life the way it was before he had come out here. It would be too bleak, too empty, too meaningless for him now. Having felt the sun, he refused to reenter the cave and do without it forever more. She'd made him take risks, emotional risks he had never wanted to take. He wasn't about to go on free-falling without her.

All the things he used to convince reluctant clients began

to fill his head in jumbled order. He planned to keep talking until he wore her down.

He took her hands in his. "Before you say anything, let me have my say. This is a perfect way to solve our bargain. Jeremy needs both of us, not just one. I've already set wheels in motion to transfer the bulk of Addison Corporation's headquarters out here. That building that you saw going up across the street from the office?"

She remembered the one he was referring to. "Yes?"

"I bought it. It's going to be Addison Corporation's new home office. Now I need a home to go to. A real home, not a penthouse apartment where I just sleep. I want a real family to come home to, not just a valet." His eyes held hers as he searched for a sign that she understood what he was trying to tell her. That he needed her. That he couldn't live without her. "I need someone who knows how to make me laugh, not who knows my suit measurements."

Jeremy laughed as he pulled the string on a dinosaur doll and it gave him another flippant answer. Drew looked at the boy over his shoulder, then turned again to Daisy. "I want to adopt Jeremy. I *need* you and Jeremy. I've never been in love before, so it took me a long time to realize what was going on. But I love you, Daisy, and I'm not about to let you say no. Tell me the word I want to hear."

She didn't know whether to laugh or cry. A little of both was happening. "Idiot."

He raised a brow. The look on her face told him it was going to be all right. "That wasn't quite the word I was looking for."

She threw her arms around his neck. "What in heaven's name made you think I'd say no?"

"Because you never say what I think you'll say." Relieved, he felt his heart slide back into position out of his throat. "Then it's yes?"

"It's always been yes." She laughed. "Right from the first moment I heard your pants ringing for me."

Drew pulled her onto his lap, his mouth finding hers. And then they both heard bells ringing, accompanied by a drumroll thanks to Jeremy's new electronic drum set.

* * * * *

SILHOUETTE® Desire®

Do you want...

Dangerously handsome heroes

Evocative, everlasting love stories

Sizzling and tantalizing sensuality

Incredibly sexy miniseries like **MAN OF THE MONTH**

Red-hot romance

Enticing entertainment that can't be beat!

You'll find all of this, and much *more* each and every month in **SILHOUETTE DESIRE**. Don't miss these unforgettable love stories by some of romance's hottest authors. Silhouette Desire—where your fantasies will always come true....

▼ *Silhouette* ROMANCE™

What's a single dad to do when he needs a wife by next Thursday?

Who's a confirmed bachelor to call when he finds a baby on his doorstep?

How does a plain Jane in love with her gorgeous boss get him to notice her?

From classic love stories to romantic comedies to emotional heart tuggers, **Silhouette Romance** offers six irresistible novels every month by some of your favorite authors! Such as...beloved bestsellers **Diana Palmer, Annette Broadrick, Suzanne Carey, Elizabeth August** and **Marie Ferrarella,** to name just a few—and some sure to become favorites!

Fabulous Fathers...Bundles of Joy...Miniseries... Months of blushing brides and convenient weddings... Holiday celebrations... You'll find all this and much more in **Silhouette Romance**—always emotional, always enjoyable, always about love!

If you've got the time...
We've got the
INTIMATE MOMENTS

Passion. Suspense. Desire. Drama. Enter a world that's larger than life, where men and women overcome life's greatest odds for the ultimate prize: love. Nonstop excitement is closer than you think...in Silhouette Intimate Moments!

SPECIAL EDITION

Stories of love and life, these powerful
novels are tales that you can identify with—
romances with "something special" added
in!

Fall in love with the stories of authors such
as **Nora Roberts, Diana Palmer, Ginna Gray**
and many more of your special favorites—as
well as wonderful new voices!

Special Edition brings you
entertainment for the heart!

SSE-GEN

WAYS TO *UNEXPECTEDLY* MEET MR. RIGHT:

♡ *Go out with the sexy-sounding stranger your daughter secretly set you up with through a personal ad.*

♡ *RSVP yes to a wedding invitation—soon it might be your turn to say "I do!"*

♡ *Receive a marriage proposal by mail— from a man you've never met....*

These are just a few of the unexpected ways that written communication leads to love in Silhouette Yours Truly.

Each month, look for two fast-paced, fun and flirtatious Yours Truly novels (with entertaining treats and sneak previews in the back pages) by some of your favorite authors—and some who are sure to become favorites.

YOURS TRULY™:
Love—when you least expect it!

FIVE UNIQUE SERIES
FOR EVERY WOMAN YOU ARE...

Silhouette ROMANCE™

From classic love stories to romantic comedies to emotional heart tuggers, Silhouette Romance is sometimes sweet, sometimes sassy—and always enjoyable! Romance—the way you always knew it could be.

SILHOUETTE® Desire®

Red-hot is what we've got! Sparkling, scintillating, *sensuous* love stories. Once you pick up one you won't be able to put it down...only in Silhouette Desire.

Silhouette SPECIAL EDITION®

Stories of love and life, these powerful novels are tales that you can identify with—romances with "something special" added in! Silhouette Special Edition is entertainment for the heart.

SILHOUETTE·INTIMATE·MOMENTS®

Enter a world where passions run hot and excitement is always high. Dramatic, larger than life and always compelling—Silhouette Intimate Moments provides captivating romance to cherish forever.

SILHOUETTE YOURS TRULY™

A personal ad, a "Dear John" letter, a wedding invitation... Just a few of the ways that written communication unexpectedly leads Miss Unmarried to Mr. "I Do" in Yours Truly novels...in the most fun, fast-paced and flirtatious style!

SGENERIC-R1